SORRY

FOR

THE

DEAD

SORRY
FOR
THE
DEAD
A JOSEPHINE TEY MYSTERY

Nicola Upson

CROOKED
LANE

NEW YORK

Published in the United States by Crooked Lane Books, an imprint of The Quick Brown Fox & Company LLC.

Crooked Lane Books and its logo are trademarks of The Quick Brown Fox & Company LLC.

Library of Congress Catalog-in-Publication data available upon request.

ISBN (hardcover): 978-1-68331-984-9
ISBN (ePub): 978-1-68331-985-6

Cover illustration by Mick Wiggins
Book design by Jennifer Canzone

Printed in the United States.

www.crookedlanebooks.com

Crooked Lane Books
34 West 27th St., 10th Floor
New York, NY 10001

First Edition: October 2019

10 9 8 7 6 5 4 3 2 1

For Val, with love.

*. . . we are at Rodmell on the loveliest spring day: soft: a blue veil
in the air torn by birds voices.
I am glad to be alive & sorry for the dead . . .*
—Virginia Woolf

1948

She waited on the step until Josephine was out of sight, then closed the front door behind her. The house seemed unnaturally quiet, and it took her a few moments to accept that she was finally alone. The book—a present she would never read—still lay on the table in the hallway. She unwrapped it and folded the brown paper neatly into a square, then went through to the sitting room to put it on the bookshelf with the others. Out of habit, she straightened the picture above the fireplace, wondering why she had lived for so long with something that she didn't really like. In a moment of defiance, she lifted the canvas from its hook and put it face down on the floor.

The pointlessness of her days stared back at her from the tidy room: the vacuumed carpet and dusted shelves, everything pathetically in its place; only the coffee table showed any sign of dissent. She stacked the plates and cups carefully onto a tray and cleared away the remains of a fruitcake made the week before. It was past its best, stale and tasteless in her mouth, but it had served its purpose, and the rest could be thrown away. She took it outside and crumbled it onto the low redbrick wall that separated her cottage from the one next door, smiling to herself when she imagined her neighbors' indignation at the thought of a week's dried fruit and sugar going to the birds. Already they thought her selfish and unfriendly, but she had been called much worse in the past, and no doubt would be again.

April was barely a week old, but the heat could have passed for early June. She sat down on a sun-bleached wooden bench that stood just outside the back door, trying not to disturb the cat, who invariably got there before her. It had taken her a long time to get used to such a small garden—just a plain, unimaginative rectangle in a terrace of the same—but she had planted it with all the things she loved most, nurturing a tiny wilderness of flowers and shrubs that had no purpose other than their beauty. A succession of warm days and spring showers had obliged her by bringing everything out before its time, and she was pleased to see the unexpected joy of early tulips. The promise of summer was everywhere, and the knowledge gave her comfort as well as pain; the rose that bore her name would be magnificent this year. Distracted by her thoughts, she stroked Percy's head as he lay stretched out in the sun, thin and arthritic in his old age. He had been with her for years, a handsome white and black hunter who arrived on her doorstep on the day she moved in, and stubbornly refused to leave. She had thought him a burden at the time, something else to care for and lose, but his company soon won her over; now, she couldn't bear the thought of being parted from him.

In the distance, the clock at St. John's struck the hour with its customary lack of urgency, and she went inside to collect her purse and shopping basket. Her front door opened straight onto the pavement, and she walked out into the narrow, leafy lane and headed for the high street, taking the most direct route to make sure of reaching the butcher's before he lowered his blinds for the weekend. She obviously wasn't the only one to be waylaid by a fine afternoon: the last-minute queue for meat stretched out of the shop door and round the corner, and she took her place in it, nodding to one or two of the customers. Whenever she found herself in a crowd these days, she was increasingly struck by the emptiness in people's faces, by a flat, going-through-the-motions air that she had never been conscious of before, not even in the depths of war. It was as if this fragile peace, no matter how longed for, lacked the exhilaration of wartime, the shared sense of purpose that had helped people forget their fear and their grief. The danger had passed, but gone too was the laughing in the street, the instinctive kindnesses from one neighbor to another—and it was these small commonplace things that mattered to most people. Now, everyone looked so tired and worn down that she wondered if the world would ever recover.

Inside, the shop smelled faintly of blood and sawdust. "Two ounces of ham, please," she said, requesting the full ration when her turn came.

The butcher nodded, and she watched as he cut thick slices from the bone and weighed them. "What else can I get you?"

"Nothing, thank you."

He looked at her in surprise. "That's all you want? I've got some of that stewing beef you like, fresh in yesterday. It'll save you queuing again if you take it now."

She looked at the meat and felt the nausea rise in her throat. "Just the ham," she snapped, feeling the eyes of the queue on her. "I really don't need anything else."

He shrugged and took her money, raising his eyes at the woman next in line, and she left the shop without another word. Across the street, a dress in the window of Jones's caught her eye, and she went over to look at it, drawn to the startling shade of green. Its tight-fitting waist and extravagantly flared skirt were so unlike anything she owned that, on a whim, she pushed the door open and went inside, conscious of her conservative shoes and the dull, shabby skirt that had seen too many summers. The counter was piled high with the new season's accessories, a flashback to the time before all the beautiful feminine things disappeared, and a young girl wearing too much rouge came over to greet her. "The dress in the window . . ." she began but was interrupted before she could finish her sentence.

"Ah yes, madam. It's only just come in, and I think you'll find the fabric is—"

"I'll take it."

"You don't want to try it on?"

The girl looked doubtful, and she wondered how many more people that day would question the fact that she knew her own mind; strange, because she had never felt more deliberate or more certain. "There's no need," she insisted. "I know it will fit."

With a shrug, the assistant went over to the window to set about undressing the mannequin, and five minutes later the dress was hers. Rather than retracing her steps, she decided to walk back via the castle. The steep climb through Castle Gate and into the Precincts beyond made her feel every year of her age, and she paused at the top to catch her breath. Beyond the outskirts of Lewes, the soft green downs spread out before her under a Wedgwood sky. It was a view she had always loved, a reminder of both the happiest and saddest times of her life, but today it was too much; she turned her back on it and headed for home.

She shook out the dress and hung it on her wardrobe door, then went back downstairs to the kitchen. Percy answered her call immediately, apparently oblivious to the strain in her voice, and she chopped the ham into a dish while he rubbed round her legs, making the small, familiar noises of appreciation that still seemed so out of place in a cat his size. The meat was as salty as brine and less tasty than it looked, and she felt a sudden surge of anger with herself for buying the wrong thing on this of all days. She picked him up and held him, and his ears flicked with irritation as he felt her tears on his fur. "I'm sorry," she said softly, choking back a sob. "I'm so sorry." He wriggled in her arms to be released, and she let him have his way, then prepared the last of the milk and put both dishes down in the sunlight just outside the back door, making sure that he had the ham first. His enjoyment was little comfort to her, and when he turned so innocently to the milk, she had to walk away.

As a distraction, she tidied the already tidy kitchen. Perhaps it was her mood, but the room seemed cheerless and neglected. When everything was as she wanted it, she found the Vim and scoured the oven until it was spotless, then climbed the stairs to change. She washed at the tiny sink in her bedroom, annoyed by the dripping tap that she had never got round to having fixed, and wondered what else had been left undone. As she took the dress from its hanger and put it on, the unfamiliar fabric felt dangerous against her skin, and she smiled to herself. She had been right to trust her instinct: the dress could have been made for her, and for a fleeting moment in the mirror she caught a glimpse of the woman she had once been. The knowledge tormented her, and she put it from her mind. "How do I look?" she asked, but the only answer was a heavy, oppressive silence.

Back downstairs, she forced herself to go outside. Percy lay in the sunshine; she could have convinced herself that he was merely sleeping were it not for the shallowness of his breath. The tears came again, more forceful than ever, and this time she made no effort to stop them. She owed him that, at least. Gently, she picked him up and clutched him to her, then set him down in the chair that he had always made his own, talking all the time to him while she made her preparations. She closed the window on the spring day and laid a wet tea towel carefully along the sill where she knew the draughts came in, then did the same at the back door and the door into the hallway. When everything was ready, she left the note where it couldn't be missed and sat by her cat while he took his final breath, then picked up the cushion from the other chair and walked over to the cooker. Astonished by how calm she felt, she turned the gas on and set the cushion in place, then put her head inside, as far as she could bear. This time, there must be no mistake.

TEN YEARS EARLIER

CHAPTER 1

It would be hard to imagine a more beautiful walk to work, Josephine thought, as she left King's Parade behind and turned into the peaceful eccentricity of St. Edward's Passage, with its old cottages and pretty churchyard. The pavements were cast in shadow by the church tower and nearby Guildhall, but the heat of the September morning was already strong enough to stay pleasantly at her back as she headed for the stage door of the Arts Theater, tucked discreetly between a café and a secondhand bookshop, and easy to miss if you were simply idling the day away.

The invitation to direct one of her own plays at Cambridge's newest theater had come out of the blue, a result of her friendship with Lettice and Ronnie Motley, who had been involved with the Arts since its opening production a couple of years earlier. At first she had hesitated, reluctant to take on a role that was alien to her, but Marta's encouragement and the opportunity to spend time with her lover in a town that excited her made her forget her reservations, and now—in the final days of rehearsal—she had no reason to regret her decision. She was enjoying every minute of the process, relishing the chance to work with a talented group of actors who wanted nothing more than to get the best out of her text, and as the opening night drew closer, the familiar nerves came with a new optimism. *The Laughing Woman*—a drama based loosely on the sculptor Gaudier-Brzeska—was the least successful of her West End productions, but the one closest to her heart. She had always been disappointed by its reception and frustrated by elements of the director's staging that were beyond her control; at least this time, if the play failed again, she would only have herself to blame.

She waited patiently at the stage door while the theater's general manager dealt simultaneously with a consignment of French linen for the restaurant and a telephone complaint about the sight lines from the back of the circle. "You're early this morning, Miss Tey," he said when the disgruntled patron had been pacified. "I thought the cast was called for midday."

"Yes, that's right, but Miss Lopokova wants to talk to me before we start the run-through. I gather she has a new idea for the last scene before the interval."

"I'm sure she has. She never does anything half-heartedly, that's for sure." Norman Higgins gave a wry smile, but his words were spoken with affection. The play's leading lady was popular with both cast and staff, and not only because she was married to May-nard Keynes, the theater's founder. A former ballerina with the Diaghilev company, Lydia Lopokova had, in her heyday, been wor-shipped by London audiences for the fiery beauty of her dancing, but her subsequent forays into acting were less successful. In *Twelfth Night* at the Old Vic, her portrayal of Olivia had been torn to shreds by the press, but she had stuck doggedly at it, encouraged first and foremost by her husband. According to the Motleys, who made it their business to know everything about anyone who had ever stepped onto a London stage, the marriage had been ridiculed by Keynes's Bloomsbury friends, but it had lasted against the odds. The Arts Theater—as well as being Keynes's gift to the town he loved—was a symbol of his devotion to his wife and her career. "Miss Lopokova is already in her dressing room, if you'd like to go and find her," Higgins added. "I've got some post here for you, and someone from the *Express* telephoned, wanting a quote from you about the play. I've got his number if you want it, but he said he'd try again later."

Josephine thanked him and took the small bundle of letters, then went downstairs to the basement. The backstage facilities—still fresh and new in comparison with most London theaters'—were unusually comfortable, with a number of good-sized dressing rooms arranged around a central green room, making it easy for the actors to socialize in a jovial, communal atmosphere. She nodded to the young assistant stage manager, who was standing by the kettle, making the first round of teas for the crew, then knocked at the door to dressing room one.

"Ah, Josephine, come in—so good of you to give up your morning. I'm sorry to have telephoned you late last night, but I was going over and over in my head the scene we had been working on—how do you say it?—wrecking my brain . . ."

"Wracking, although the effect is probably the same."

"Yes, *wracking* my brain, when it came to me that we could do something different just before the sculpture falls to the floor, and I was so excited that I had to talk to you about it." The heavily accented voice, which Virginia Woolf had once famously compared to that of a parakeet, was sometimes hard to understand, and Josephine could see why Shakespeare might not have been the ideal vehicle for Lydia's talents, but with Ingrid Rydman—her character in *The Laughing Woman*—the broken English simply added to the authenticity of her portrayal. In fact, the first time she had met Lydia—or Loppy, as her friends called her—Josephine was struck by the extent to which the actress could have walked straight out of her own stage directions: the wide, finely cut mouth and slightly hollowed cheeks, the dark hair scraped back from a high forehead, the expressive eyes that moved so swiftly between curiosity and apprehension—all were exactly as she had imagined her character to look while she was writing the play. By her own admission, Loppy wasn't attractive in the conventional way, but her movements were still graceful and full of energy, and Josephine loved the sense of nervous energy that she brought so naturally to the part. "Here, sit down and let me show you what I mean in the script."

The scene in question was the emotional climax to the first half, a passionate argument between Ingrid and her soul mate, René, in which the destruction of a clay model hinted at the tragedy to come. They ran through the lines, engrossed in the intensity of the exchange, until a knock at the door interrupted them. "Is this a good time to borrow you for a moment?" Keynes asked. "There's something I'd like to show you."

Loppy gave a squeal of delight. "Ah, Maynard darling, you have our wonderful surprise." Josephine looked at her curiously and followed the couple upstairs to the stage, where a sack barrow stood waiting in the wings, half-covered by a red blanket. Keynes gestured toward it with a flourish, like a magician performing his favorite trick. "A little something to bring you all luck," he said, his eyes twinkling over half-moon glasses. "By all means take a look."

Josephine did as she was told, at a loss to guess what the talisman might be. She removed the covering and stared in disbelief at the pale stone sculpture beneath, a bust of a woman's head that glistened brilliantly in the harsh stage lighting. "Is this really what I think it is?" she asked.

"If you mean is it a genuine Gaudier-Brzeska, then yes," Keynes said, winking at his wife.

The economist was a shrewd collector of art—the first time that Josephine had visited his office, she'd fallen in love with a Cezanne on the wall by his desk—but still the gesture astonished her. She knelt down to be level with the woman's face and put her hand on the cool stone, feeling the contrast between its rough and polished surfaces. "I don't know what to say. It's absolutely exquisite."

Keynes smiled, pleased by her reaction. "Well, we want to do everything we can to make this one a success," he said, squeezing Loppy's hand. "I know it's not exactly like the piece you describe in the play—more abstract, I suspect, than what you had in mind . . ."

"It's perfect," Josephine said, interrupting him. "I don't know how you managed it, but I couldn't be more thrilled that you did."

"A generous donation from the wine cellars at King's to a friend of mine did the trick. That, and two tickets to the opening night. Apparently, he's a fan of yours. He tells me he saw *Richard of Bordeaux* fourteen times."

"Then he must come as my guest and let me buy him dinner. It's the least I can do."

"I'm sure he'll be delighted."

"I don't know—we go to all this trouble to make every scene sparkle, and what thanks do we get? Upstaged by a bit of bloody stone. When was the last time you bought *us* dinner?"

Josephine turned and smiled at Ronnie as the Motleys struggled in with a pile of costumes. "The night before last, if my memory serves me correctly," she said. "But pull something like this out of the bag and I'll gladly do it again."

"It *is* stunning," Lettice said, dropping the clothes onto a chair to take a closer look. "What a tragedy that he died so young."

"Let's just hope that Loppy doesn't get carried away in the heat of the moment and smash the wrong sculpture," Ronnie said. "That really would be a showstopper."

Keynes laughed and turned back to Josephine. "Do you mind if I stay and watch for a while?"

"Of course not. You can keep an eye on our new prop. I'm already worried about the insurance, or does the wine cellar solve that problem too?"

A bell rang in the wings before he could answer, and the stage manager called the company to order. "Five minutes, ladies and gentleman. Opening positions, please."

Loppy hurried off to change for her first scene, and Josephine followed Keynes and the Motley sisters into the front stalls. The theater itself was far more beautiful than anyone might have guessed from the modest entrances—simple and elegant, with rich, unadorned wood and pale paintwork. Already, in rehearsals, Josephine had come to appreciate the unique intimacy between the stage and auditorium, and she could hardly wait to see it in action with a full house. She chose a seat in the middle of a row halfway back and watched as two members of the stage crew lifted the sculpture carefully onto a plinth for the opening scene, set in a London gallery. It looked magnificent, and if the seamless first act was anything to go by, Keynes's lucky charm was beginning to work its magic.

She had just finished giving notes to the cast when she noticed Marta slipping quietly into the back of the stalls. "This is a nice surprise," Josephine said. "You can't have finished the first draft already?"

"I've barely started it. Nothing was going right, so I went out for cigarettes and bought a couple of newspapers."

"And the next thing you knew it was lunchtime?"

"Something like that, yes, but I'm pleased I went. There's an article in the *Daily Mirror* that you really need to see."

"Can't it wait until tonight? We've only just got underway with the run-through, and I . . ."

"No, Josephine, it can't. I wouldn't disturb you unless it was important. Who is Elizabeth Banks?"

Josephine stared at her, unsettled by her tone of voice. "I've no idea," she said. "Why? *Should* I know her?"

"Probably. She's saying you killed her sister. Well—you're on the list of suspects."

"What?" Josephine laughed, then realized that Marta was serious. "I don't understand. What on earth are you talking about? I've never met anyone called Banks."

"Banks is her married name. At the time in question, she was called Norwood. Betty Norwood." Josephine sat down, feeling suddenly faint. "Her sister was called Dorothy," Marta added, "and she died at a farmhouse in Surrey during the war."

"Sussex, not Surrey. The farmhouse was in Sussex."

"So you *were* there? She's not lying?"

"Not about that, no. It was the end of my first term at Anstey, and I had a placement at a school called Moira House in Eastbourne. They sent some of their girls to a nearby farmhouse to learn horticulture and help with the war effort, and I was one of the chaperones. It was my job to keep them fit and look after their moral welfare, as the principal put it, even though I wasn't much older than they were." She smiled ruefully. "As you've probably read, it wasn't exactly a glittering start to my teaching career, but Dorothy's death was an accident. It was a terrible thing to happen, and Betty was devastated by it—we all were—but it was nobody's fault. Is that what this woman's saying? That my negligence killed her sister?"

"That's not exactly what she's saying . . ."

Josephine snatched the newspaper from Marta's hands and unfolded the double page spread, which pictured a glamorous blonde woman next to the headline "*Real Life* School for Scandal: *a* Mirror *exclusive by Faith Hope.*" A little further down, tucked among a group of smaller photographs in the bottom right-hand corner, she was horrified to see her own face looking back at her. "I don't understand. This was all so long ago."

"God knows why she's waited until now to dredge it up." Marta was about to go on, but Josephine stopped her.

"Just be quiet for a minute," she said, hating the panic in her own voice but unable to do anything about it. "Let me read it first."

She turned to fetch her glasses, frustrated by the lack of light in the auditorium, but Marta caught her arm. "I'm sorry, I shouldn't have sprung this on you here, but I was so surprised that I didn't really think. Can't you take a break, and we'll talk about it somewhere more private? I'm sure there's a simple explanation, but you won't be able to concentrate on the play until you know what this says."

Josephine hesitated, but she knew that Marta was right. "I suppose we could stop for lunch now. They'll have to reset for the next scene, so we might as well combine the two."

"Good idea. Go and fix it. I'll take the paper and meet you outside."

By the time Josephine had made the arrangements and refused Lettice's offer of a bite to eat in the restaurant upstairs, her imagination had created so many terrible scenarios that she was almost relieved to confront the reality of the article. She found Marta on a bench outside the church and gratefully accepted a cigarette. "Sorry I snapped at you," she said. "It was just such a shock. I haven't thought back to those days for years, and I never dreamt that anyone would make something of what happened. I suppose that *is* bad of me—to dismiss a girl's death so easily just because she wasn't someone I was close to or particularly liked."

"Perhaps, but we all do that. It doesn't give anyone an excuse to make sensational accusations."

"Is it really that bad?" Josephine asked, picking up the paper at the page that Marta had left open for her.

"Oh, it's cleverly written—all suggestion and implication, and nothing that a very expensive lawyer hasn't been through with a fine-tooth comb, so I doubt you'll be able to sue the bitch. It's what people make of it that counts, though, and I'm afraid I have no faith in the intelligence or generosity of the British public—not the ones who buy a rag like that, anyway." It would have been churlish to point out the irony of Marta's last comment, and in any case Josephine appreciated her loyalty. "Read it first; then we'll talk about what to do."

Guessing now that the quote the *Express* was after had nothing to do with her play, Josephine skimmed the opening paragraph, which was a master class in selective reporting. The gossip columnist wrote:

> *When the actress Elizabeth Banks walks on stage each night in Lillian Hellman's scandalous play of deviant love, she carries her own ghosts with her. Avid theatergoers will remember that* The Children's Hour *caused a sensation when it was originally produced on Broadway back in 1934, with its depiction of a young girl who claims that two of her schoolmistresses are guilty of sharing an abnormal attachment. At the time, no leading lady would touch a*

role that might justifiably tarnish her career—and there were fears that the police would close the play as soon as the curtain rose.

"'A scandalous play of deviant love,'" Marta muttered, looking over Josephine's shoulder. "And no mention of the fact that the young schoolgirl is eventually exposed as a lying little minx. Who the hell does Faith Hope think she is, making moral judgments on the rest of us? Pay her twenty-five pounds a week and suddenly she's Jesus."

Josephine sighed. "Call me selfish, but right now I'm far more worried about the rest of the article. I'm sure Lillian Hellman can look after herself."

"Yes, of course. Sorry. I won't interrupt again."

She lit another cigarette, and Josephine turned back to the story.

When Miss Banks welcomed me into her colorful, feminine dressing room at the Gate Theater Studio to discuss her new role, I had no inkling of the revelation she was about to share—and neither did she. Only when the intense emotions of the drama began to over-whelm her did she admit that they had a highly personal resonance, and one that she could no longer ignore. Twenty-three years ago, almost to the day, her twin sister died at the age of sixteen—just hours after making a similar accusation!

"We were always so close," Miss Banks recalled, fighting back her tears. "When she died, a part of me died with her, and I never believed it was an accident—Dorothy was so clever and so careful. But no one took me seriously, and in the end I stopped trying to be heard. I suppose I was afraid that something similar would happen to me." The actress, who plays the character of Martha Dobie in the London revival of The Children's Hour, *which opened last week, went on to confide that she sees her new role as a gift from fate, a second chance to do the right thing. "My opening lines in the play are 'What happened to her?' And the first time I said them out*

loud in front of an audience, I felt a shiver down my spine. It was as if Dorothy was standing right next to me, reminding me of my debt to her memory. I owe her the truth, and it's my intention to prove what really happened all those years ago. Perhaps then we can both find some peace."

"Miss Banks refuses to be drawn on whether or not she suspects anyone in particular of the crime, saying only that there were a number of people staying in the house at the time, all of whom were present when her sister died; intriguingly, she adds that "some of them obviously had secrets." The tragedy took place at a farmhouse in East Sussex, which was run as a celebrated horticultural college and smallholding by Georgina Hartford-Wroe and her close friend, Harriet Barker. The two women—who also operated a lodging house on the premises—had recently been entrusted with the charge of schoolgirls keen to study garden design and the management of the land. After Dorothy Norwood's death, and other accusations of impropriety that remained unproven at the time, Miss Hartford-Wroe and her companion were forced to close their disgraced establishment and move away from the area.

In more recent years, the farmhouse (which is situated just a few miles outside the pretty and historic town of Lewes) has enjoyed a different sort of notoriety as home to a number of prominent artists and members of the Bloomsbury group. But the mystery that surrounds the summer of 1915 grows deeper by the day—and its shadows continue to haunt Miss Banks in all their tragic fascination whenever she speaks those poignant opening lines: "What happened to her? She was perfectly well a few hours ago."

"Is it accurate?" Marta asked, when Josephine had finished reading.

"Broadly speaking, yes. The only thing I could argue with is the sprinkling of melodrama. Dorothy's death happened days after she made those accusations, not hours. But that's a minor detail compared to everything else, and I suppose people would think me pedantic to point it out."

"It's important, though. It undermines the idea that one was a direct result of the other."

"Yes, I suppose so."

"And these dangerous accusations—they were about the women who ran the place, presumably?"

Josephine nodded. "Amongst other things. There was a lot of unpleasantness flying around, and not just inside the house. Farmers didn't like women playing on the land, and their wives didn't like women playing with the farmers. It was very early in the war, and resentment hadn't quite been trounced by grief."

"What happened to the two of them after they were forced to leave? The article doesn't say."

"I've no idea—we were all hauled back to Eastbourne. There was no way that the principal of Moira House was going to allow its girls or its reputation to be touched by the scandal any more than they had been already." She glanced down at the newspaper again, looking this time at the photograph of Georgina Hartford-Wroe, a woman she had once admired. She was pictured outside in the garden, giving the day's orders to one of her students, and there was something in the eagerness on the young girl's face that brought the sadness of that summer back to Josephine in a way that all the *Mirror*'s sensationalizing never could; it had all been so hopeful, she thought, so new and exciting.

At the end of the article, there was a collection of photographs, including her own, grouped together under the loaded question *"Who else was there?"* She scanned the faces, but there was no image of Harriet Barker, and Josephine remembered how she had always shunned the limelight, even though her contribution to the work of the college had been just as great as her friend's. Someone in the *Mirror*'s art department had diligently tracked down the Moira House school photograph for 1915, but the newspaper had stopped short of identifying individual pupils, and Josephine's memory couldn't do any better; the girls were virtually indistinguishable in their school hats and uniforms—and anyway, as she had said to Marta, it was all so long ago. Dorothy Norwood's photograph was curiously absent from a story that was allegedly about keeping her memory alive; as far as Josephine could recall, the relationship between the two sisters had always been an unsettling mixture of dependence and rivalry, and she wondered if the latter had lingered; now that the limelight was quite literally hers, perhaps the actress in Elizabeth Banks refused to be upstaged by her long-dead twin.

Her eyes fell on the final picture. Jeanette Sellwood had been a teacher at Moira House and the other chaperone to the girls. Like Josephine—whose recently taken photograph was the one she used in theater programs and anything else to do with her writing—Jeannie was shown as an older woman, but she had hardly changed at all in the intervening years. Her long, auburn hair was more styled, her face a little fuller, but still she had that wry smile and those dancing eyes that always seemed to want to know more than anyone could tell her. The picture was so familiar that it was easy to imagine her now, poring over the same page at home or at work, floored by this abrupt resurrection of half-buried memories. Suddenly, with an urgency that took her completely by surprise, Josephine longed to know what Jeannie had done with her life.

"I bet the box office at the Gate has never been busier," she said, casting the paper aside with a heavy sigh. "It's the best publicity a play could ask for. I wish I'd thought of it." She looked at Marta in despair. "What on earth am I going to do? Thousands of people will see this, and there's no opportunity to answer back because it's all so slyly done. They might have avoided actually using the word *suspects*, but that's exactly what this little collection of photographs is. The whole nation will be playing Poirot over their evening cocoa, and I'll be odds-on favorite."

"Josephine, that's not true."

"Of course it is. Listen to this." She picked up the paper again and read the caption beneath her photograph. "'*The former teacher was present when Dorothy Norwood died and has since gone on to become one of our best-known writers of detective stories, whose most recent novel was filmed by none other than Mr. Alfred Hitchcock! Could her flair for fictional crime be inspired by more than just a rich imagination?*'" And I see I'm the only one with a special footnote. I suppose I should be flattered."

"Why not use that to your advantage?" Marta suggested. "Any editor would happily print your side of the story if you wanted to write it."

"And fan the flames even higher than they are already? That would just make things worse. As it is, I don't believe for one moment that this will end here. All that nonsense about guests in the house having a secret—that's just license to speculate. People are bound to pick it up and start snooping around, and God knows what rubbish they'll print when that happens. What on earth will my family think, Marta? Or my publisher? Or my neighbors in Inverness?" She stopped before the list became too horrendous to contemplate. "You know I'm right. This is just the *Mirror*'s opening gambit. They're fishing for people to come forward and stir up more trouble, and if that happens, there'll be a new revelation in the papers every day."

"You should talk to Archie about it. You know he'd want to help, and if you've got a friend at Scotland Yard, you might as well call on him."

Josephine hesitated. Her friendship with Archie Penrose was only now recovering from a crisis the year before, when Archie discovered in the most tragic of ways that he had a child, and that Josephine had—with the best of intentions—kept the secret from him. "I don't want to bother him when he's in Cornwall," she said. "This is the first chance he's had to take Phyllis to meet his family, and he's waited long enough for some time with his daughter."

Marta didn't argue, but seemed deep in thought. "Don't bite my head off," she said after a while, "but do you think this Banks woman could be right in one respect? *Could* it have been murder?"

"Of course not. This is all about boosting her career. As you said, if there were any truth in her story, why would she wait twenty-three years to bring it up? Shouldn't she have been shouting from the rooftops to get justice for her sister?"

Marta shrugged. "You'd think so, but sometimes things resurface when you least expect them to."

"All those emotions miraculously triggered by one brief line in a play?"

"So you're sure there was nothing strange about it at the time?"

Josephine shook her head in exasperation. "I really don't remember. So much has happened since then—it's like trying to make out a faded photograph." The church clock began to whirr into life, and she glanced at her watch. "I've got to go, or they'll be starting the second act without a director. We'll talk about this later."

"All right, but try not to let it get to you. No one in his right mind would believe you capable of murder just because you write books about it. People don't kill to make themselves famous."

"Don't you think so? That doesn't say much for my last novel." She tried to smile but failed miserably. "Anyway, it's not just the girl's death, is it? Let's not forget the deviant love. What if people start looking more closely at my life? At you and me? They don't have to tie me to a murder to destroy my reputation."

"But it's the murder they're interested in, not your private life."

It was unlike Marta to say something she didn't believe simply to be kind, and somehow it made Josephine even more fearful. "Really?" she demanded. "There were two men staying in that house at the time, but I don't see their pictures in the rogues gallery. It's obvious what the *real* crime is here. Lillian Hellman was spot-on about that." She was on the verge of tears but managed to force them back, angry with herself for feeling so vulnerable. "You have no idea what it was like for those two women once the rumors started, and it absolutely destroyed them. It wasn't just one girl who couldn't keep her mouth shut. It was the village, the farmers, the local papers. I can still feel it now—all the hate and the suspicion, the violence that was just below the surface. No one even felt the need to hide it. On the contrary, they wore it like a badge of honor. I couldn't live through that shame the way they did."

"I thought you said you couldn't remember?" Marta said gently, taking her hand. "It sounds to me like everyone suffered that summer." She didn't press the point, and Josephine was grateful to her. "And scandal fades, you know. Trust me on that. It's just a question of holding your nerve." Marta was such a strong, confident presence in her life that Josephine occasionally forgot how much grief and shame of her own she had lived through. "And do you know what really helped me to hold my head up again? Other than you, of course. It was facing it—going back to all the places that had caused the pain in the first place. People used to whisper about me in these streets, and I thought I'd never be able to come back here, but I was wrong. They're just streets."

"What are you saying?"

"I assume the farmhouse they're talking about is Charleston?" Josephine nodded. "Well, let's go there. Loppy can get you an invitation—she and Maynard are friends with the Bloomsbury lot, and they've got a house just down the road. In fact, didn't she invite you last week, and you were funny about it?"

"I wasn't funny about it," Josephine said defensively. "I just hate that sort of party. And why would I want to go back there now, with all this going on?"

"Because it's just a house, Josephine. A house where an accident happened nearly twenty-five years ago. You need to remind yourself of that and move on." Josephine hesitated, and Marta looked curiously at her. "Unless there's something you haven't told me. You're *not* sure it was an accident, are you?"

"I've never doubted it before."

"But?"

"But now I've got over the shock, it doesn't seem impossible. That's all. I can't explain why, but it doesn't."

"Then all the more reason to go back. You have nothing to fear from the truth of what happened to Dorothy Norwood—we both know that—so why not try and find out? Play the *Mirror* at its own game and get to the bottom of it. If I wanted to be cynical, I'd say that's exactly the way to get people on your side and deflect them from what you really don't want them to know about. Sleight of hand—it works every time." She grinned and gave Josephine a kiss. "I've got to get back to my script. See you later, and don't come home without an invitation to Sussex."

Josephine watched her go, then walked back to the theater, deep in thought. In the green room she found the post she had been too busy to read earlier, knowing now why the handwriting on one of the letters looked familiar. She opened the small, blue envelope, forwarded from her London club. The note was brief and oddly polite, but it helped her make up her mind. "Loppy!" she called, as the actress passed by on her way to the stage. "I never thanked you properly for the invitation. If the offer's still open, Marta and I would love to come to Sussex at the weekend."

The actress smiled at her. "You have changed your mind about parties, Josephine? You surprise me."

"Am I that transparent? No, I haven't changed my mind. I didn't tell you before, but I spent some time at Charleston when I was younger, and I'd like to see it again."

"You were there before Vanessa and Duncan? When the house was even colder?"

Josephine laughed. "It was summer when I stayed there, but now you mention it, home comforts were few and far between."

"How wonderful! Then you must come and look round. They will all be so pleased to meet you and hear about the old house, and I can introduce you to Grace."

"Grace?"

"She is the housekeeper, and we are the best of friends. You will love her, I promise. Now, shall we go and smash some clay?"

CHAPTER 2

The house was less forbidding than she remembered it. As soon as they left the Lewes to Eastbourne road, Josephine was struck anew by the utter peace of the place, by a gentleness that the soft colors of a fading summer only served to enhance. Despite the intervening years, the setting felt every bit as remote as it always had. The dusty old farm track was still just that, and several times Marta had to swerve to avoid cracks and potholes in the parched earth. For a while the track skirted a scruff of woodland, but then they were out into open farmland, with barns and other outbuildings visible across the fields. Finally, the house gave itself up to their search, its distinctive, rectangular chimneys standing tall through the trees.

Several cars were parked behind the orchard, where the shepherds' huts once stood, and Marta pulled up alongside them. "I thought we'd never get here," she said. "You didn't tell me it was in the middle of nowhere."

"It's a farmhouse. Surely you weren't expecting to find it just off Lewes high street?"

Marta laughed. "No, I suppose not, but how on earth did you get around? Presumably you didn't have a car."

"Miss H had a battered old van for deliveries, and we were allowed to borrow it occasionally, but mostly we just walked across the fields to the village." It was the first time that Josephine had used the familiar term by which Georgina Hartford-Wroe had been known among the girls, and it brought back those days as vividly as seeing her photograph in the newspaper had. "It's a lot quicker as the crow flies."

"And you were all so sickeningly fit, of course. I keep forgetting that."

"Fitter, and much younger." She got out of the car and looked round, pleased that the countryside could still stir in her the strange mixture of sadness and delight that was her customary response to places she loved. The scene in front of her hadn't changed, but then how could it, subject to the cycle of the seasons and nothing more? Firle Beacon, the highest point of the downs, rose suddenly out of an otherwise flat landscape, and the dark ribbon of hills formed an austere backdrop to the house, making the green of the trees more brilliant.

"Ready to go in?" Marta asked.

"No, but we might as well get it over with." She led the way, memory taking her easily to the narrow path that ran alongside the walled garden. The house ambushed you suddenly; she had forgotten that. Even with a generous autumn sun to bring color to its walls, the façade remained a sober, unfussy mixture of brick and flint, and the only adornment was a gabled porch jutting out onto the gravel. The Virginia Creeper that once ran wild across the front had been stripped away, exposing six wide sash windows, all thrown open to the air, and Josephine glanced up at the room that had once been hers—east-facing, so that she woke each morning to a haze of sunlight filtering through the silver branches of the willow tree by the pond.

"It doesn't look like a house of scandal," Marta said, looking appreciatively at its solid, simple form. "That must be a great disappointment to the *Daily Mirror*."

She was right, Josephine thought; there was a dignity about its lack of pretension. "Perhaps they'll dig up an old picture," she said. "It looks much friendlier now than it used to." The front door stood open, and the contrast continued inside. From the hallway, she could see that the house's rambling interior remained essentially unchanged since her last visit, but the atmosphere in the downstairs rooms had been utterly transformed. The old, overbearing wallpaper was replaced now by a soft gray distemper that soaked up the light and emphasized the colors of the paintings on the walls. A gramophone record was playing deeper in the house, something by Haydn or Mozart, and Josephine was relieved to find that the party was a more relaxed affair than she had imagined—a handful of guests who all seemed very much at home, talking in small groups and drinking tea.

Loppy waved as soon as she saw them, and ushered them into the dining room, where a round table—hand-painted in delicate pastel shades—was laden with sandwiches and freshly baked cakes. "Ah, Josephine, Marta—you are here at last. Come, have some tea and let Grace get you something to eat." She beckoned the housekeeper over from the other side of the room, an attractive woman with stylish, well-cut brown hair, whom Josephine would have assumed to be one of the guests had she not been working so hard. "Grace, these are my friends from Cambridge: Josephine—she has created the wonderful play you are coming to see next week; and Marta—she writes scripts for the movies and works with all the best directors."

The housekeeper nodded and smiled at Josephine. "Mrs. Keynes was telling me you stayed here during the war." Her voice was light and disarmingly girlish, with the faintest hint of a Norfolk accent. "Is it nice to be back?"

"Very nice, if a little strange after all this time." She looked round, noticing that the old fire grate and its surrounds had been removed to reveal a large open hearth, big enough for an armchair on either side of the chimney breast. The room was comfortable and welcoming now, with windows on two sides, floral chintz curtains, and an array of brightly colored plates on the mantelshelf, but still she found it hard to shake off the tension she associated with this part of the house in the old days, when angry words across the breakfast table had made the space seem tense and claustrophobic. "I was only here for a summer," she added, conscious that both Grace and Loppy were hoping to hear more from her, "but it was my first time in this part of the world, and I've loved it ever since. I suppose it's because I associate it with my first real taste of freedom."

Grace looked at her with interest. "That's strange," she said, "but someone else said that to me recently."

"Really? Who?"

"A woman turned up out of the blue last week. Tuesday or Wednesday, it must have been, because Mrs. Bell and Mr. Grant were still away. She said she'd lived here once, like you, and asked if she could have a look round for old time's sake. I let her see the garden, but not the house—told her she'd have to write and make a proper appointment if she wanted to come in."

"Did she give a name?" Marta asked, and then, when Grace shook her head, "Can you remember what she looked like?"

The housekeeper thought for a moment, absentmindedly playing with one of her round, blue earrings. "Fair hair, slim, and about my height. Nice clothes, but nothing out of the ordinary."

"Could it have been this woman?" Josephine took the newspaper article out of her bag and showed Grace the photograph of Elizabeth Banks. "She was here with me that summer, and she's been talking about it in the papers recently."

"Is that right? We had a couple of people snooping round with cameras yesterday, but I didn't know why." Grace scanned the article with obvious skepticism. "Not a bad way to get yourself noticed," she said. "I suppose it could have been her, but the woman I spoke to was wearing dark glasses, so I can't say for sure. She wore her hair differently too, but no doubt this one's done herself up for the press."

Josephine smiled in agreement. "She certainly wasn't blonde the last time I met her."

"I dare say." Grace handed the article to Loppy, who had been trying to read it over her shoulder. "As far as I know, the woman I met hasn't bothered writing here like I told her to, but if I hear anything else, I'll tell Mrs. Keynes, and she can pass it on. Now—what can I get you to eat?"

She filled their plates, then headed back to the kitchen to make more tea, and Josephine retrieved her newspaper. "Are Ronnie and Lettice here yet?" she asked, changing the subject.

"Oh yes. Vanessa took them through to the sitting room. Come, I will show you—it is just across the hall."

"I can't believe I'm about to meet Virginia Woolf's sister," Marta whispered as they followed Loppy into the next room.

"Hasn't it crossed your mind that Virginia Woolf herself might actually be here?"

"Of course it has. I lay awake all last night, terrified you might let slip what you think of her work."

Josephine laughed out loud. "I promise not to embarrass you—not unless I'm really provoked. And anyway, it's only the novels I can't stand. When you gave me *The Years* to try, I thought it was a title, not an estimate of how much time I should put aside to read it."

As it turned out, there was no need for Marta to worry. Except for Maynard and another man, who were deep in conversation by the window, the Motley sisters were alone in the room. "You're a sight for sore eyes," Ronnie said, looking approvingly at Josephine's black and white dress. "All this color is giving me a headache." The house's unconventional decorative scheme was certainly more in evidence here than it had been in the dining room. A row of wooden panels below the window was painted with flowers that mirrored those in a vase on the table, and the top half of the door had been embellished with a similar design in stronger colors. In theory, it was a strangely modern vision to impose on an old Sussex farmhouse, but the miracle for Josephine was that it didn't seem more alien. Ronnie looked pointedly at the fireplace surround, which boasted a striking combination of circles and crosshatching. "Those repeating patterns don't *exactly* repeat, do they?" she said. "And as for the lampshade . . ."

Lettice glared at her sister and put her empty plate down on one of the bookshelves. "Have you found anything out about the murder yet?" she asked eagerly.

Josephine looked sharply at Marta, who held up her hands in a protestation of innocence. "Don't look at me. I haven't said a word."

"She didn't have to. We *do* read the papers, you know."

"Then you'll know the whole thing is four parts gossip and one part speculation," Josephine said firmly. "And I don't think we should make too much of it while we're here. They don't seem to know anything about it at the moment, and I'd rather keep it that way."

Lettice looked disappointed. "All right, but if you want us to dig anything up, you know where we are. It wouldn't be the first time you'd sent us in undercover. I seem to remember we were quite good at it."

"Who do you think Grace's visitor was?" Marta interrupted, ignoring Josephine's stipulation. "It was before the newspaper came out, so she obviously wasn't just someone who'd read the article and fancied a look at the crime scene."

"I wish you'd stop calling it a crime scene," Josephine said as Lettice and Ronnie drifted off in search of more tea. "We don't know that, and coming back here hasn't made me change my mind. But my money would be on Faith Hope, having a look round before she wrote her article. That, or Betty herself."

"If it *was* Betty, that remark about the house being her first taste of freedom is interesting."

"Why? I'm sure that was true for most of us."

"Yes, but she could have meant that it was her sister's death that set her free."

Josephine was about to argue with Marta's stretch of the imagination, but now she thought about it, Betty *had* always walked in her sister's shadow. If both girls had lived, it would have been Dorothy, surely, who was the more likely to find success as an actress. Before she could answer, Loppy came back into the room with another woman, obviously their host. "Josephine, Marta—this is Nessa. She has been very keen to meet you."

Vanessa Bell must have been in her late fifties, but she was still a strikingly beautiful woman—tall, with strong features, long fair hair, and a natural grace to every movement that she made. "Welcome to Charleston," she said warmly. "It was good of you to make the trip from Cambridge. Maynard was telling me how busy you've been with the play."

Whether consciously or not, a single sentence had effectively marginalized Loppy from the conversation, and Josephine began to understand how difficult it must have been for the new Mrs. Keynes to break into her husband's close-knit group of friends. No wonder she seemed to spend most of her time gossiping in the kitchen with Grace; they were natural allies—intimates and outsiders at the same time. "Yes, it's been hard work to get everything together in a couple of weeks," she said, "but we're blessed with a very fine cast, and the theater itself is beautiful."

"And we had a mutual friend in Cambridge too, I understand. Bridget Foley? What a terrible thing to happen."

Josephine hesitated, caught off guard by the mention of Archie's lover, who had died the year before. Her own relationship with Bridget had been fraught with complications, dogged by buried secrets and their respective attachments to Archie; she would never have described them as friends, but it seemed churlish to say so now. "Yes, although we didn't have very long to get to know each other. I only met her when she and Archie grew close again."

"She often used to come here with Carrington in the early days," Vanessa said. "We've got one of her paintings upstairs, and I've always loved it. Her death was such a shock, but then last year was nothing but sadness."

It was impossible to ask what she meant when they were

obviously expected to know, and Josephine's curiosity had to wait until Vanessa moved on to greet other guests. "Her son died in the Spanish war," Loppy explained. "Grace says it is the only bad thing she has ever known to happen here. Nessa was devastated. There was nothing anyone could do to help, not even Virginia."

"No one can touch you when you've lost a child," Marta said, and Loppy looked at her, sensing the strength of feeling behind the comment, but too discreet to probe further.

"Was he Vanessa's only son?" Josephine asked.

"No, there's Quentin—he's an artist—and she has a daughter with Duncan called Angelica. You must meet Duncan. He's such a sweet boy, and Grace is devoted to him. He and Maynard were once so in love."

The comment was made without any of the complications or resentment it implied, and Josephine looked at Marta, who simply shrugged. "You've got to give them credit for their understanding," she said as they wandered out into the walled garden for some time to themselves. "I used to think our love life was complicated."

"That's because it was." Josephine smiled and briefly took Marta's hand. "Worth it, though. Shall we have a look round?"

They set off down the nearest path, lined with roses on both sides. It was still early afternoon, but the air had been quick to acquire the chill of an autumn day, and Josephine shivered, wishing she had thought to bring her coat in from the car. The old elm trees, which used to shield the garden on two sides from northerly winds, had either been felled or succumbed to disease, leaving the garden more exposed, and the extra light seemed to have drawn every ounce of drama from the soil in an explosion of color and growth. "This is stunning," Marta said, admiring a blaze of dahlias and hollyhocks that jostled for position in the same patch of earth. "You can tell it's been designed by an artist. It's all about color and form, and very little to do with gardening."

It did seem as if the decoration on the walls inside had forced its way out through the windows, and Josephine wondered what Miss

H would have had to say about the beautiful disorder that now blurred her strict lines and carefully contained borders. She marveled at how little time it had taken to obliterate something that had once seemed so functional and productive. She left Marta in her element by the flower beds and headed for the wooden gate that led out through the crumbling redbrick wall to the paddocks beyond. The paint was the same pale gray color that it had always been, sun-scorched and peeling away from the wood, and as she pushed it open, she heard the familiar rising squeal of rusty hinges that no amount of oil had ever silenced; back then, it had been a useful way to monitor the girls' comings and goings; she had always known how many were passing through by the time it took the gate to slam shut.

With a mixture of relief and disappointment, she saw instantly that there was nothing left of the old greenhouse. In its place was a compost heap, overrun with nettles and a few newly planted fruit trees with clusters of lords-and-ladies around the trunks. The potting shed was still there, filled with damaged garden furniture and things discarded from the house over several years. Josephine peered through the window at the miscellany of boxes, filled with broken crockery and colored glass, all presumably waiting to be made into mosaics like those she had seen dotted around the walled garden. Everything was covered by a silver labyrinth of spiders' webs, miraculously strong enough to hold the past in place.

A path to her left took her the long way round to the front door, down by the side of the house and past the old dairy and kitchens. She paused by the gate that separated the gardens from the farm and looked back at what had once been the college office, very much Miss H's domain. If her visit had been designed to bring those people back to life, it had not disappointed. Standing here, with the solid red brick at her back and the sound of voices through the open window, it was easy to conjure up an image of the girls at work in the gardens or to relive the conversations over supper. But that still didn't answer any of Marta's questions or satisfy her own niggling doubts about Dorothy Norwood's death. Had the barely suppressed hostility in that community really ended in violence? Would two women—women she had liked and admired—stop at nothing to protect their reputation? Or was that simply a convenient smoke-screen to hide a different motive altogether? There was only one way to find out, and she knew now that she would have to try to track them down and speak to them.

She shivered again and went back to find Marta, half-wishing that she hadn't come. A sadness had taken hold of her as soon as she crossed the threshold, partly because of memories that she would rather not revisit, partly because of the way the house felt now—grieving, in spite of its color and its laughter; talking constantly to keep the despair at bay. There was no sign of Marta in the garden, so she went back inside to look for her, but on her way through the downstairs rooms, curiosity about the rest of the house got the bet-ter of her. The steps to the first floor were steep and narrow, but she took them boldly, prepared to ask for the bathroom if anyone chal-lenged her. As she had hoped, the bedrooms were quiet and obvi-ously empty, so she followed the dimly lit landing round to the front, surprised to see that the ceramic number plates that had been above the doors when Charleston was a guesthouse were still there.

The door to her old room was closed, and her nerve stopped short of trying the handle, but Jeannie's old bedroom—number five, a little further down—was more obliging. The hinges creaked as she pushed at the half-open door, and she guessed that the room must now be used for guests, because there was a suitcase on one of the twin beds, its contents strewn hurriedly across the bedspread. She looked round at the motley furnishings and walked over to the window, catching the scent from a pot of lavender that was drying on the sill. The view to the west was disappointing, but if the maze of outbuilding rooftops lacked beauty, they made up for it by offer-ing an alternative means of entry and escape that she had often taken advantage of. Immediately below, the noises from the kitchen were familiar, and she remembered the early morning sound of

Harriet Barker's footsteps on the attic stairs, which ran immediately behind the bedroom wall, a warning that the household was about to come to life.

The curtains billowed in the breeze, bringing Josephine back to the present. She heard someone coming and hurried to the door, only to find herself face to face with a man on the landing. "Hello there," he said, apparently unsurprised to see her. He probably assumed that she was staying the night in the guest room, so she returned the greeting as casually as possible and introduced herself. "Ah, you're Loppy's friend—the playwright? Very nice to meet you. I'm Duncan Grant."

His words were muffled a little by the cigarette hanging from his lips, but his voice was warm and surprisingly gentle. Josephine looked at Loppy's "sweet boy" and knew exactly what she meant. Even as a middle-aged man, Grant was exceptionally attractive, with thick, dark hair parted at the side and piercing blue eyes; in his youth, he must have been beautiful. She was about to say something complimentary about the house, when she noticed a picture hanging on the landing wall opposite; she hadn't seen it coming up in the gloom, but the light from the spare room behind her dispelled the shadows on the canvas, and she stared in surprise. Grant looked at her curiously. "I'm sorry," she said, "but I suddenly recognized that painting. I don't know if Loppy told you, but I stayed here during the war, and the man who painted it was one of the other lodgers. I watched him working on it, but I've never seen it finished."

"Then be my guest." He threw open the other bedroom doors to allow more light onto the landing, then came to stand beside her. "Good, isn't it?"

The image was certainly very powerful. A soldier stood in the foreground, looking gravely into the distance as he prepared to put on his gas mask. Behind him, other members of his platoon wrestled with their kit, helping one another with straps and buckles in a simple but touching gesture of friendship. The painting was a somber palette of browns and khaki, lifted here and there by a metal object picked out in gold metallic paint. In the darker shadows on the left hand side, a soldier stood apart from the rest, distant and impersonal, with his mask already on, and Josephine was struck by the picture's quiet but eloquent statement on the dehumanizing effects of war. "Do you know Peter Whittaker?" she asked, wondering if the artist was now one of the many regular visitors to the house.

"No, we never met him. This was hanging in the hall downstairs when we moved in, and it seemed wrong to get rid of it. Nessa's not so keen, but she'll just about tolerate it up here in the dark."

"So Whittaker was killed in the war?" Josephine asked, picking up on his use of the past tense. "He was convalescing when I knew him, and waiting to be recalled."

"To be honest, I don't know for certain, but I've always assumed he was killed. So many of them died, and with a talent like that, I think we would have heard about it if he were still painting." He hitched his trousers up, and Josephine noticed that they were held up with a red tie rather than a belt. "We've got some sketches of his downstairs that might interest you. At least I think they're his— they're not signed, but the style is quite distinctive. We found them in an old portfolio when we were building the studio—they must have been lying around in that shed for years. Would you like to take a look if I can lay my hands on them?"

"Yes, I'd love to."

"Come on then."

He ran down the stairs like a boy on Christmas morning, and Josephine followed—through the old dairy, which was now a garden room, and into a light, open space whose high vaulted ceiling was completely in contrast to the proportions of the rest of the house. "This used to be the chicken run," she said with a smile.

"Yes. We converted it about ten years ago, when the lease was extended, although I suppose you could say we're still scratching around in it." He grinned at her and began to rummage through a

cupboard piled high with prints, sketchbooks, and gallery cata-
logues. "They're here somewhere, but I haven't had them out for
years."

Josephine looked round in fascination as he began to throw
more and more paper down onto the floor. Despite its inevitable
clutter, the studio was a peaceful room, filled with a cool, still
light that was fading now as the afternoon went on. The gunpow-
der walls were hung with canvases that she assumed were Duncan's
and Vanessa's, and everything that had contributed to their creation
was scattered like shrapnel about the room: easels and paint boxes;
brushes in jam jars and bottles of linseed oil; palettes and tubes of
paint; plaster busts, photographs, and a collection of curious objets
d'art that lived in unlikely harmony on the mantelpiece. Ashtrays
overflowed on every surface, and the air was heavy with the smell
of tobacco mixed with turpentine. A vase of flowers and a gramophone struck a more homely note, the latter decorated with a
painted nymph, and an armchair stood on either side of a large
black stove. The easels too stood in companionable proximity, and
Josephine tried to imagine herself and Marta working together like
that and sharing a table to write. It would be a battleground, she
realized: arguments over music or silence, with Marta constantly
irritated by the noise of a typewriter and she by the scratching of a
pen or the fug of cigarette smoke. Neither their careers nor their
relationship would last the month, and she began to understand the
respect and tolerance that must exist between the two artists.
"When exactly were you here?" Duncan called over his shoulder
as the pile of sorted papers began to dwarf what was left in the
cupboard.

"The summer of 1915. It was a horticultural college for girls,
part of the war effort."

"Ah, that explains why the grounds were nothing but a sea of
mud and potatoes. It took us ages to get the garden round, but
thinking about it, we should have left it as it was. We'll all be growing our own food again soon."

"Was it really that bad when you arrived?"

"Yes, although that wasn't until the autumn of the following year, and I think there must have been other tenants in between. They'd kept animals in all the downstairs rooms, and that doesn't sound like a ladies' college." He smiled again and scratched his head, ruffling hair that was already unruly. "The place was going to wrack and ruin, with damp everywhere and the most awful wallpaper you've ever seen. Just as well it was falling off the walls, and we certainly helped it on its way."

"How did you find the house? Were you living round here already?"

"No, but Nessa's sister was. She and Leonard were down at Asheham, and she saw Charleston one day when she was out walking. We were in Suffolk at the time, but Bunny and I were conscientious objectors, and growing raspberries in Wissett wasn't arduous enough to constitute essential work, so we took farm work here instead and rented the house. It was that or prison." Josephine had no idea who Bunny was, but there was a triumphant cry from the cupboard before she could ask. "Here it is. I knew I'd kept them."

He took the old leather portfolio over to a table and without ceremony dumped a sheaf of his own sketches onto the floor. The first drawings that he pulled out were single studies, some for the painting on the landing and others for work she didn't recognize. Duncan passed them over to her, occasionally commenting on some small quirk or detail, and she noticed how the pictures came to life in his hand. He possessed that unself-conscious charm of someone who had always known what he wanted to do in life and now had the luxury of doing it, and Josephine could easily understand why people fell so easily under his spell. "These are so different," she observed suddenly, shocked by the next series of sketchbooks that came out of the folder. "They're so . . ."

"Accurate?" Duncan suggested wryly as she searched for the right word.

"Yes, I suppose that's exactly it." She turned the pages slowly, trying to come to terms with their anger. All the violence that had been so carefully suppressed in the finished painting upstairs was here given a free rein, and she stared down at images of dead bodies on the battlefield and war-torn landscapes, of men's faces filled with hate. Somehow, the carefully controlled beauty of the draftsmanship only served to emphasize the horror. She looked at Duncan, but he was staring fixedly down, his jaw set, and she wondered if the drawings were a rebuke to his conscience for the safety of his own war or simply a confirmation that he had been right all along. "You never know what people are feeling, do you?" she said quietly, remembering the young man who had sat across the breakfast table from her, white-faced whenever a letter was delivered that might recall him to the front, but stoically accepting its inevitability. Occasionally, there had been outbursts of temper that she had put down to fear or frustration, but nothing to suggest the darkness that had found its outlet on these pages.

"They shouldn't be hidden away," Duncan said, taking a small sketch of a gas victim and pinning it to the mantelshelf, where it sat incongruously next to postcards, invitations, and children's drawings. "Not ever, but especially not now. Something's got to show these bloody idiots what we're heading for."

"You really think that would make a difference?" Josephine asked cynically, putting the sketchbook down. "I can't help but remember the last time I was in Germany. It was a beautiful warm night, and someone was playing a violin in the darkness under the trees—all very sweet and nostalgic except for the Nazi rally in the background. Long after I went to bed, I could hear the marching and the chanting, and if *I* could have seen what was coming . . ." She gave a bitter laugh, surprised by her own strength of feeling. "We've had plenty of warning if we wanted to listen, and no matter how many times you remind yourself that more people are killed on the roads each year than in Spain, you can't rationalize war. It's an idiot's delight."

There was a noise behind her, and she turned to see Vanessa

standing in the doorway. "Desmond is here, Duncan," she said. "He wants to speak to you." She smiled at Josephine, but there was no warmth in it, and Josephine wondered how long she had been there.

"I'm so sorry," she said as Vanessa went back to the party. "That was tactless of me."

He accepted her apology without judgment. "She couldn't even paint after it happened," he said, as if that was the most telling sign of Vanessa's grief, a secondary casualty of her son's death. "I suppose what happened to Julian disabused us all of the notion that by doing no harm to anyone, we could avoid the suffering." He shook his head at his own naivety, absentmindedly straightening the drawings as he asked, "Did you lose someone in the war?"

She knew what he meant, but the melancholy that had been playing on her mind all afternoon came from the realization that something precious *had* been lost that summer, and it had nothing to do with the war. "Yes," she said, choosing the easy answer. "At the Somme. He died helping a friend, which was a great comfort to me and a constant torment to the friend."

Duncan nodded but avoided the usual clichés, and she appreciated his lack of sentiment. "I'd better go," he said, "but take as long as you like here. It's been nice to meet you."

He switched a lamp on for her as he left, and she began to look quickly through the remaining sketches, conscious that Marta would be waiting for her. There were two more books in the portfolio, smaller than the others and tucked into a side pocket. She opened one, expecting to find more of the same, but stopped in astonishment at the first page. Though similar in tone, these drawings had a very different subject matter to the others. The body she was looking at was Dorothy Norwood's—not on a battlefield this time, but recognizably where she had died. Josephine flicked through the next few pages, increasingly disturbed by what she saw: a girl's mutilated corpse, drawn from every angle and in forensic detail, killed in a multitude of ways in scenes that must have come from Peter Whittaker's imagination, scenes that bore no resemblance to how she had actually died. She forced herself to go on: Dorothy's contorted face with a strong hand at her throat; her bruised and beaten body hanging from the rafters in the barn; and finally her head held under the water in the pond outside the door.

Shaken, she turned to the other book. To her relief, it was harmless, consisting mainly of drawings of the girls at work in the gardens or sitting round a campfire on a summer's evening, all very much alive. She turned the final page, glad to have reached the end, but there was one more surprise waiting for her: the figure on the right was unmistakably her, and the tenderness between the two women in the picture was in such stark contrast to everything else that it took her breath away. She sat down, feeling suddenly faint, and looked at the picture again. They had been so careful, she thought, so discreet. How could he possibly have known? Ashamed of herself, but not ashamed enough to be deterred, she closed the sketchbook and slipped the two slim volumes into her bag.

She was too shocked for the moment to think logically about what the drawings might mean or what she should do with them. Outside, the Sussex light was working its magic over the pale golden stubble fields, and she used its peace to settle her thoughts. When she was less afraid of what the past might hold, she went to look for Marta.

SUMMER 1915

CHAPTER 1

If Josephine had ever wondered what a London station looked like at five in the morning, she couldn't have imagined anything quite as miserable as this dim and drafty depository for lost souls. The sense of busyness and purpose that animated travelers during the day was entirely absent here. People lay asleep on the platforms, something that would never have been allowed in peacetime, and soldiers rested on their packs, listlessly turning the pages of a newspaper. One or two of them were drunk, shouting and swaying as they passed the bench where she sat, hoping not to draw attention to herself and struggling to remember a time when the hours had passed more slowly. Only the fresh morning air was a relief after the packed train from Birmingham. She shivered, more at the thought of continuing her journey than from anything the early dawn could throw at her, and stood up to stretch her legs.

Victoria was obviously the central station for soldiers traveling to and from the front. As the daylight strengthened outside, it brought with it a swarm of uniformed men heading for the early leave train, and the station sprang to life as suddenly as if a film had started halfway through. Relieved to have something to do, Josephine followed the crowd to one of the sidings, where a private train was waiting to take soldiers on the first leg of their journey back to France. It was a train like any other, identical to the one that had brought the men home, and yet somehow everything about it was different. The carriages were dark and somber, as if in deference to a fated journey, and Josephine couldn't help but feel that black drapes at the windows would have been appropriate; even their luggage—long bolsters rather than cases or trunks—marked these passengers out from ordinary travelers, and the flowers that some of them clutched had an ironic, funeral feel.

The platform had filled up quickly, with no one willing to board the train before the last possible moment. She scanned the faces of those who had come to see their loved ones off: wives who talked too much to hide their fear; fathers standing strict and silent; children for whom a uniform hadn't lost its glamour. A small boy stood by his brother's kit, beating it like a drum to a refrain of "Let 'em have it!"; the sentiment sounded shrill and unsettling in the high-pitched voice of a child. As for the men themselves, their faces were set and impassive, and she noticed how few of them dared to look for long at the people they loved.

The sound of a whistle cut through the air, signaling departure. There was a silence as the final goodbyes were said, and a succession of banging doors brought the scene to a close. The train pulled out of the station—slowly, as if reluctant to play its part in the drama. As the waving khaki-clad arms grew more distant, Josephine was shocked by the loneliness on the faces of the women who turned and drifted away, back to homes which must have seemed so briefly normal again. There were very few tears, but some of them seemed to have aged beyond recognition the minute their men were out of sight.

Her trunk was where she had left it, and a train now stood at the platform, ready for boarding. There was no porter in sight, so Josephine hauled it across to the luggage van and went to find a third-class carriage. This leg of the journey showed no sign of being as busy as the last, and she settled comfortably into a seat by the window, exchanging pleasantries with the middle-aged woman opposite until it was time to leave. The warmth of the carriage reminded her of how tired she was, and when her companion took a magazine out of her bag and began to read, Josephine allowed herself to doze, encouraged by the gentle motion of the carriage as it left the city behind and moved out into the countryside, heading south. When she woke, the sun had worked its magic, drawing every ounce of color from the fields and wooded hills until it seemed as if the gentle English landscape had been laid out solely for her approval. Perhaps it was the beauty of the morning, perhaps simply the knowledge that each mile took her farther from home than she had been before, but she couldn't remember ever being quite so entranced or excited by her first impressions of somewhere new.

The countryside she had pored over on a map for weeks materialized in ways she could never have dreamt of: the kaleidoscopic patterns made by fields among hedgerows; the pretty villages and soft, undulating hills; and then, across the border into Sussex, the county's defining glory, a vibrant chalk and green escarpment that rolled into the distance like a vast, breaking wave. Suddenly, her college life in Birmingham seemed as unreal as if it had belonged to someone else. The trams that broke down in the dark of an unknown suburb, the smell of the gasworks, the crowds in Steelhouse Lane on a Saturday night—all of it vanished beneath these clean, fresh skies, and the homesickness for the Highlands which had colored every minute of her time in the city was suddenly absent. With no logic or justification that she could think of, she felt a powerful sense of belonging, a certainty that here was somewhere she could call home.

As the train drew nearer to Eastbourne, her thoughts turned to the job that had brought her south—a summer posting before her second year at college, and a chance to put into practice everything that she had learned so far. She had never once regretted her decision to turn down art college in favor of something more practical. Anstey was one of the finest physical training schools in the country, with professional links to a number of institutions all over England, including the school that had arranged her current placement. Over the last twelve months, she had been drilled in everything from gymnastics, sports, and dance to physiotherapy, nursing, and the theory of teaching—but now, as her first real job beckoned, she was painfully aware that "theory" was all it had been. The very thought of standing before a group of young women only a few years her junior, and issuing even the most basic of instructions, made her long to catch the first train home.

A guard passed down the corridor, announcing the next stop, and Josephine waited eagerly for her first glimpse of the sea. The downs surrounding Eastbourne were dotted with the familiar white tents of army camps that had begun to appear in wide-open spaces, for training and increasingly for convalescence, and she marveled at how quickly such a sight had become a natural part of the landscape. At first glance, the town itself was more modern than she had expected, with handsome new villas eventually giving way to the established civic buildings, but it had a bright, fresh feel to it that seemed to suit the morning sunlight. The station was busy, and Josephine looked anxiously at the clock, conscious that her train was ten minutes late; her confirmation letter had promised someone to collect her and take her to the school for a meeting with the principal, but there was no one waiting at the barrier, and she wondered if her lift had given up and left. With a sigh, she tried to attract the attention of a sweating, overworked porter, then gave up and dragged her trunk out to the front, hoping to find a bus that passed by Moira House. She was just trying to make sense of the timetable when she heard the sound of a car horn, used repeatedly from the road, and someone calling her name. "Josephine? Josephine Tey?"

Josephine glanced round and saw a young woman waving at her from a dusty delivery van parked awkwardly on the pavement. The girl opened the door and jumped out, much to the annoyance of a cyclist passing by on the driver's side, and made a beeline for Josephine through the bus queue. She was tall, with long auburn hair scraped back into a ponytail, and she wore a striking outfit of tunic, breeches, and mud-caked boots. "I knew you straightaway," she said, answering Josephine's puzzled expression. "Not second sight, I'm afraid—just the Anstey uniform. Once worn, never forgotten." She held out her hand. "I'm Jeanette Sellwood, but most people call me Jeannie. I've been dispatched to take you to the madhouse."

Josephine smiled. "That's very kind. My train was delayed, so I hope I haven't kept you waiting."

"Not at all. It's been a bloody awful morning, and I've only just got here myself." She looked round in vain for a trolley, then grabbed one end of the trunk and signaled to Josephine to take the other. "Have you got any more luggage to collect?"

"No, just this."

"Good. Let's get it loaded up, and we can be on our way." They dragged the trunk over to the van and wrestled it into the back, which was already stacked with empty vegetable crates. "That's a lovely accent, by the way," Jeannie said, moving things about to make more room. "Edinburgh?"

"No, but you're on the right coast. Inverness. Apparently we speak the King's English better than he does."

"I think even the King might struggle to make himself heard in front of our lot. It's a bit like a hurricane passing through when those girls get together." Jeannie brushed some soil and a few carrot tops off the front seat. "Hop in. It's hardly traveling in style, but at least it's reliable."

"I'm not bothered about style. After all those hours cooped up in a carriage, it's just nice to have room to breathe." Josephine climbed aboard, noticing that the vehicle was newer than its bruised and dented bodywork had led her to believe.

"Don't get too used to the space. We've got to make a detour on the way." She offered no explanation but threw an admiring glance at Josephine's white blouse and full-length navy-blue skirt. "I don't know how you manage to look so fresh after that journey. My recollection of Birmingham is spending the first three weeks of every holiday trying to get the grime from the steelworks out of my skin."

"Well, that certainly hasn't changed," Josephine said, pleased to have some common ground to break the ice. "When were you at Anstey?"

"I graduated in 1912 and came back down here straight afterward."

"Back?"

Jeannie nodded. "That's right. I'm a local girl. My family lives in Firle."

"Isn't that where Charleston Farmhouse is?"

"Just outside, yes. I was a student at Moira House before I started teaching there. It wasn't quite what I intended, staying so close to home, but they had a vacancy, and I'd always been happy there, so I thought I'd give it a try while I wait for something more adventurous to come up." She looked wryly at Josephine. "I suppose that sounds feeble to you, when you're so far away from your roots. Does your family still live in Scotland?"

"Yes."

"And do you miss it?"

"Very much, but it's nice to be away for a while—somewhere different, where people take you at face value without any history. And from what the teachers at Anstey tell me, Moira House keeps its staff busy. I imagine there's very little time to notice if you're five miles from home or five hundred."

Jeannie nodded. "That's true enough, and it means I can help out in the pub during the holidays, so it keeps my parents happy." She caught the look of surprise on Josephine's face. "My father's the landlord at the Ram Inn. I know pulling pints isn't quite the thing for a teacher with young ladies in her charge, but as the great and the good of Eastbourne don't seem to drink there, I've got away with it so far. And the countryside around the village is beautiful. I'll give you the grand tour once you're settled in."

"Thank you. I'd like that." The roads became steeper as they left the town center behind, leafy avenues with majestic houses on either side and, in the distance, the longed-for glimpse of a sparkling sea. "You called the school a madhouse," Josephine said, wondering how carefully the word had been chosen. "Was that just a figure of speech?"

"You'll have to decide for yourself, but I was actually talking about Charleston. We're heading off there after lunch, as soon as you've had your orders from Miss Ingham." She stopped at a junction for a bus to pass, then continued. "I was so pleased when I heard you'd be joining us. There's a lot to do, and apart from anything else it'll be nice to have some ordinary company for a change."

Josephine laughed. "I'll try to live down to that."

"Sorry. That didn't come out quite as I intended." Jeannie smiled apologetically and considered her next words more carefully. "I don't want to give you the wrong impression. It's a wonderful place, and I'm sure you'll love it."

"But . . . ? You might as well warn me now. My principal couldn't say enough about Moira House, but she was very vague about the farm post, other than to say that it was 'pioneering work.'"

"Well, for a start you must never call it a farm," Jeannie said. "It's a horticultural college for young ladies. Miss Hartford-Wroe and Miss Barker are very particular about that."

"And they run it together?"

"That's right. Miss Barker looks after the house and runs the business side of things, and the gardens are very much Miss H's domain. They bicker like an old married couple at times, but it seems to work."

Josephine was intrigued. "Is this the moment to admit that I know nothing whatsoever about gardening?"

"That doesn't matter. There's nothing Miss H likes better than a clean slate to work with. By the time you leave, those fingers will be the brightest of greens." She smiled at Josephine's doubtful expression and spoke more seriously. "I mean it. She's a born teacher—and very ambitious for what the college could become. I've learnt as much from her in three weeks as I did in two years at Anstey. She's got us all eating out of her hand, and the girls can't do enough to please her. It gets quite competitive at times."

"What are the girls like?"

Jeannie considered her answer. "They have that Jekyll-and-Hyde quality peculiar to all adolescents—charming one moment and the devil incarnate the next. Mind you, I can't say that I was any better behaved at their age, and I'm sure you weren't either." Josephine thought back to her sixteen-year-old self, trying in vain to find the rebel and the saint that Jeannie obviously imagined. "It doesn't help that Miss Barker's cousin is staying with us at the moment," she added. "He's very attractive if you like the broken hero type. Back from the war, all angry and vulnerable." There was a sudden edge to her voice, which surprised Josephine. "Speaking of which, here's our diversion." She pointed up ahead and to the left, where the huts and tents of an army convalescent camp were nestled into the downs. "Welcome to Summerdown."

"Why are we here?"

"To round up a couple of strays. I'm sorry to involve you in some subterfuge on your very first day, but it will give us both a quieter life in the long run, I promise." She stopped the van at the gate and jumped out as the soldier on duty came over to greet them, and Josephine admired her confidence as she showed him some papers and charmed him into waving them through. "You can add lying to the British army to my ever-growing list of misdemeanors," Jeannie said, as the gates closed behind them.

"What did you tell him?"

"That we've come to teach the patients gardening." She caught Josephine's bewilderment and laughed. "It's actually not as ridiculous as it sounds. Gardening is one of the things they do here alongside the medical treatment—it's supposed to get the men physically and mentally fit to go back. And look at how I'm dressed. I could hardly convince him that we ran the basket-making workshops."

"This surely can't have been here very long?" Josephine said, amazed by the camp's size. Rows and rows of round white tents stretched out in straight lines across the hillside, and in a large area of ground on the other side of the makeshift road, the small canvas structures were already being replaced by larger, inauspiciously permanent wooden huts. Very quickly, Summerdown seemed to have become a community in its own right, part of the landscape and peopled by wounded men in badly fitting blue uniforms.

"They opened it in April, but it's already three times the size it was originally," Jeannie explained. "You'll see that uniform every-where about the town. Blueboys, they call them, although I can't help feeling that's a misleadingly romantic name for people whose bodies or nerves have been shot to hell. Still, at least it marks them out from the cowards."

It was hard to tell if she was being serious or sarcastic. They came to a crossroads, and Jeannie turned right, apparently knowing exactly where she was going. "You've obviously been here before," Josephine said.

"Yes, it's not the first time I've saved those girls' necks, and I dare say it won't be the last, although today I feel more like wring-ing them." She swerved suddenly onto the grass by the side of the road and pulled up near a motorbike and sidecar. "And there's the telltale clue. Do you want to wait here? I won't be long."

Josephine nodded and watched as she walked off toward the huts. From the chatter of conversation and a smell of frying bacon, the nearest clearly functioned as a canteen. She got out of the van and looked round, realizing suddenly how hungry she was. The day was heading for noon, and its warmth had brought several soldiers outside to make the most of it; they sat around in deckchairs with their eyes closed and faces lifted to the sun, now gloriously high in a clear blue sky, while seagulls whirled overhead. Were it not for the predominance of crutches and bandages, she could almost be fooled into accepting the holiday atmosphere at face value.

The van was an object of curiosity, and she noticed two soldiers in standard khaki uniforms looking at her as they headed toward the canteen. "You look a little lost," one of them said, breaking off from his friend. "Can I help?"

Josephine couldn't help smiling. "With an accent like that, I think we're both a long way from home."

"An Inverness girl! I'm right, aren't I?" She nodded. "Ah, the answer to all my prayers." He laughed and beckoned the other man over to join them. "See, Archie? I told you it was going to be a beautiful day. This young lady and I are practically neighbors." The news didn't seem to hold any particular interest for the soldier called Archie, who was considerably less affable than his companion. "I'm Jack Mackenzie," the Scotsman said, "and my English friend here is Archie Penrose."

"Nice to meet you. I'm Josephine Tey." She shook hands with them both. "Whereabouts in the Highlands are you from?"

"Daviot, just a few miles down the road from you. You must know it?"

"Know it? I spent every summer there until I was eighteen. My parents are good friends with the Patersons."

They talked about mutual acquaintances in the small village that Josephine loved so much, and she was surprised by how welcome she found this unexpected connection with home. Conscious that Archie was excluded from the conversation, she gestured toward the book in his hand, a well-read copy of an Edgar Wallace mystery. "I think that's one of his best," she said. "Are you enjoying it?"

"It's not bad, as far as it goes. I don't really like thrillers, but Jack insisted I give it a go."

"So what *do* you like?"

Archie shrugged. "Something with a bit more realism, I suppose."

Josephine looked round at the wounded men. "Don't you have enough of that already?"

Her tone was faintly mocking, and she regretted the words as soon as they were out, but Archie didn't rise to the bait. His aloofness unsettled her, and she was glad when Jack filled the silence. "Are you one of the volunteers here?" he asked, still smiling at her gibe to his friend.

"No, I'm here with a colleague to . . . well, if I'm honest, I'm not quite sure why we're here. But I'm training to be a teacher, and I've got a summer posting with a girls' school in town. We're heading off there now."

"That's a pity."

Josephine felt herself blush. "What about you? You don't look injured, so . . ."

"Neither do lots of the men here," Archie interrupted. "Not all the damage is on the surface."

He delivered the point politely, but there was a spark of defiance in his eyes that she read as a challenge. "We're medics," Jack explained before she could retaliate. "We were studying together in Cambridge when we signed up, and we've got a spell of work here before they send us out to the front."

"When will that be?"

"It could be any time, but I doubt we'll be here longer than a month. Probably best if we go sooner rather than later—the facilities here are spoiling us, and we won't have anything like it out there."

"We'd better go, Jack," Archie said, looking at his watch. "I'm on duty in half an hour, and I want to get something to eat."

"All right. You go ahead if you want to." He turned back to Josephine as Archie nodded to her and headed for the canteen. "Would you like to go out one evening, Miss Tey? When you've had a chance to settle in?"

She hesitated, reluctant to make any arrangements before she had even reported for duty, but she was flattered by his interest and attracted to his good humor. "All right," she agreed, surprised by how at ease she felt in his company. "I'd like that very much."

"Good. So would I. Where can I contact you?"

"We're staying at Charleston Farmhouse in Firle, or you can

send a note to the school and it will reach me—Moira House, on Carlisle Road."

"I'll do that." He ran to catch up with his friend, and Josephine was struck again by the contrast between the two men. Tall and dark, his lean features tanned by the sun, Archie would have been the more conventionally handsome were it not for Jack's readiness to laugh, which transformed his pleasant but ordinary face into something much more memorable. She watched as they disappeared into the hut, intrigued by the brief encounter. To Josephine's surprise, it was Archie who looked back at her and raised his hand.

She wandered back to the van, just in time to see Jeannie marching two sullen-looking girls across the grass. Their uniforms, like their expressions, were identical: pale brown coat and skirt, with matching soft-rimmed felt hat and crisp white shirt. A silk sailor tie in red and blue, together with a corresponding cord around the hat, provided what Josephine assumed were the colors of the college. "Sorry to have kept you waiting, Miss Tey," Jeannie said, her face as black as thunder, "but Miss Lomax and Miss Norwood appear to think we've got nothing better to do than to chase all over the countryside rounding up lost souls who are old enough to know better."

"We weren't lost," the blonde girl objected, and as she lifted her head, Josephine noticed traces of a vivid red lipstick that had been hurriedly wiped off. She seemed about to develop her argument, but Jeannie raised her hand.

"In that case, Miss Lomax, would you like to explain to Miss Hartford-Wroe and then to your parents exactly what you *were* doing?" The threat was enough, and Josephine looked forward more than ever to meeting the woman who inspired such respect—or fear. "Good. At the end of term—and believe me, I'm looking forward to it every bit as eagerly as you are—you will be free to decide what you are and what you are not. Until then, you will both defer to me on all subjects, including your own minds. Is that understood?"

"Yes, Miss Sellwood." One young voice echoed the other, and Josephine stared at them with what she hoped was a mirror image of Jeannie's authority.

"Excellent. Now this is Miss Tey, who will be with us until the end of our time at Charleston. Introduce yourselves, and then perhaps we can get on with our day."

Again, it was the blonde girl who spoke first. "Charity Lomax, Miss Tey. Very pleased to meet you."

She smiled easily—a little too easily for Josephine's liking—but her face was honest and open, and Josephine found her easier to warm to than her tight-lipped friend. "I'm Betty Norwood," the dark girl said, barely meeting her eye.

"Right—let's get you back to school." Jeannie walked round to the back of the van and opened the doors. "Get in."

"What?" Charity cast her eyes over the cramped, dirt-strewn interior, and the mixture of disgust and indignation on her face was a picture. "Surely you don't expect us to travel in there?" she said, looking to Betty for support. "We'll get absolutely filthy, and it reeks of cabbages. Peter will bring us back on the motorbike."

"Peter will do no such thing, and it's Mr. Whittaker to you. Now get in the van. I won't tell you again."

This time they did as they were told, although not without protest. Jeannie slammed the door shut and winked at Josephine. "I shouldn't be enjoying this, but I am."

"What *are* they doing here?"

"Making eyes at Peter bloody Whittaker."

"Who's he?"

"Miss Barker's cousin. I told you about him earlier."

"Oh yes—the broken hero. I thought you said he was staying at the house, though."

"He is, but some of his regiment are convalescing here, so he's back and forth all the time, and it amuses him to lead the girls astray. Charity, especially—she's a law unto herself, and as you might have guessed from her reaction just now—growing vegetables doesn't really fit with the future she imagines for herself. Apart from any-thing else, the soil plays havoc with her nails." Her grin faded as she glanced back toward the huts, where a young man was lounging in one of the doorways. "Talk of the devil. I swear he only does it to infuriate me."

The edge in her voice was there again and Josephine looked curiously at the man who had provoked it, but the only sin she could lay at his door was an air of detachment that bordered on arrogance. As she watched, he blew a theatrical kiss to the girls in the back of the van, whose humiliation was obviously increased by his having witnessed it; their faces quickly disappeared from the rear window. "Why would he want to infuriate you?"

"Why do you think? He made me an offer I could refuse, and that didn't sit well with him."

She got back into the front seat, and Josephine joined her. "What is he convalescing from?" she asked. Whittaker was wearing the Blueboy uniform, but—as if to give weight to Archie's reproof—there were no obvious signs of injury, and he was clearly fit enough to ride a motorbike.

The question seemed to irritate Jeannie. "Gas. He was caught up in the attack at Ypres." She turned the van round, reversing quickly and deliberately over the grass until she was perilously close to the sidecar. "Please don't tell me you *are* the broken hero type. You seem to have more sense than to fall for the first attractive man in uniform."

"Of course I have," Josephine said, smarting a little from the accusation and omitting to mention that she had already disap-pointed Jeannie's expectations. "I'd also have more sense than to give him the satisfaction of damaging his motorbike and having to apologize."

Jeannie laughed, and the tension between them vanished as quickly as it had arrived. "I'm sorry. I don't know you well enough yet to give you the third degree. You've probably got someone back at home, and anyway it's none of my business."

It wasn't, but Josephine still felt inclined to answer; she liked Jeannie for her humor and frankness, and didn't want to alienate a potential friend by giving less in return. "There isn't anyone," she said, hoping that the students in the back of the van couldn't hear their conversation over the noise of the engine. "At the moment, I'm just enjoying my freedom, and I have every intention of keeping it that way."

Summerdown Camp was on the same side of town as Moira House. The school occupied a large corner plot with a distant view of the sea, and Josephine looked admiringly at its imposing redbrick grandeur, surprised by its size. A tall, square turret at one end crowned what was already a lavishly designed building, and a generous number of windows overlooked immaculately kept playing fields and tennis courts. Everything spoke quietly of discipline, stability, and order. "Impressive, isn't it?" Jeannie said as she drove through the gates and parked close to the entrance. "Miss Ingham's father was the architect as well as the founder, and no expense was spared."

Josephine got out and looked round, breathing in the fresh sea air and instantly drawn to the tranquility of the grounds. "I can see why you were happy to come back here," she said. "It would be hard to imagine a starker contrast to Anstey. Not a factory in sight."

"No, and I love being so close to the sea." Jeannie went round to the back of the van and banged on the doors. "Come on, you two. Out you get." Betty emerged first, sulkily brushing the soil from her uniform, but any complaints she had were instantly overshadowed by her friend's sense of melodrama. "I honestly thought I was going to die in there," Charity gasped, inhaling deeply as if she had been holding her breath for the last ten minutes. She rubbed the cramp from her limbs and glared at her captor. "Did you have to drive over quite so many potholes?"

"Sorry about that. Have ten minutes in the front to recover, but I don't want either of you to leave this spot until we come and fetch you for lunch. Is that clear?" Charity opened her mouth to argue, but Jeannie turned her back and walked away.

"You found them, then?" An older woman, presumably another teacher, had been watching them from the window and she raised an eyebrow as they walked through the entrance hall. "Good luck upstairs. All hell's broken loose here since someone from the college telephoned to say they were missing. Miss Ingham would have reported them to the police already, I think, but for Lomax's parents."

"Well, there's no need for that now, Miss Frobisher. They're safe and well, and they've been with me all the time."

"Of course they have."

Miss Frobisher went about her business, still with a wry smile on her face, and Josephine followed Jeannie up an elegant, open-plan staircase. Like the entrance hall, the first-floor landings were tastefully decorated with rugs and select pieces of good, if unostentatious, furniture; plants or vases of flowers brightened dark corners, and highly polished floors and banisters filled the air with the faint smell of lavender. The overall impression would have been of a graceful, upmarket boarding house rather than a school, were it not for a series of framed photographs that provided visitors with an eloquent history of the school's beginnings and philosophy: the founder and his family pictured on the lawn and in their private quarters; well-behaved young ladies playing in an orchestra or dressed for the gym. Strangely enough, there was no photographic record of Moira House students playing truant in army camps, and Josephine wondered if this very individual contribution to the war effort would remain their secret. "Why is Miss Ingham concerned about Lomax's parents?" she asked, as Jeannie stopped in front of a mirror to check her hair and straighten her tie.

"Because they own half the Cotswolds, they're extremely generous with their donations, and there are three younger daughters who are all set to board here. She has a very pragmatic streak, our principal. And in fairness to her, it's not the first time that Charity's done a bunk, but she always turns up again."

"What are you going to tell her?"

"You're about to find out. Just back me up."

She knocked on a door at the end of the landing, and a voice responded immediately, a command rather than an invitation to come in. Gertrude Ingham was a small, neat woman in her thirties, with light brown hair parted in the middle and caught in a bun, and a style of dress that managed to be both feminine and authoritative. The desk she stood up from to greet them was perhaps the most productive that Josephine had ever seen, with the day's correspondence growing in tidy piles on one side of a vast blotter, and sheaves of paper—efficiently sorted—waiting for attention on the other. No ornaments or personal photographs had been allowed to encroach on the space devoted to work, but she noticed that the walls behind the desk were hung with a number of theatrical production shots—both professional and amateur—which suggested that the principal was a passionate fan of the stage in whatever leisure time she allowed herself. At least they would have that in common, she thought, as long as she managed to get beyond her initial interview without being dismissed for her part in the morning's deception. "Where have you been, Miss Sellwood?" the principal demanded. "We've been waiting."

"I'm so sorry, Miss Ingham, but Miss Tey's train was nearly an hour late." Josephine resisted the temptation to glance at Jeannie, and the lie went unchallenged. "I'm afraid I have another apology to make too. I took Lomax and Norwood with me to the station because there were some deliveries to do on the way, and I thought a couple of extra pairs of hands would save time. I assumed they'd told Miss Barker where they were going, but I gather that wasn't actually the case. I should have checked with them before leaving Firle, and I'm very sorry for all the trouble and worry I've caused."

"So you should be. Miss Tey, it seems to have been your misfortune to arrive on a day when we can show you how things are *not* to be done—but you're very welcome here all the same. I hope you will find your time with us both productive and enjoyable."

"Thank you, Miss Ingham. I'm sure I will."

The principal turned her attention back to Jeannie. "So Miss Lomax and Miss Norwood have been with you all the time?"

"Yes, Miss Ingham—other than a brief period at the station while I was looking for Miss Tey."

"I see. And they will tell me the same story if I get them in here now?"

Jeannie's hesitation was barely perceptible, and Josephine could only admire her nerve. "Of course, Miss Ingham. Shall I go and fetch them?"

"No, there's no need for that. I've wasted quite enough time on them already this morning, but make sure it doesn't happen again. Now, Miss Tey—let me tell you a little about the Moira House family. As you may know, my father founded the school thirty-five years ago because he was horrified by the education that was offered to my mother and my aunt, and indeed to women in general. He was inspired to do better by his travels in America, and we follow the pioneering ideas he introduced to this day: no arbitrary rules, no marks or prizes, no forced preparation for external exams, no punishment, and no bells to announce the beginning of the day or a change of lesson." Admirable as they were, the methods sounded like a recipe for chaos to Josephine, but she said nothing. "Such rigid markers are never necessary when intelligent, knowledge-loving children are involved, and we treat our girls like the sensible adults we hope they will become."

An image flashed into Josephine's mind of two young women surrounded by soldiers with only one thing on their minds, but Miss Ingham had paused in her address and clearly expected some sort of endorsement from her newest staff member. "So Miss Sell-wood was telling me on the journey here," Josephine said, feeling Jeannie stiffen by her side in an effort not to laugh. "It's a very inspiring atmosphere to learn in, and I'm sure the girls benefit from it enormously."

The principal nodded approvingly. "Indeed. We encourage indi-vidual and collective aspirations through music and a participation in team sports, and are particularly proud of our cricketers. Moira House has one of the first all-female teams in the country. Do you play?"

"Not cricket, I'm afraid, but I like sport very much, and I'm willing to try most things."

"Good. That's the spirit. I'm sure you'll fit in very well, and your teachers at Anstey certainly speak very highly of your achievements." She paused, considering for the first time what to say next. "Do you know why we chose our name?" Josephine shook her head. "Ah, you must study your Greek mythology. The Moirai are the three fates who guard the destiny of us all, and that is our responsibility to the girls in our charge. With that in mind, I would like to talk to you in confidence about your work with us this summer. The college placement at Charleston is both valuable and rewarding, but it is not without its pitfalls."

"Can I ask what they are?"

"Well, for a start there are the physical dangers that horticultural work inevitably throws up, and I would ask you to ensure that all our girls observe the rules they've been taught when working on the land. Then there is the more delicate matter of their moral welfare." She stopped again, looking meaningfully at Jeannie, and Josephine realized that the principal was perfectly aware of the lie that had been invented in her honor. "There are two men living in the household, as well as a number of laborers and conscientious objectors working on the surrounding land. We were all sixteen once, and know how exhilarating a small taste of freedom can be, but I'm sure I don't have to stress how important it is that you keep those girls safe from outside influences and, where necessary, safe from themselves."

"Of course, Miss Ingham."

"And finally to the most sensitive matter of all—your hosts. Miss Hartford-Wroe is a woman of great ambition and achievement, and a role model for us all. She has a unique vision and an unwavering determination to pursue it, which is why we value our connection with her work—but those same qualities can also lead to what might best be described as single-mindedness. What I'm about to tell you must not be discussed outside of this room, and I hope I can rely on your discretion." Josephine nodded and stole a glance at Jeannie, who was obviously as surprised as she was. "I have recently received a complaint about Miss Hartford-Wroe's treatment of one of the students in her care."

"But that's nonsense," Jeannie began, obviously bewildered by the accusation. "Yes, she works them hard and believes in discipline, but I've never known her to overstep the mark. Who is the complaint from?"

"I'm not at liberty to say just yet. The matter may come to nothing, and I wouldn't want either of you to be prejudiced against the person concerned. I hope very much that Miss Sellwood is right and that it will prove to be a simple misunderstanding, but it's my duty to investigate the matter thoroughly, and I need your co-operation as the people best placed to do that."

"You'd like us to come to you if we see any sign of bullying or cruelty?" Josephine said, trying to clarify exactly what the accusation was.

"I'd like both of you to be vigilant and report to me anything you think is . . . well, unseemly. Anything that betrays the trust that Moira House has placed in the college as a temporary custodian of its students. Is that clear?"

"Yes, Miss Ingham."

"Good. And please remember—you represent this school and I expect your conduct to be exemplary at all times, day and night. Now—lunch is about to be served downstairs. You may eat here, and then go straight back to the college."

"Of course, Miss Ingham. Thank you."

"Do you really have no idea at all what she was talking about?" Josephine asked when they were outside the office.

"None whatsoever. As I said to you on the way, the girls all love Miss H—at least I thought they did."

"Perhaps that's the trouble." Jeannie looked at her questioningly. "Does Miss H have favorites?" Josephine asked. "You said it was competitive. Perhaps someone's getting her own back for being overlooked."

"I hadn't thought of that. It's possible, I suppose." She stopped by one of the first-floor windows that overlooked the front gates. Charity Lomax and Betty Norwood were standing by the van, deep in conversation, and Josephine saw Charity put a hand briefly on the other girl's arm, as if to reassure her of something.

"Why did you take the blame for them?" she said.

"Because I like Charity's spirit and I feel sorry for Betty. She's a twin, and she spends all her time trying to live up to her more brilliant sister. Sometimes I think that's why she gets herself into trouble—just to be noticed for a change." She sighed. "Come on. I hate the idea of being asked to spy on them all, but I suppose we'd better get on with it."

CHAPTER 2

The residents of Charleston might have made a careful distinction between a farm and a horticultural college, but any visitor arriving for the first time would have struggled to pinpoint where one finished and the other began. The yard where Jeannie parked was a sea of mud, suggesting that the countryside owed its rich, fresh greens to a recent spell of poor weather, and only a narrow track separated the house from a clutch of farm buildings—barns, a pigsty, and an impressive wooden granary, which sheltered hay wagons and tumbrels of varying sizes. Another lane led off to the left, deeply rutted by cows going to and from their pastures to be milked; the enclave nestled comfortably in its pleasant, rural surroundings, with cornfields and straggling hedges pushing out toward the low curve of the downs. Josephine looked up at the house, which was around a couple of hundred years old and substantial if straightforward—square and solid, with an ordinary façade rendered in an unattractive shade of brown and partially covered by a Virginia creeper. Beyond its limits, the harsh colors softened a little in a long flint and redbrick wall—presumably surrounding the gardens—which sang with the warmth of the day.

"I'll tell our strays to take your trunk upstairs," Jeannie said, getting out of the van, "then we'd better go and eat humble pie with Miss H. Why don't you go and introduce yourself to Harriet?

She'll be in the kitchen, just down there on the right." She pointed to a side door, which stood ajar. "And don't forget—Lomax and Norwood have been with us all the time. Wish me luck."

Jeannie beckoned to her students, leaving Josephine to present herself at the tradesman's entrance. She hesitated, feeling suddenly shy of a strange household, then walked purposefully across the yard in case anyone was watching her from inside. As she passed the main gate, she noticed a sign with the words "The Hartford-Wroe Horticultural College for Ladies" painted in a circle around a deep pink rose and thought about what Jeannie had told her. If the two women really *did* run the college together, there was not much evidence of it in the name, and she wondered if that set the tone for their partnership in general. She knocked and waited, then knocked again, but the only response was the leisurely buzzing of a bee as it moved from one hollyhock to another, so she pushed the door wider. A small vestibule filled with oilskins and gardening boots led to the kitchen, but there was no one there. The room was pleasantly cool, with a stone floor and tiled walls, which were more than a match for the afternoon sun. A range took up most of one wall, and the sweet smell of stewing fruits came from a large copper pan. In the middle of the floor there was a freestanding scrubbed table with accounting books and paperwork at one end and mixing bowls at the other, arranged around a slab of marble that was liberally sprinkled with flour. Onions and garlic hung in strings from the ceiling, and a battle-scarred ginger tomcat was fast asleep on one of the chairs, oblivious to the arrival of a visitor.

Josephine hovered on the threshold, wondering if she should go round to the front door and ring the bell there instead, but someone was obviously in the middle of making pastry, so she decided to wait. Sure enough, after a minute or two she heard the sound of footsteps coming down a passageway from the other side of the house. The woman jumped when she saw Josephine, then smiled. "You must be our new recruit. How nice to have you here." She put the bags of flour and sugar down on the table and wiped her hand on her apron before offering it to Josephine. "I'm Harriet Barker. Welcome to the college."

Her host was a slender woman in her late thirties, with a combination of self-assurance and youthful energy that could have placed her five years either side of Josephine's estimate. She had wavy, shoulder-length dark hair that she wore tied loosely at the neck, and a complexion that obviously had a natural affinity with the sun: her arms and face were pleasantly tanned, even though she was probably the only person at Charleston who spent most of her working day indoors. Her greeting was formal but genuine, and Josephine warmed to her immediately. "Thank you, Miss Barker. I knocked a couple of times, but . . ."

"Oh, I'm sorry about that. I was in the larder, so I didn't hear you. I've often thought that whoever designed this house must have despised women; otherwise, why would he have put the pantry in the most inconvenient place imaginable? I swear I walk miles every day." She took a kettle from the range and filled it at the sink by the window. "And please feel free to call me Harriet whenever the girls aren't around. Have you and Jeannie had lunch?"

"Yes, we ate at the school. My train was delayed, so I'm afraid we're later than expected."

"It doesn't matter. Nothing about today has gone according to plan, and I'm running late with supper, as you can see. The girls take it in turns to help me out in the kitchen, but this morning happened to be Miss Lomax's turn, and she made alternative arrangements, so I've had to do everything myself." Her eyes, which were a deep honey-brown, twinkled as she looked at Josephine. "I'll have to decide how she's to make it up to me. They *are* with you, I presume? No other errands to distract them on the way back from Eastbourne?"

Josephine smiled. "No, they're both here. Jeannie took them straight back to work."

"Good. I suppose I overreacted by alerting the school so quickly, but we can't be too careful at the moment." Was the comment a coincidence, Josephine wondered, or did Harriet have some inkling of the charge laid against her friend? "Let me take you up to your room while the kettle's boiling; then you must come down and have some tea. You'll be tired from your journey, and George will want to meet you. She'll be in from the garden at five." She glanced past Josephine to the vestibule. "Are your things still outside?"

"No, the girls took them upstairs."

"Then come with me."

Josephine followed her out of the kitchen and along a series of dark, short passageways to the main staircase. "Do the students sleep here too?" she asked as they climbed up to the first floor.

"No, not during the summer. There's a row of shepherd's huts in the field by the orchard, and the girls share those, with Vera keeping an eye on them. That way, we can have the house for paying guests and visitors like you who are connected to the college."

"Is Vera another teacher?" Josephine asked, wondering why Jeannie hadn't mentioned her.

"Oh no. Vera is our right-hand woman." She spoke with an affection that offset the faintly tongue-in-cheek description. "Vera Simms. The place needed a lot of work when we first took the lease, so we advertised for someone to help out. Vera soon made herself indispensable." The landing was narrow and a little claustrophobic, dark except for the occasional shaft of daylight through the keyholes of closed bedroom doors. "As for the other guests, we've got a chap from the Board of Agriculture with us at the moment," Harriet continued. "George is hoping to get the college included in some sort of government support program, which would mean we could expand, so he's here to inspect our work. My cousin Peter is in the room at the end, but he'll be going back to the front soon." There was very little emotion in her voice, and Josephine wondered if that was because the cousins weren't close or if—like most of the population—she had simply resigned herself to the inevitable comings and goings of war. "And we have our rooms in the attic," she continued. "George insists on overlooking the garden, of course. It means she can check that the planting lines are straight while she gets dressed in the morning."

Josephine smiled, although she sensed that the comment wasn't entirely a joke. Her trunk was waiting outside room number three, and Harriet let her in. "I'll leave you to unpack and make yourself at home," she said. "Come back down to the kitchen when you're ready."

After the dim and rambling passageways, the light, airy room was a relief. It was generously proportioned and furnished with nothing more than was necessary: a large chest of drawers to the left of the window and a narrow bed to the right; two rush seats, one in better condition than the other; and a small oak desk with a pot of blue anemones to welcome her. She pushed her trunk into the corner, ready to unpack, and walked across to the window. It overlooked the pond at the front of the house and was partially enclosed by the vigorous green leaves of the vine. Cattle were drinking at the far side of the water, where a stream entered the pond, but otherwise the surface was still and clear, reflecting the chimney pots and red-tiled roof; to her left, a line of dark yew trees made the silver of an enormous willow even more intense. Josephine wasn't an early riser by nature, but even she would have very little trouble in getting up every morning to a view like this. Without wasting any more time, she removed the bare essentials from the trunk and looked with satisfaction at the small signs of ownership—the book on the bedside table, the dressing gown hanging from the hook on the door. It was the first time that she had ever had a room of her own to retreat to—a far cry from the dormitories of Anstey or the inevitable give and take of sharing with her sisters.

She went back downstairs, taking a wrong turn before eventually finding the kitchen again. The fruit pie was now made and stood waiting to be cooked, while its place on the table had been taken by a tea tray and half-eaten Madeira cake. "Have you got everything you need?" Harriet asked, looking up from the accounts.

"Yes thank you, and the flowers are lovely."

"I'm glad you like them. I've given you what I would have chosen for myself, but feel free to pick something else when they need refreshing. Flowers are something we're never short of."

"Do you work in the garden too?"

"As a hobby, not a religion. The borders outside the windows are mine to play with, but I don't interfere with anything else. Come on, Byron—let our guest sit down." Harriet scooped the cat up from the chair, offering a saucer of milk by way of compensation, and gestured to Josephine to take his place. "When George and I started the business, we each had our own strengths, and we tend to stick to them. It's best not to compete. I learnt that quite early on."

"How long have you been here?"

"At Charleston? Only for three years or so, but we had another place before that—just two or three students at a time, but enough to find out what worked and what didn't. Here, we can take up to twenty girls and teach them over a longer period—enough to make a real difference. No one learns gardening in a day." She poured two cups of tea and cut Josephine a generous slice of the cake. "I'll wager George will tell you that at least three times before the cock crows."

"What am I being so predictable about?" The woman who stood at the kitchen door, scraping mud off her boots, was exactly like the Georgina Hartford-Wroe that Josephine had imagined—so much so that for a fleeting moment she wondered if they had actually met. The founder of the college would have been a distinctive presence in any gathering just because of her height, but everything else about her carried a similar air of authority—her voice, her age, the confidence with which she entered a room—and Josephine stood up, understanding immediately why she commanded such respect from her students. She walked across the kitchen to put a trug of carrots and potatoes down on the table, and shook Josephine's hand, covering it with soil. "Excellent to have you with us, Miss Tey," she said. "You've arrived at a very exciting time for the college." George was a little older than her friend, her fair hair already tinged with silver, and Josephine was intrigued by the contrast in their dispositions: one face animated by humor, the other inclined to earnestness, even when she smiled. "I expect you'll be keen to look round."

Harriet laughed. "Give the poor girl a chance to settle in, George," she said. "I've only just made some tea."

"There'll be plenty of time for that later. Keep it hot for us." She beckoned to Josephine, who hesitated, unable to decide which of her hosts it was ruder to ignore. In the end, her curiosity got the better of her, and she followed George out of the kitchen, with an apologetic glance over her shoulder.

Her guide set off at a brisk pace round the front of the house, and Josephine hurried to keep up. "The marvelous thing about being here is that we've finally got enough land to teach women everything they need to know about gardening," George said, passing the pond and taking a narrow path that led to the right of the walled garden. "The students who come here expect the sort of grounding that will help them to make a living from it. That's what makes us different—a woman's interest in horticulture shouldn't begin and end with a vase of bloody flowers." Her outspokenness amused Josephine, and she wondered if George was as direct with the girls in her charge. "And we've got the potential to expand too," she continued. "Our landlord is renting us a few acres of agricultural land, so at last we'll be able to work on a decent scale."

She stopped suddenly by an orchard, whose trees were too mature to have been planted during the life of the college. "We're lucky with these," George said, reaching up to thin one of the branches that was particularly laden with young fruit. "There are more than twenty varieties here already, and we're going to turn the next field over to more in the autumn. If we convert one of the outbuildings to a cool room, we can store the fruit over the winter months and supply our customers for most of the year."

"Which varieties grow best here?"

"Worcester Pearmain, Egremont Russet, Beauty of Bath . . ."

"Charles Ross?" George looked impressed by her knowledge, and Josephine was sorry to disillusion her. "Nothing to do with growing them, I'm afraid. My father's a fruiterer in Inverness, and apples are one of his specialties. I was brought up on some of those names."

"Ah well, we're all in the same game, whether we grow the food or sell it. If your father were a little nearer, I'd be looking to do business with him." She smiled and wandered farther into the orchard, unable to pull herself away from a task now that she had noticed it needed doing. Josephine watched as she thinned apples out wherever the growing fruit would make the branches too heavy, choosing her sacrifices quickly and without sentiment, and letting them fall to the ground. Her passion for her work—the single-mindedness that Miss Ingham had referred to—was already obvious, and Josephine envied her for it; one day, she hoped to find a vocation that gave her the same degree of satisfaction, although she knew in her heart that it would not be teaching.

Seeing that the tour had been temporarily sidetracked, she selected a tree of her own to work on and followed George's example, using a straightforward task to get her bearings and soak up the atmosphere of her new home. Through the apple trees on the far side of the orchard she could just make out a row of rounded rooftops, which she assumed belonged to the shepherd's huts that Harriet had mentioned. "Is that where the students sleep?" she asked.

"That's right. If I were younger, I'd be tempted to join them. There's something joyous about an outdoor life, don't you think?"

In moderation, Josephine thought to herself, but voiced a more tactful answer. "There must be a lot to worry about, though."

"Yes, it can be hard work at times, but it's not without its rewards." She came over to inspect the tree that Josephine had been working on and nodded approvingly. "You learn quickly, but this had better wait for another day. I expect you want to meet your girls."

George walked on and the extent of the college's operation

became more obvious as they rounded the corner of the garden wall and came out into an area of orderly greenhouses, potting sheds, and cold frames, with a large stretch of land beyond that was obviously a work in progress. "Was this already here when you arrived?" Josephine asked, curious to know how so much had been achieved in what seemed to her a very short space of time.

"Good grief, no. We had the orchard and one or two dilapidated outbuildings, but the rest we've built up from scratch."

"So where on earth did you start?"

"Well, the real genius was in choosing the right spot," George explained, "and that was entirely down to Harry. She's from this part of the world, so she suggested we should look here. I knew as soon as I saw Charleston that it would be ideal—sheltered and sunny, so we could force the produce on and make it saleable in the early season, and we're only a spit from Glynde Station so nothing is a problem to transport. It wasn't perfect, by any means, and I'd have ruined us in a fortnight by expanding too quickly, but Harry is a hard taskmaster when it comes to balancing the books." It was another reference to the individual strengths that Harriet had mentioned, and Josephine listened, impressed by the way that each woman acknowledged the other's importance in the business. "Rome wasn't built in a day, I suppose, but then we weren't in charge of that." She laughed, then spoke more seriously. "It feels wrong to profit from the war, but we've got to be hard-headed about it. The longer it goes on, the more urgent the issue of food production is going to become. Do you realize that we still import half of our food from abroad?" Josephine shook her head. "Ludicrous, in war or peace, when we have everything we need to grow it ourselves. But that's got to change—the German U-boats will make sure of that—and when it does, we'll be ahead of the game here. There are no limits to what we can do in the future if we work hard now."

"Miss Barker—Harriet—said something about getting support from the government."

"That's right. They've sent someone down to scout us out—odd sort of chap if you ask me. Not very forthcoming, but he knows his stuff, and at least he takes the situation more seriously than Asquith seems to. I'm confident he'll give us a favorable report. We've got the ideal site here, as I said, and a long lease if we want it, with the potential to take students for proper two-year courses. That's what's really needed. You can't teach gardening overnight."

Josephine smiled to herself, mentally striking off a third of Harriet's predicted tally. She followed George through a creaky wooden gate to the walled garden adjacent to the house, and was instantly struck by the atmosphere of ordered peace. It was a large area, divided naturally into sections by paths or low boxed hedges, and the students were engrossed in their respective tasks, working in pairs or small groups. To Josephine's untrained eye, the various plots seemed to offer perfect examples of almost every fruit and vegetable under the sun: onions and broad beans in the straightest of rows; potatoes earthed up in neat trenches; cane wigwams supporting runner beans and peas; and tender young leaves of things she didn't recognize, all protected by yards of netting and a scarecrow dressed jauntily in college colors, with a face painted to look uncannily like George's. Around the walls, various fruits were espaliered against the brick, with the crowning glory of an enormous fig tree on the south side. Close to the house, where its colors and scent could be better appreciated, a flower garden flourished in shades of purple, pink, and white, with painted sage and lavender spilling out onto the paths.

"You should have seen this when we first arrived," George said. "They must have let it run wild for years—completely overgrown and impossible to walk from one side to the other."

"That's hard to believe. It looks so productive."

"It is now, but it took us a good six months to make it fit for any sort of planting. Have you met Vera?"

"No, not yet."

"She's the person to talk to about what this used to be like. She did a lot of the hard work in the early days. I don't know what we'd have done without her." The garden gate flew back again with a screech of impatience at being disturbed, and Jeannie winked at Josephine over the pile of seed trays that she was carrying through from the greenhouses. "Ah, Miss Sellwood—perfect timing. Go and round the girls up, will you? I'd like to introduce them to Miss Tey and give them the good news about their extra morning lessons."

Jeannie did as she was asked, and one by one the students downed tools and gathered round their principal. Charity Lomax—apparently recovered from the humiliation of being hauled home in a delivery van—held no grudges and greeted Josephine as if they were lifelong acquaintances, and even Betty Norwood managed a faint smile of acknowledgment. As the stragglers from the furthest parts of the garden took their place in the group, Josephine looked with interest at the girls, trying in vain to spot Betty's twin, but only when each student introduced herself did she identify an attractive, fair-haired girl in the front row as Dorothy Norwood. The sisters could scarcely have been more different, and Josephine was reminded of a weather house that stood on her mother's mantelpiece at home, with its contrasting rain and shine figures, each of whom could only take prominence by pushing the other back into the shadows. When everyone had given her name, she thanked them for her welcome and talked briefly about her work at Anstey, hoping that experience would give her some authority over girls who were almost her contemporaries.

"Now, since you started here at Charleston, some of you have complained about the physical nature of the work," George said with a glint in her eye, looking directly at Charity. "Gardening *can* be strenuous and tiring when you're new to it, so with that in mind, I've asked Miss Tey to devise a morning class that will better equip you for the tasks that you face every day. As you've heard, she specializes in fitness and physiotherapy, so from tomorrow your day will begin forty-five minutes earlier than usual with an exercise class at a quarter past six exactly." Her announcement was met with a universal groan of protest, which Josephine could heartily have echoed. "Really, you don't have to thank me—never let it be said that I don't take your complaints seriously." Several of the girls glared at Charity, and Josephine guessed that she would not be quickly forgiven for giving Miss H the excuse to do what she was going to do anyway. "I expect you to take these classes on with a good grace and to work as hard for Miss Tey as you do for me," George continued. "That's all for now. You're free to carry on with what you were doing."

Josephine watched them go, noticing that they all returned to their tasks with an eagerness to please that bore out what Jeannie had told her about George's teaching. "They're not a bad lot," the principal said, "and one or two of them have shown a natural flair for horticulture since they arrived—enough to make a good living from it if they choose to."

"What sort of posts do your students go on to?" Josephine asked.

"It varies. There's more demand for them now in the big houses, for obvious reasons—and in increasingly senior positions. I've had girls who've thrown their lot in together and formed co-operatives to make more profit out of the land, and there are plenty of temporary positions. One woman came here last month looking for someone to care for her country garden while she's in London. Another single lady wanted some guidance on landscaping and thought it would be nice to have a companion to share the work." She bent down to rescue a seedling that had been partially pulled from the ground by a bird. "There's no shortage of opportunity for women who are well trained—and not before time. An eye for detail, gentleness, the instinct to nurture—those are the qualities that make a good gardener, and in my experience they tend to be found more reliably in women than in men, wouldn't you say?"

The comment was distinctly at odds with the ill treatment that

Miss Ingham had warned them about; in fact, everything about life at the college so far had been an unconscious defense against the accusation, and Josephine was more curious than ever about what might have inspired it. George obviously misconstrued her lack of response, because she pressed the point. "Patriotism, powers of organization, unbounded enthusiasm—there are great things expected of women now, and these are the qualities that will help them succeed. Are you excited by the opportunities that suffrage has given you, Miss Tey?"

"I've always been very lucky," Josephine admitted, considering the question. "I'm one of three daughters, and we've had every opportunity to succeed because my father is ambitious for his children to have a better life. He's worked his way up from nothing to own property and provide for his family, so the struggles I've grown up with are about class, not gender. If he thinks differently about us because we're girls, I've never noticed it, but I doubt he'd recognize that as suffrage."

George nodded, giving Josephine the impression that she respected an honest answer more than an easy one. She led the way out of the garden, following the path to the right of the house, which took them past a chicken run and through a wooden archway smothered by cascading pink and white roses. "These are stunning," Josephine said, stopped briefly in her tracks by the fragrance. "I can see why you've chosen a rose as the college emblem."

"Not just any rose. We named these two varieties ten years ago when we first started the business, the pink after Harriet and the white after me. The fact that they flourish here seems to be a good omen." They had come almost full circle to the kitchen door, but instead George crossed the yard to a small single-story building opposite the main house. "We'd better get you kitted out," she called back over her shoulder, unlocking the door and ushering Josephine into what was obviously her office. The room was dark and smelt faintly of wood and polish, like a vestry in a church, with a large desk in the middle, a workbench down one side with cupboards below, and piles of logs next to a small fire in the corner. The wall above the bench was lined with shelves—row after row of jars and bottles containing everything from seeds and beans to weed killer and other poisons, all carefully labeled. George took a Hessian apron, a pair of secateurs, and a pruning knife out of a cupboard and handed them to Josephine with a smile. "These are yours. All we've got to do now is teach you how to use them."

CHAPTER 3

There were two new faces at breakfast the next morning. Neither Simon Cassidy nor Peter Whittaker had been present at supper on Josephine's first evening, and she was introduced to them both as soon as she came downstairs. The government official was, as George had said, an odd sort of chap—a middle-aged man with receding gray hair and dandruff on his collar, stiff and formal in a dark suit that belonged to a different age and was starkly at odds with the youthful energy of the morning. Cassidy was obviously uncomfortable with the forced intimacy of lodgings and did nothing more than return Josephine's greeting. By contrast, Peter Whittaker—still dressed in the blue uniform of the convalescent camp—grinned at her with an easy familiarity, no less cocky without his friends to egg him on, and she gave what she hoped was a passable impression of seeing him for the first time.

"How did you sleep?" Jeannie asked as Josephine joined her by the sideboard, where breakfast was laid out in silver dishes. "I came to say goodnight, but your lamp was already out."

"Sorry about that. I was gone as soon as my head hit the pillow. Then I woke with the light and couldn't go back to sleep for fear of missing my own class."

"It went well, I gather. I heard Lanton and Macdonald singing your praises as they passed by my window earlier."

"Whoever they are. I don't think I'll *ever* remember all their names."

"Coffee will help. Take mine and I'll pour another one."

"Thank you." Josephine looked round at the room that she had been too tired to take in properly the night before, wondering if the floral pattern on the wallpaper—a peculiar hybrid of poppy and daisy that had no actual counterpart in nature—had been Harriet's choice or George's. She sat down next to Jeannie, pleased to be able to get on with her breakfast while George took the lead in the conversation. "It's all very well to have these voluntary outfits all over the country," she was saying, with Simon Cassidy firmly in her sights, "but the government should be coordinating what they do, or their work will overlap and waste the charitable funds we're raising for them. If you ask me, the railways would be a good place to start. Growers should get together and bulk-send their produce with cheaper transit. That way, we could improve the quality of the food for people living in the cities and keep most of the profit where it rightly belongs—with the person who grows it in the first place. That's just common sense, and you could make it happen overnight if you wanted to."

Cassidy cleared his throat and straightened his spectacles. "As a precaution during the war, we might consider—"

"Bugger the war. You should be doing it anyway. At least the war might teach us to be a bit more resourceful about the amount of food we grow and the way we store and preserve it."

"Let's keep it going for as long as possible then, shall we?" Whittaker's voice was heavy with sarcasm. He stared defiantly at George, who ignored him, and Josephine got the impression that sparring such as this was a common feature of mealtimes. "Men are dying in the thousands, but it's worth it because the nation is finally making jam."

The provocation got its intended reaction. "For God's sake, Peter, grow up," George said, losing her patience. "I don't suppose the name Hilda Horsley means anything to you, does it? Or Florence Kay? No, I thought not. Well they died too—in a Zeppelin attack, along with fifty other women, and I dare say they won't be the last. Women are making sacrifices as well, even though they have absolutely no say in this war or how it's being fought. It's not good enough any more to ignore us and point to the battlefields. Things are changing."

"For some women, perhaps, if they're privileged to begin with. It's interesting, isn't it, that *your* lot think of working on the land as patriotism, while working-class women just call it the same old slog they've been doing for years."

"I'm sure it suits *you* to believe they think like that," George argued, 'but they're foolish if they do. We're fighting against lower wages for *all* women. Everyone benefits, irrespective of class."

"Except the men who still rely on the land to feed their families. All you're doing is forcing their rates of pay down by taking the labor from under their noses."

The row was threatening to get out of hand, and to Josephine's ears there was a personal quality to the exchanges. Whittaker seemed to inspire the same sort of dislike in George as he obviously did in Jeannie, and she wondered why he chose to stay at the farmhouse rather than at Summerdown; perhaps Harriet kept the peace, but there was no sign of her so far this morning. Simon Cassidy pushed his empty plate away and sat back in his chair, and Josephine noticed how intently he was listening to everything that was said. "Soon there won't be any men left to work the land," George pointed out. "As you said, they'll be needed to fight."

"'The women of Britain say go'?" Whittaker gave a mock salute as he quoted the enlistment posters that had begun to appear all over towns and villages. "Nice of you to give us your blessing. I suppose if you had your way, every last man would be on the next boat out. You really do hate us, don't you?"

George shrugged. "You're a necessary evil. Nothing more." They glared at each other for a moment, and Josephine caught

Jeannie's eye, wondering if it was possible for the atmosphere to get any more uncomfortable. To her surprise, it was George who backed down first. "Anyway, it's not about men and women," she said, turning her attention back to Simon Cassidy. "It's about what's best for the nation as a whole—and that is most certainly to become more self-sufficient than we are at the moment. We shouldn't be giving our money to the bloody foreigners for food that we're perfectly capable of growing ourselves—in war or in peacetime."

"Do you agree with that, Mr. Cassidy?" Jeannie asked, more, Josephine suspected, from a desire to dissolve the tension than a genuine interest in the answer.

Cassidy cleared his throat again. "Well, Miss Hartford-Wroe is correct when she says that we could learn from some of our friends in Europe. Take Belgium, for example . . ." He launched into a lengthy sermon on imports and exports, and Jeannie muttered an apology under her breath.

Out of the window, Josephine saw the postman cycle up to the front door, his wheels skidding a little on the gravel as he braked. She noticed the color drain from Peter Whittaker's face, his quarrel with George temporarily forgotten, and he leapt up to rush into the hallway, arriving at the front door almost before the letters had a chance to clatter to the floor. Harriet came through from the kitchen with more toast and coffee, and she looked questioningly at her cousin as he sorted through the post. "Is it your call-up?" she asked.

Whittaker shook his head. "Another stay of execution."

He grinned at her and left the room, but his bravado didn't entirely eclipse the panic of a few seconds earlier, and Josephine could only begin to imagine what it must be like to live each day in constant fear of that official envelope. Cassidy got up to help Harriet with the tray, and the smile he gave her was the first time that Josephine had seen his expression change. "How was your class this morning?" Harriet asked, clearing away some of the empty dishes.

Before Josephine could answer, there was a cursory knock at the door, and a young woman wearing the college uniform handed

George a sheaf of papers. "Sorry to interrupt you, Miss H," she said, "but this is the inventory you asked for."

"Ah, good—thank you, Vera." Josephine looked with interest at the "right-hand woman," mentally revising the image of someone older and more experienced. Vera was around twenty, with closely cropped fair hair and a lean, wiry figure. She wore her gardening clothes easily, as if she had been born to an outdoor life, but her face—though striking—carried the insecurities of someone who was always waiting to be judged. Josephine wondered if she knew how much she was valued at the college; sometimes women who were as confident in their own abilities as George and Harriet forgot that those who worked for them needed encouragement. The young woman hovered in the doorway, unsure of whether to stay or go, until George solved the problem for her. "This is excellent news," she said, getting up from the table. "We're already well ahead of last year. I'll come out with you now, Vera, and we can check the orders together. There's just about time before I give the girls their instructions for the day."

Vera beamed and followed George outside, and Josephine watched them head toward the gardener's office, noticing how often the girl glanced over at her employer. Harriet collected George's half-eaten breakfast and added it to the tray, then disappeared into the kitchen without another word. Through the open doorway, Josephine saw her give the abandoned bacon to the cat, then heard the rest of the food being scraped into the bin. Simon Cassidy excused himself from the table and retreated upstairs with his newspaper, leaving Josephine and Jeannie to finish their breakfast in peace.

"What time are we all summoned for duty?" Josephine asked, just as the sound of a vigorously rung bell cut through the air.

Jeannie smiled and pushed her chair back. "Does that answer your question? Come on. Out to the garden, and just pray it's not your turn to fetch the muck carts."

It wasn't, and Josephine couldn't help but feel that George was breaking her in gently by putting her in charge of preparing vegetable boxes for the college's private customers. Lanton and Macdonald—her new disciples—immediately volunteered to help her, and gave her a cheerful smile when their offer was accepted. In fact, everyone seemed to take on the tasks they were assigned with a good grace. Josephine looked round at the twenty young women gathered together on the lawn by the house, notebooks in hand for any special duties, their faces turned as one toward their teacher, and she realized that the lessons they were learning went well beyond the confines of horticulture. The mood that George had established here—and it seemed to come so naturally to her—was very much one of mutual trust and responsibility, and Miss Ingham's concerns seemed to Josephine more unfounded than ever.

Eight of the girls, including the Norwood sisters and Charity Lomax, were dispatched under Vera's supervision to dig a large patch of uncultivated ground beyond the greenhouses. It was Jeannie's job to sell produce at the Thursday afternoon market in Lewes, and she was given two students to help her with the picking and loading, although Josephine couldn't remember their names. The rest of the girls were directed to various parts of the walled garden for watering, planting, and pruning, and the air gradually filled with distant young voices as they drifted off and went about their work.

"Come on, Miss Tey—we'll show you the ropes," Lanton offered, and she led the way through the bottom gate to a stone-built lean-to, attached to the garden wall, which doubled as a potting and packing shed. The building was long and low, rich with the pungent smell of earth, and three windows at the front gave it a soft, pleasant light. A wooden bench ran all the way down the window side, scuffed and scarred by the work that had taken place there, and against the back wall stood rack after rack of tools: shovels, forks, rakes, dibbers, sieves, and a multitude of sharp-pronged, peculiarly shaped implements whose purpose was a mystery to Josephine. At the far end, flanked by bunches of wooden canes, several rows of terracotta flowerpots had been laid on their sides like a honeycomb, and watering cans of all sizes hung from the beams, interspersed at regular intervals by oil lamps. Sweet peas stood in a jar by the window, giving off the faint but unmistakable scent of summer, and under the eaves just inside the door there was a house martin's nest; Josephine ducked her head as the bird flew past to feed its young, apparently unconcerned by the company.

"Right," said Macdonald, picking up a file of letters that lay ready on the bench and waving them enthusiastically in the air. "These are the new orders, and this is Vera's list of all the produce that's ready for harvest. All we have to do is put the two together, but God help us if we pick a bean that's too young, or a radish more than we need. All hell will break loose."

"Waste and neglect are the enemies of a civilized society," chimed in Lanton, and Josephine smiled to herself, already sufficiently familiar with George's oratory to give the impression the credit it deserved.

"I suppose that goes for time too," she said, "so you'd better show me where everything is, and we can get started."

They did as she asked, and the three of them spent a productive hour collecting all the produce that was needed, finishing with the salad crops, which were grown in cold frames next to the shed. The girls were easy company and had been friends since childhood, traveling to Moira House together from their hometown in Essex, and with ambitions to concentrate on physiotherapy as a career and perhaps start a clinic together. They quizzed Josephine on her own training and the pros and cons of a place at Anstey, and she saw in them the sort of camaraderie that she had enjoyed with her own school friend, Marjorie, who had been at her side in all but this most recent placement. When everything had been gathered from the different parts of the garden, they laid it all out on the workbench, arranging the fruit and vegetables according to the quantities required by every customer, then took a box each to pack. A companionable silence fell over the shed as they concentrated on their orders, broken only by regular cries from the nest as the young birds scrambled for the latest delivery of food. The windows looked out toward the glasshouses and beyond them the patch of new ground, and Josephine watched the digging as she worked, impressed by the students' application to their task. Peter Whittaker was sitting on the grass by the wall with a sketchbook in his lap, squinting against the sun as he drew the girls at work, and Josephine noticed how self-consciously most of them behaved whenever he glanced in their direction; even the diligent Vera wasn't immune to his attention.

"Not the Little Gem for Mrs. Needingworth," Macdonald said, catching Josephine's arm as she reached for a head of lettuce to complete her order. "She can't bear them. Nothing but a Webb's Wonder will do."

She pointed to another variety, and Josephine corrected her mistake, amused by the familiarity with which the girls talked about their customers, as if they were personal friends rather than women they would never meet. "Is Mr. Whittaker an artist?" she asked, closing the box and taking a new order from the top of the pile.

"Yes, he is," said Lanton, seizing quickly on the topic of conversation. "He's always drawing something or other, and he's really very good."

Macdonald rolled her eyes. "I'm afraid you'll have to excuse Joyce, Miss Tey. She's been sweet on Mr. Whittaker ever since he rescued her glove from the pond and told her to call him Peter. Now there's simply no saving her."

"Mags!" Lanton blushed and glared good-naturedly at her friend. "Just ignore her, Miss Tey. She hasn't got an artistic bone in her body, so she judges everyone by her own standards, which are straight out of the gutter. I'm not sweet on him—nothing of the sort. That wouldn't be right. He's Miss Barker's cousin."

"Hmm. So he says . . ."

Macdonald left the remark dangling provocatively in the air.

The girls seemed to have completely forgotten that Josephine was a teacher, and she couldn't decide whether to take that as a compliment or a strike against her authority. "What do you mean?" she asked, too curious to care.

"Just that they seem very *close* for cousins. Very protective of each other, if you know what I mean."

"Nonsense!" Lanton sighed wearily and looked to Josephine for support. "There must be fifteen years at least between them, don't you think, Miss Tey? And anyway, if Miss Barker *is* interested in anyone, it's that chap from the Ministry. He's far closer to her age, and I saw him take her flowers the other day."

"Well, if that isn't coals to Newcastle, I don't know what is," Macdonald said dismissively. "He's such a creep, Joyce. And anyway, Norwood says he's married, although how she knows that I've no idea. But either way, I doubt that someone like Miss Barker would look twice at him. She's got too much sense. What do *you* think, Miss Tey?"

Josephine was just remembering Simon Cassidy's smile at breakfast that morning, but she was saved from coming down on either side of the argument by the sight of George emerging from the largest of the glass houses with a face as black as thunder. "Look out—Miss H is on the warpath again," Macdonald said, and then, when George reappeared a few minutes later with the bell, added, "What did I tell you? Someone's for it."

"What does that mean?" Josephine asked, as the clanging cut through the air, angry and relentless.

"Like Mags just said, one of us is in trouble," Joyce explained, "and if it's to do with the glass house, it's bound to be serious." She took off her gloves and brushed the soil from her tunic. "Every week, one of us is put in charge of ventilating the greenhouse and watering all the plants."

"Twice a day, morning and night," Macdonald continued. "It's supposed to teach us responsibility, because a lot of the college's most precious plants are there—expensive fruits and flowers, seedlings coming on for the new season, all that sort of thing."

"It's ridiculous," Lanton admitted, "but even though I know it's not me this time, I still feel guilty."

"And I can't afford another fine," Mags groaned. "Why did this have to happen?" She caught Josephine's bemused expression and explained. "When one of us does something that causes the college to lose money, we all have to pay a token fine, even if it wasn't our fault. Miss H is a great believer in collective responsibility, so everyone suffers. I don't mind telling you, I'll happily dole out the punishment on her behalf when we find out who it is this time. It's just not fair when everyone's skint, and we *so* wanted to go and see *The Tramp* on our afternoon off."

The bell continued to ring, and Josephine noticed that all the girls were dropping their tools and hurrying toward the glass house. She led her charges out to join them, falling in with the circle that had gathered round to receive its reproof. Everyone seemed nervous, and she caught Jeannie's eye; for once, there was no mischief or sparkle in the face that looked back at her. George stood silently by the glass house door, waiting for the last girl to arrive, breathless, from the furthest parts of the garden, and Josephine couldn't help but feel that missing out on Charlie Chaplin's latest film was the least of anyone's worries; criminal misdemeanors must have been met with less fury and recrimination than were currently evident on the principal's face. "Who was in charge of closing the ventilators last night?" she demanded, her voice low and even. Nobody answered, and Josephine noticed how much younger the girls suddenly looked, like children about to be scolded by an angry parent; even the worldly-wise Miss Lomax had temporarily lost her composure. "I'll ask you one more time," George said, "and I would advise you not to make things worse by compounding negligence with deceit. Who should have been on duty in the glass house last night?"

There was a movement to Josephine's right as someone—she didn't see who—gave Dorothy Norwood an accusing shove in the back. Reluctantly, the girl raised her hand. "It was my turn, Miss H, but I swapped with Betty because I wasn't feeling well. She said she'd do my shift for me."

"Liar!" Betty shouted, and the outrage on her face was either genuine or one of the most gifted performances that Josephine had ever seen. "I don't know what she's talking about, Miss H. She didn't ask me to do anything of the sort."

The twins stared at each other, and the hostility between them was palpable, although Dorothy had the self-control necessary to use it to her advantage. "I swear I'm telling the truth," she said without even raising her voice. "Betty must have forgotten that she'd agreed to take over for me." She looked at George and smiled, and Josephine was reminded of her grandmother's cat, who always seemed to be asleep on a cushion when a dead bird was discovered in the house. "Either that, or she never had any intention of helping me at all and only said she would to get me into trouble."

"You bloody bitch!" Betty launched herself at her sister, but Vera Simms stepped forward quickly to intervene. "You've been doing this ever since we were little," Betty shouted, red in the face and struggling to free herself. "Well, you might have fooled our parents with your butter-wouldn't-melt act, but you won't get away with it this time."

The unfolding family drama was threatening to overshadow the breach of college rules, and Josephine realized that she still had no idea what sin had actually been committed. George held up her hand in a bid to regain control of the situation, and both girls fell silent, waiting for her judgment. "Dorothy, I'm surprised at you. Your conduct here so far has been exemplary, but even if you are telling the truth about last night, you had no business to ask anyone to do your duties for you. If you were feeling unwell, you should have come to me or to Miss Barker, and we would have appointed someone to take over the work for you. And Betty, we only have your word to counteract your sister's, and I'm sorry to say that your word has not always proved trustworthy in the past. As for your language and behavior just now, that is not what I've come to expect from a Moira House student, and you've left me no choice but to report the incident in its entirety to Miss Ingham. Now, you will both come to my office at the end of the day, when I've had a chance to consider how best to deal with you."

The Norwood sisters nodded in unison—the only time as far as Josephine could see that they had ever been in agreement—and George addressed the group as a whole. "I neither want nor can afford to see a repeat of last night's carelessness," she said gravely. "Because nobody closed the windows, the rain has destroyed some of our most precious plants—months of work and a significant part of the college's potential income." She reached inside the glass house and took out a trug of soaking wet bulbs. "These have been drying out across the summer, ready to plant for the new season. We have a reputation for the quality of our cut flowers, and these should have made us upward of a hundred pounds. As it is, they're worthless—completely ruined and only good for the compost." She paused, and the ensuing silence was excruciatingly uncomfortable. "All acts of indifference or forgetfulness when they affect the welfare of our plants must be punished, and I'm appealing now to your sense of duty. I shouldn't have to remind you that the men in your families are away fighting, and—in some cases—making the ultimate sacrifice. The least you can do is live up to the new responsibilities that you have been given in their absence, and prove yourselves worthy of the trust your country is placing in you."

"That's a bit strong," whispered Jeannie, who had maneuvered her way round to stand next to Josephine. "I hardly think we're going to lose the war over a basket of freesias."

Josephine agreed but was interested in the skill with which George adjusted her rhetoric to suit whichever battle she was fighting. The girls shuffled their feet and looked at the floor, expecting to be dismissed, but the principal had one more blow to deliver. "I don't know how you let this slip through the net, Miss Simms," she said, catching Vera's arm as she prepared to lead her students back to their digging. "You should have checked the glass house last night before you turned in—or at least brought the matter to my attention when you did your inspection this morning. I'm very disappointed in you. Everyone else is still learning, but you've been with me long enough to know better. Now, get out of my sight—all of you."

It would have been kinder if George had shown more discretion in front of the girls, but Josephine sensed that it wasn't the very public nature of her dressing down that wounded Vera; the emotion in her eyes as she turned away was pain, not humiliation—and a deep pain, at that. The students went back to their work in silence, and Josephine noticed that both the Norwood sisters were subtly shunned by their colleagues, although their shared lack of favor didn't seem to heal the rift between them. Vera Simms took up a spade and worked her feelings out on the land, digging furiously in a way that might have impressed George had she been in the mood to notice.

The quiet of the potting shed was a welcome contrast to the unpleasant turn that the morning had taken. Josephine resumed her task, wrapping vegetables carefully in tissue paper and layering them in boxes according to weight and size. The work was methodical but hardly taxing, and it gave her plenty of time to consider what had happened in relation to Miss Ingham's concerns; punishments were yet to be decided, but George's reaction so far to a costly mistake seemed measured and reasonable, and neither of the Norwood girls would have had grounds for complaint. She felt sorry for Vera, though, caught between the pupils and the teachers but belonging to neither camp—and perhaps the worst thing of all was that George seemed oblivious to how devastating her rebuke had been.

"Poor V," muttered Lanton, obviously sharing her thoughts. "She always tries so hard, but it's never quite good enough."

"I got the impression that she was indispensable," Josephine admitted. "Miss H told me what a help she'd been when they first took the place on."

"It's not so much that. There's no shortage of responsibility handed out to her—or credit, when it's earned. It's hard to explain what I mean." Joyce paused, squinting hard as she concentrated on threading a long needle with string, then proceeded to sew some fruit tightly into a jute bag to protect it from damage in transit. "The trouble is, Vera absolutely worships the ground Miss H walks on, so she's always looking for something more than praise—something more personal, I mean." She had taken her eyes off her sewing and winced as the needle pierced her skin. "Ouch! That was stupid of me. But I suppose what I'm saying is that Vera wants to be *someone* as far as Miss H is concerned, but really she could be *anyone*."

"It's a shame," agreed Macdonald, taking the needle from her friend and offering up her own handkerchief to stop the blood. "Vera's a really nice person when you get to know her, but that sort of attachment is never healthy. It'll end in catastrophe, mark my words."

On that positive note, the last box was sealed, and Josephine collected all the paperwork, making sure that every parcel had been correctly addressed and entered into the sales book. "I'll take these to Miss Barker so that she can get the bills ready," she said. "Why don't you two shift this lot round to the van? Miss Sellwood will drop it all off at the station on her way to Lewes."

"Righto." Macdonald went in search of a trolley, and the parcels were soon on their way.

Josephine tidied the workbench, then returned the letters to the file in date order and headed to the kitchen. Lunch preparations were well on the way, but there was no sign of Harriet. She checked the pantry and the dairy without success and was just on her way back to leave the paperwork on the kitchen table when she saw Peter Whittaker waving at her from the front porch. "Are you looking for Harriet?" he called, and she nodded. "She's round by the shepherds' huts. You know where they are?"

"Yes, but I won't bother her now. I can just leave these on the table."

"It won't be a bother. In fact, she'd probably appreciate a hand. She's been back and forth, setting up lunch for the girls, and she's a bit behind."

If she'd been braver, Josephine might have asked why Peter hadn't given Harriet a hand himself rather than providing a running commentary on her timekeeping; from what she had seen so far, he didn't lift a finger to help around the house or garden, and she doubted very much that he was paying for his bed and board. As it was, she simply thanked him and walked through the orchard to the field beyond. It was the first time that she had seen the students' distinctive accommodation, and—in spite of her aversion to any sort of makeshift living—there was a carefree sense of romance about the scene in front of her that she found very tempting. The huts stood in two rows, one of five and one of six, facing each other, and each was made of wood with a corrugated iron roof and heavy-duty cast-iron wheels, originally made to withstand the constant movement from field to field. Settled now in a more domestic environment, they had all been painted either red or green, with a reverse trim around the windows, and some were more weathered than others. The top of each stable door had been left open to air the hut inside, and she could see from the nearest one that they were sparsely furnished, with a narrow bed down each side, a simple foldout table, two locker-sized cupboards, and a small stove just inside the door. There were flowerpots on some of the steps, and as she walked down the row, she noticed the occasional flourish of a personality she recognized: film posters that smacked of Lanton or Macdonald; a bedspread that almost certainly belonged to Charity Lomax and must have cost more than a shepherd earned in a whole year. Thinking back to the dispute of the morning, she wondered if the Norwood sisters shared with each other.

A long trestle table stood in the middle of the grass, and the girls ate their meals there together—unless it rained, when they decamped to one of the barns. As Peter Whittaker had said, the beginnings of lunch had arrived in the shape of plates, glasses, and four large bottles of homemade lemonade, but Harriet herself was still elusive. Josephine went further along the line of huts to make sure, but stopped when she heard voices coming from the end of the row. She crouched down to look between the wheels and saw two pairs of legs standing behind the final hut; the summer print dress that Harriet had been wearing at breakfast was easily identifiable, but the other person was dressed in the brown boots and leggings of the college uniform and could have been anyone. Josephine listened more carefully, and—although she didn't know it very well—she thought she recognized the second voice as Vera's, raised now in anger. "We can't go on like this any more," she shouted, "or at least I can't. I'm going to tell her."

"Don't be reckless, Vera," Harriet said, confirming the other girl's identity. "It's not the right time, and we agreed to wait. If you tell her now, God only knows how she'd react, and do you really want to risk everything? Because we'll both suffer, you must know that."

"Then when? How much longer do I have to wait?"

Harriet said something that Josephine couldn't quite catch, and Vera must have calmed down too, because the next part of the conversation was too muffled for her to hear. She turned to go, fearful now of being seen, but Vera's voice rose again and held her where she was, shocked by the violent sobs that locked the words in place. "I'm *not* going to be ashamed of this—why should I be? You're making me feel like we're keeping some dirty little secret, and that's just not fair. I'm going to tell her right now, and you can't stop me."

"Can't I?" Josephine didn't wait to hear any more. She ran back over the grass to the orchard, turning at the safety of the hedge to see if anyone was following, but there was no sign of Vera or of Harriet, and she hoped they'd had no inkling of their audience. She waited a moment to catch her breath, then strolled back up the path toward the front of the house, trying to look unconcerned and hoping above all that she didn't bump into George. Peter Whittaker was lounging on the grass by the pond, and he looked up when he heard her footsteps on the gravel. "Did you find Harriet?" he asked.

"No, she wasn't there," Josephine said, wondering if he had known what she would stumble on. "I'll leave this paperwork on the kitchen table, and if Miss Barker does want some help serving the lunch, tell her I'll be out in the yard, loading the van."

Chapter 4

The rest of the day passed without incident, but Josephine was glad to retreat to her room after supper. She wrote a chatty letter home, enthusing over the landscape and sharing selective first impressions of the college, then tried to read a novel, but the words refused to make any lasting impact, and she realized that she had read the first ten pages without concentrating on anything but the argument she had overheard at lunchtime. The book was too good to waste, so she put it down and was just about to get undressed and blow out her lamp when she heard footsteps along the landing and a soft knock at the door. Jeannie stuck her head round and smiled. "Oh good, you're still up. Am I disturbing you?"

"No, not at all—come in. How was supper with your parents?"

"Nice, but hardly an evening off. My brothers enlisted together last month, so my dad's been left in the lurch, and I ended up helping out in the bar—again. I swear it's the only reason they ever invite me." She grinned and held up a bottle of stout and a packet of potato crisps. "I did bring something back with me, though. We could probably both do with a drink after this morning."

"That's the best idea I've heard all day."

Josephine pulled another chair over to the window, but Jeannie shook her head. "I thought we might go outside. The garden's always beautiful on a night like this."

"But won't the house be locked up by now?"

"Yes, but there are ways round that. Come with me and I'll show you." Josephine followed her across the landing to her own room. "Sorry about the mess," Jeannie said, glancing apologetically at the spare bed, which was covered with magazines, discarded clothes, and more supplies from the Ram Inn. "It's tidiness or breakfast for me, and I always choose breakfast. God knows how you manage, having to drag yourself out of bed even earlier."

"I'll get used to it eventually."

"Then you're a better woman than I am. Now, hold this open for me." She handed Josephine a rucksack and packed two bottles of stout, a bottle opener, and the crisps, then pushed the window up as far as it would go. "Your view is lovely, but the one advantage of staring out over the rooftops each night is that you can plot your escape. Watch where I put my hands and feet, and do exactly the same. You're not worried about heights, are you?"

"I dare say the Guinness will help. Going down, I'll just have to take my chances."

Jeannie swung herself out onto the ledge and dropped to the flat roof that sat obligingly just below her window. Josephine followed, watching where her guide trusted the trellising sufficiently to get her to the next level down, and then from there to the ground. The sky was clear, with no hint of the summer rain that had caused such trouble the night before, and Jeannie was right—the garden was utterly transformed as darkness fell. Flowers were suddenly of secondary importance to the dramatic shape of trees and bushes, and the dominance of color gave way to other senses. They took the long way round the walled garden, avoiding the telltale gravel by the door, and Josephine mapped the path by a succession of strong scents—roses giving way to honeysuckle, and then the sweet smelling rosemary bush that was the jewel of the herb patch—all more intense and more sharply defined than in daylight. "Where are we going?" she asked.

"Miss H's bench, over by the greenhouses. It's a lovely spot, but more importantly it's one of the few places that can't be seen from her attic rooms. Omniscient doesn't even begin to describe her."

"You've obviously got this down to a fine art," Josephine said. "Do you come out here often at night?"

"Now and again, when I can't sleep. It's such a beautiful place, but there's never any time to appreciate it during the day. That's the only thing I hate about this way of life—there's no peace and quiet to be had, and you never get a moment on your own. Not unless you sneak around under cover of darkness."

Jeannie's deep connection to the landscape she'd grown up with was very similar to her own, and Josephine liked her all the more for it. Most of the people she knew at Anstey threw themselves wholeheartedly into the bustle of a communal life, far from home, but Jeannie's craving for solitude and stillness was all too familiar, and Josephine was pleased to have found someone with whom she had so much in common. They rounded the corner, where the glasshouses glinted like crystal in the strengthening moonlight, and Jeannie stopped by a bench that faced out to the downs. "Just look at that," she said. "What more could you ever want?"

Very little, Josephine thought, captivated by the scene in front of her. The long, low outline of the downs was more subtle by moonlight, but somehow more striking. Without the colors or moving shadows of the day to take the eye, every small rise and fall of ground was distinctive, moving rhythmically toward the high, bold line of Firle Beacon. Jeannie followed her gaze, apparently satisfied by her reaction. "The view from up there is extraordinary," she said. "Firle and Charleston and Glynde all laid out for you on this side, then Newhaven and the sea on the other. We'll have to do the walk while you're here."

"I'd like that. You can show me your pub."

"I will, but tonight it's come to you. All except the glasses, I'm afraid—I forgot those." She deftly opened the bottles and passed one to Josephine, then took a long swig from her own. "So tell me what I've missed. Have Dorothy and Betty been sentenced for their crimes?"

"They have. A double fine for each of them, and George has written to Miss Ingham, as she said she would. Both of them have had their afternoon off cancelled this week, and neither of us needs to worry about muck cart duties for the next few days—that plum has gone to Betty. Miss H drew a rather compelling comparison with the filth that came out of her mouth."

Jeannie winced. "Betty will hate that."

"The look on her face was very expressive, but mercifully she had the sense not to argue."

"So all this was done publicly?"

"Just before supper, yes."

"And Dorothy? Anything else for her?"

"Greenhouse duties until further notice. Not surprisingly, the ventilators have been well and truly closed tonight. I have to admit, I thought she got off lightly with that. Is it really such a harsh punishment?"

"It's very time consuming, and doing it last thing at night is a drag—most of the girls are exhausted by then, and all they want to do is fall into bed. It's not just a matter of closing the windows either. There's all the watering, which takes ages if you do it properly, and you have to inspect everything for pests or diseases and treat it accordingly. Those poisons are vile, especially when it's so hot and stuffy in there. I swear that Lomax honestly thought she was dying the first time she had to spray a tomato for whitefly." Josephine laughed, easily picturing the scene. "No, on balance I'd take the muck spreading. You know where you are with that."

"Well, I suppose the most significant thing is that they've both received a formal warning. One more mistake and they're back to Moira House in disgrace."

"I wouldn't put it past them to goad each other into it," Jeannie said, looking concerned. "We'd better keep an eye out for that. It would be a shame if they didn't see the thing through—Dorothy because she's genuinely good at it, and Betty because she isn't, if you know what I mean. And apart from anything else, it would be nice to have a few days in the sun without any drama." Josephine agreed, with the row between Vera and Harriet still playing on her mind. "We virtually sold out at the market today," Jeannie continued. "The shops are getting more expensive now, so people like to buy direct from the grower—especially if you drape a few patriotic flags around the veg boxes. I had to borrow two bicycles from the White Hart and send Rogers and Nicholson back for more supplies. You should have seen them, balancing the trugs on their handlebars." She looked at Josephine, suddenly aware of her silence. "Are you all right? You seem bothered about something."

"What do you think of Vera Simms?" Josephine asked.

Jeannie looked surprised by the sudden change of subject but considered the question. "She's hard to get to know, so I'm not sure I think much about her at all. It's strange, because in lots of ways we're in a similar position—senior to the girls, but not in charge of the place—and you'd think that would make us natural allies, but it hasn't. I already know you far better than I know Vera—and that's not a complaint, by the way."

Josephine smiled. "Macdonald thinks Vera has an "unhealthy attachment" to Miss H."

She let the comment stand without any context, interested in Jeannie's immediate response. "Macdonald has a cinematic view of the world," she said, almost admiringly. "Everything in black and white, and explained afterward in simple sentences. Sometimes I envy her that."

"But you disagree?"

"Not about the attachment, no. But I'd call it unfortunate rather than unhealthy, just like anything that's one-sided. Which of us hasn't been hopelessly infatuated with someone at an impressionable age? I know I was. Anyway, why do you ask?"

"One more question before I explain. You're sure that Vera's attachment is to Miss H, and not to Harriet?"

"Harriet? Good God, no. Why on earth would you think that?"

Josephine repeated what she had heard by the shepherd's huts. "They seemed very close, and it sounded to me as if the two of them were keeping a secret that Vera wanted George to know about and Harriet didn't."

Jeannie thought about it but eventually shook her head. "I really can't see that. Vera's rave on George is a standing joke amongst the girls, and I think Harriet finds the whole thing mildly irritating, but that's as far as it goes."

The emotions she had witnessed seemed to Josephine to run deeper than irritation, but she didn't argue. "Does George encourage Vera?"

"I'm not sure she's even noticed. You saw what happened today. Does that seem like encouragement to you?"

Josephine shook her head. "No, not at all. It just occurred to me that this might be what Miss Ingram meant by 'unseemly.'" She didn't say 'harsh' or 'cruel' or 'bullying,' and 'unseemly' is the kind of word that people use when they don't know what else to call it."

"Tell me exactly what Vera said again," Jeannie said, and then, when Josephine had finished, "So we don't actually know that she was going to tell *George* something, because she didn't mention any names. Perhaps she was threatening to tell Miss Ingham *about* George and the way that she'd been humiliated by her."

"But Miss Ingham isn't responsible for Vera's welfare. And anyway, why would Vera confide in Harriet about it first?"

Jeannie had no answer to that, and they lapsed into silence. "Where have your brothers been sent?" Josephine asked.

"Gallipoli. They sailed last week. From what I read in the papers, it's got more than its fair share of casualties, so they'll get the responsibilities they were hoping for." There was a bitterness to her voice again, just as there had been the day before when she talked about the war, and Josephine sensed the fear that she must be living with—always there, no matter how much she tried to put it to one side; not for the first time, she was thankful to have only sisters. "They've got to go—I understand that, and if I were in their shoes, I'd want to do my bit too. But they're just kids, Josephine—both younger than me, and Freddie's only just had his sixteenth birthday. Occasionally, when I'm working here, I look round at the gardens, and it's like catching someone out in a lie—all the peace and the order and the straight lines, as if we're still in control, as if the world still makes sense. It's such false comfort."

"Do you really think so? Or are you just feeling guilty because it *does* comfort you? There's no shame in that, you know. Sometimes I think that's the worst of this war—it makes everything that's right and natural and beautiful look like the aberration." She stopped, not wanting to preach to someone she liked but barely knew. "That's easy for me to say, I suppose. No one I love is at risk—only a way of life."

"You're right, though, I do feel guilty. I can't look my mother in the eye at the moment—she's literally sick with worry, although she has to hide it for the sake of the pub. We went into Eastbourne on my last day off. I thought it might cheer her up, but I could see what she was thinking every time we passed one of those blue uniforms—for every soldier who's convalescing here, there are a hundred who won't come back at all. It just made things worse, and it's driving a wedge between my parents because my father encouraged them to go. I hate seeing my mother and father at odds."

"I don't suppose having breakfast every morning with Peter Whittaker and his fear helps either," Josephine said shrewdly. "Is that partly why you resent him so much? Because he reminds you of what your brothers will have to go through?"

Jeannie didn't admit it, but her smile told Josephine that she was right. "I can see I'm not going to get much past you," she said. "You're not ordinary company at all, are you? Anything but." No one had ever studied her face quite that intently before, and Josephine felt herself blush. "It's so nice to have someone to talk to, you know. Right now, a proper conversation about something other than soil temperatures and the Ministry of bloody Food is the answer to all my prayers. I didn't realize how much I'd missed it."

Josephine smiled. "You're the second person to call me that in forty-eight hours."

"Who was the first?"

"One of the soldiers at Summerdown yesterday—Jack, his name is. I met him while you were off looking for Lomax and Norwood, and we got talking. He was friendly, and he's from Inverness, so we had people in common."

"You didn't mention it. That was fast work."

"Well, if you will leave me on my own in the middle of an army camp . . ." Jeannie didn't laugh, obviously still preoccupied with her own worries, and Josephine played her encounter down. "He said he'd write, but I don't expect he meant it. He'll be off to the front soon, anyway, so what's the point in getting to know someone when they're only passing through?"

"I can't argue with that," Jeannie said, and her mood seemed suddenly more despondent than ever. "What *is* the point?" She finished her drink and put the bottle back into the rucksack. "It's getting late," she said. "I suppose we'd better call it a night."

CHAPTER 5

Josephine woke early, as had become her habit during the first couple of weeks at Charleston. She surprised herself by wanting to make the most of every day, sneaking down into the garden with Jeannie as dusk fell and talking long into the night, then rising with the first hint of sunlight through the willow tree outside her window. The only person to beat her to the morning was Vera, who was always at work in the garden when the dew was still heavy on the plants. Josephine watched her from the front lawn while she waited for her students to join her—putting soot on the crops before the sun's rays grew too strong, moving from row to row of peas and stooping every now and then to pick up a mousetrap and reset it. There was no doubting her diligence or dedication, but it seemed to come from duty rather than love, almost as if she were doing penance for something, and Josephine couldn't help but contrast it with the passion that George communicated so effortlessly for even the most mundane of tasks. She wondered what had made Vera answer that advertisement in the first place. Gardening was hard work if you didn't love it, and there must be easier ways of earning a living. She glanced up toward the attic and saw George standing by the large window on the left-hand side of the house, looking down at the garden and watching Vera's every move intently. She had been kinder toward her protégé recently, and there had been no repeat of the incident that had clouded Josephine's first day. Perhaps Harriet had intervened on the girl's behalf, or perhaps Vera had simply been more conscientious; either way, the threatened revelation had come to nothing, and Josephine was beginning to think that she had misconstrued the incident completely.

Her class flew by, with everyone now knowing the routine, and she went back inside to change for breakfast. "Ah, Josephine—I'm glad I've caught you," Harriet called from the dining room. "George and I have got to go into Eastbourne this morning. Gertrude Ingham wants to talk to us about something, and I've no idea how long it will take, so would you and Jeannie oversee lunch for the girls if we're not back?"

"Yes, of course."

"Thank you. I'll leave it all ready, and Vera knows where everything is if you have any problems."

Josephine went upstairs and met Jeannie on the landing coming the other way. "Harriet and Miss H are off to Moira House this morning," she whispered. "Harriet's just told me. Do you know what it's about?"

Jeannie shook her head. "It's the first I've heard of it. Perhaps there's been another complaint. Did she seem concerned about it?"

"No, not particularly. Anyway, you and I are on lunch if they're not back."

Lunch came and went, and there was still no sign of George and Harriet. "Perhaps they've gone into Eastbourne to shop," Jeannie said as she and Josephine helped Vera take the dishes back to the kitchen. "If it was anything serious, surely they'd have come straight back to sort it out?"

"It depends what it is, I suppose, but you're probably right. We'll just have to wait and see."

Josephine's job for the afternoon was to prune back the spring-flowering shrubs in the ornamental garden, and she set about the forsythia when the washing up was done, trying to stick to what George had taught her the day before. She could hear music as she worked: a gramophone record played over and over again in a way that she found infuriating, and on a trip to the compost, with a barrow full of cuttings, she traced its source to one of the sheds next to the chicken run. Intrigued, she looked through the open doorway and saw that Peter Whittaker was using the space as a studio. The arrangement had obviously gone on for some time because the floor and parts of the wall were covered in drips and splashes of paint. There was a stack of canvases against the wall, next to the gramophone, and Whittaker was busy at an easel by the window. He beckoned her in when he noticed her, and she was about to refuse when curiosity got the better of her. "You obviously like this part of the opera," she said, walking over to see what he was working on.

"What? Oh, I see what you mean. To be honest, I haven't really been taking much notice of it, but it's easier to concentrate with something on in the background."

"I'm sure the composer would be thrilled to hear that."

He laughed, and she noticed how easily the humor reached his eyes. "By all means put the final act on if you want to," he said, "but I doubt it ends happily. Opera never does."

Josephine looked at the canvas, and anything she was about to say died in her throat. For some reason, perhaps because she had mixed feelings about the artist, she hadn't expected to admire the painting, but she couldn't have been more wrong. It was the colors that struck her first—or rather the lack of them. The tone of the picture was set by heavy black and gray skies above a deadened land-scape, in which everything—trees, earth, uniforms, flesh—looked harsh and monotone. Here and there, flashes of gold paint brought a welcome contrast to the overall starkness, but any relief was decep-tive because the color only served to highlight things that had been fashioned to kill—the shaft of a bayonet, the barrel of a gun. There were three human figures in the painting—soldiers preparing for battle—but they were dominated by their surroundings, defeated even before the fighting began. Josephine stared at the painting, unable to look away or to imagine a more powerful depiction of the way in which war sapped the beauty from a landscape.

"You're interested in art?" Whittaker asked, sensing her reaction.

"Yes, very much. I thought about going to art school, but in the end it wasn't for me."

"Why not?"

"Because it isn't enough just to be able to draw well. I could sketch a face and you'd recognize it, but that's all it would be—a copy. If I want to express myself and say something original, I choose words, not pictures. And any sort of art should add to the world, not just reflect it. Otherwise, there's no point." He looked approvingly at her, and she pointed to the stack of canvases. "Do you mind if I look at the others?"

"Help yourself."

He carried on working while she took her time, and when the record came to an end, he didn't put it on again; in the silence, she could hear the soft, rhythmic sound of his brush against the canvas. "What's it like over there?" she asked, knowing how inadequate the question was, but unable to think of any other way to phrase it.

"If you've looked at those and you still have to ask that, then I've failed."

Josephine flushed. "I didn't mean . . ."

"I know what you meant."

"No, I don't think you do." She stood her ground, and he waited for her to explain herself. "I look at these and they're so immediate and so powerful, but they're just moments. I still can't begin to imagine how it must feel to live with it day in, day out—or how it must change you when you have."

"Why would you want to?" It was a genuine question, less aggressive than it sounded, and Josephine realized that she had no answer. "You're right, though—there is something missing," he said. "The twenty-second of April, to be precise."

"The gas attack?"

Whittaker nodded. "It was a beautiful sunset, I remember that very clearly. As it began to get dark, you could see the flash of shrapnel to the north and the occasional flare from a rocket, but that was nothing special, nothing we hadn't seen a hundred times before. Then a low cloud of yellow-gray smoke appeared, and that *was* new—we couldn't explain it at all. We heard a murmuring in the distance, growing louder all the time, and then suddenly a load of horses came over the horizon toward us, frenzied and out of control, until the road was just a mass of dust. I remember thinking— really believing—that it was some kind of apocalypse, that the whole damned thing was going to end there and then. When the horses got closer, you could see that some of them were carrying two or three men, poor devils—and there were more chaps behind on foot, throwing off their guns and their tunics so they could run faster."

"What did you do?"

"Nothing, at first—we just watched. Then we noticed the smell—very faint to start with, a tickling in the throat and smarting eyes, like the beginnings of a cold, but it soon became pungent and nauseating. One of our officers pulled his revolver out and yelled at the cowards to turn back, but they'd reached the lines by then, and we could see what was happening—we could see them frothing at the mouth and writhing on the floor, and that's when we ran too." He took a sketchbook from the top of a pile and handed it to Josephine to look through. "As you can see, I've tried and tried to paint that day, but it never works. It might be just another moment, as you said, but that *is* what it's like out there. It's all there is—a series of horrific moments. The normal bits in between, the eating and the sleeping and the friendship—they don't matter any more. In fact, they're so out of kilter that they seem absurd."

The sentiment reminded Josephine of what she had said to Jeannie that night in the garden, and she was moved by it. She picked up another sketchbook, but he took it quickly from her hands. "Those aren't finished yet," he said. An envelope that had been tucked between the pages fell to the floor, and she realized what he had been trying to hide. "It came this morning," he admitted, picking up the letter that had recalled him to the front. "I managed to intercept the post before Harriet saw it. I'd be grateful if you didn't tell her. She'll have to know next week, but I want to save her a few days of anxiety if I can. She's got enough to worry about at the moment, and she doesn't need me to make it worse when George does that so efficiently."

"Why do you dislike George so much?" Josephine asked bluntly, feeling sure now that whatever Harriet's concerns were, they revolved around the visit to Moira House.

"I don't dislike George. I *despise* her. I hate the way that she treats Harriet like a servant. She'd be nowhere without my cousin, but she takes her for granted and has done from the moment they first met, as far as I can see." He must have caught the look of surprise on Josephine's face, because he added, "You probably think I'm being indiscreet in telling you this, but it's nothing I wouldn't say— haven't said—to George's face. I've never made any apologies for encouraging Harriet to go her own way and find a different life." Harriet had never struck Josephine as someone who was remotely dissatisfied with her life, but she had no opportunity to say so. "She's got more spirit and more kindness than anyone else I know," Whittaker continued, "but she's changed. I can't remember the last time I heard her laugh." He took a tin of tobacco from his pocket and began to roll a cigarette. "Harriet has always given me a home whenever I've needed it—even when she had nothing, and even when George fought against it. I have to stand her corner because she's her own worst enemy." He threw the envelope angrily down on the floor again. "Except now I won't be around to look out for her."

There were so many questions that Josephine wanted to ask, but she didn't have time for any of them. The sound of an engine outside brought the conversation to an abrupt end, and she followed Whittaker round to the yard, noticing that Simon Cassidy was watching from the sitting room window, as if he had been waiting for the women to return. Harriet got out of the driver's seat and hurried toward the house, and it was obvious to Josephine that she had been crying. George followed, her face pale from an emotion that might have been rage and might have been shock; whichever it was, it seemed unapproachable, and although Whittaker made a move to go after them, something in the women's demeanor made him hesitate and turn back. A door slammed inside the house, and then there was silence.

CHAPTER 6

"It was good of Harriet to let us borrow the van," Josephine said as Jeannie waited to turn left onto the narrow lane that would take them to Firle.

"I think she just said yes to get me out of the kitchen. She and George were deep in conversation over the morning post."

"Not more bad news?"

"You say that as if we knew what had happened already." A horse and cart made its leisurely progress toward them, and the farmer waved his hand in thanks. "Let's hope that's all the traffic for a while," Jeannie said, seizing her opportunity to take the road. "There's no room to let anything pass down here, and reversing— as you know—isn't my strong point."

The open parklands of a manor house gave way to woodlands on either side, and a dense canopy of dark green hues marked the passing of spring into summer. The shade was a welcome interlude in a day of unrelenting sunshine, and Josephine relaxed her eyes, pleased to stop squinting against the glare. Nothing had been explained after George and Harriet returned from Moira House, but the behavior of both women had changed. Harriet was tight-lipped and less visible than usual, barely speaking unless it was to answer a question or give an instruction; George carried on working as tirelessly as ever, although Josephine thought she detected a new watchfulness about her whenever she was around the girls, as if she were trying to catch them out—but perhaps that was simply her own imagination, fed by what Gertrude Ingham had said on her arrival. There was a definite distance between Harriet and George, though—that much she *hadn't* imagined. The small moments that she had witnessed—a private joke or a hand on the shoulder, the myriad things that had spoken of their mutual respect and unshakeable unity—all that had gone, replaced by an awkward detachment, and Josephine could count on one hand the number of times that she had even found them in the same room. In the days that followed the meeting, she had half-expected some sort of official communication from Moira House, an endorsement of their orders, but nothing had been forthcoming.

"I think it's Lomax, you know," Jeannie said thoughtfully.

"Why do you say that?"

"Because there was a letter on the kitchen table from her parents—that *was* the morning post. I couldn't read what it said, obviously, but the letterhead was unmistakable. And if Lomax's family is kicking off about something, that really *will* get Miss Ingham worked up."

"But kicking off about what? I haven't noticed Lomax getting the rough end of George's tongue, mostly thanks to your covering for her. What's she got to complain about? Unless Betty put her up to it, of course. You're right—those two are as thick as thieves."

The lane curved round to the left, with another road leading straight ahead, rising steadily toward the ramparts of the downs. "That's the route to the Beacon," Jeannie said, "but we'll park at the pub, and you can meet my parents."

The Ram Inn was an attractive old building that meandered over three stories, built of brick and flint, and beautifully kept, with fresh white paintwork and flower tubs by the door. A small crowd had gathered at the front to watch a Morris side perform, resplendent in matching flannels, with bells and ribbons tied to their calves. "What's the occasion?" Josephine asked. "It's not a festival day, is it?"

"Doesn't have to be round here," Jeannie said, parking the van on the other side of the road. "We're a pagan lot when it comes down to it, and we never need an excuse to flick a hanky in the eye of the devil." They watched until the accordion player brought the dance to an end, and the men—with one final clash of sticks—disbanded to enjoy a well-earned drink. "And I suppose it *is* a festival day of sorts—for them, at least. It's the last dance they'll do for a while. They're off next week, all six of them. That's why most of the village has turned out to wish them well."

"I thought it was busy, even for a Sunday."

"Oh, it always is. There used to be four pubs in the village until they built the main road. Now ours is the only one left."

"Good news for your father."

"Yes, and my mother never stops. She's always got a sideline on the go—teas in the summer and shooting parties during the season." They got out and Jeannie led the way to the nearer of two entrances, exchanging greetings with some of the villagers, and Josephine noticed how pleased people seemed to be to see her. "Come and say hello," she called back over her shoulder. "We won't stay long, though, or I'll find myself with an evening shift."

There were three rooms inside, each of a slightly different character but with scrubbed tables and polished wooden floors in common. Most of the tables had been deserted in favor of the sunshine outside, and the drinkers left gathered at the bar were all farmworkers—middle-aged men whose faces had been prematurely aged by the weather and whose bodies were so accustomed to hard physical labor that they seemed incapable of relaxing, even on a precious day off. The men were talking loudly and were clearly in high spirits, and the arrival of two young women did nothing to dampen their mood. "That'll be enough now, gentlemen," said the woman behind the bar—obviously Jeannie's mother—and Josephine was impressed to see that the chorus of wolf whistles and teasing died away immediately, even though the landlady had barely raised her voice. Mrs. Sellwood was an older version of her daughter, and Josephine liked her immediately. Her face was naturally serious, giving her the authority that she had just used to such good effect, but her eyes—the same cornflower blue as Jeannie's—were full of humor, and there was a twitch at the corner of her mouth that suggested a smile was never very far away. She finished pouring a pint of beer and took the money for it, then came out from the bar to give her daughter's friend the warmest of hugs, as if they had known each other for years. "It's lovely to meet you, Josephine," she said, squeezing Jeannie's hand affectionately. "Jeannette's talked about you so often since you started. How are you finding it up at the college? Have you settled in all right?"

"Yes thank you, Mrs. Sellwood. It's interesting work—and every day is different, which is what I really love about it."

"Nice to be out in the open air too at this time of year. I wouldn't mind a bit more of that myself." A man at the bar cleared his throat and waved an empty glass pointedly in their direction, and Mrs. Sellwood looked at Jeannie. "Just mind the bar for a bit, love, while I pop to the kitchen. I won't be a minute, I promise."

Jeannie raised her eyes at Josephine. "What did I tell you? Do you want a drink while I'm busy?"

"I'll have whatever you're having."

"Don't tempt me." She poured two glasses of mild, and Josephine took hers over to a table to wait. A heady scent of geraniums drifted in through the open window, mingling with the beer and tobacco smoke that seemed ingrained in the walls of the room, and she watched while Jeannie dealt with the barroom banter almost as effortlessly as her mother, envying the quick retorts that gave as good as they got but always stayed just on the right side of courtesy. Three more men came in to join the others, and Jeannie's face changed as she turned to serve them, losing its easygoing welcome in favor of something much more forced. "Given up playing at a man's work, then, have you, Jeannette?" one of them said, as she poured the beer he had ordered. "Quitting the bonnet brigade and leaving the land to those who know what to do with it?"

His friends laughed, and Josephine noticed the barely suppressed hostility in Jeannie's voice as she answered. "We're not playing at anything, Mr. Farrell—at least the man from the Board of Agriculture doesn't think so. He'd hardly be supporting the college if he didn't take its work seriously."

"And what does he know about it? Sitting in his office in London and never getting his hands dirty. I wouldn't mind, but you're not even teaching *our* women. Most of the girls who pass through that college aren't from around here."

"Living just over the county boundary doesn't exactly make them foreigners, does it? Anyway, isn't Mrs. Farrell from Norfolk?"

Farrell's friends sniggered again, but this time they were laughing *at* him. Jeannie took his money and turned away, but he obviously wasn't the sort to allow a woman the last word when she had embarrassed him in front of his peers. He eyed her up and down, and said in a loud voice, "And that's no way for a girl to dress either. I'm surprised at your father, letting you bring that sort of getup in here. It's enough to turn the beer."

She handed him his change and looked him squarely in the eye. "I'm a bit confused, Mr. Farrell. Which offends you most? The bonnet brigade or the breeches? When you've quite made your mind up, I'll know what *not* to apologize for."

There was more laughter, and while Josephine admired Jeannie's spirit, she wished she would stop provoking Farrell. He was becoming increasingly angry, on the verge of losing his temper altogether, and the other men at the bar were enjoying the sport sufficiently to goad him. "She's got you there, Jim," one of them said. "And anyway, speak for yourself. I've no objection to seeing the shape of a woman's legs every once in a while. Makes a nice change."

"So what else are they teaching you up at that college, eh, Jeanette?" Farrell continued, his tone now even more aggressive. "Fucking man-hating bitches, the lot of them."

A man came through from the other bar, carrying a tray of

empty glasses. "Watch your language around my daughter, Jim," he said. "You're not in the fields now."

"No, and I won't be tomorrow or the day after that if they carry on like this. I've got to look out for my boys, George—if people can get away with paying women eighteen shillings a week, where does that leave them?"

"You could always do the decent thing and let them sign up, like my father did."

"Jeannie . . ." There was a warning note in the publican's voice, and he gave a flick of his head to dismiss her from her bar duties. "I'll take over here now. You get on your way."

"You know I'm right, though," Farrell insisted, a dog with a bone now that Jeannie had been cautioned. "It's not natural, two women running a house without a man in sight, doing just as they like in front of all those girls—and *very* close, by all accounts. I wouldn't let a daughter of mine anywhere near them."

"You take too much notice of gossip, Jim. What those women get up to is their business as long as they keep it to themselves, but it's got nothing to do with my daughter. We've already waved two of our kids off recently, and it would break Annie's heart to lose the other one, so I'd appreciate it if you could leave your filth at the door when you come in here. Jeannie knows what's right and what's wrong, and I won't have you saying any different. Now, do you want another one in there?"

The speech was meant to be supportive, but when Jeannie came over to Josephine's table, all her defiance was gone, and she looked upset. "Let's get going," she said. "I've had enough of village life for one day."

To Josephine's relief, the men at the bar had already moved on to another topic of conversation, and they were able to slip out of the pub unnoticed. They hadn't got far when a voice called them back, and she turned to see Mrs. Sellwood hurrying toward them with a basket. "I've made you a picnic to take on your walk," she said. "You'll need something to eat if you're going all the way up there."

"Thanks, mum, but you needn't have gone to any trouble."

"It's no trouble to spoil my daughter once in a while." She handed over the food and gave them both a kiss. "Have a lovely afternoon, and it was nice to meet you, Josephine. I hope we'll see you again."

"That was kind of her," Josephine said as Jeannie's mother waved over her shoulder and disappeared back into the inn. "They seem nice, your parents. I can see where you get it from."

"My charm and my unwavering sense of right and wrong, you mean?"

Josephine smiled. "He was only looking out for you."

"Then I'd hate to be there when he's sticking the knife in. Come on—it's far too nice a day to hang around here."

The road climbed gently at first, and then—as they left the last few houses of the village behind—it became more punishing, rising steadily from one bend to the next, but always with another small joy up its sleeve to lure them on. The dense, springy turf on either side was awash with banks of pink and purple flowers, and the occasional scrub of gnarled hawthorn gave the landscape a dramatic, weatherworn twist. High above them, Firle Beacon crowned the whale-backed downs that until now Josephine had been familiar with only from Kipling's poetry, and she noticed that the hills lost their soft lines and gentle grace once she was among them, becoming steadily more oppressive as they ate into the sky. For a long time she resisted looking back, wanting to extract every ounce of surprise from the scene below, and when she finally gave in to temptation, it didn't disappoint. The Weald was laid out before her, a checkerboard in every shade of green, and she stared at it in delight. "Stunning, isn't it?" Jeannie said, linking her arm through Josephine's. "I can never decide whether it's better to be down there looking up at these hills, or up here looking down."

"It's beautiful either way." It seemed an inadequate description for this fresh, new world that had made such an impression on her. The instinct to call it home that Josephine had first felt on the train coming down had proved more accurate than she could have imagined, and what began as a simple aesthetic response to the countryside was growing into something much richer—a sense of ownership and belonging which couldn't be entirely separated from Jeannie's friendship. "Can we see the farmhouse from here?" she asked, trying to plot its location from where Firle nestled in the valley, its church peeping out through the trees.

"Easily on a day like this." Jeannie pointed to the right, and Josephine recognized the striking tall chimneys that had been her first acquaintance with the house. "More peaceful from a distance at the moment."

They walked a little farther, then left the road to find a shady spot to eat. The sedge rustled in the breeze, and they chatted about Scotland or Birmingham, lapsing occasionally into a lazy silence that suited the heat of the day, but as the afternoon wore on, something remained unspoken between them, and Josephine sensed that Jeannie was waiting for her to bring it up. "Is it true what that man was saying?" she asked. "Harriet and George—are they more than good friends and business partners?"

She hated her own euphemism, which was only marginally less vague than "unseemly," but Jeannie didn't mock her for it. "Yes, I think so," she said quickly, as if she had been expecting the question. "I've always assumed they are, anyway. Not that they've been anything other than discreet, but you can tell sometimes, can't you?"

It was true, Josephine thought. She hadn't needed village gossip to tell her that the two women were in love, although she would have found it hard to say what had given it away; something in her as much as in them, she suspected, and perhaps simply the fact that she was capable of imagining it. "So is that why they're in trouble with Miss Ingham?"

Jeannie shrugged. "Not necessarily. Not everyone's as ignorant as Jim Farrell and his cronies, thank God."

"But if one of the girls had seen something and reported it, that would explain why George and Harriet were hauled over the coals at Moira House—and why they've been behaving so strangely toward each other."

"Yes, I suppose so." There was a long pause, and this time the silence was less comfortable. "Does it shock you?" Jeannie asked eventually. "Their relationship, I mean."

"No, it doesn't shock me. The only thing that shocks me is that they have the courage to follow their feelings." Without meaning to, Josephine had given herself away, and she felt something slip from her grasp, something dangerous, as if she were taking a leap into nothingness. Her stomach tightened, and she could see from the expression on Jeannie's face that the implication of what she had said had not gone unnoticed. "If I were in their position, I know I could never be that brave," she added, making a clumsy attempt to distance herself from her honesty. It was hard to tell if Jeannie took the words as a warning, and even harder to know if she had meant them as one, but she got up before the conversation could take a more personal turn. "We'd better get on. It would be a shame to come all this way and not make it to the top, and you promised me a glimpse of the sea."

The intensity of the sun was fading as they reached the summit, and Josephine was struck by how abruptly the birdsong stopped. It had been such a feature of the walk that its absence seemed ominous, a reflection of the sudden awkwardness in conversation, and the only thing that filled the silence now was the strengthening breeze and occasional bleating of sheep. The view from the Beacon stretched out for miles in every direction, quite literally as far as the eye could see, and although Josephine had been expecting the stark contrast between the countryside on one side and the English Channel on the other, it still took her breath away. "I'm so glad you brought me here," she said, knowing how much it meant to Jeannie and touched that she had wanted to share it. "It's magical."

"It is, isn't it? And it does me good to see it through your eyes.

Lately, whenever I've come up here, all I've been able to think about is what's happening on the other side of that water. It feels so insubstantial now. Funny, because when my dad brought me here as a kid, that sea seemed to stretch so far that it might as well have been the end of the world." She gave a wry smile, mocking her own sentimentality. "Thinking about it, I don't suppose that's changed so much."

Josephine looked at her, seeing straight through the cynicism. The childhood memory had sparked the same sadness in Jeannie that she had noticed earlier, when her father's defense of her at the bar had had the opposite effect to the one he intended, and she understood how deep-rooted Jeannie's love was for her family and how frightened she was of destroying it. "Sometimes you only realize how strong something is when you test it," she said. "It looks solid enough to me. You might be surprised."

They fell quiet again, and in the distance Josephine could just make out the dull thud of the guns from France. "Did you ever hear from your soldier?" Jeannie asked. The question came out of the blue, but its phrasing was too deliberately casual to be entirely spontaneous.

"Yes. I got a letter from him last week, with an invitation to go and see Vesta Tilley. In fact, right now I could be belting out 'Six Days Leave' in the Hippodrome."

"So why aren't you?"

"Because I'd rather be with you."

There was laughter from somewhere behind them, and another couple with two young children appeared over the ridge. Josephine and Jeannie turned away and began to walk back the way they had come, instinctively wanting to be alone. The sky was streaked with swaths of a pink so intense that it seemed artificial, and they stopped by a five-barred gate to watch the sunset, tucked away from the road and standing as close as it was possible to stand without touching. Then Josephine felt Jeannie's hand on her back, and a jolt ran through her as she realized that it was what she had been waiting for. It was a cautious gesture, easily laughed away if necessary, and yet so different from any touch that she had ever known. She stood stock-still, unable to remember a moment when she had been quite so aware of everything around her—the scent of the grass and Jeannie's breath faint against her cheek, the racing of her own heart. It was still not too late to pull away, she told herself; all she had to do was smile and turn for home, and nothing more would be said. Then Jeannie moved her thumb a fraction of an inch, caressing Josephine's spine, and suddenly they were kissing—shyly, almost stealthily at first, and then with no self-consciousness between them, no conscious thought of anything at all.

Josephine lost all sense of time, but when they eventually broke apart, the rose tint in the western sky had faded. The long line of hills was slowly losing its natural tint and taking on the darker blues of the evening, and it seemed to her that everything was different, everything had changed. "Is this all right?" Jeannie asked.

Josephine smiled. "Can't you tell?"

"Yes, I suppose I can." She laughed softly and stroked Josephine's cheek. "You're obviously much braver than you give yourself credit for."

She wasn't brave at all, and too much thought about where this could lead and who might find out would have been enough to make her change her mind, but tonight—with the freedom of being so far from home and the unfamiliar thrill of this new love—it was easy to put her fears to one side and live for the moment. The moon was visible just above the hill now, waiting for the darkness which would give it its true glory, and only the faint but persistent rumbling of gunfire threatened the evening's peace, striking such a jarring note that Josephine could easily have believed it was a figment of her imagination. "Are the guns always this loud?" she asked.

"It's not just the guns." Jeannie pointed to the sky above Firle, and this time the thunder was accompanied by a streak of lightning. "Something tells me we should make a dash for it."

Josephine drew Jeannie close, breathing in the smell of summer on her skin, feeling her tremble a little as she kissed her neck, her shoulder, her throat. "I don't want this to end," she whispered.

"No, neither do I."

The rain held off until they were on the outskirts of the village, but then the storm broke with a vengeance and they were glad for the canopy of trees, which gave them shelter as far as the inn. As they reached the van, the thunder vied for attention with a harsh cacophony of sound from the rooks overhead, and Josephine was astonished at how quickly the serenity of the day had disappeared. To her relief, Jeannie showed no sign of wanting to call in at the pub to say goodbye, apparently as eager as she was to preserve the illusion that the world really did exist for the two of them alone. All too soon, though, they were turning in off the main road, and the lights from the house shone dimly through the trees. "If we leave the van by the orchard, we should be able to sneak round the back without anyone knowing we're home," Jeannie said, reading her thoughts. She switched off the engine and turned to Josephine again, pulling her into a long, deep kiss. The rain hammered harder than ever on the roof of the van, and lightning forked the sky, and Josephine tried not to read a judgment into nature's sense of timing.

Long before they reached the side path, they heard the ominous clamor of the bell. "What on earth's going on?" Josephine asked, raising her voice so that Jeannie could hear her above the deluge.

"It must be a call to arms. This storm has come from nowhere. There'll be things to put away and protect, and it's all hands on deck—including ours, unfortunately." She squeezed Josephine's hand. "Just our luck. We'd better go and help, but it shouldn't take long. Why don't you go back to the van for a minute while I fetch some coats from the house?"

"I'm not sure there's much point in sheltering," Josephine said. "I'm already soaked through. Anyway, I need to check the cold frames. I left some of them open this morning, and I want to make sure that someone closed them at the end of the day."

"All right. I won't be a second." Jeannie ran off through the greenhouses to the garden gate, and Josephine headed for the potting shed. The rain stung her hands and face, coming down with such ferocity that it felt like a thousand needles against her skin, but she was pleased to find that all the lids on the cold frames were down, and the plants had been properly protected. Behind her, she heard the creak of the garden gate but was too slow in turning to see if someone was coming or going; either way, there was still no sign of Jeannie. The bell had stopped ringing; in its place she could just make out George's voice, shouting instructions from the walled garden, and she went over to help. Shadowy figures with lamps were moving round the vegetable plots, collecting tools or covering the most recently planted seedlings with sheets to prevent the rain from uprooting them, and she envied the girls their sou'westers and thick oilskin coats, buttoned high to the neck so that only the smallest of gaps was left to see through. She was about to pitch in when something made her glance back over her shoulder, and she noticed to her horror that several of the top windows were still open on the main greenhouse. Fearing for the damage she would find, and wondering who was responsible this time, Josephine turned back and ran toward the entrance, hoping to be in time to salvage something.

She heard the screams before she got there, rising high and shrill above the pounding of the rain. The door was wide open, and oil lamps lit at intervals threw out a soft, welcoming glow that jarred with the chilling sound of fear and despair. The greenhouse was long and narrow, with low walled beds on either side, and had been partitioned by more glass to form three separate houses. One of the girls was standing just beyond the first section, bending low over the flower bed on the right-hand side, and were it not for her obvious distress, Josephine could easily have believed that she was merely tending the plants. As she drew closer, she saw to her horror that the glass partition had been shattered. The girl turned toward her, and although her face was in shadow from the hood she wore, her words gave her identity away: "Please," she begged, her voice hysterical with fear, "please help my sister."

Dorothy Norwood lay on her side, surrounded by broken glass, and Josephine guessed that she had fallen from the low wall while she was reaching to close the windows in the roof; rain had soaked the bricks, leaving them perilously slippery, and one careless move in her panic to save the plants would have been enough to make her lose her footing. The greenhouse was unbearably hot, even with ventilation from above, and Dorothy's heavy oilskin coat lay discarded on the floor, where she had presumably taken it off to complete her task more easily—a natural move, but one which had left her without any protection against the glass except for a thin cotton blouse. She was unconscious—Josephine's mind refused to admit the possibility of anything worse—and her arms and face were covered in cuts of varying depths and sizes; most of the wounds looked superficial, but a quick glance was enough to suggest that two were potentially fatal. Dorothy's right arm had taken the brunt of the impact as she put out her hand to save herself, and the glass had severed all the tendons; another shard—dagger-like in its shape and deadly effectiveness—was lodged in her neck.

"Move out of the way," Josephine said, trying to keep the panic out of her voice, but Betty seemed incapable of understanding instructions, let alone following them. She began to scream again, and Josephine took her by the shoulders and half-helped, half-dragged her away from her sister. Fighting a wave of revulsion and nausea, she bent over Dorothy as the blood poured from the wound in her neck, matting her blonde hair in thick, viscous clumps and soaking into her blouse. Her pulse was weak, her face already pale and lifeless, and there was very little time left to save her. "Pass me that twine," she shouted at Betty, but the girl was rooted to the spot, so Josephine fetched it herself, using a piece of the glass to cut a length off before tying it as tightly as she could around Dorothy's upper arm. Still there was blood everywhere, refusing to be cleansed by the incoming rain, running in rivulets down the wall and into the metal drainage grille that ran the length of the floor, and covering Josephine's hands and clothes until it seemed for a moment that she was viewing the whole world through a film of deathly red. She tore off her cardigan and pressed it to the girl's neck, making sure not to touch the embedded glass, but in seconds the fine merino wool was drenched with blood. Her heart was beating so fast that it hurt her to breathe, pounding in her chest with tactless vigor as Dorothy's life seeped inevitably away from her. She could have wept with fear and frustration. "How long has she been here like this?" she asked.

Betty's answer was only just audible above the pounding of the rain on the roof, coming down so hard that Josephine half-feared another shower of broken glass. "I don't know," she said. "That's how I found her."

"And when was that? *Think*, Betty!" The only response was a pathetic, forlorn whimper, like the cry of a helpless animal, and Josephine knew in her heart that it was too late; Dorothy had already lost far too much blood to live. "Go and fetch some help," she screamed, finally giving in to her horror.

"What in heaven's name is going on?" George stood at the entrance to the greenhouse, tearing off her oilskin, and Josephine saw the color drain from her face. "Good God, no," she said, her voice low with shock. "Please tell me she hasn't . . ."

She stopped, unable to say the word, and Josephine tried to explain. "She must have slipped off the wall and fallen through the glass while she was closing the windows. We need an ambulance."

"But what was the stupid girl doing on the wall? Why didn't she use the pole?"

George looked round, as if the missing implement were somehow the most urgent matter, and Josephine did her best to stay calm. "We need an ambulance," she repeated firmly. "Someone needs to drive to the village to get help, and it has to be done *now.*"

She heard footsteps outside and looked at the door, praying that Jeannie would arrive in time to be sent to Firle, but it was Harriet, soaked through to the skin. "George? Oh my god, George, what have . . ." She trailed off, just as George had done, and the two women looked at each other for the briefest of seconds as an understanding passed between them. It was Harriet who regained her composure first. "I'll go to the post office and telephone from there for an ambulance; then I'll bring Dr. O'Brien back with me. The van's not in the yard, though—is Jeannie still out?"

Josephine didn't answer. She looked at Dorothy's face, noticing a subtle but unmistakable change, and—although it was something that she had never seen before—she knew that this was death. The sharp, metallic smell of blood seemed to cling to her, mixed with the sickly sweet scent of hothouse lilies in full bloom, and it was all that she could do not to retch in horror and disgust. "It's too late," she said quietly, releasing the pressure on the girl's neck. "Dorothy's gone, Betty. I'm so sorry."

Betty stared at her, then down at her sister's body, and the expression of blank bewilderment gave way first to disbelief and finally to shock. Without warning, she launched herself at George, hitting out at her and screaming uncontrollably. "You fucking bitch! This is all your fault, and I'm going to make sure you pay!"

The tirade was a poignant echo of Betty's recent anger toward her sister, and the words seemed to shake George more than the blows. She stood motionless, her hands by her sides, allowing Betty to vent her rage until Harriet pulled her away and calmed her down. "We'll have to let someone know," George said, and even her voice sounded older; in the few minutes since she had entered the greenhouse, Georgina Hartford-Wroe seemed to have added ten years to her age. "I'll go to the village and telephone the police . . ."

"No," Harriet objected, interrupting her. "I'll send Vera to fetch Dr. O'Brien, and he can deal with the police. You and I are needed here, looking after the girls." She paused, apparently recognizing the irony of what she had just said; on that score, she and George had fallen woefully short of their responsibilities. There was an air of fear and defeat about them both, as if they realized that this was the end of all their dreams. "The school will have to be told too, of course," Harriet added. "They'll want to notify Dorothy's parents as soon as possible."

At the mention of her parents, Betty began to sob—a violent, tortured sound that wracked her whole body but brought no tears. "They'll blame me for this," she said, choking on the words as she struggled to control herself. "I was only ever enough for them when they had Dorothy as well. It's always been the same, and now she's gone, they'll resent me more than ever." Josephine pitied her, but all the energy had drained from her body, and she couldn't even summon the strength to go over and comfort her. Feeling suddenly faint, she sank back against the wall for support, longing for some fresh air to dispel the suffocating heat and the images now fixed so clearly in her mind that she doubted they would ever fade.

"Josephine? Jesus, what the hell has happened? Are you hurt?" Jeannie pushed past Harriet and Betty, oblivious in her panic to anything other than Josephine's bloodstained clothes.

"I'm all right," Josephine said, wanting to reassure her. Perhaps she was being oversensitive, but it seemed to her suddenly that Harriet was staring at them, as if she knew exactly what was going on. "It's not me who's hurt—it's Dorothy. She's had an accident. I tried to save her, but I couldn't." All the emotions that had been kept at bay until now were released by that one simple statement, and Josephine put her hands to her face and wept. Ashamed of the tears when the true grief belonged to someone else, she allowed Jeannie to put her arm around her and lead her out into the rain.

1938

CHAPTER 1

To Josephine's relief, although the original *Daily Mirror* article had been picked up and reworked by other newspapers, no fresh revelations emerged to fan the flames, and she managed to avoid the handful of requests from journalists for a comment. With a bit of luck, Marta would be proved right, and the story would fade from view before it developed into a full-blown scandal. If she was ever to satisfy her own curiosity about those days, she needed to find out what had happened to the people involved; it seemed sensible to start at the source of the rumors, with Betty Norwood—or Elizabeth Banks as she now was. *The Laughing Woman* was due to open on the weekend, and Josephine's days were taken up with final rehearsals and last-minute decisions over costumes and lighting, but Cambridge was close enough to London to get to an evening performance of *The Children's Hour*, and it would make a refreshing change to sit in a theater without worrying about every single thing that happened on stage.

The Gate Theater Studio was on Villiers Street, underneath the arches and close to Charing Cross Station, and they arrived early. "Do you remember the last time we came down here together?" Marta asked as they walked along the Strand to pass the time.

"How could I forget?" She thought back to that cold March night, more than four years ago now, when she and Marta had only just met. A colleague of hers—the producer of her first play—had been murdered at the theater during a performance of *Richard of Bordeaux*, and Josephine, Marta, and another friend had walked through the London streets in the early hours of the morning, too shocked to go to bed and finding solace in one another's company. She and Marta had been virtual strangers, with no hint of the love that would soon develop between them, but the emotions of the night had made the conversation more intimate than it might otherwise have been, and they had talked about the war and those who had been lost. Funny, she thought, that it should be those very same years that brought them back here today. "I remember telling you about Jack," she said. "I've been thinking about him a lot lately."

"That's understandable. It's the anniversary of his death soon, isn't it? I'm the same every April, even now." Marta rarely spoke about the wartime affair that had destroyed her marriage and cost her her children, perhaps because it had resurfaced later on with such tragic consequences. "I don't suppose first loves ever really go away, especially when they were cut off before their time."

Josephine chose not to correct the assumption that Jack Mackenzie was her first love. For some reason—mostly guilt on her part over how the affair had ended and a need to resolve that in her own mind—she had shied away from telling Marta about Jeannie when the story first appeared in the newspaper. Now she was reluctant to mention it at all in case Marta saw something suspicious in her silence, and she wished that she had been more honest at the outset. She hated the idea of a secret coming between them, particularly one that was so unnecessary. "It's not just that," she explained, conscious of missing another opportunity to put things right. "I met Jack during that summer at Charleston."

"Really? I always assumed you met in Scotland."

"No, in Sussex. He was training at the convalescent camp just outside Eastbourne that I told you about. Archie was with him."

Marta smiled. "And what was a young Archie Penrose like?"

"Very similar to an older Archie Penrose. Handsome, thoughtful, serious—the complete opposite of Jack. I remember being a little intimidated by Archie, but Jack was so easy, right from the start. Very kind and very funny and very gentle—and he managed to stay that way, which always astonished me. He was a pacifist and the war horrified him, but somehow he didn't let it change him."

"That's rare," Marta said, "and obviously not an achievement that Peter Whittaker aspired to."

After their visit to Charleston, Josephine had shown her one of the stolen sketchbooks, and Marta had been shocked by the violence of the drawings. "Yes, although to be fair, I didn't know him well enough to say whether his anger was down to the war or to something more innate."

"Either way, those sketches of Dorothy's body are quite damning."

Josephine agreed, although she had grown to like Peter Whittaker during her time at Charleston. "If we accept for a moment that Dorothy's death *was* murder, they're almost a rehearsal," she said. "It's as if he was trying out different ideas or different fantasies until he found one to suit him."

"Why might he have wanted to kill her?"

"I can't think of a single reason except to bring George down. He hated her, by his own admission—but he must have also known that he couldn't destroy George without destroying Harriet, and I don't think he'd have risked that."

"You said Betty was one of the girls that he was running about with."

"Betty and Charity, yes."

"What if there was something going on between them, and he resented the way that Dorothy treated her sister? Or maybe Dorothy found out that Betty and Peter were having an affair and threatened to tell their parents. Perhaps he'd even got her pregnant."

"I doubt that. She just didn't seem the type. I could believe it of Charity, perhaps, but not Betty. She was always so . . ."

"Quiet? You know what they say."

They dropped the subject for a moment as the crowds outside a cinema forced them into single file. "Do you think you and Jack would have lasted?" Marta asked when they were on the other side of the street.

Josephine hesitated, thrown by Marta's question when she had spent the last few days preoccupied by thoughts of Jeannie and Jack, and whether—in some fundamental way—she had betrayed them both. "I don't know," she said truthfully. "We weren't together for very long, and you're right—when things end suddenly and far too soon, it's tempting to be sentimental about them." Once again, she could just as easily have been referring to her love for Jeannie, although the sense of regret that had resurfaced with the newspaper article hinted at something more troubling than sentiment.

They turned into the busy, narrow street that linked the Strand to the Embankment, and found their destination halfway down on the right. The Gate had begun life in Covent Garden before moving to its current home, a former skittle alley, music hall, and restaurant, which—like many buildings used for different things—had lost its claim to any particular architectural style. Over the years, it had been designed by thrift and necessity rather than aesthetic vision, but it had the nobility of a survivor against the odds and Josephine had loved its spirit since her first visits here in the late twenties. Like the Arts Theater Club, where her own plays had been tried out over a few nights before transferring to the West End, the Gate championed experimental or controversial plays and works by lesser-known writers, avoiding censorship from the Lord Chamberlain by calling itself a club and financing less commercial productions with a series of popular theatrical revues.

The Children's Hour needed no help in that department. Demand for tickets was so great that they were rationed to two per member, and Josephine had been lucky to get a couple of returns. The play's notoriety—already well established by its subject matter—had been further enhanced by the *Daily Mirror*'s focus on one of its leading ladies, and the foyer was packed to the gills. "I'd better find stage door and deliver this," Josephine said, taking the note she had written for Betty out of her bag.

"Do you think she'll agree to see you?"

"I can't see why she'd refuse. After all, she's the one who's been raking this up again—you'd think she'd be keen to have an audience with one of the main suspects."

Marta smiled at her sarcasm. "I doubt you're the only one who's upset at having your name dragged into it, though. If she's had flak from anyone else, she'll be keeping her head down."

"Yes, but don't forget, I've got a professional advantage over the others." She waved the envelope with a smile. "I may inadvertently have hinted at a part in a future play, and we both know that no actress can resist a part. I won't be long."

Josephine didn't often pull rank with her own celebrity, but she knew that most stage doorkeepers subscribed to a type and treated other members of their professional club with a respect which wasn't afforded to the general public. As she hoped, the doorman at the Gate knew her name—he'd taken his wife to see *Richard of Bordeaux* four times, he said; such lovely costumes—and promised to deliver her note to Miss Banks immediately and in person. She thanked him and made her way back to the foyer to find Marta, but stopped in her tracks when she saw Jeannie standing in the queue for the stalls. Perhaps she shouldn't have been so surprised—it was natural that she too might be curious to see her former pupil, and her letter had carried a London address—but Josephine still found it hard to imagine her anywhere else but in the Sussex countryside that she loved so much and which had been the backdrop to their time together. She watched from a safe distance, knowing that she would have recognized Jeannie instantly, even if she hadn't seen a photograph of her as an older woman; it was the gesture even more than the face or the hair—a wave across a room, which was so familiar that Josephine half-lifted her hand in response, even though she knew that the greeting was not for her. She looked for the intended recipient, but it was impossible to single anyone out in the crowd, and by the time she glanced back, Jeannie was gone.

"There you are!" Josephine jumped and found Marta behind her with two glasses. "We've just got time to sink a gin before it starts. Is something the matter? You seem a bit on edge."

"No, I'm fine. I was just looking for you." She accepted the drink gladly, wondering why—after all these years—she was still hiding her feelings for Jeannie, even if the reasons had changed. "I've ingratiated myself with the man on the door," she said, raising her voice above the hubbub. "By fair means or foul, I think we'll get backstage."

"Good. I'm looking forward to meeting the woman I've heard so much about." A bell rang for curtain up, and Josephine drained her glass, hoping that fate hadn't seated them anywhere near Jeannie. Though small, the auditorium had been skillfully designed to please both actors and audience, with a generous stage and steeply raked stalls that offered excellent sight lines. There was no sign of an auburn head in the first few rows, and Josephine wondered if Jeannie had noticed her walk past. If they *were* to meet again, she hoped it wouldn't have to be here, in the middle of a crowd, with all the awkwardness and affectation that entailed; after the way that things had ended between them, the last thing she wanted was to pretend that their love had meant nothing.

"I was reading the program notes in the bar," Marta said when they were settled in their seats, "and apparently Lillian Hellman based her story on an exclusive girls' school in Edinburgh called something I can't pronounce."

"Drumsheugh."

"So you've heard of it?"

"Yes. I bought a true crime book a few years ago for an article on Deacon Brodie, and ended up being much more interested in Miss Pirie and Miss Woods."

"The program says they lost every single one of their pupils within forty-eight hours of the rumors starting."

"Are you surprised? Two women making love in a bed next to their students? They'd be drummed out of town today, let alone in 1810."

"*If* that's what they were doing. The girl had a grudge against them, apparently, and they won their slander case against her grandmother—eventually, after it went to appeal."

"It still ruined them, though. They never taught again." Now, just as it had when she first read about it, the story reminded her of George and Harriet, and she wondered if their love had survived the scandal and if they'd ever been given a chance to rebuild their lives.

"Do you think Pirie and Woods *were* lovers, or was it all just a terrible misunderstanding?"

Josephine looked at Marta, one eyebrow raised. "The girl said the bed shook every night—do you really believe that it was a massage for rheumatism?"

"No, I suppose not, although come to think about it, my back has been killing me lately." She grinned, and opened the program again. "This bit made me laugh, though. One of the judges said that sex between women was as likely as 'thunder playing the tune of "God Save the King."'"

"He wouldn't be the first Scotsman to disregard anything that happens south of the border."

Marta was still laughing when the lights went down. The curtain rose on a comfortable room, part study, part lounge, where a group of young girls was gathered around an older woman, all sewing or engrossed in their schoolbooks. After a few innocent exchanges, the conversation began to expose Mary Tilford—the girl who would eventually make the fatal accusation—as a liar and manipulator, and Josephine could only admire the subtlety with which Hellman was laying the foundations of her tragedy. She took against Mary instantly, as she was supposed to, but there was nothing so far in her personality to suggest the comparison with Dorothy Norwood that had supposedly left her twin so shaken.

The character of Martha Dobie entered through the center stage door, carrying a couple of books that she returned to a bookcase, and Josephine nudged Marta. "That's Betty," she whispered, noticing that several other people were responding in exactly the same way. When Betty spoke her opening line—"What happened to her? She was perfectly well a few hours ago."—there was an audible stir as the audience recognized the words from the newspaper, and it seemed to Josephine that a deliberate pause had been built into the script to allow the words maximum impact. It had been unfair of her to assume that Betty would be at best a mediocre actress; she was actually very good, instantly conveying her character's nervous, highly strung nature and delivering her lines with a perfectly judged restraint. Her American accent was convincing too—so convincing that Josephine began to wonder if she had spent some time there. She took the program from Marta's hand to check the actress's credits, but the stage lights were far too dim to be able to read by, and she sat back to enjoy the production.

As the play progressed and the actors began to relax, the intimacy of the small theater really came into its own. The proximity of the audience to the stage required a particular sort of performance, Josephine noticed. There was no room for melodrama when even those at the back of the auditorium were privy to subtle gestures and changes in facial expression, and the actors could speak as they would on a film set or in a broadcasting studio, without any need to strain their voices. The effect for everyone watching was to be uncomfortably caught up in the emotions of the play, and Josephine was struck by how accurately it portrayed the infectious nature of fear and suspicion as a young girl began to exploit her power to hurt. The helplessness of the accused women in the face of prejudice and waning trust reminded her so acutely of the aftermath of Dorothy's death that she felt it physically, a return of the nervous tension that had been her constant companion during those terrible weeks. It was exactly the same: a scandal grows and takes on a life of its own until it's virtually unstoppable, like a forest fire extinguished in one spot, only to burn twice as strong somewhere else. Suddenly, she felt less skeptical of Betty's claim that the play had brought back the horror of her sister's death with an over- whelming sense of déjà vu.

"Do you want another drink?" Marta asked at the interval, when the curtain had fallen on a damning piece of evidence that seemed certain to seal the teachers' fate. "I have a feeling we'll need something to get us through the final act."

Josephine glanced back toward the foyer, imagining Jeannie in every queue and every doorway. "It's a bit of a crush," she said. "Why don't we wait until afterward?"

"All right, but I've got to do battle for the cloakroom. I may be some time."

While she was gone, Josephine flicked through the program, fumbling irritably in her bag for her glasses when she realized that she still couldn't see well enough to read it properly. "Infuriating, isn't it?" said a voice beside her. "I was so angry when my eyesight went, but glasses suit you." Jeannie sat down in the seat that Marta had left vacant. "Hello, Josephine. How are you?"

All Josephine could do was return the greeting, and even that sounded forced. She realized that her lack of surprise probably gave her away, but if Jeannie suspected that she had seen her and looked the other way, she didn't seem to resent it. "Did you get my letter? I wasn't sure how to get in touch with you, but I found the name of your club in *Who's Who*."

"Yes, they sent it on, but I'm away at the moment, so it's been up and down the country. That's why I haven't had the chance to reply."

"It doesn't matter. Really, it doesn't. I just wanted to warn you of what was coming."

She stopped abruptly as if she had run out of everything that was prepared and harmless, and the two of them looked at each other in silence. It was astonishing how little Jeannie had changed, and had she been a casual acquaintance, her ability to defy her age might have been a cause for envy; as it was, the telescoping of time into a merging of then and now felt dangerous, and Josephine found herself struggling for safer ground. "How did you know about the article?" she asked. "You must have written the letter long before it came out."

"Charity tracked me down through the school's old girl system. We meet every few years, so my address was . . ."

"*Charity* did?"

"Yes."

"What's she got to do with it?"

"Faith Hope is her pen name. Didn't you know?"

Suddenly the sly, knowing tone of the article made much more sense. "No, I had no idea," Josephine admitted. "I suppose I should have guessed, though. It's not the subtlest of jokes."

"No, especially when none of them are virtues that she's *ever* possessed as far as I can remember."

It was the first departure from Jeannie's carefully neutral tone, and it reminded Josephine of the defiance that she had always found so attractive. She smiled and said, "There was a time when you fought Charity's corner. You were sticking up for her the very first day we met."

"Perhaps, but we're all allowed to change our minds." The veiled accusation hung in the air between them, and Josephine realized that she had ventured too close to old wounds. "This brings it all back, doesn't it?" Jeannie added, as if reading her thoughts. "I almost wish I hadn't come. Except for this, of course. It's nice to see you, whatever the circumstances."

Her graciousness was more than Josephine deserved, and although she longed to ask Jeannie about her life and what she had done with those missing years, something in her felt that she had waived the right to idle curiosity. "I'm hoping to talk to Betty after the show," she said instead. "Did Charity give you any indication of why this has all been dragged up again now? Obviously those two have kept in touch."

"No, she only gave me the line about the play bringing back old memories."

"And do you know where Harriet and George are? They must be terrified by all this publicity."

Jeannie's eyes looked past her as she shook her head, and Josephine turned to find Marta coming back to her seat. She stood to make the introductions, and obviously did a reasonable job of hiding any awkwardness because Marta smiled warmly and shook Jeannie's hand. "The other teacher," she said, making the connection with the article.

"Yes, the *other teacher*." Her sarcasm was obvious to Josephine, but thankfully not to Marta, and they were saved from any further small talk by the two-minute bell. "I should go back to my seat," Jeannie said. "It was nice to meet you, Miss Fox." She turned to Josephine, who could tell from the subtle change in tone that Jeannie had correctly guessed the nature of her relationship with Marta. "Give my regards to Betty when you see her," she said, "and I hope we can catch up properly sometime. Come and see me when you're next in town. You've still got my address on the letter?"

Josephine nodded, feeling Marta's eyes on her. Jeannie bent to pick up her bag, and her hair fell across her face; she brushed it back with another familiar gesture, and Josephine noticed for the first time that she was wearing a wedding ring. She would have found it impossible to explain the rush of conflicting emotions that ambushed her—relief, confusion, jealousy—but Jeannie seemed to see them all pass across her face. "Funny how life turns out, isn't it?" she said. There was no bitterness in the words, only regret, but Josephine would have found anger far easier to deal with. Jeannie stepped forward to give her a parting hug. "I need to see you," she said, so quietly that Josephine could hardly hear her. "Please come."

They watched her walk back down the row. "She's obviously as upset by all this as you are," Marta said, taking her seat again. "I didn't know that she'd written to you."

"Didn't I mention it? It must have slipped my mind in all the fuss about the play. She wanted to warn me, but the newspaper had already come out by the time I got the note, so it didn't seem important." The response was far too defensive for a comment that had held no reproach, and Josephine forced herself to stop. She longed to look round again to see if Jeannie was with her husband, but didn't trust herself to be casual enough about it, and the lights went down before she had the chance.

"Is she still teaching?" Marta whispered.

"I doubt it. She's married now."

When the curtain rose again, the play had moved forward a few months to the aftermath of the scandal. As in the original story, the teachers had won their court case, but their business was in ruins, and the action built inexorably to a tragic conclusion, as Betty's character—in despair about the true nature of her feelings—took her own life. "Well, that was uplifting," Marta said while the actors were taking their second curtain call. "Did that happen in the real thing?"

"Not as far as I know. I think they just parted and lived their separate lives." She watched while Betty and the actress playing Karen Wright came back for one final bow. "This will make her career, you know, provided she chooses carefully from now on. Hers *and* Charity's if the story gets any bigger."

"What?" Marta listened as Josephine told her about the pen name. "Do you think that's all this has been, then? A cynical bid for the limelight, and damn anyone else who gets hurt in the process?"

"I'm not sure, but I doubt that crumbs off my casting table would be enough to turn her head now. In hindsight, I probably should have tried a different approach."

She was right to be skeptical. As soon as they arrived at the stage door, jostling for position with a gaggle of fans and reporters, the man on duty shook his head apologetically. "I'm sorry, Miss Tey, but Miss Banks sends her regrets. She simply doesn't have time to see you today."

Josephine had been half-expecting the rejection, but she wasn't used to being on the receiving end of such a casual dismissal, and her frustration got the better of her. "Perhaps if you could explain to her that we just need a few minutes . . ."

She was interrupted by Marta's hand on her arm. "What my colleague is too discreet to mention is that we've come here today on behalf of someone else. My name is Marta Fox, and I work for Mr. Hitchcock and his wife . . ." She let the words hit home before continuing, and Josephine stared at her in astonishment. "Miss Tey, as you may know, has recently provided the source material for one of Mr. Hitchcock's finest films, and she and I are currently working on a new project that may be of interest to Miss Banks. Knowing of Miss Tey's past association with her . . ."

"Wait a minute—did you just say Hitchcock?" The American accent was pronounced, and Marta turned to the man who seemed so proud of his own voice that he obviously wanted everyone to hear it. He was in his fifties, heavily built and expensively dressed, and Josephine took against him instantly.

"That's right."

"*Alfred* Hitchcock."

Marta suppressed a smile. "And Alma Reville, yes. Who are you?"

"Teddy Banks, Betty's husband. Delighted to meet you, Miss Fox."

Josephine was used to fading into the background whenever a certain type of man set eyes on Marta, and it amused rather than offended her, but today she felt obliged to speak up, if only to corroborate her lover's outrageous ruse to get them backstage. "Mr. Banks, perhaps you could persuade your wife to give us five minutes? That really is all we need, lovely as it would be to talk about old times."

"Hell, you can have as many minutes as you like if you're here for Alfred Hitchcock. Even better—why don't you join us for dinner?"

"That's very kind, but I'm afraid we have other plans, and time is pressing."

"Then I'll go and tell Betty you're on your way. Wait right here."

He disappeared toward the dressing rooms, ready to groom his wife for her future film career, and Josephine took Marta to one side. "When did you think that one up?" she whispered, half-admiring and half-accusing.

"During the curtain call, when you pointed out that Betty was far too grand to see us. And don't look at me like that—it worked, didn't it?"

"Up to a point, but how on earth are we going to carry it off? You've virtually promised her a role in Hitchcock's next film."

"I've done no such thing. If you think about it, I didn't actually tell any lies. If she—or rather her husband—chooses to jump to conclusions, that's their problem, not ours."

"I'll remind you of that when he's on the phone to Hitchcock's office, threatening to sue for breach of contract."

"He wouldn't dare." Marta looked less confident than she sounded. "You don't really think he'd do that, do you?"

"He strikes me as the type who'll do anything for his wife's ambition. He almost tripped over his own desperation on his way to tell her about us."

"Oh well, it's done now. If necessary, I'll just have to come clean with Alma."

Banks reappeared and beckoned them through to the dressing rooms. He opened Betty's door without knocking, and the actress glanced up at their reflection in the mirror, which covered the whole of one wall. She finished removing her makeup and rose to greet them, dismissing her husband with a wave of the hand. "It's all right, Teddy. I'll see you outside."

"Don't you want me to—"

"No, darling. Why you don't go on to the restaurant? I won't be long." To Josephine's surprise, Banks melted away without any further argument, and Betty gestured to them to sit down. "Bless him—he's rich and he adores me, but he's not very bright. You don't really work for Alfred Hitchcock, do you?"

"Actually, yes," Marta said. "I'm a screenwriter and assistant to his wife. Right now, I'm helping her destroy *Jamaica Inn*, although I'd be grateful if you didn't pass that on to anyone called du Maurier."

Betty smiled. "But that isn't why you're here."

"No, it isn't."

The actress looked at Josephine, waiting for her to speak, and Josephine was struck by how poised and confident she seemed; the likeness to her twin, which she had always struggled to see, was much more obvious in the older woman than it had been in the sulky, uncertain sixteen-year-old, and not just because her dyed blonde hair gave her a physical resemblance to Dorothy. Betty seemed to have grown into the life that was always meant for her sister, and Josephine wondered if her self-assurance was down to a successful career or a shrewd marriage, or if she had simply—as Marta suggested at Charleston—found freedom in shaking off Dorothy's shadow. "Why did you agree to see us if you knew we were lying?" she asked, genuinely curious about Betty's motives.

"I thought about it, and I remembered how hard you tried to save Dorothy's life." She walked over to an ice bucket surrounded by flowers and poured three glasses of champagne from the open bottle. Josephine looked at the bouquets and wondered how Betty could bear to have lilies anywhere near her when they were such a powerful reminder of that terrible night; to this day, they were the only flower that she herself disliked. "It's a terrible bond to have with someone, but only you and I really know how that felt—to watch her die, I mean. I don't think I ever thanked you, did I?"

"No, but there was no need. And anyway, I couldn't save her."

"But you tried, which was more than I did." She held out the glass and stared at Josephine, challenging her to tell the truth. "You thought at the time that I wanted her to die."

Josephine nodded. "Not consciously, perhaps, but—"

"No? There wasn't a small voice somewhere telling you that I'd plunged that piece of glass into her throat?"

"I honestly don't remember thinking that. It crossed my mind that your life might be easier without Dorothy around to over-shadow it, but nothing more than that." The conversation wasn't at all as Josephine had envisaged it, and she had never expected to be the one under interrogation, but she was interested to see that Betty had obviously spent a great deal of time analyzing her own reactions to that night and thinking about how they might appear to other people.

"So why didn't you do more to help her?" she demanded, justi-fied now in asking the question that had seemed too insensitive at the time. "You must have got to her a few minutes before I did. If you'd reacted more quickly, she might have stood a chance. Or *did* you kill her?"

"Josephine!" Marta turned to her in surprise, but Betty didn't seem in the least bit unsettled by the question; on the contrary, she seemed to welcome it.

"No, I didn't kill Dorothy, but I didn't save her either, and I've spent the last twenty-three years wondering what that makes me." She drained her glass, and in the context of their conversation there was something disturbing about the way that the crystal caught the light. "I was shocked when I found her—shocked and frightened. For as long as I could remember, I'd hated and needed Dorothy all at the same time. Do you know what that's like?"

"No."

"Then you're lucky. I seem to have had that my whole life—first with Dorothy, then with my parents and my friends, and now my husband. Never quite strong enough to stand up for myself, but not too helpless to resent my own dependence. Perhaps all twins are like that. But in answer to your question, when I found her lying there, it was as if someone had offered me a choice—my life or hers.

That's what I was thinking about when you got there. That's what I've been thinking about ever since."

"So why now? Is this Charity's doing? Is it her fault that we're all having our lives rolled out for public inspection?"

Betty seemed genuinely surprised by the strength of her objection. "You're in the public eye already. Why would that bother you?"

"Being well known for your work is one thing. Having your personal life played out in the newspapers is completely different." Betty looked at her curiously, and Josephine continued quickly, before she had a chance to ask what was so dangerous about Josephine's personal life. "Being linked to an old crime—*if* it was a crime—might be good for your career, but I'd prefer it if you left me out of it."

"But nobody is seriously going to think I meant you."

"Really? *'Could her flair for fictional crime be inspired by more than just a rich imagination?'* With lines like that, it's a miracle I haven't already been hauled in for questioning."

"Yes, I'm sorry about that," Betty said, suddenly less at ease. "I didn't know she was going to go that far."

"So this *is* Charity's fault."

"It was her idea. She suggested it when I got the part, but she didn't have to hold a gun to my head. I needed a break, and this has given me just that." She threw Marta a wry glance and refilled her glass. "I might not have turned Hitchcock's head yet, but I'm not without offers."

"They would have come eventually. You're very good."

"Thank you, but we both know that's not how it works."

Josephine smiled, conceding the truth of what Betty had said. "Just out of interest, what made you go into acting? We didn't know each other very well, but it's not the career I'd have predicted for you."

"In a funny sort of way, I've got Dorothy to thank for that. After she died, everyone wanted me to be like her, so I acted the part as best I could. It turns out I was rather good at putting on a performance. Now, even I'm not sure where the join is."

Betty had become very adept at cynicism—thinking about it, Josephine didn't know a successful actress who hadn't—but every now and again she caught a glimpse of the girl she had known, frightened and insecure, and she had much more sympathy for those qualities now that they were tempered with spirit rather than sullen resignation. She'd had no time for Betty Norwood, but to her surprise, Josephine felt a grudging respect for Elizabeth Banks. "What happened after the inquest?" she asked. "Did your parents sue for negligence like they threatened to?"

"Yes. They were advised against it because the other side could prove that Dorothy had been taught all the proper safety procedures and had simply chosen to ignore them, but my father wouldn't listen. We were never a rich family, but he spent everything he had on bringing those women to court, and then he lost. Even then, he wouldn't let it go. He hounded them for a while, and in the end my mother left him because he wouldn't see reason. He died shortly afterward of a heart attack."

"And your mother? Is she still alive?"

"No, but we were virtually strangers anyway—her choice, not mine. She remarried, and my stepfather had children of his own— boys, who weren't expected to live up to a dead sister."

She spoke the words as if they offered a perfectly rational explanation of why her mother had abandoned her, and Josephine began to understand how deeply scarred Betty had been by her childhood, even before Dorothy's death. "Where did Harriet and George go?" she asked.

"Devon at first. After that I don't know. My father lost track of them eventually, which was probably just as well."

"Does Charity know where they are?"

Betty hesitated. "No, not yet."

"But she's looking for them?"

"Yes."

And God help them when she struck lucky, Josephine thought; suddenly her wish to talk to the two women took on a new urgency. "Who else have you kept in touch with, apart from Charity?"

"No one, really. I lived in America for a while after I met Teddy. I still get a Christmas card every year from Joyce, which is very sweet of her, but that's about it."

"Joyce Lanton?"

"Joyce Thorpe now."

It was tempting to ask more about a girl she had liked very much, but there were more pressing questions, and Josephine moved on. "And what about Peter Whittaker? Do you know what happened to him?"

"He was killed during the war—in the final few days, I believe."

It was hardly an unexpected response, but still it saddened Josephine—so much so that she began to ask herself if the mission she had set herself to get to the bottom of Dorothy's death was really worth all the grief it entailed. She had never been the sort to attend school reunions or sustain friendships beyond their natural course, preferring to leave the past where it was; anything else—as she had been reminded today already—was just too painful.

"How did Whittaker and Dorothy get on?" Marta asked, taking part in the conversation for the first time. "Were they ever an item?"

Betty looked at her in bewilderment. "No. Why would you ask that?"

"Because he often sketched her."

"Oh, I see. No, that was nothing special. He sketched us all, and gave some of us lessons too. It didn't mean anything." She looked to Josephine for corroboration, and Whittaker's image of her with Jeannie came instantly into her mind; it wasn't the first time she had thought of it, but after the recent embrace, it had become more than just a harmless, two-dimensional memory. "If Peter liked anyone, it was Charity. That's how I heard of his death. She was very cut up about it."

Betty glanced at her watch, and Josephine knew that their time was almost up. "Do you *honestly* believe that Dorothy was killed?" she said, getting back to the point, "or did you just say that for dramatic effect because Charity told you to?"

"No. I do believe it." She paused, as if deciding whether or not to trust them. "There was someone else in the greenhouse when I got there, you see. I heard them running away."

"What? Why on earth didn't you say so at the time?"

"Because I was frightened that something would happen to me. Charity was the only person I trusted, and she agreed that we should keep quiet about it."

It was a pity that Charity's sense of discretion had died with Dorothy, Josephine thought, but she said nothing. "What exactly do you remember?" she asked, and then, pre-empting Betty's response, "I know it's a long time ago, but do your best."

"Well, I was down by the sheds, checking all the cold frames, when I saw the van come back and park by the side of the orchard. You'd been out with Miss Sellwood that afternoon, if you remember?" Josephine nodded, desperately hoping that Betty wasn't about to say that she had seen them together. "I saw you running toward the potting shed, and I was about to come and warn you that Miss H was on the warpath about you being out so late when we needed all hands on deck, but then I heard the crash of broken glass from the greenhouse. I knew that Dorothy was there, so I went to see what had happened. That's when I heard the footsteps, and then the gate. You know how it always used to squeal?"

"But you didn't actually see anyone?" Betty shook her head. "Jeannie had gone to fetch some oilskins from the house for us," Josephine said carefully. "Are you sure it wasn't *her* footsteps that you heard?"

"They were definitely by the greenhouse. That's all I know. I went inside and found Dorothy lying there. You arrived shortly afterward."

"And you think this was directly connected to the accusations she made about Harriet and George?" Josephine clarified, aware of how serious things would look for the two women if Betty was telling the truth. Seeing the actress hesitate, she continued. "That's what the article said. Charity claimed that—"

Betty held her hand up to interrupt, and Josephine saw to her surprise that it was trembling. "Dorothy didn't make those accusations," she said, her voice much quieter now. "I did."

Josephine stared at her, wondering if she had misunderstood. "Miss Ingham told Harriet and George that *Dorothy* had complained about them," she said, but even as she was speaking, another small piece of the mystery fell into place.

"I telephoned Miss Ingham, pretending to be Dorothy," Betty admitted. "Our voices were similar, so she believed what she was told."

"Why would you do that?"

"To pay them all back for the way they treated me. I was so miserable at that farmhouse, and no matter how hard I tried, I couldn't compete with Dorothy. Then Miss H humiliated me after the row about the greenhouse, so I thought I'd teach her a lesson. I'd expose them for what they were and turn them against their precious Dorothy at the same time." She gave a bitter laugh at her own childishness and shook her head in disbelief. "So perhaps now you can understand why I'm doing this. If my sister was killed because of those accusations, that really was my fault, and it should have been me. That's why I can't rest. I need to put it right."

"But you're still using Dorothy as a cover—how can that be putting it right?" Josephine argued. "Think of the lines you've been speaking all night: a girl tells a lie, and it destroys everyone."

"It wasn't a lie, though, was it? Not completely. We're not talking about a child who makes something up out of spite. I shouldn't have done it, I admit that, and I wish to God I hadn't—but it *was* the truth. Those women *were* lovers. How other people judged that wasn't my fault."

Rightly or wrongly, there was no argument to that, and

Josephine didn't waste time on trying to find one. "And I'm assuming you think it was one of them who killed Dorothy, even though the damage was already done and it wouldn't have saved their reputation?"

Betty hesitated. "Perhaps, but there were other accusations, other secrets. Charity had a knack for finding things out and turning them to her advantage, even then."

"So who else is she planning to destroy?" Josephine asked, deciding to brazen it out. "Or do I have to wait for the morning edition?"

"I can't tell you that. As it is, she'll kill me if she finds out how much I've said, but I'm not sure I care any more. I've carried this guilt around for years, knowing that it should have been me people hated, not Dorothy. I deserve whatever I get."

"You're lucky you've been able to decide that for yourself," Josephine said. "Not everyone has that luxury."

"Have you been back to Charleston recently?" Marta asked. "The housekeeper mentioned a visitor who had been there during the war."

"No, that was Charity. She wanted me to go with her, but I couldn't face it. I wish I'd never seen that place. I'll never go back."

Josephine stood to leave, knowing exactly how she felt. "Do give my regards to Charity," she said on her way out. "It's nice to know that she's doing something worthwhile with her life."

It was good to be out in the air. They walked toward the river to hail a cab from the Embankment, and Marta took Josephine's arm. "Well, that was a lot to take in. What do you make of it?"

"I'm not sure I know what to think. Part of me feels sorry for Betty. It was a stupid, spiteful thing to do, but I can also understand how she felt, and she couldn't possibly have foreseen the consequences. And she's still being manipulated by Charity, of course— that relationship hasn't changed, no matter how successful she's become."

"Are you convinced it wasn't an accident now?"

"More convinced than I was, yes. I wish I knew how to get in touch with Harriet and George, though."

Marta looked at her doubtfully. "Be careful, Josephine. The way I see it, one or both of them could have done this. Don't stir things up and put yourself at risk."

"I wouldn't be at risk."

"How can you be so sure? And why are you hell-bent on protecting them when you don't know the facts?"

"Because I liked them," Josephine said, knowing how naive that sounded but unable to think of anything more convincing. "Particularly Harriet. I honestly don't believe they were capable of hurting any of the girls in their care, and they don't deserve another witch hunt."

The words alone brought back the horror of that time, and Marta seemed to sense her strength of feeling. "All right," she conceded, "but if you're insisting on going any further with this, I really do think you should talk to Archie. He's got more ways of tracing people than you *or* the *Daily Mirror*, and he could probably find these women straightaway if you asked him to."

"I told you—Archie's in Cornwall, and I don't want to disturb him."

"A telephone call is hardly going to wreck his week." She sighed impatiently. "It's been months since he found out about Phyllis, and you know he's forgiven you. Isn't it about time you forgave yourself?" As usual, Marta had seen straight through her excuses, and Josephine didn't try to argue. "This isn't just a question of curiosity any more; it's about justice, and the stakes are very high. If someone out there really did get away with murder, you shouldn't go plowing in without some sort of official help. It's too dangerous. Give him a call, or better still, come down to Cornwall with me on Thursday when I go to talk about the film."

"And spend the day with the Hitchcocks? I've had quite enough of them to last me a lifetime, thank you. No, I'll talk to Archie when he's back in London. I'm too busy to go chasing round the country until the play opens, anyway, so it won't hurt to wait."

She fell silent, thinking about everything that had shaken her that night, from Jeannie's urgent parting request to Elizabeth Banks's confession that she, not Dorothy, had set in motion such a destructive chain of events. If those accusations had never been made, would Dorothy still be alive, she wondered? And if that death hadn't unleashed a tide of hatred and prejudice, would she have been brave enough to acknowledge her love for Jeannie? The strengthening breeze carried a fresh, salty tang from the river, which seemed out of kilter with the heart of a city. The unsettling beauty of the Thames at night always filled her with a mixture of wonder and fear, and today its dark, impenetrable depths seemed to chime with her mood more than ever.

They were lucky with the third taxi along, and soon heading back to King's Cross. "As much as I hate to give Charity any credit, contacting Moira House for some addresses is a really good idea," Josephine said. "I don't know why I didn't think of it myself. It might be useful to talk to some of the other girls about what they remember from that night."

"You just promised me you wouldn't take any risks before you've spoken to Archie."

That wasn't quite how the conversation had gone, but Josephine decided against splitting hairs. "I think it's very unlikely that I'd ever be in danger from someone like Joyce Lanton. It would be nice to see her again and find out if she and Mags ever started their clinic."

"What could she tell you, though? Betty was in the greenhouse and you were nearby, and yet neither of you saw anything incriminating. If everyone else was in the main garden, how could they possibly help?"

"By telling us who was missing," Josephine said. "I know it's doubtful, especially in the chaos of the storm, but it's got to be worth a try."

Chapter 2

"Will he film any of it here?" Marta asked, looking out of the window as Alfred Hitchcock and his art director tramped around the inn that lent its name to his latest project.

"I doubt it, but he's found a stretch of rough track on the moor near Altarnun for the coach scene, and an old post office in Tintagel to base some interiors on, so it hasn't entirely been a wasted trip." Alma Reville smiled and joined Marta by the window, more than used to her husband's painstaking approach to his work; if anything, as the person in charge of continuity on his films, as well as some of the script work, Alma's attention to detail was just as demanding as his. "I never imagined it would be quite so difficult to find a hundred yards in Cornwall without a telegraph pole or a stretch of tarmac," she said. "You've been very patient, and I'm sorry about the rewrites."

"You don't need to apologize to me. I'm not the one who'll object to them." Marta gathered together the research materials that she had used during the script meeting—scores of photographs of Cornish architecture, old maps of the county, and books on wrecking or the history of Falmouth's Packet ships; everything, in other words, but the novel that had inspired the film in the first place. "Fowey's not far down the coast, if you wanted to speak to Miss du Maurier in person."

Alma laughed and shook her head. "If we started doing unpleasant things like that for ourselves, what would be the point of agents? Anyway, there's no choice in the matter. If the film is to play in America, we have to change the villain. Daphne will forgive us eventually."

Marta had her doubts about that, although she didn't argue. She knew how much Josephine still resented the changes that Hitchcock had made to her book, and if Marta had written *Jamaica Inn*, the changes to the plot would be the least of her objections; it was the loss of atmosphere that she felt du Maurier would hate most, the taming of the novel's raw brutality to accommodate an actor of Charles Laughton's stature, and she was surprised that Hitchcock was allowing it to happen, no matter how keen he was to get the film done and make his move to Hollywood. "And talking of America," Alma continued, "are you sure you won't come with us? There's always a place for you—you know that."

Marta was aware that Hitch and Alma would no longer be as free to pick and choose their team once they were part of the Hollywood system, but still she appreciated the offer and the respect it implied. "Don't think I haven't considered it," she said, "but I'm settled here now and happier than I've ever been—and when you've been as *un*settled and as *un*happy as I have, that counts for a lot. Too much to give up, no matter how tempting the offer." Alma nodded, accepting her answer. She had become a friend and confidante in the time that Marta had known her, and it was that as much as the work that Marta would miss when she left. "In the meantime, I'll redraft those scenes in time for you to share them with the other writers next week."

"Good." Alma glanced back to the window and said, "It looks like they've seen enough, so we'll be off. Are you sure we can't give you a lift anywhere?"

"No, thank you. I'm meeting Archie here, and he'll run me back to the station afterward."

"Do give our regards to Chief Inspector Penrose," Alma said with a twinkle in her eye. "We didn't part on the best of terms after that terrible business at Portmeirion, but he made quite an impression on us."

She went out to the car, and Marta looked at her watch, trying to decide what to do with the half hour she had left before Archie was due. There was no time to do any work, so she went for a walk instead, soaking up the atmosphere while she had the chance, even if it wouldn't be required for her script. It was a day of constantly shifting sun and cloud, and occasionally the light chased the shadows from the hills with such dramatic speed that it was as if someone had taken a cloth and wiped the landscape clean. The inn occupied a high vantage point with spectacular views across Bodmin Moor, but its remoteness was chilling, even on a warm autumn day; other than a tiny chapel farther down the road, the bleak, gray stone of Jamaica Inn was the only landmark for miles around, and Marta didn't have to walk far to find the harsh, mournful landscape of du Maurier's novel.

She headed back in time to see Archie's car pull up by the inn. To her surprise, Phyllis was with him, and she watched, unobserved, as they got out and walked over to look at the view. From a distance, they seemed at ease in each other's company, and although Marta couldn't have been more pleased for Archie, she felt a sharp pang of envy, so painful that it stopped her in her tracks; her own daughter had been a stranger to her and had died before her eighteenth birthday, younger than Phyllis was now, and not a day went past when Marta didn't long for a second chance to get to know her. She waited until the emotion passed, then waved and walked across to join them. Archie introduced Phyllis, and Marta saw a look of vague recollection pass across the girl's face as Phyllis tried in vain to place her. "It was at Cambridge railway station," she said, reminding Phyllis of where they had met before. "You were with Bridget, and I was on my way back to London." The recognition was immediately blurred by sadness at the memory of a time when Phyllis had taken her mother for granted. "It's nice to see you again, but I'm so very sorry for what happened."

"Thank you. How did your meeting go?"

The deflection of sympathy—polite but standing for no argument—was uncannily like Bridget's, and Marta could see from the look on Archie's face that the likeness between mother and daughter was still painful for him. "As well as could be expected. I'm not convinced it will be the greatest film ever made, but Alfred Hitchcock's mediocre is still better than most people's finest, so I haven't given up hope."

"It must be exciting, though."

"It has its moments, but I couldn't help remembering when I was on my way down here that the last time I was in Cornwall, Hitch had me chasing off to Newlyn for buckets of fish because the seagulls wouldn't do what he wanted them to. Don't ever accuse me of being in it for the glamour."

Archie laughed. "That was for Josephine's film, wasn't it?"

"Yes, but as she'd never written that scene in the first place, I didn't get much sympathy for it. Shall we go inside?"

"I fancy a walk first," Phyllis said, "and it'll give you two a chance to talk."

"You don't have to . . ."

"I know, but I'd like to. I love the book, and there's a Jem Merlyn out there for me somewhere. I'll see you in awhile."

"How are you two getting on?" Marta asked, watching her stride off in search of *Jamaica Inn*'s romantic hero. "It must be so difficult for both of you."

"It is," Archie admitted. "I haven't the faintest idea how to be her father, any more than she has of how to be my daughter, but it helps that we seem to like each other."

"That's a good start."

"We still can't talk about Bridget, though."

"Give it time. It's all so new."

"I know, but I see how much she's hurting, and I want to help."

"She'll be hurting for years, Archie—for the rest of her life—so don't rush her. And you have to accept that helping Phyllis with her grief for Bridget might *never* be your job. There's a big enough mountain to climb there with your own feelings. She'll let you know, when and if she's ready."

"I know, but . . ."

"But we all want the impossible."

He smiled. "This must be hard for you. It must bring things back."

Not many people would have thought of that, and Marta realized how important Archie's friendship had become to her, regardless of his connection to Josephine and in spite of a difficult start. She took his arm and said, "The fact that you even said that makes it easier. Let's have a drink."

The Inn's low ceilings and a bewildering number of rooms were disorientating after the openness of the moor, and there was an overpowering smell of wood smoke. "What would you like?" Archie asked.

"If they do anything but rum, I'll have a gin and tonic." She chose a table in the corner, away from everyone else, and Archie soon joined her with the gin and a pint of beer. "It was good of you to come here and save me the extra miles," she said.

"My pleasure. Phyllis was dying to see it, and I was pleased to get your call, although I can't help wondering why Josephine didn't make it herself."

"She still feels guilty about what happened, Archie. She wanted to tell you about Phyllis as soon as she found out, but I persuaded her to wait for Bridget to do it."

"And you were right. I can see that now."

"It's not just that, though." She paused, wondering how honest to be. "Josephine never really trusted Bridget where you were concerned, any more than you trusted me when she and I first met." Archie smiled but didn't argue, and Marta added, "I think she always believed you'd get hurt somehow, and from what she's told me, she was very hard on Bridget during their last meeting, perhaps unfairly so. She urged her to be honest with Phyllis about who her father was, and there's a part of Josephine that will always believe that if Bridget hadn't gone to see her daughter that day, she'd still be alive."

"You could also say that Josephine gave Bridget the chance to save her daughter's life."

"I know, and I've told her that, but she'll only believe it coming from you."

She offered him a cigarette, but he shook his head and took out a pipe. "I'll talk to Josephine as soon as I'm back and find a way to put it right," he promised. "I miss her."

"And she misses you. If I'm honest, that's why I really wanted to see you today. This newspaper business just gave me an excuse, although I *am* worried that she'll go too far with it. You know what she's like when she gets the bit between her teeth about something, but I can't work out why this is affecting her the way it is. It was all such a long time ago, and the fuss seems to have died down after the first flurry of interest."

"I'm not surprised it's run out of steam. I found the article after you called, and it's a masterpiece of suggestion, but very thin on facts."

"Were you aware of the story back then?" Marta asked. "Josephine told me it happened around the time you first met, when you were both in Sussex."

"That's right. I vaguely remember the accident because Josephine mentioned it to Jack afterward, but she never talked about it in much detail. I always got the impression that she wanted to put it behind her, and to be honest, I was too caught up in going to war to take much notice of anything else."

"That's understandable."

"If a little selfish. Tell me what else you've found out."

Marta explained in as much detail as she could everything that

Josephine had told her about the murder and the days leading up to it, then recounted the visit to Charleston and their conversation at the theater, including the revelation about Faith Hope's real identity. "I've made a list for you of all the people who were there in 1915, as not everyone is mentioned in the article. The starred names are the ones we can't trace ourselves, and Josephine is especially keen to track down the women who ran the place. The others are pupils from the school."

"Have you spoken to them already?"

"No, but Josephine thinks she can get their addresses from Moira House. The only person she's talked to is Jeanette Sellwood, the other teacher. She was at the theater when we went on Tuesday."

"Was she? What did Josephine tell you about her?"

The phrasing of the question struck Marta as odd, and Archie's tone was suddenly more guarded. "Not much," she admitted, realizing how little Josephine had actually said about her old friend. "Why?"

"Oh, no reason, really," he said, far too casually. "It's just that I met her once or twice. She came to Summerdown Camp with Josephine when she was seeing Jack."

He flushed, and Marta suddenly understood what he had meant. "Ah, you mean Josephine was trying a spot of matchmaking?"

"Something like that, although I think it was more Jack's idea, and we never really hit it off." He looked down at the list again and changed the subject. "Well, I can help you with Simon Cassidy for a start. He died in prison about five years ago."

"Really? I don't suppose it had anything to do with a nasty accident in a greenhouse?"

"I'm afraid not. Just a common or garden financial scandal. Cassidy was a member of parliament for one of the home counties constituencies during the 1920s—quite high profile and a cabinet minister for a while, but he fell from grace when a journalist exposed him for swindling his way to a fortune by selling bonds and siphoning off most of the cash. I can't remember all the details or when he went to jail, but I do know that they eventually traced his misdemeanors back to the war—and this will interest you. He might have got over the bonds business—people don't really care about that sort of financial fraud—but nobody was going to forgive him when it came out that he'd been abusing his position in the Ministry of Food, taking backhanders from foreign farmers to downplay the urgency of British food production."

"My God, so that means he'll have had things to hide during the period we're talking about?"

"Yes, although I'm not sure how a sixteen-year-old schoolgirl would have worked that out when he managed to fool the government."

"But if she did, it would have given him a motive to silence her."

"Hard to prove now that they're both dead." He drained his glass and grinned at her. "I don't know how you've got the cheek to say that Josephine's taking this too far. You seem quite keen on getting to the bottom of it yourself. The same again?"

"Yes, but I'll get them. Can I get Phyllis a drink while I'm there?"

"She seems to have something different every time we go out, so you'd better wait and see."

"Right, let's talk about Harriet and George," Marta said when she got back from the bar. "My money would be on one of them having killed Dorothy, which is why I'm worried about Josephine seeking them out. How easy is it to trace someone after so long?"

"Not very easy at all. There are electoral registers, of course, so you could start with Devon—where you know they were living, at least for a while—and work from there. It has to be said, though, if someone really doesn't want to be found, the chances are that they won't be, and if they've been harassed to the extent that you say they have, they might even have changed their names. Leave it with me, and I'll see what I can do." He made a note on the piece of paper she had given him, then asked, "Who's Vera Simms? You've starred her, so she's obviously not a Moira House girl."

"She worked for Harriet and George. There's a possibility from something Josephine overheard that she and Harriet were conspiring over something, perhaps even having an affair."

"So Vera would be a suspect if that was one of the secrets that Betty and Charity found out?"

"I suppose so, but the implication of what Josephine heard was that Vera *wanted* George to know, so on that tack we're back to Harriet again—or her cousin."

"That must be Peter Whittaker," Archie guessed. "He's the only name left on the list."

"Yes, and he hated George, apparently. Perhaps Dorothy too if these are anything to go by." She reached for her bag and took out the sketchbook that she had borrowed without Josephine's knowledge. "We've just found out that Whittaker died in the war, but these are his. Josephine described them as rehearsals for Dorothy's murder, and she's got a point."

Archie studied them closely. "*If* he did them," he said, flicking through the pages.

"What do you mean?"

"Well, look at the picture of the body in the greenhouse compared to the one hanging in the barn—one is much more confident than the other."

Marta looked again and saw that he was right. "One is pencil and the other is pen and ink, though," she argued. "That makes it harder to compare them."

"It might just be that, I suppose. You'd have to get an expert to be sure." He fell quiet, and she knew what he was thinking; the person who would have known—Bridget—was no longer here to ask.

"You didn't know Whittaker, I don't suppose? He was

convalescing at Summerdown, even though he spent most of his time at the farmhouse."

"No, but there were thousands of soldiers passing through that place." He returned the sketchbook and said, "I'm glad you told me about this, and I'll do my best to help—but Josephine certainly shouldn't go and see anyone on her own. Why do you think she's so set on it?"

Marta shrugged. "I know she liked George and Harriet, but I think the fact that they were so badly hounded makes her more sympathetic to them than she might otherwise be. There was a lot of prejudice against them, apparently, and she can't help putting herself in their position and wondering what people will find out about her."

"Yes, I suppose she must have been terrified."

Marta looked at him, confused. "I meant now—with our relationship. She's frightened that someone will make that public."

"Of course."

He had backtracked quickly, but not very convincingly. "You didn't mean that, though, did you?" Marta persisted. "You said she must have been terrified, and you meant at the time. Is there something she's told you and not me about that summer?"

"No."

"Don't lie to me, Archie."

"I'm not lying. Josephine hasn't told me anything."

"But . . . ?" His silence gave Marta time to think, and she remembered how awkwardly Josephine had behaved at the theater, how she had kept Jeannie's letter to herself and how emotionally charged—in hindsight—some of Jeannie's comments had been. "It's Jeanette Sellwood, isn't it?" she said. "They were more than friends."

"I don't know that."

"But you suspect it. That's why you asked me what Josephine had said about her. You thought she'd have told me."

"Yes, and the fact that she hasn't probably means I'm wrong." He surprised her by taking her hand. "Look, Marta, I've probably misled you, and I shouldn't have. It was very clear to me at the time that Jeannie had no interest in me, despite Jack's best efforts, but she obviously cared a great deal about Josephine." Coming from some men, Marta might have seen Archie's reasoning as a way of protecting his ego from a woman who simply wasn't attracted to him, but Archie wasn't like that, and she believed him. "She was upset and angry about Josephine and Jack," he added, "but that doesn't mean that her feelings for Josephine were reciprocated."

"No, I don't suppose it does," Marta said, relieved to think that an unrequited love would also explain everything that had worried her, "and I honestly think she'd have told me if there was more to it. There's no reason not to, for God's sake. It was years ago, and we've always talked about the people in our past without any jealousies."

"Exactly, and if you still have doubts, just ask her. Josephine would never do anything to jeopardize what you have—you've both fought too hard for it." He looked at his watch. "We'd better leave for Bodmin soon if you're to get your train. Shall we go and look for Phyllis?" She nodded and followed him to the door. "Is there anything else you want to say about the case before you go? We were rather sidetracked just now."

"I can't think of anything except perhaps to ask you what it would take to reopen it. Do you think, from what you've read, that there's any chance of another investigation? An official one, I mean—not trial by the press or amateurs like us shuffling round in the dark."

"I doubt it, and certainly not without at least one piece of tangible new evidence."

"Like?"

"A witness coming forward who saw what happened—but even that would be circumstantial. There's no chance of any new medical evidence now, and anyway, there's no confusion over how

Dorothy died. Did anyone check for fingerprints on the glass, by the way?"

"I've no idea. I don't think it was mentioned at the inquest, so probably not."

"I can have a look at the file for you and find out exactly what was said. But short of a confession—which seems unlikely after all these years—I really don't think we'll ever know."

CHAPTER 3

There was silence in the auditorium as the final scene of *The Laughing Woman* drew to a close in front of a rapt full house. Josephine sat in one of the boxes, her attention equally divided between the audience's response and the action on stage, where her character, Ingrid—now fallen on hard times—sat in an art gallery by the sculpture that gave the play its title, forced to listen as a party of school children talked casually about the bust of her younger self and René's death on active service. She had feared during rehearsals that the ending might prove too sentimental, but the shadow of the war was still strong, particularly in the current climate, and as the curtain fell, the audience was visibly moved. Keynes was first to his feet to applaud his wife, but the rest of the stalls soon followed, and the cast enjoyed three enthusiastic curtain calls before the lights came up in the auditorium, and a satisfied crowd filed out into the crisp night air.

Marta squeezed Josephine's hand. "Absolutely brilliant," she said. "Congratulations. Are you pleased?"

"I'm just relieved at the moment, but I will be when I've had a chance to take it in. The cast was wonderful—every single one of them worked so hard. I just hope the critics agree."

"Bugger the critics, darling." Ronnie leaned forward from the seat behind to give Josephine a hug. "What do they know?"

"At least you won't have to wait until you're dead to get the recognition," Lettice said bitterly, still emotional from the sculptor's fate in the closing scenes. "Poor René. All that talent and passion, and what does he get? A cursory glance and a cardboard label."

"Yes, well, that's life for you," muttered her sister, ever the more philosophical of the two. "And I bet they even spelt his name wrong, but at least we can still have a drink in his honor. Come on. Two solid hours of clay and angst has made me thirsty."

The Motleys headed upstairs to the theater's restaurant for the first night party, and Josephine rolled her eyes at Marta. "Well, that's the best review of the night so far. I'm going downstairs to thank the cast. Come with me."

"No, tonight's for you and them, so go and make the most of it. I'll join Ronnie and Lettice and see you up there."

Josephine watched her go, concerned by how preoccupied she had seemed since her trip to Cornwall. She knew that Marta was worried about the work she would lose when the Hitchcocks went to Hollywood, and it was typically unselfish of her not to want to dampen the celebrations around the opening night by raising the subject, but Josephine was glad to have the play up and running so that they would have more time to talk.

"Congratulations, Miss Tey. A tour de force, if I may say so." Josephine glanced automatically toward the voice at stage door, but her smile froze when she saw whom it belonged to. "Or should I be calling you Miss Daviot tonight?" the woman continued. "That's your stage pseudonym, isn't it? So many names, so many masks. If I had a suspicious mind, I might wonder what you were hiding."

"When it comes to false identities, you make beginners of us all," Josephine said with a deadly civility. "How are you, Charity? I had a feeling we might be bumping into each other."

"Very well, thank you, and yes—this meeting is long overdue." Charity looked her up and down, and Josephine was ashamed of how relieved she felt that her former pupil had sought her out on a night when she could at least begin to compete with the exquisite Schiaparelli dress and expensively styled hair that Charity wore so well. As Faith Hope, Charity might have sunk to the gutter with her work, but the social advantages which had made her stand out so awkwardly at Charleston had obviously not deserted her in later life; Josephine found herself wondering if Miss Ingham had ever had the dubious pleasure of educating the younger members of the family. "Betty was right," Charity said. "You *have* changed— although not in all respects, I gather. How is your friend? Is she here tonight—or far too busy with the Hitchcocks?"

It couldn't have been more than a stab in the dark, but Josephine silently cursed herself for how many details of her life she had already given away. She obviously should have thought more carefully about having that conversation with Betty Norwood, but it was too late now, and she was determined not to let her concern show. She walked up to Charity, conscious that several other people were milling around by the stage door, waiting to speak to her. "It's ironic how life turns out, isn't it?" she said, paraphrasing Jeannie's observation from the other night. "There was a time when you'd do anything you could to avoid spreading the muck. Now you make a living out of it. It was nice to see you again, but I must go and speak to my cast."

Charity put a hand on her arm. "Just a minute—I thought we might have a little chat first. I've come a long way."

"Have you? From where I'm standing, you've hardly moved at all, and the only thing I've got to say to you is this: if you publish one damned thing about me, I'll sue you."

"That's really not very friendly, Josephine. And you'll want to hear this, I think—it's about you and Mrs. Priestley."

"Who?"

In her panic, Josephine didn't even think about Jeannie's married name, but Charity took great pleasure in clarifying what she meant. "I've got my version of what you and Jeanette Sellwood were doing on the night that Dorothy Norwood was killed. This is your chance to give me yours."

"You've already spoken to Mrs. Priestley," Josephine said,

gambling on Jeannie's discretion. The name fell awkwardly from her lips, utterly disconnected from the person to whom it belonged, but she tried to put her feelings about that to one side. "I've got nothing more to add."

"So you're still in touch? How nice, after all these years, but then you always were very close."

Josephine longed to wipe the knowing smirk off Charity's face and give her a genuine grievance to write about, but she knew when she was beaten. "All right," she said. "I'll give you five minutes, but not in here." She led the way out to St. Edward's Passage and walked past the church, lighting a cigarette to buy herself some time to think. "What do you want to know?" she asked, turning to face Charity.

"If you can give Mrs. Priestley an alibi for that night. She very nobly refused to commit you to one, but I thought—as you obviously once cared about her—that you might want to help."

"An alibi?" Josephine stared at her in astonishment, beginning to feel as if she had walked straight out of one theater and into another. "Why on earth would she need an alibi?"

"Well now, let's see. What she might or might not have told you is that several of us knew exactly what was going on between the two of you. Girls pick up on things, don't they, especially at that age, and you surely don't think that we stayed dutifully in those shepherd huts on a beautiful summer's night? No, you weren't the only people sneaking out into the garden under the cover of darkness, and we'd see you having heart-to-heart conversations and God knows what else."

"But we weren't doing anything—"

Charity held up her hand to interrupt. "Betty and I weren't terribly pleased about the way we were treated, at the college and at Moira House."

"Jeannie stuck up for you."

"She humiliated us in front of Peter, and—"

Now it was Josephine's turn to interject. "Is that what this is really all about? Some adolescent grudge because you found out that Peter Whittaker had made a play for Jeannie and you were jealous?"

"We're not here to discuss my motives. To get back to what I was saying—we sent her a note, threatening to say something to Miss Ingham about the two of you . . ."

The news stunned Josephine. "And making her think it was from Dorothy, I suppose."

Charity smiled, neither confirming nor denying the accusation. "We even said that we might pop into the Ram Inn and tell her parents. I imagine that made her quite angry."

Josephine was about to insist again that there was nothing to tell at that time, but of course it wasn't true; their affair might have begun on the day of Dorothy's death, but the attraction and the intimacy—even the love—were there long before that, and there was no point in trying to deny it. She remembered how hurt and upset Jeannie had been in the bar that afternoon, as her father so innocently deflected the gossip, and wondered why she had never said anything about the threat from the girls that hung over them both. The obvious answer was that she didn't want to frighten Josephine away, and it hurt her now to realize how predictably she had justified Jeannie's lack of faith in her. "Get to the point, Charity," she said, more defiantly than she felt. "Your time's running out."

"Very well. Let's talk about the night of the murder. Betty heard you and Jeannie coming back in the van together, and you told her the other day that Jeannie had gone to the house to fetch some coats."

"Yes, that's right."

"Was she a long time fetching those oilskins?" Josephine hesitated, knowing that Charity was right. "Did she even have them when she eventually got back to the greenhouse? Betty says that she didn't. So what was she doing in between leaving you and coming back?"

To her dismay, Josephine realized that Jeannie was damned

either way; she knew too that she could save herself simply by telling the truth and saying what Charity wanted to hear—that Jeannie had been missing at the time of Dorothy's death—but the words would have choked her. "Let me make this very clear," she said, scarcely daring to think of what the consequences might be. "Jeannie did leave me to go and fetch some coats, but she came back almost immediately because the rain was torrential. We sheltered together, and you can read into that what you like, but I doubt that many people would find anything shameful in two women taking refuge from a storm. Then we heard the screams coming from the greenhouse, and I went to see what was wrong while Jeannie went to find Miss Barker or Miss Hartford-Wroe. So you have your alibi. Jeannie was with me."

"If that's the way you want to play it."

"How can you live with yourself, Charity?" Josephine demanded. "You've used Betty's relationship with her sister to get your own back for every imagined slight you've ever felt, and have you even considered what this might be doing to her? She's wracked with guilt over Dorothy's death, and really it should be you because you've been pulling the strings all this time. Dorothy's blood is on *your* hands, not Betty's or George's or Harriet's, and certainly not on Jeannie's."

"Josephine? What the hell's going on? Are you all right?"

Josephine turned round to find Marta looking concerned, and wondered how much she had overheard. "Yes, I'm fine," she insisted. "We're finished here. Miss Lomax was just leaving."

CHAPTER 4

Try as she might, Josephine couldn't get the conversation with Charity out of her head. She lay awake for most of the night, struggling to answer some of the questions it raised and worrying about the possible consequences of her lie. She found it impossible to believe that Jeannie had had anything to do with Dorothy's death, and yet—now that the seed of suspicion was planted—she couldn't quite dismiss the idea altogether, particularly as she knew something that Charity didn't: when Jeannie eventually returned to the greenhouse that night, she had changed her clothes, and Josephine remembered wondering at the time why she had bothered to discard wet things only to be soaked all over again; now, the explanation took on a more sinister possibility. She heard again the urgency in Jeannie's voice when she was asking to see her, and began to fear what she might be about to confess. If their love turned out to be the reason for a young girl's death, Josephine would never forgive herself.

The next day, she wanted to raise the subject with Marta and try to explain why she hadn't been honest about Jeannie from the outset, but Marta went to her study early to work, so Josephine decided to do something practical instead. A telephone call to Moira House brought the good news that Gertrude Ingham was still there, and Josephine left a message for her, explaining what she wanted and why. An hour later, she was rewarded with a response from Miss Ingham's secretary, who informed her that the principal was in a meeting with the school's governors but sent her warmest wishes and hoped that they might meet again before long as she was a great admirer of Josephine's work for the stage. In the meantime, she was more than happy to pass on addresses from their files, and to save time, Josephine took them down over the phone. As she had hoped, Joyce was one of the girls who kept in touch with her old school, and Josephine was intrigued to see that her address wasn't a clinic, but a teashop in Southend. There were no contact details for Mags, but she didn't doubt that Joyce would be able to help her there if necessary.

Even the formal brevity of a telegram couldn't entirely obscure Joyce's delight at the suggestion that they meet, and as Josephine set out for Essex early the following morning, she found herself looking forward to seeing her again. Marta had said very little about her plans, other than to reiterate the dangers of meddling in something that was getting out of hand, and showed no interest in going with her; knowing how quickly her lover worked when she was engrossed in a project, Josephine wasn't at all convinced that she couldn't spare the time, but she didn't argue, hoping that a day apart would either clear the air between them or bring on the row that had been brewing for days.

The Essex seaside town was bigger than she expected, and—as the nearest coastal resort to London—bustled with holidaymakers keen to make the most of a summer that, though fading, seemed reluctant to leave altogether. A sign at the railway station proclaimed the benefits of Southend "for health and pleasure," and Josephine wouldn't have argued; as she took a leisurely stroll to the seafront, where Joyce had her café, she was impressed by the way in which the town had managed to combine its fine streets and beautiful old buildings with the feel of a modern resort. She soon located the address she was looking for on Marine Parade. The teashop looked busy, and Joyce had asked her to avoid the lunchtime rush, so she walked past and crossed the road to sit in the sun for a while. The promenade was still popular at the fag end of the season. Some of the more adventurous visitors were enjoying a trip out to sea, and Josephine followed their progress as they sailed toward the grand iron pier—the longest in the British Empire, according to advertisements she had noticed on the way, and served by its own electric railway. There was something precious about a warm day in September, when the sun could never be taken for granted, and she wished that she had tried harder to persuade Marta to come with her.

Plans for a physiotherapy clinic might have fallen by the wayside, but Joyce was obviously as passionate about the cinema as she had always been. Her café was called The Reel Thing, and its walls were lined with film stills and movie magazine covers, some of them signed by the stars they celebrated. It was the only glitzy note in what was otherwise a typically English setting—understated yet welcoming, with crisp white cloths, flowers on every table, and an irresistible smell of home cooking coming from the kitchen. Josephine took her place in the queue to be seated and looked round for Joyce, eventually spotting her by the till. She looked very different as an older woman, and—had she passed her in the street—Josephine doubted that she would have recognized her, but the smile which she lavished on her customers was familiar enough to overshadow the fuller figure and permanent wave, and she wondered if Joyce would find her much changed by the twenty-odd years that had passed since they last saw each other. Her reaction suggested not: she rushed out from behind the counter at the first glance in Josephine's direction, dispensing with any formal greeting in favor of a hug. "How lovely to see you again," she said. "I was so surprised to get your telegram, but I often think about you—it's not everyone who can say that their old teacher hobnobs with Derrick de Marney."

Josephine had actually never met the actor who starred in Hitchcock's film of her book, but it seemed churlish to admit as much when Joyce was so excited; in truth, she was just as starstruck by the film world as her former pupil, and she looked round the walls with a genuine fascination, impressed by the collection of autographs. "I'll have to get you his picture," she said, hoping that Marta could pull some strings. "Hitchcock's too, although I know whose cheek-bones I prefer."

Joyce laughed. "That would be wonderful. Now come and sit down."

"Thank you, but don't let me interrupt. You're still busy, and I'm very happy to wait."

"There's no need." She ushered Josephine to a table with a reserved sign on it, much to the annoyance of two elderly women who were ahead of her in the queue. "I've been saving my lunch break for you, and the girls can easily manage without me while we talk. To be honest, I think they could manage without me altogether if I let them. They're a good bunch." Joyce looked proudly at her staff, half a dozen girls who—without exception—were young, hard-working, and polite. "We always choose the ones who haven't had much of a chance in life," she said. "That was very important to us when we started out, and I've never had one who's let me down yet. Now—what would you like?"

"Whatever you recommend. It all looks wonderful, and I'm famished."

"Good. I won't be a minute." She disappeared into the kitchen, leaving Josephine to wonder who the "we" referred to. She found the answer in a photograph on the wall above the table that Joyce had chosen for them—not a film still this time, but a picture of the café with two young women standing by the door, about to cut a ribbon; the one on the right holding the scissors was Mags, and Josephine was delighted that they had fulfilled their ambition of running a business together, even if it wasn't the one they had talked of originally.

"This is lovely," Josephine said when Joyce returned a few minutes later with a tray of tea. "And obviously very successful. I'm so pleased for you."

"I'm glad you like it," Joyce said, arranging the cutlery and cups. "And two cottage pies coming up." She took the seat opposite Josephine and removed her apron. "It's nice to sit down for a minute. We haven't stopped all summer, what with the heat wave last month and now this. We had visitors sleeping out by the pier because all the hotels were full, and quite frankly they had the right idea. I've never known it to be so hot. In the end, we took the kids and went down to join them. They thought it was a hoot."

"How many children do you have?"

"Three—two girls and a boy. They're a bit of a handful, but David's great with them, and he often works nights, so he can have them while I'm busy here."

"It's quite a change from physiotherapy."

"Fancy your remembering that. Are you disappointed in us?"

Josephine laughed. "Of course not. I couldn't wait to get out of teaching in the end, so who am I to criticize? And I'm willing to bet that this is considerably more entertaining. Harder work too." She paused while one of the waitresses set down two delicious-looking plates of food. "Who does the cooking?"

"Me, mostly—in the evenings, once the kids are in bed." She encouraged Josephine to eat while she poured them both some tea and went back to her story. "We did try the physiotherapy idea for a while after college."

"Did you go to Anstey like you were planning to?"

"No. We chose Chelsea in the end because it was closer to home."

"And it's a good school."

"Yes, we learnt a lot and had a few interesting placements, but to be honest, it wasn't really what either of us wanted to do. Then Mags's father died and left her a bit of money. I already had some savings from a trust fund, so we decided to pool our resources." She smiled and preempted Josephine's next question: "We always used to come here on the way home from school, and one night we were walking back from the pictures and noticed it was for sale. We bought it the next day, even though neither of us had the faintest idea about running a restaurant, and we never regretted it."

It was a lovely story, and Josephine was pleased that things had worked out for them. "How long have you had it?" she asked.

"Nearly fifteen years now."

"And how is Mags? Is it her day off?"

Joyce's face clouded over. "You don't know . . . Of course you don't. Why would you? Mags died, I'm afraid. It was three years ago now, but it still feels like yesterday."

She looked down awkwardly, as if the news were somehow her fault, and Josephine was mortified. "Joyce, I'm so sorry. Whatever happened?"

"She was hit by a car, just outside here. One of our regulars forgot her change and Mags ran across the road after her without thinking." Joyce smiled sadly to herself. "I always used to joke with her about being too honest for her own good. Told her we'd never make our fortunes if she carried on like that." Josephine put her fork down, her appetite suddenly gone. "The bastard didn't even stop," Joyce added, her anger barely diminished since the day of the accident. "They never found out who it was."

"Were you here when it happened?"

Joyce nodded. "I heard the screech of the brakes outside, and then people started screaming. I ran out to see what was wrong, telling myself not to panic, but I think I knew already. She died in my arms. David couldn't get here in time. They didn't even have a chance to say goodbye."

Josephine was confused. "But I thought David was *your* husband?"

"He is now, but we only got married after Mags died. She was the love of his life. I've never known two people to be so happy."

"So the children . . ."

"Are Mags's, yes. The youngest was only six months old when she died."

"What about you? Didn't you have anyone?" Josephine stopped

abruptly, before the words "of your own" followed. She was deeply moved by the unselfish way that Joyce had put her own life to one side to do the right thing by her friend's family, and the last thing she wanted was to sound judgmental.

"Not since the war, no. He was killed at Passchendaele, and no one else quite measured up after that. When Mags died, David and I—well, I was the only one who could console him, and vice versa. And she asked me to look after him and the children—it was the last thing she said to me. I had to promise, to give her some peace."

"That must have been difficult."

"It was at first. There were times when David was so beside himself with grief that he'd think I was Mags, and I would have given anything to grant him his wish, but that passed in time. He's a good man, and the children are a joy. We've found a way to be happy." She glanced up at the photograph, and Josephine couldn't even begin to imagine the thoughts that must be going through her head. "What about you?" Joyce asked making an effort to lift the mood. "Did you get married?"

"No, I didn't." It was a relief to have her answer taken at face value, without any further interrogation, and she remembered how refreshingly immune Joyce and Mags had been to any of the troubling undercurrents at Charleston. "I wanted to talk to you about the night that Dorothy Norwood died," she said.

"Because of that ridiculous piece in the paper?"

"That started it, yes, but I've spoken to Betty since then, and I think she might be right. There may be more to it than we thought." Joyce looked skeptical, and Josephine continued, "Will you tell me anything that you remember?"

"Of course I will, but I don't know that I can be much help." She thought for a moment, giving Josephine the opportunity to carry on with her lunch. "It had been such a hot day, and everyone was irritable and getting on one another's nerves. It was Dorothy's turn to help Harriet and Vera with supper, and it took longer than usual, so she was in a terrible mood when she got back, and she and

Betty started bickering. There was nothing new in that, of course, but there was an edge to it—there had been since that business about closing the greenhouse windows—and in the end Betty flounced off with Charity, which only made Dorothy more angry. She was always jealous of how close those two were."

"Dorothy was? I didn't know that. I always got the impression that she was perfectly happy with her lot. The words 'cat' and 'cream' spring to mind."

"You'd think so, wouldn't you, but being good at everything doesn't often win you many friends. Whenever I think of Dorothy, at school or at the farmhouse, I always picture her on her own. Yes, she was the model pupil, but who at that age wouldn't swap their teachers' approval for some genuine affection from a friend or two? And Charity used that by playing up to Betty."

It was funny, Josephine thought, but both twins had been desperately unhappy in their own way, each wanting a friendship—or at least some sort of recognition—from the other that they had never had. "She's still playing up to her. Did you know that Charity wrote the newspaper article, using a pen name?"

"No, but it doesn't surprise me. She always used to say the most outrageous things just to get a reaction, and occasionally one of them would turn out to be true—then she really had you where she wanted you. It seems like nothing's changed."

Joyce could have no idea how right she was, Josephine thought. "You said Dorothy was angry when she came back—not frightened or worried?"

"I suppose indignant would be the best word to describe it. Just like she was over the greenhouse."

"As if she'd been blamed for something else she didn't do?" Josephine asked, wondering if Harriet had confronted her about the accusations to Miss Ingham.

"Yes, that's exactly it." She paused, looking over Josephine's shoulder, and a smile lit her face. "Here's David now, with the children. I'm so pleased you'll get to meet him."

Josephine turned to see a uniformed policeman coming through the door with a toddler in each arm and a girl of eight or nine by his side. "Ah, so it's that sort of working nights."

"Yes, David's a bobby. He's taking his sergeant's exam next month." She looked at him proudly and gave him a kiss, and it was immediately clear to Josephine that the love Joyce felt for her husband was far more than duty. She suspected that Mags had known that too and that her final request to her friend had in fact been a blessing.

"Lovely to meet you," Josephine said, standing to shake his hand.

"And you. When Joyce said she was having lunch with her teacher, I expected someone older."

"We were more like friends, the three of us, weren't we?" Josephine nodded, happy to take the compliment now that she didn't have to pretend to be in charge. The younger girl looked up at her shyly, then held out her arms. "You've got a fan there already," Joyce said. "It's a shame you live so far away. We could do with another babysitter."

"What's her name?"

"Ruby."

"Hello, Ruby." Josephine sat the child on her lap and found her a napkin to play with. She watched Joyce with her family, realizing how wrong she had been to assume that Joyce had sacrificed her own life for her friend's memory; the way that she and David had found to be happy obviously worked for all of them.

"Right, where were we?" Joyce asked when David had left for work and the children were packed off to the kitchen for something to eat.

"We were talking about Dorothy," Josephine reminded her. "Where was everybody when the storm broke?"

"We'd just turned in for the night. The next thing we knew, there was an almighty clap of thunder, and the heavens opened. Mags and I watched it from our bunks for a bit, but it wasn't long before that bloody bell started ringing, and up we had to get."

"Who was ringing the bell? Miss H?"

"Or Vera. I honestly can't remember."

"And you were in the walled garden?"

"Yes, covering as many of the seed beds as we could with tarpaulins."

"I know this is a tall order after so long, but can you remember if anyone was missing?"

Joyce shook her head. "I honestly couldn't say for certain. I remember Miss Barker coming out at one point and asking where Miss H was, but that could have been later, when they'd found Dorothy's body. And most of us were wearing those wretched oil-skins too, so you couldn't tell who was who."

"Did you see Jeannie come back and go to the house for some coats?" Josephine asked casually.

"Mags said she saw her running up the path. Miss Barker called after her, apparently, but she didn't take any notice. Or didn't hear—the storm was so loud." It was a logical explanation, but Josephine couldn't help but consider another possibility: that Jeannie hadn't wanted to be seen until she'd had a chance to change her clothes. "Have you spoken to Vera about that night?" Joyce asked. "She might know who was missing from the garden."

"She might, but I've got no idea how to get hold of her."

"Well, I can help you with that. She came to Mags's funeral. They got on quite well, if you remember."

"How did she know that Mags had died?"

"There was a piece in the Eastbourne paper about it, what with her being an old Moira House girl. Miss Ingham came to the funeral too. She's hardly changed at all. Hang on a minute, and I'll dig Vera's address out for you. We said we'd meet up again and talk properly, but you never do, do you, no matter how much you mean it at the time."

So Vera must still be in Sussex, Josephine thought, and her guess was soon confirmed when Joyce returned with an overburdened address book. "They'd only just moved back up country when I saw her," she explained, tearing out one of the few blank pages and copying the details down for Josephine, "but as far as I know that's still current."

"They?"

"Yes. I know we used to joke about Vera and Miss H, but she stayed loyal to them all those years, in spite of the trouble. She's married with children of her own now. Apparently, Miss Barker's like a grandmother to them."

CHAPTER 5

Josephine had intended to stay at the Cowdray Club overnight and return to Cambridge by the morning train, but something happened at breakfast to change her mind. Thursday, as she knew only too well, was the day that Faith Hope's column appeared in the *Daily Mirror*, and she picked up a copy of the newspaper on her way through to the dining room. The club was always busy at this time of day, as its restaurant served both private members and women from the adjoining College of Nursing, and she was lucky to find a free table. She ordered some coffee and helped herself to breakfast from the buffet that ran the length of one wall, then settled down anxiously to see how much of her encounter with Charity had found its way into print. To her relief, there was no mention of her at all this week, either by name or by implication, but the embers of the story were very much alive. There was a small piece on the imminent transfer of *The Children's Hour* to the West End following its unprecedented success at the Gate, and the columnist had been quick to use the news as an excuse to resurrect the story, revealing that more information had emerged following the original "heartbreaking" interview with Elizabeth Banks. One account in particular gave the actress reason to hope that her sister's murderer would finally be brought to justice, and the fact that the newspaper now felt confident enough to use such an inflammatory word frightened Josephine. She knew that Charity hadn't believed for one moment in Jeannie's alibi, and it was only fair to warn her.

The self-satisfied, faintly threatening tone of the article managed to make even the Cowdray Club's studied elegance feel tarnished and grubby, and Josephine pushed her plate to one side. She finished her coffee, then took Jeannie's letter out of her bag and went to the telephone, waiting impatiently to be put through. Perhaps it was her imagination, but when it came, the voice at the other end already sounded guarded and suspicious.

"Hello, Jeannie. It's Josephine."

There was a long pause, and Josephine began to wonder if Jeannie had actually hung up. "I really wasn't sure if you'd call," she said eventually.

"To be honest, neither was I. It was such a shock to see you the other night. I wouldn't have chosen to meet that way after all this time."

"If you'd chosen to meet at all."

It would have been asking too much of Jeannie to make this easy, but still Josephine found her coolness disconcerting. "We didn't have the chance to talk properly, and I thought we might do that now—if it's convenient? You said you wanted to see me, and I'm in town. I could come to you, or we could meet somewhere . . ."

"Somewhere neutral? I'm not sure, Josephine. I've been thinking about it, and it would probably be a mistake. It's too difficult—for both of us."

"Have you seen this morning's paper?"

"No." Even in that one syllable, the fear in Jeannie's voice was palpable. "Why? What's she saying about us now?"

"Nothing, at least not yet. It's what she might be leading up to that bothers me." Perhaps it was foolhardy, but now that she had committed herself to the phone call, Josephine was determined to hold Jeannie to the meeting she had asked for; there were things she needed to say, no matter how difficult they proved. She knew that this was her only chance to confront some painful memories and do her best to make amends. "It's important, Jeannie, but I don't want to go into it over the telephone."

"All right. I'll be here all day, but don't come between twelve and one. Robert comes home for his lunch."

Josephine looked at her watch. It was still only half past nine, but it would take her a while to cross London, and she didn't want the meeting to be hurried, with one eye always on the clock. "This afternoon, then," she said. "I'll be there as close to . . ."

"I'm sorry, I've got to go." The line went dead, and Josephine imagined Jeannie composing herself in the hallway, setting her face to a smile as if nothing out of the ordinary had happened, lying to her husband about who was on the phone and chatting absentmindedly about what she might do with her day when she had waved him off to work. She wanted to call Marta but decided against it, knowing that the conversation would involve telling a lie that was just as reprehensible as those she was attributing to Jeannie, and with far less justification. Whatever happened this afternoon, and even if her worst fears about Dorothy's death were confirmed, Josephine resolved to share everything with Marta as soon as she got back to Cambridge.

It was just as well that she hadn't attempted a morning visit. The journey to Greenwich from Cavendish Square seemed designed to be as complicated as possible, and by the time she got out at Maze Hill Station, it was already a quarter to one. She resisted the temptation to take the short walk to Jeannie's house in time to catch a glimpse of Robert and skirted the park instead, wondering how Jeannie coped with living in the city. The avenues of chestnut trees and gentle green slopes leading up to the Observatory still had a countrified feel, reminiscent of former days, but it was impossible to ignore the tall chimneys and gasometers which were creeping in on every side, and in the distance she could map the curve of the Thames by the industrial settlements now lining its banks. After half an hour of aimless wandering, Josephine judged it safe to head for Greenwich Park Street and found Jeannie's address on the corner with Old Woolwich Road. The house was a handsome three-story building with a steeply pitched roof. As far as Josephine could see, there was no garden.

Jeannie opened the door quickly in response to her knock, and they stood awkwardly in the narrow hallway, each of them waiting for the other to speak. A copy of the newspaper lay next to the telephone, and Josephine nodded toward it, glad to have something to break the ice. "You've read the latest, then."

"Yes. I went out to get a paper as soon as Robert left for work."

"What does he do?"

"He's a doctor—a GP. I was teaching at a school in Tunbridge Wells for a while, and one of the other mistresses introduced us. We married about fifteen years ago, when he took the job here." She spoke quickly, giving Josephine far more information than she had asked for, as if she wanted to get the circumstances of her life out of the way. "I'm sorry I was so abrupt when you called earlier, but I couldn't possibly talk to you in front of him and behave normally." Jeannie smiled for the first time, and once again Josephine found it alarmingly easy to forget about the years that had passed since they were last alone together. "You seemed very composed at the theater the other night. I hope our meeting by chance like that didn't cause trouble with your friend?"

"No."

"Because she trusts you or because you haven't told her everything?" Josephine felt the color rise to her cheeks, making any other answer redundant, and her response obviously intrigued Jeannie. "Go through and sit down. I'll make us some tea."

The sitting room was tidy and comfortably furnished, and Josephine looked round for a photograph that would fit a face to Robert's name. There were just two, a formal wedding portrait and another taken in front of a French hotel at around the same time, perhaps while Jeannie and her husband were on their honeymoon. Robert was tall and broad-shouldered, and he looked a little older than his wife, with fair hair and a strong, determined face; his expression was naturally earnest, even in the more relaxed of the two photographs, but his eyes had a kindness to which Josephine immediately warmed, and Jeannie seemed genuinely happy by his side. If she didn't know any better, Josephine would have taken it for granted that she was looking at a couple very much in love— and she realized suddenly that she *didn't* know any better; she had no right to assume a knowledge of Jeannie's feelings after all this time, or to imagine that the marriage was anything other than a success.

She moved away from the photographs, embarrassed by how predictable her curiosity was, and sat down on the sofa. The alcoves on either side of the fireplace were filled with books, but it was the picture above the hearth that drew Josephine's attention—a print by Eric Ravilious of the South Downs, with paths zigzagging across the hills and a hauntingly empty landscape, so typical of the artist's work. She stood up again to take a closer look, admiring the way that—in the absence of any human figures—it was each slope and chalk path that seemed particularized and individual. A fence strung across the fields led her eye deep into the picture until she felt as if she were actually standing on the crest of a hill looking down into the valley, and although Ravilious had chosen soft, pale colors to bring his landscape to life, there was a radiance to the scene which she couldn't help but associate with that June afternoon when she and Jeannie had become lovers.

"I miss it."

The words connected naturally with Josephine's thoughts, and it took her a second to realize that Jeannie was talking about the countryside she had grown up in. "So do I," she said. "Do you go back very often?"

"When we can. My brother runs the pub now, but my parents are still in Firle, and they can't help but interfere. Robert's mother lives up north, though, so we have to spend time there too."

She set the tea tray down, and Josephine joined her on the

sofa. "What about your other brother? Did they both get through the war?"

"Yes, they were lucky. They're married now, with a gaggle of children between them, so that took the pressure off me."

"You didn't want children?"

Jeannie shrugged. "It just never happened, but I think that was more of a disappointment to Robert than it was to me." She poured the tea and passed a cup to Josephine, not needing to ask how she took it. "And to his mother, of course—Robert's the only son of an only son, so that's the end of the Priestley line."

Before they could fall irretrievably into small talk, Josephine forced herself to broach the question that had brought her here. "What did you want to see me about, Jeannie? It sounded important." The change of subject was abrupt to the point of rudeness, and Jeannie smiled. "I'm sorry," Josephine said, trying to explain. "It's not that I don't want to talk about your husband, but . . ."

"That wasn't why I was smiling. Nobody calls me that anymore, that's all. It's nice that you still do." She put her cup down and clasped her hands, looking anywhere but at Josephine. "And you're right, this is important, so we might as well get it over with. There's something I've never told anybody about the day that Dorothy died, and when all this started up again, I didn't know who else to talk to."

"What is it?" Josephine asked, although it was the last thing that she actually wanted to hear. She felt the knot tighten in her stomach as she braced herself for a confession, knowing that—no matter how wrong it was and how hard it would be to live with the guilt—she would never be able to betray Jeannie; not in that sense, at least.

"It was after breakfast that morning, before we set off for the Beacon. I went to the kitchen to ask what Harriet wanted us to pick for lunch, and I overheard her and George having a row. They were talking about what had happened with Miss Ingham at Moira House and how the complaints against them could destroy everything they'd worked so hard for. Both of them were very bitter about it, and understandably angry with the girl who had made them, and I heard George say that she wanted to have it out with her. At the time I thought it was Charity because I knew she'd accused them of bullying and told tales to her parents."

"Is it wicked of me to wish that it *had* been Charity?"

"If it is, then we're both guilty. In hindsight, though, they were obviously talking about Dorothy."

Josephine would have to tell Jeannie that it was actually Betty who had been responsible for the trouble at Moira House, but she didn't want to interrupt her story. "What exactly did you hear?" she asked instead, trying to hide the relief in her voice now that her worst fear had failed to materialize.

Jeannie hesitated. "Harriet said that she could kill her. She was so angry, Josephine. I'm not sure I've ever heard someone quite so beside herself with rage, before or since. She kept saying that she'd like to beat the girl from dawn until dusk every day for a year. That's when George stepped in."

"And said what?"

"That it would be the easiest thing in the world to shut Dorothy up, once and for all, and teach her a lesson. She said there were enough death traps lying around, and no one need ever know. Then suddenly they both went quiet because Vera came in through the back door and interrupted them."

"Do you think she heard anything?"

"I don't know. She didn't react as if she had, and we were out shortly after that so there was no opportunity to talk to her, even if I'd been brave enough to raise the subject. Then later, when I got to the greenhouse and saw you covered in blood, I thought for a moment that they'd hurt you, and it would have been my fault because I hadn't warned you."

"Why didn't you tell me what you'd heard?"

"I'm not really sure now. Partly because I didn't think for a minute that they were serious. We all say things we don't mean when we're angry, and most people vow to kill someone at some point in their lives, but they don't actually go out and do it. And I suppose part of the reason was more selfish than that. I didn't want to cause trouble when you and I were so close. If there was any suspicion that Dorothy had been murdered, I knew that the college would be closed down immediately, and you'd probably be sent straight back to Birmingham. I loved you, and I couldn't bear the thought of losing you. That was more important to me than any consideration of right and wrong for Dorothy. I suppose I should be ashamed of it, but I'm not."

Josephine remembered how fearful they had both been of anything that jeopardized their time together; the summer had felt so fleeting and so precious, and perhaps they had both known deep down that it was all they would ever have. "I would have done exactly the same," she admitted, "but what I don't understand is why you're still keeping their secret even though Charity is knocking on your door and threatening to pin the whole thing on you."

"How do you know that she threatened me?"

"Because she paid me a visit too. She offered me the chance to give you an alibi, as she put it. Why didn't you just say you were with me when Dorothy was killed? It would have been so easy."

"It wasn't true, though, was it? I *did* leave you as soon as we got back and I *was* gone a long time." She accepted a cigarette and fetched an ashtray from the mantelpiece. "Charity took a gamble on that and decided to twist it, and I could hardly put her right about the real reason. It's perfectly harmless, but to admit to it would have given us away. It's our secret I'm keeping, not theirs. We've all got something to hide now. That's about the only part of Charity's article that was true."

"So why were you gone for so long?"

"I wasn't the tidiest of people back then—you know that."

"What's being tidy got to do with anything?"

Josephine stared at her, confused, and Jeannie blushed. "I hoped you'd come back with me that night. I hoped we'd make love, but the room was a tip so I went upstairs to tidy it and change. I wanted everything to be perfect."

She hadn't needed to revisit Jeannie's old room at Charleston for the image of it to be as fresh and vivid in her mind as it was twenty years ago—the neatly made bed and the bunch of delphiniums that must have been gathered in the rain, the cool breeze through the window that seemed to cleanse everything after the storm. Coming so soon after the horror of Dorothy's death, the peace and beauty of that room had felt like a sanctuary, and Josephine allowed herself to remember just for a moment how gently Jeannie had removed her bloodied clothes, how loving and tender she had been. "It was perfect," she said quietly. "It would have been perfect whether the room was tidy or not."

"Don't, Josephine. Please."

Jeannie got up and walked over to the window, and although Josephine longed to say more about how much that night had meant to her, she knew it wasn't fair. "I told Charity that we were together all evening. I don't think she believed me, but she can't prove otherwise."

"Thank you. That was kind of you, especially when you must have wondered if she was right to be suspicious."

There was no point in denying it. "Everything was so intense . . ."

"You don't have to make excuses. Why wouldn't you wonder if I killed Dorothy? After all, we barely knew each other."

The comment hurt Josephine, and despite her best intentions she couldn't resist rising to the bait. "How can you say that?" she demanded. "It simply isn't true."

"Isn't it? All right then, perhaps I should just say that I didn't know you." She turned round and Josephine saw that she was crying. "Was it all my doing, our affair?"

"Of course it wasn't."

"Did I put too much pressure on you? Make you commit to things you weren't ready for?"

"No. You know it was never like that."

"Then why, Josephine? Why did you just cut the strings as if nothing had happened between us? One minute you were telling me how much you loved me, and the next you were out with the boy from the army camp. For a while there I honestly thought I was going mad. I told myself that I must have imagined everything that we'd ever said or done, because how could someone change so quickly? Except I could still feel your skin against mine. I could still smell you on my pillow whenever I tried to sleep. And then to see you the other night after all that you'd said, laughing and talking with an attractive woman on your arm. Can you even begin to imagine how that felt?" Josephine went over to hold her, but she pulled away as if someone had scalded her. "Don't touch me. I can't bear it."

She stood by, helpless to do anything but watch as Jeannie's grief brought back every emotion that had been so new and raw to her at the time. Josephine had cried for days when the affair ended, avoiding everyone until she could trust herself to pretend, and it was a sorrow that she had never been able to share; even now she carried it alone, too shamed by Jeannie's pain to point out that she had also suffered. "Do you want me to go?" she asked.

Jeannie shook her head, and Josephine waited for her to speak. "I need some air," she said when she was calmer. "Do you mind if we go for a walk? Sometimes I just have to get away from these four walls."

They headed for the park, walking in silence until they were well within its boundaries. It seemed to Josephine that Jeannie was following a familiar route, and she wondered how much time she spent here on her own. Although she had expected a confrontation, the intensity of their exchange still shocked her, and she knew that she had underestimated how destructive it might be for both of them to revisit the past. Greenwich was one of London's most beautiful parks, with a spectacular view of the city's skyline, but she could find no pleasure in it, and she was glad when Jeannie broke off from the path and led them toward a bench by the boating pool at the foot of the hill to the Observatory. "You must think me such a hypocrite," she said.

"I did begin to wonder if someone had played a very bad joke on me," Jeannie admitted. "When I married Robert, I was settling for a perfectly nice man, just as I thought you had—only to find out that you didn't do anything of the sort. It was my decision, though, and I've only got myself to blame. What happened to your soldier?"

Even now, Jeannie couldn't bring herself to say Jack's name, but the resentment with which she used to refer to him was gone.

"He died at the Somme."

"And would you have married him if he'd lived?"

"I don't know. Probably. It would have been so simple, and he *was* a nice man. We would have made it work, just like you did."

Jeannie looked at Josephine, her anger softened by resignation. "She's beautiful, I'll give you that, and you don't have to spare my feelings. Tell me about her."

"What do you want to know?"

"How did you meet?"

"She tried to kill me." Jeannie started to laugh, then realized that Josephine was serious. "It was a little more complicated than that, but let's just say it wasn't easy at first. In fact, it's never been easy, and we've both done our damnedest to destroy it, especially me. Marta's been brave enough for us both at times, although she shouldn't have to be."

"And you love her, so it's worth the risk."

"Yes. I love her very much." If Jeannie was throwing back some of the words that Josephine had used in the past to justify her own fears, she was doing so without any recriminations, but still Josephine felt the need to explain. "It's not love that makes the difference, though," she insisted. "I loved you. You must have known that." Jeannie nodded. "It just didn't seem possible, and I don't know how else to explain it. I couldn't see a way that you and I could ever be together. My family would never have understood. It would have destroyed them."

"Yes, I know. It was my father who compared having a lesbian to losing a child in the war, if you remember, so I do understand all that."

"Then you must know why I was so frightened. And this might sound silly, but when we were together, when I was young, it never occurred to me that I could lie—and lying is what makes it possible. You think that the world is going to adapt to you because you're not doing anything wrong, and then, when it doesn't, you change instead. Even now, I have to be two people. I don't talk about Marta to my family. I hide her letters and pretend that her flowers have come from someone else. I'm not myself when I talk to her on the telephone, just in case someone's listening. She's never been anywhere near me in Scotland, and she never will. We met in Keswick once, and it was so far north that I spent the whole weekend looking over my shoulder."

Jeannie laughed. "Is Marta happy with that?"

"Marta accepts it, and before you say it, I know that's not the same thing." A clock in the distance struck the half hour, and Josephine saw Jeannie glance anxiously at her watch; she would have to go soon, before Robert got home from work, and Josephine was surprised by how much she resented that. "This business with Charity has brought it all back," she said, more bitterly than she had intended. "You and I saw firsthand what happens when the lies aren't convincing enough, and we both know that George and Harriet weren't just being punished for what happened to Dorothy. It could have been us, and that terrified me."

They lapsed into silence while a man sat on the end of the bench to tie his shoelace, and Jeannie seemed lost in her thoughts. "I thought about it for a while, you know," she said when the man had gone. "Taking a lover, finding a way. There was a woman who used to walk here every day, and we started to talk. Robert works hard and he's out a lot. It would have been possible."

"So why didn't you?"

"Because in the end it wasn't what I wanted. Sex in the afternoons while my husband was at work. Snatched meetings whenever she could get away, and the rest of the time spent wondering. Sooner or later, I would have wanted more, so perhaps you were right to end it. We could never have had a life together, and I wouldn't have been satisfied with less."

"But I shouldn't have done it the way I did, without any explanation or warning. I know how much it hurt you, and I'm sorry. That was never what I wanted."

Jeannie turned to look at her, the first time that she had held Josephine's eye for any length of time. "I know. Still, I wish you'd been braver. Perhaps then I might have been too."

The words reminded Josephine of the last thing that Harriet had said to her, a piece of advice that she had emphatically failed to take. Before she could apologize again, Jeannie stood up to leave. "I'd better get home. Will you walk with me to the end of the street?" She put her arm through Josephine's, taking refuge in an innocent gesture of friendship. "I still haven't decided what to do about George and Harriet. Do you think I should tell anyone what I heard? It's so long ago, and God knows where they are or what they're doing."

"They've gone back to Sussex, of all places."

"How do you know?"

Josephine told her about Joyce. "I've decided to go and see them before Charity finds out. Why don't you wait until I've been and then decide?"

"Will you come back and tell me what happened?"

The promise would have been such an easy one to make, but Josephine hesitated, troubled by the hope in Jeannie's voice and by her own strong desire that they should see each other again. As much as she wanted to believe that there was no danger in another meeting, she knew how many people might be hurt by it, and this time there was only one way to do what Harriet had asked of her.

"I'll write," she said, and Jeannie nodded, understanding what she meant and accepting it.

Instinctively, they both slowed their step as they neared the park gates, and it was Jeannie who stopped and turned first. "I'll say goodbye here. Be happy with Marta." She took Josephine's hand and held it to her face, kissing the palm of her hand. "Just out of interest, why haven't you told her we were lovers? Because it was over and done with?"

Josephine shook her head. "Because it wasn't. Not until we'd seen each other again. Not until we'd made our peace."

"So you can tell her now."

"Yes. I can tell her now."

SUMMER 1915

CHAPTER 1

Harriet looked at George's face and knew that there was no going back. Whatever they did from now on, wherever they went and however hard they tried, nothing between them would ever be the same. She remembered their last conversation, so full of bitterness and rage, and the shock of what they had each seemed capable of hit her again like a blow to the stomach. It was ironic, she thought, but at the very moment that threatened to tear them apart, she had never loved George more. "We'll have to get the girls inside and let them know what's happened," she said, resorting to practicalities.

"Yes, of course."

There was a speck of blood on George's cheek and Harriet reached across to wipe it off, but George turned away, unable even to meet her eye, and Harriet's hand hovered awkwardly in the air. "I'll send Vera to the village to get help," she repeated, trying not to show how hurt she was. "Where is she?"

"I've no idea. In the gardens, I suppose."

"It'll be quicker if we go." Josephine stood just inside the door with Jeannie, sufficiently recovered from her ordeal to face its aftermath. The "we" wasn't lost on Harriet, and she wondered if the growing closeness that she had noticed between the two women had come to anything more than friendship.

"The van's just over by the orchard," Jeannie agreed. "We can be halfway to Firle in the time it would take you to find Vera and explain what's happened."

George nodded her agreement, but still nobody moved, and it seemed to Harriet that the glass house had become a twisted sort of sanctuary that they were all afraid to leave, as if to make contact with the world outside would be to acknowledge the reality of Dorothy's death. Except for Betty, who sat on one of the low walls with her head in her hands, they all stood staring at the young girl's body, taking in the enormity of what had happened. Outside, the rain was beginning to ease, but a steady drizzle of water still found its way through the open windows, splashing onto Dorothy's face, and Harriet looked round for something to cover her with.

"Did anybody find the pole?" Josephine asked into the silence.

Harriet glanced sharply at her. "What?"

"The window pole—it was missing. That must be why Dorothy climbed on the wall. We should close the ventilators if it's here somewhere."

"I'll do it," George said.

"But surely that doesn't matter at the moment," Harriet objected. "And it's probably best if we keep things as they are . . ."

"I said—I'll do it." It was hard to tell if the harshness in George's voice was due to anger or fear, but there was no arguing with it. "Get out—all of you," she insisted. "I'll go and break the news to the girls, then come back here to wait for the police."

"Let me wait with you," Harriet offered, clutching at the chance to talk to George alone.

"No, I don't need you here. Take Betty back to the house and put her to bed."

Harriet helped the girl to her feet, and Betty allowed herself to be gently led away from her sister's body and out into the fresh summer night. The storm had passed, and only when she felt the cool breeze on her face did Harriet realize how humid and suffocating the greenhouse had been; she took several deep breaths, hoping to think more clearly again, but the air did nothing to dispel the confused images that crowded her mind or the faint sensation of nausea that accompanied them. Betty slumped against her as they walked, clinging blankly to the only refuge left to her, and her trust seemed so misplaced that it sickened Harriet.

Suddenly she couldn't be alone with the girl's grief, and she called back over her shoulder to Josephine. "Come to the house with us and change out of those clothes. You've had a terrible shock too, and you need a hot drink and some rest. I'm sure Jeannie can manage on her own."

Jeannie seemed to agree with her, but Josephine shook her head. "Thank you, Miss Barker, but I'll be all right. I'd rather keep busy, at least for now."

Defeated, Harriet let them go and headed for the house, glad of a generous moon to guide her up the narrow yew-lined path between the pond and the garden wall. There was a light on in Simon Cassidy's room, and she could see him through the gap in the curtains, standing back from the window and watching their approach across the gravel; by the time they reached the landing, he was waiting at his bedroom door, and Harriet noticed that his hair was wet, even though he was wearing his dressing gown. "I was out for a walk and got caught in the storm," he said, answering a question that she hadn't asked. "I haven't been in long myself. What on earth has happened?"

"There's been an accident in the garden—a terrible accident, I'm afraid. One of the girls has been killed, and Miss Sellwood has gone to Firle to fetch help."

"Which girl?"

"Dorothy, Betty's sister." An odd expression passed across Simon Cassidy's face, and had the circumstances been different, Harriet might have said it was relief. "It wasn't George's fault," she added, then realized as soon as the words were out how suspicious they sounded. "What I mean to say is that it could have happened anywhere, and I wouldn't want it to affect your view of the college. We have very strict rules on safety, but Miss Norwood doesn't seem to have been following the methods she was taught, and I . . ." He was looking at her curiously and Harriet faltered, appalled by her own tactlessness in blaming Dorothy Norwood for her death in front of her grieving sister. She started to apologize, but Betty was staring into space, apparently oblivious to the conversation.

"People in glass houses," she said suddenly.

"What?" Harriet stared at her in horror.

"That's what they say, isn't it? People in glass houses shouldn't throw stones, but that's what you thought Dorothy was doing. You thought she'd told tales to Miss Ingham, that she was threatening to tell—"

"Now, Miss Norwood, you've had a dreadful shock, and you mustn't upset yourself even more by worrying about what your sister did or didn't do," Cassidy said. "Miss Barker will take good care of you, so go along with her now and get some rest."

Harriet tried to thank him, grateful for his intervention, but the words came out as an awkward, choked sob, and she turned quickly toward the spare room, feeling his eyes on her back all the way down the dark landing. She lit a lamp and pulled the blankets back on one of the beds, then sat Betty down on a chair and began to help her out of her wet clothes, but the girl seemed more distracted than ever. "Dorothy always did things properly," she insisted, and Harriet began to wish that she had never implied otherwise. "She wouldn't have been so careless. All our lives, she's been the one who followed instructions and kept to the rules. I've never known her to put herself in danger." Betty clutched at Harriet's hands, and there was an expression of such utter desperation in her eyes that Harriet was suddenly afraid for her. "It should have been me," she said. "I lied when I said—"

"When you said what? And why on earth would you think that it should have been you?"

Still Betty hesitated, and when she eventually spoke, Harriet couldn't decide if she had changed her mind about what she was going to say originally. "It should have been me in the greenhouse.

I lied before when Miss H called us out about it. Dorothy *did* ask me to close the windows for her that night, but I forgot."

"Oh Betty, is that what this is all about?"

Betty nodded. "She came to me that afternoon because it was her time of the month and she had terrible stomach cramps. I didn't want to do the shift for her, but she said I'd get into trouble if I refused. Now she's dead, and it should have been me."

She began to cry again, and Harriet led her over to the bed and held her close, wanting to take away her pain and tell her that her sister's death had nothing to do with a stupid lie over gardening duties. "It was an accident," she said firmly, trying the words out for herself as much as for Betty. She took the girl's face in her hands and made her listen. "You have nothing to feel guilty for, I promise. We all tell lies now and again, and what you did was wrong—but that doesn't change the fact that Dorothy's death was a terrible, tragic accident that none of us could do anything about."

She heard footsteps running along the landing, and the bedroom door was flung open without a knock, crashing against the wall. "Betty, darling, how awful for you—" Charity Lomax stopped in her tracks when she saw her friend sitting so close to Harriet on the bed, wearing nothing but a slip. The look of disgust was so spontaneous and so sincere that Harriet withdrew her hand from Betty's face as if it had been burned, hating her own instinct for shame when she had nothing to hide, but unable to help herself. "I'm here to look after you now," Lomax said, and there was something almost threatening in her attitude. "You shouldn't be on your own with *her*, Betty. None of us should. It's not safe."

Harriet stood up, determined to keep her dignity. "And what exactly do you mean by that?" she asked. The words were defiant, but there was something in the brazen confidence of Lomax's rudeness that told her that the battle was already lost. It was all beginning again—the insinuations and the name-calling, the nudges in the street spilling over into outright hostility—and she doubted this time that she had the strength to fight it.

"I'll stay with my friend." Lomax sat down next to Betty, and Harriet longed more than anything to wipe the sly smirk from her face. "Shouldn't you go and be with yours?"

Harriet felt a crimson stain of humiliation flood her neck and face. She left the room without another word, wondering why she and George had ever imagined that the shame might stop just because one person had been silenced. The memory of George's ashen face in the greenhouse refused to go away, and her mind played tricks on her, obscuring even the most innocent of mental images with Dorothy's blood. She got to the bathroom just in time and retched over the sink, but the fear and disgust she felt refused to be so easily banished, and she sat for a long time on the edge of the old tin bath, waiting for something to happen.

"Harry? Harriet, what the hell's going on? I've just passed a police car in the lane, and there's an ambulance outside the house." Peter stood in the doorway, staring at her as if she were mad, and she wouldn't have argued with his judgment. "Are you all right?" he asked, crouching down and taking her hands in his. "Has something happened to George?"

She shook her head. "No, George is all right."

"Then why are you so upset? Christ, Harry, what's she done now?"

"How do you know she's done anything?" Harriet snapped defensively.

"Because she's the only person in this world who can make you cry."

The sound of another vehicle pulling up outside saved her from having to respond. It was followed by hurried footsteps on the gravel and voices shouting instructions, and she got up to go and look, hoping that Peter wouldn't come with her. The window in Josephine's room afforded the best view, and she opened the door, feeling like an intruder in her own home as she noticed how tidy everything was, scarcely more lived-in now than on the day she moved in; how long ago that seemed, she thought, although it was not yet a full month. She stood in the darkness and looked down into the yard, taking in the ominous outline of an ambulance and the police car next to it. There was no sign of the college van; Jeannie and Josephine were either still out or had parked by the orchard again, but she recognized the blue Bifort from its customary position outside the doctor's house in Firle, and another small piece of privacy slipped from her grasp. "You still haven't told me what's happened," Peter said, coming up behind her.

She replied without turning round, watching her reflection in the glass as she spoke the words, testing herself for the ordeal to come. "Dorothy Norwood is dead. She fell through some glass in the greenhouse, and Betty found her there. Josephine tried to save her, but her injuries were too serious. She bled to death in front of them."

"And where was George?" Her silence seemed to anger him, and he repeated the question. "Where was George while all this was going on? You can't blame yourself for everything, Harry. Those girls are in her care when they're in the garden, not yours. If anyone should be feeling like this, it's George, so don't let her shrug her shoulders and leave you to pick up the pieces like she did last time. Even better, walk away while you still can."

Two ambulance men carrying a covered stretcher came from the direction of the garden, and there was a terrible finality about their lack of urgency. Harriet closed her eyes, but not before she had noticed a group of farmworkers with lanterns standing over by the barn, silently watching the comings and goings. The landlord would have been told immediately, of course—there was no way to avoid that. And soon everyone would know—the village, the newspapers, perhaps even the government, with one of its civil servants on the premises. "It was Dorothy who caused the trouble for you at Moira House, wasn't it?" Peter said, piecing together a story in spite of her refusal to help. "Do you think George had something to do with this? My God, you do, don't you? That's why you're so upset. You can't keep this quiet, Harry, or George will destroy you completely."

Harriet didn't trust herself to answer. "I've got to go down. People will be wondering where I am." She pushed past him and stood at the top of the stairs, watching while strangers gathered in her hallway—the doctor and two uniformed policemen, one of senior rank to the other. O'Brien looked up, and Harriet was struck by how shaken he seemed. "Miss Barker, please forgive us for arriving unannounced, but Miss Hartford-Wroe said to come up to the house."

"Where is she?"

"Securing the glass house. She'll be here in a moment."

The sergeant cleared his throat. "My name's Chadwick, ma'am, and this is Constable Rees. We need to ask you a few questions, if we may."

"Of course, but there's not much I can tell you. Dorothy was dying as I got there. One of our teachers—Miss Tey—was at the scene before me." She bit her lip, conscious of sounding as if she were already defending herself in the dock, when she hoped to God it wouldn't come to that. "I'm sure she'll give you an accurate report. She's very competent."

"So I understand, and I've already had a word with Miss Tey, but we'd still like to speak to you and to Miss Hartford-Wroe—just to confirm one or two things. I'll try not to take too much of your time."

"Very well. Come through to the kitchen, and I'll make some tea."

She ushered them through the dining room and held the door open for O'Brien, but the doctor shook his head. "I'll be on my way, Miss Barker. I'm not needed here any more." He hesitated, as if there were something he wanted to say, and her stomach tightened again. "Do you and Miss Hartford-Wroe have a solicitor?" he asked eventually.

"A solicitor? Why on earth would we need a solicitor?"

"It might be a sensible precaution, under the circumstances."

"But the circumstances are quite straightforward, Dr. O'Brien. Dorothy's death was an accident—we had nothing to do with it."

"I'm not suggesting you did." He looked genuinely taken aback by the idea, and Harriet realized too late that she had completely misread his advice. "But there will still be an inquest and a police inquiry. The publicity will be extensive, and of course there will be the question of . . . well, of negligence. The girl's parents may want to pursue that, and you would be wise to be prepared." Harriet wasn't sure if her urge to cry was down to his kindness or just the hopelessness of her situation; furious with herself, she blinked back tears, and he put a solicitous hand on her arm. "Don't give up, Miss Barker. As you know, my wife and I are great admirers of the work you do here. You gave our daughter a sense of purpose in life when we were at our wits' end with her, and we'll always be grateful to you for that. If you ever need someone to speak up for you, please don't hesitate to ask."

His loyalty gave Harriet some of her spirit back. "Be careful what you agree to, Dr. O'Brien," she said wryly. "You may find yourself on the wrong side of the witch hunt."

He smiled. "It's a risk I'm happy to take. In the meantime, there's a solicitor in Lewes I can recommend. He's a smart chap, and beyond the sphere of local gossip, if you know what I mean. I'll telephone him in the morning and ask him to consider taking your case—if it comes to that, of course."

"Thank you. You've been very kind, and we're eternally grateful, both of us."

"Not at all. Now—chin up." He disappeared into the night, and Harriet went back to the kitchen. The policemen were standing awkwardly by the table, trailing mud all over the floor that she had recently cleaned, and George had just come in from outside. "I'll put the kettle on," she said. "Unless you'd like something stronger?"

"No thank you, Miss Barker. Please don't go to any trouble on our account."

"It's no trouble." She filled the kettle, if only to prove that the choice was still hers to make, and George was obviously of the same mind because she fetched a decanter of whisky from the sideboard in the dining room and poured four glasses. "Do sit down," Harriet said, irritated by the self-conscious formality that had suddenly taken over her kitchen. "What do you want to know?"

The sergeant took the chair next to her, and Byron jumped onto his lap, oblivious to any etiquette where the law was concerned. The dark blue trousers were soon covered with ginger fur, and Harriet suppressed a smile in spite of the circumstances. "We wanted to let you know that Miss Norwood's parents have been notified, and they're on their way down from Nottingham," Chadwick said, his authority somewhat compromised by the purring from his lap. "They'll be here in the morning."

"Then they must come to us and stay as long as they like. They shouldn't be in a hotel at a time like this, and they'll want to be with Betty."

"Harriet, for God's sake don't be so bloody ridiculous!" George slammed her empty glass down and glared across the table. "Their daughter's *dead*—don't you understand that? A warm bed and a good meal isn't going to fix everything."

Harriet's hand shook as she reached for her whisky, and she realized that she had been waiting for the outburst; she had only ever seen this sort of rage once before in her lover, and then—as now—it was the product of fear. "Mr. and Mrs. Norwood won't be coming here, Miss Barker. Their other daughter will be back at school by the time they get to us. One of my colleagues has spoken to the principal there, and she feels it best if all the girls return to Eastbourne as soon as possible. Arrangements are being made to collect them in the morning."

"All of the girls?"

"Yes, ma'am, I'm afraid so."

"But that's really not necessary. Tell them, George—surely you haven't agreed to that?"

"I think we've rather forfeited our right to an opinion, don't you?"

Harriet fell silent, afraid of provoking George into saying something indiscreet. Chadwick drew breath to continue, but he was interrupted by a knock at the kitchen door. Vera hesitated when she saw the police, but George waved her in and introduced her. "What do you want?" she asked.

"Just to say that everyone's turned in now except for Lomax."

"She's upstairs with Betty," Harriet said. "They'll both sleep in the house tonight."

"How are the girls?" George asked.

"Upset, obviously, and still very shocked, but they're comforting one another. I'll make sure to keep an eye on them."

She turned to go, but Chadwick called her back. "Just a minute, Miss Simms. While you're here, perhaps you could give us your version of tonight's events?" Vera glanced quickly at Harriet but nodded her agreement. "Where were you when the accident happened?"

"In the walled garden with the girls. Miss H rang the bell as soon as she realized how serious the storm was going to be, and we all did what we could to protect the plants."

"And that includes Miss Norwood?"

"Yes, Dorothy was there."

"So how did she come to be in the glass house?"

"She offered to go," Vera said quickly. "I asked for a volunteer to check the sheds and greenhouses, and she put herself forward. She'd been on those duties recently, and she knew the routine, so it made sense for me to choose her." Harriet stared at her, thrown by the lie; she had heard George order Dorothy to the glass house herself as soon as the girls reported for duty, and Vera had had nothing to do with the decision. "I think she felt guilty about something that happened a couple of weeks ago," Vera continued, looking the policeman in the eye. "She let herself down and wanted to make up for it. I wish now that I'd gone instead of her, but I honestly didn't think there was any danger."

"Of course not, Miss—why would you? Did you notice anyone else near the greenhouses at around that time?"

"No, but I wasn't really taking much notice of who was where. The rain was pouring down, and we were all so busy—and everyone looks the same in those oilskins anyway. It would have been impossible to keep tabs on individual girls."

If the sergeant found that a convenient excuse, he didn't say so. "Do you have any idea why Miss *Betty* Norwood would have gone out to the greenhouse?" he asked.

Vera shrugged. "I've no idea. You'll have to ask *her* that. There was certainly no love lost between her and Dorothy—I know that much."

"Vera!" Harriet objected.

"It's true, though—they hated each other. We all witnessed that the other day."

Chadwick made a note and asked Vera to explain. When she had finished, he turned to Harriet. "You said Miss Norwood was upstairs, Miss Barker. Perhaps you could take me up to her?"

"She's asleep, Sergeant, and she's had a terrible ordeal, regardless of how she might have felt about her sister. Do you really have to see her now, or can it wait until the morning?" The thought of Betty being questioned by the police, with Charity on hand to embellish her answers, terrified Harriet, and she added in what she hoped was a voice of reason, "It's not as if she's going to run away, is it? And she'll be stronger in the morning with her parents or Miss Ingham to stand by her."

"Very well, Miss Barker, we'll do as you suggest and leave you all to get some sleep." There was precious little chance of that, Harriet thought, relieved to be rid of them. "Just one more thing," Chadwick said at the door. "I understand from Miss Tey that the top windows in the greenhouse are usually opened with a pole that was missing tonight. Do you have any idea where it is?"

"Yes, I found it myself just before you arrived," George said. "Miss Tey was right about it not being in the usual place, but it was standing just inside the next section—perfectly visible to anyone who looked properly. I've no idea why Dorothy didn't see it. Perhaps she was simply in too much of a panic. It's still there now if you'd like to go and look."

"No, that won't be necessary. We have everything we need for now."

George stood up to see the policeman out to their car, and Vera watched them go from the window. She drew the curtains and walked over to the table. "It's going to be all right," she said, putting her arms around Harriet's neck and kissing the top of her head. "If we all stick together and try to behave normally, no one can touch us."

With a shock, Harriet realized that Vera knew—or thought she knew—everything that had happened. She turned to face her, trying to decide if she could be trusted not to falter, and understood that—of the two of them—Vera was the stronger, at least for now. The kettle had been boiling for some time, and Vera took over making the tea. She fussed around George when she came back in, and Harriet tried not be hurt by how much more willing George seemed to engage with Vera than she was with her. It was funny, but she hadn't noticed until now what a lot they had in common. For the first time in her life, she knew how it felt to be jealous.

"I'd better go and check on the girls," Vera said after a while. "I'll see you in the morning."

She left them alone with each other, and although it was what Harriet had been craving all night, she found no comfort in it. "Dr. O'Brien thinks we should get a solicitor," she said, unable to stand the tension any longer. "He's going to talk to a man in Lewes on our behalf." She studied George's face, looking for the smallest sign of acquiescence, but there was nothing. "George, we've got to talk about this, or we're going to lose everything we've worked for," she pleaded. "I know you're upset—we both are—but we can't just let it go. Otherwise, what was the point—"

"—of her death? Funny, I was just thinking that myself." George got up without another word, and Harriet watched her go. She poured herself a drink and took it over to the window, waiting for a light to appear in the office across the yard and wondering why—after all that had happened—she was still the one who seemed to be asking for forgiveness.

In the stillness left behind, she heard the soft murmur of voices coming from Jeannie's room just above. Even though it wasn't hers to cling to, the companionship was soothing, and she let it drift over her until the voices eventually fell silent. She listened for the sound of footsteps across the floor and the click of a door closing as Josephine went back to her own room, but they never came, and she envied the women their solace in each other—the thrill of another body and the fleeting illusion that nothing could ever come between you and the person you loved.

CHAPTER 2

Harriet woke late to the sound of the morning bell, and for one glorious moment it was just like any other day. She sat up in bed, waiting for the whisky fug to clear, and the events of the last few hours fell back into place with all the scattered logic of pebbles coming to rest on a beach. George hadn't come to bed, and Harriet was surprised to hear her summoning the girls for duties so soon after the tragedy, but perhaps it was a welcome sign that she intended to fight after all. Daring to hope, she went to the window and looked down into the garden, but it was Vera ringing the bell, not George, and the response was understandably half-hearted. The girls gathering together on the lawn seemed to embody everything that had changed in the last twenty-four hours. They looked defeated and vulnerable, as if they had already had the life knocked out of them, and the idea that they were to carry the hope of a generation seemed suddenly forlorn and ridiculous.

She dressed and went downstairs to make a late breakfast. A hearty meal was hardly appropriate, but she was determined to go through the motions, if only for appearance's sake, when Miss Ingham arrived to collect her students. As predicted, the mealtime was a tense and thankless affair. Peter's concern for her fought with his natural anger to make every word he uttered brittle and volatile; Simon Cassidy treated her with a mixture of pity and distaste, as if any regard he might previously have shown her was now an embarrassment to him; and Josephine and Jeannie made such a show of appearing separately and inquiring after each other's sleep that she longed to bang their heads together. Unable to face any more insults, Harriet sent Jeannie upstairs with breakfast for Betty and Charity, neither of whom had put in an appearance, but the food was returned untouched. The morning milk delivery had failed to arrive as usual from the farm, something which had never happened before, and its timing was too much of a coincidence for Harriet to believe in her heart that it was a genuine mistake.

The car from Moira House arrived promptly at ten, just as she was finishing the dishes. It pulled up in the yard, and Harriet was grudgingly impressed to see that Gertrude Ingham at least had the courage and decency to do her own dirty work, when she could so easily have sent someone else to recall her students. She wiped her hands on a tea towel and went out to greet her, missing George at her side but at the same time hoping that she would have the sense to stay away; another row at this stage would only make things worse. The driver got out and opened the car door, and she and the principal faced each other just as they had a week ago in Miss Ingham's rooms at Moira House. The awkward memory of that scene hung palpably in the air between them, with shame on one side and embarrassment on the other, and she heard again her own feeble protestations at the accusation, felt George's anger as she sat with her fists closed tightly in her lap. She had been surprised to hear that the charge came from Dorothy, who had always worked so hard and flourished under George's teaching, but that only made it more difficult to dismiss: an "unnatural influence" on the girls in their care. How strange, she remembered thinking, that a phrase could be so vague and ambiguous, and yet at the same time impossible to misconstrue.

Miss Ingham seemed no more anxious than she was to make a repeat encounter last longer than necessary. "Is Miss Hartford-Wroe here?" she asked, dispensing with the usual formalities, which would have seemed absurd under the circumstances. "I need to speak to you both in light of last night's tragic events."

"She's working in the gardens," Harriet said. "Both of us are devastated by what happened to Dorothy, but it's vital that we keep things running normally wherever possible." Her words sounded more callous than she felt, but they were the simple truth, and she'd had enough dealings with Gertrude Ingham to know that—wherever possible—the truth was what she should stick to. "Whatever you have to say, you can say to me, and I'll be sure to discuss it with Georgina."

"Very well. You know why I'm here, and I don't intend to make this any more difficult by raising issues that we have discussed in the past, when Miss Norwood's accident alone would be sufficient to determine my course of action. I can no longer allow Moira House to continue its association with the College, no matter how worthwhile I have found our partnership until now. You know, I hope, how much I respect your achievements here, and the students who have come to you in past terms have returned to school with a sense of industry and purpose that does you both great credit." She paused, and Harriet braced herself for the blow to which the praise had been building. Out of the corner of her eye, she noticed Jeannie and Josephine at the head of the path by the pond, listening intently, and she wondered if they—as the school's appointed chaperones—would be forced to take any of the blame; if necessary, she would do what she could to protect them. "However," Miss Ingham continued, "where safety is concerned, good intentions are not enough, and there is no room for second chances. Miss Norwood and Miss Lomax will come back to the school with me now, and we will make arrangements with our teachers here to have the other students collected later this afternoon."

Harriet could see how well earned the principal's reputation for fairness was; the speech would have left no reasonable room for objections, even if she'd had the heart to raise them. She nodded, and Gertrude Ingham seemed relieved that the occasion was at least going to remain dignified on both sides; the regret in her face seemed genuine, and Harriet sensed a sympathy for their situation, if not an understanding. She turned to Jeannie and Josephine. "Miss Sellwood, Miss Tey—perhaps you would be kind enough to bring the girls down. We can send their things on if they haven't had a chance to pack."

They headed for the house, and Harriet felt obliged to invite her guest to follow. "Would you like to come inside and wait?"

"No, thank you. I'm sure they won't be long, and it's a lovely day."

Not the weather, Harriet thought to herself; please God, anything but that. "Are Dorothy and Betty's parents here yet?" she asked as the lapse in conversation became more strained.

"We expect them on the eleven o'clock train."

"Please give them our sincerest condolences if you feel it's appropriate."

"Yes, of course."

Betty and Charity had obviously been ready and waiting, because they emerged quickly from the house and walked to the car with all the enthusiasm of two captives released from jail. Gertrude Ingham gestured to the back seat and turned to take her leave, but Harriet stopped her. "Just a moment," she said, putting her hand on the driver's arm. "There's something I wish to say, and I'd like them to hear it before they leave." She looked directly first at Charity and then at Betty, and Charity took a theatrical step forward to protect her friend. "I'm terribly sorry for what happened to Dorothy last night. I wish more than you can ever know that I had done something to prevent it—please believe me when I tell you that. She died on these premises while she was carrying out the duties of the college, and that is something both Miss Hartford-Wroe and I must live with, and—to a certain extent—take responsibility for. There will be an inquest in due course that will determine who, if anybody, was at fault, and we will abide by its decision. However, I would like to put it on record here and now that, until last night, no young woman has *ever* come to harm whilst in our care. We have always striven to put out students' physical and moral welfare first, whether they come from Moira House or anywhere else. To my knowledge, not a single girl has had cause to complain about the treatment she received from us. In fact, should we need to, we can produce plenty of testimonials to the contrary." She caught Charity's gaze and held it, defying any dissent. "There will no doubt be a glut of speculation and rumor about last night's events before the inquest makes its official judgment, and I hope I can rely on all of you to ask yourselves what is just and fair before contributing to it."

Betty nodded and glanced nervously at Charity, and her expression wasn't lost on Gertrude Ingham. "Thank you for your honesty, Miss Barker," the principal said. "Please believe in mine when I say how truly sorry I am that things have had to end this way. Now," she added, turning to Josephine and Jeannie, "make sure that the other girls are ready by three o'clock. The school vehicle will collect you all then and bring you back to Moira House."

"May I speak to you first?" Jeannie asked.

"Can't it wait until later, Miss Sellwood?"

"I'd rather do it now, before you take the girls away—just in case it makes a difference."

"I doubt that, but go on."

Jeannie hesitated, and Harriet guessed that any intervention she was about to make hadn't been planned. "I just wanted to say that most of us will be very sorry to leave Charleston," she began, looking to Josephine for solidarity. "We came here expecting to study horticulture, whether we wanted to or not, but we're actually learning things that are much more important, things that will last us a lifetime, like trust and friendship and a sense of responsibility. I've watched our students flourish here because they're respected as young women. They've come of age and stepped up to everything that's been asked of them—working hard and taking decisions and making a tangible contribution to the war. They're a credit to Moira House and to the College, and you would be so proud if you could have seen them at work here every day like I have.

"Most of them have proved themselves worthy of the freedom they've been given, and Dorothy more than most—but sometimes freedom means you make mistakes, and what happened last night *was* Dorothy's mistake, no matter how tragic it is. All of us work with dangerous situations while we're here, but not once have I ever known a girl to be asked to do something that she hadn't been fully prepared for by Miss H and supervised until it was safe to leave her. Dorothy knew the procedures for glass house work, but she didn't follow them; she panicked and forgot what she'd been taught—but that isn't Miss H's fault. As Miss Barker said, there's going to be an inquest and everything will be out in the open. At least let us stay until there's an official verdict, and if you don't like what you hear, you can remove us then. You know we'll all be more careful than ever after what's happened, but think about what message it might send out to haul us back now in disgrace. You'll just prove the critics right—women aren't up to the job."

Harriet was so touched that she could have wept. She knew that part of Jeannie's motivation was selfish; whatever was going on between her and Josephine would be impossible to continue at Moira House, and there was even a chance that Josephine might be sent back to Birmingham immediately, but it was still obvious that the words were sincere, and she wished that George had been present to hear them.

"That was a very eloquent speech, Miss Sellwood, and I admire your courage, but my mind is made up. I'm sorry. I simply can't take the risk where lives are at stake, no matter how persuasively you argue that I'm wrong."

Charity got into the back of the car, as if to demonstrate that the debate—for her, at least—was over, but Jeannie hadn't quite finished. "Then at least ask the girls what *they* want to do, and how safe *they* feel," she said, pushing her luck. "You've always encouraged us to think for ourselves, Miss Ingham. Surely you're not going to refuse them the chance of doing what you've taught them to do?"

To Harriet's surprise, the principal allowed herself the slightest flicker of a smile—of pride or sheer incredulity, it was hard to say. "Very well," she agreed. "Take me to speak to them."

Josephine led the way to the walled garden, where the girls were peacefully at work in small groups, methodically restoring order after the storm. Harriet looked round, trying to picture the scene through the eyes of someone who had only been there once or twice before, and she knew that any first impressions must be favorable. The lethargy that she had witnessed earlier was entirely gone, replaced by an air of companionship and quiet purpose; without exception, the girls seemed to be taking refuge from their sadness in their work and in one another, unconsciously supporting everything that Jeannie had said. Josephine rounded them up, saying very little to them in case Miss Ingham suspected a conspiracy, and the principal addressed them with a simple statement.

"You've been through a terrible ordeal, and you have my deepest condolences for the loss of your colleague and friend. After what happened last night, my instinct is to take you all back to Moira House, where I know you will be safe. Miss Sellwood thinks I'm wrong, and believes that it's in your best interests to stay and continue your work. The one thing we agree on is that you should be allowed to decide for yourselves. I will now ask each of you to tell me your verdict, and you will abide as a group by the wishes of the majority."

Macdonald was the first to step forward, and her testimony was brief and to the point. "As you can see, Miss Ingham—there's a lot to do here, and we can't just abandon it. That wouldn't be right. I vote we stay and finish the job."

Lanton backed her up. "Mags is right, Miss—and I don't think Dorothy would have wanted us to throw in the towel either. She loved what we do here, and she was better at it than the rest of us put together." Joyce hesitated, giving Harriet time to consider what she had just said; the complaint that Dorothy had leveled against them made even less sense if she was really as happy at the college as Joyce claimed.

"She once told me that she'd found something she wanted to do for the rest of her life," Lanton added sadly, "so I think we should stay and make a success of it for her."

Rogers spoke next, then Mitchell, Williams, Gale, and Jackson, all in support of staying. One by one, the students stepped forward to endorse the college, paying tribute to how well they had been treated and their enjoyment of the work, and—in one or two cases—using Dorothy's memory as the rationale for their argument. Harriet heard George's influence in some of the more strident declarations about women and the war, and the young voices speaking up with such passion took her back twenty-odd years to the time when she and George had first met, and any battle seemed theirs to win. When the girls had all said their piece, there was not one dissenting voice.

Gertrude Ingham turned to Harriet and smiled. "I can't remember ever being quite so pleased to be put in an impossible position," she said. "Clearly, Miss Sellwood is right, so I will allow my students to stay with you until the inquest—under certain conditions."

"Of course. What are they?"

"No girl should ever be sent to do a task on her own, and either Miss Sellwood or Miss Tey must be on the premises at all times, day and night. I will expect a daily written report from one of them, and they will notify me immediately of anything—anything at all—that concerns them. And it goes without saying that, should the verdict at the inquest throw the slightest doubt on your professionalism or standards of safety, the girls will be brought back to Moira House immediately, with no further discussion." Harriet nodded her agreement, and the principal addressed her students. "The decision I have made will no doubt be unpopular in some quarters, but I'm relying on you all not to let me or yourselves down. Now you may get back to your work."

They did as she asked, chattering among themselves about the unexpected turn of events, and Harriet saw Josephine give Jeannie a hug. "I can't thank you enough," she said as she walked Miss Ingham back to her car. "I know what a risk you're taking by putting your reputation on the same line as ours, and you have my word that we won't let you down. Do you mind if I ask you something?"

"Go ahead."

"The other complaint about us . . ."

"As I said when you came to see me, I can't pretend to understand your relationship with Miss Hartford-Wroe, but I'm willing to concede that it's a private matter—as long as you keep it away from the children."

"Yes, but that's not what I meant," Harriet said quickly, her hackles beginning to rise at the very memory of the conversation. "I just wondered how Dorothy made her accusation. You never told us."

"What do you mean?"

"Did she come to see you?"

"No," the principal admitted. "She telephoned me from the post office in Lewes on her afternoon off."

"Out of the blue?"

"Not exactly. That was the first I knew of it, but the matter had obviously been playing on her mind for some time. She was very upset."

"And that was enough for you to call us in to see you? One telephone conversation?"

"On its own, perhaps not, but we had already had a complaint about bullying from Miss Lomax's parents."

"Lomax thinks that being asked to get out of bed is bullying."

"What are you driving at, Miss Barker?"

"All I want to know is if you're absolutely *sure* that it was Dorothy who made that call." Gertrude Ingham stopped by the garden gate and stared at her in bewilderment. "If she was as happy here as the other girls say she was," Harriet argued, "why would she cause trouble for us?"

"I admit it's curious, but why would anyone else pretend? Surely that's even more unlikely?"

"Perhaps." Harriet looked over at the two uncertain faces in the back of the car, and a chill went through her when she considered the implications of what she was suggesting. Whatever happened, George must never know. "I'm sure you're right, and we've taken enough of your time," she said, suddenly keen to get the car away from the house so that she could be on her own to think. "Thank you again for what you've done today. We're deeply in your debt."

"I've done what was fair, Miss Barker. Nothing more."

She watched as the car drove away down the track, and George joined her from the office. "What are they going to do?" she asked.

"The girls can stay until the inquest. After that, we're dependent on the coroner and his verdict. You should have heard them speaking up for us, though, George—every single one of them, and Jeannie too. They were magnificent."

"And so were you." Harriet looked at her in surprise. "I heard everything you said from the office. I'm sorry for the way I behaved last night, but I just couldn't believe that—"

"It's all right. You don't have to say anything else. We need never talk about it again if you don't want to." She saw the relief on her lover's face and had to look away. "In fact, it's probably best if we don't."

CHAPTER 3

When Thursday came round again, Harriet decided to go to the market herself. As tempting as it was to hide away at Charleston, with only taunts from the farm laborers and the odd anonymous letter to contend with, she knew she would have to face the outside world eventually, and experience told her that the longer she left it, the harder it would get. Far better to show her face now and get the measure of people's hostility than wait until the inquest, when she and George really would be the center of attention. The van was loaded with enough produce to meet the high demand of the last few weeks, and she took Josephine and Mags Macdonald with her, leaving Jeannie at the farmhouse to comply with Miss Ingham's conditions.

It was a relief to get away for a bit. As she left the college behind and headed out on the Lewes road, she felt herself breathe out, and realized for the first time what a strain she and George had been living under. The girls chattered away about films and music hall, which they both seemed to love, entering into a spirited debate about the respective talents of Max Linder and John Bunny. Harriet joined in at first, relieved that the general topic of conversation among the students had moved on from Dorothy's death, but after a while the countryside demanded her full attention, as it invariably did. It was the landscape of her early childhood, this patchwork of fields and farms and tiny churches, and even now she found something enchanted in these green-tunneled lanes and hazy blue skies, something that spoke to her as nowhere else did. Returning here with George had been one of the happiest times of her life, and the country had woven itself even more deeply into the fabric of her being by charming the person she loved. For a while, she had thought they might settle here. For a while, it felt like home.

The old market town of Lewes stood on raised ground, with the beauty of the Downs lapping at its feet, and she never tired of its narrow streets and pretty cottages. The town was defined in most directions by the stark silhouette of a castle, which appealed to her love of history, but still there was a softness about it, a safe, homely feel to the mellow redbrick houses and peaceful walled gardens that—in another life—she could see herself tending. Today it was looking its picturesque best, with the sun bringing a clean, fresh dignity to the high street, warming the pavements, and adding a sparkle to the old bow-fronted windows that encroached at regular intervals.

There was no town square as such, but stalls had established a regular twice-weekly spot at the point where the high street widened and converged with Market Street, whose name suggested the continuation of a long tradition. The center had struggled to come to terms with motor transport of any sort, and a combination of medieval lanes and steep inclines was perilous to drivers. Harriet made careful progress up School Hill, suddenly conscious that her arrival was a matter of great interest to the passersby on either side of the street. The van was well known in the town by now, and with the exception of a small group of children who refused to be distracted from a game of hopscotch, everyone stopped what they were doing and turned to stare. "Looks like we're going to be the afternoon attraction," she said, her tone more defiant than she felt. "I suppose we should have expected that."

"Then we'd better put on a decent show."

Harriet smiled at Josephine, encouraged by her boldness, but she couldn't entirely shake off the ominous feeling that to show themselves in town like this was a terrible idea. The queue at the butcher's fell silent as the van parked in its usual place outside, and she heard the quiet but unmistakable whisper of "brazen bitch" as she got out. She looked at the line of women, trying to shame the culprit, but it could have been any one of them and the comment proved contagious, giving rise to a stream of muttered insults which grew steadily more audible as she opened the back door and began to unload. The girls came round to help, and Harriet felt guilty for involving them in something so uncomfortable; this was her battle, not theirs, and one glance at Josephine's face was enough to show how fragile her bravado was. Mags just seemed bewildered, as if she couldn't understand why anyone would behave so rudely, and Harriet envied the girl her innocence.

Across the street, she noticed that their designated space was filled with empty crates and other rubbish, all spilling over from the stall next door. "Obviously we weren't expected," Harriet said. "Either that, or they're trying to tell us something. I'll go and ask them to move that before we take anything over. You wait here and look after the van."

"Perhaps we should go somewhere else instead," Mags suggested. "There's a space free farther up the road, just outside the post office."

"Why should we? People know where to look for us here." Not that there would be much of that today, she thought to herself; they would be lucky to sell a quarter of what they had brought. Still, the principle and a determination not to lose face drove her across the road. The neighboring stall sold hardware, a motley selection of dusters, pegs, mops, nails, and other ironmongery, and Violet—the woman who ran it—was in her seventies, born and bred in the town. Harriet knew her reasonably well, as she was never short of a story and loved to talk about the old days in a lull between customers. She often brought her young grandchildren with her while her widowed daughter was out at work, and Harriet let them arrange the fruit and count the money, making sure that they took plenty home for themselves at the end of the afternoon. Today, Violet was on her own, and stony-faced, and she looked steadfastly past Harriet as if she didn't exist.

"Good afternoon, Violet," Harriet called, determined to keep things as normal as possible. "We're a little late today, so you might have thought we weren't coming, but we're here now, and we'd like to set the stall up. Perhaps you'd be kind enough to move your things?"

"We don't want you here—not today or any other day."

The blunt certainty of the statement threw Harriet, but she recovered quickly. "I'm afraid that's not your decision to make. We're here, and we have every intention of staying, so I'll ask you again—please move your things. If you'd like any help, just ask."

Violet ignored her, turning to straighten a basket of doorknobs that were already arranged with military precision, so Harriet began to move the crates herself, piling them up on the pavement in between the two stalls. Josephine and Mags brought the produce across, and she arranged it as it arrived, all the time knowing that people were watching her every move. When it was done, they sat together on upturned boxes, waiting in vain for some trade, but no one came anywhere near them; meanwhile, the rival stall at the bottom of the hill—whose produce was always inferior to theirs and far more expensive—was doing a roaring trade.

Harriet shifted her seat to follow the sun and noticed how many soldiers were walking the streets; occasionally they gave her a smile or a nod, strangers to the town and ignorant of her outcast status, and she despised herself for feeling grateful. In the distance, a bell sounded from the rose-red tower of Southover Church and was answered immediately by St. Michael's in the High Street, but even these sweet summer chimes sounded strangely discordant in the hostile atmosphere. It was only two o'clock, and she doubted her ability to see the afternoon out; although she would never have wanted to show it in front of the girls, she felt more vulnerable and exposed than she ever had in her life, and she didn't need the ugly

Martyrs' Memorial to remind her that people had been burnt at the stake on this very spot for lesser crimes than the ones of which she was suspected.

"As we're not exactly rushed off our feet, I might as well go and do some shopping," she said, unable to bear the idleness any longer. "If the doors aren't mysteriously closed in my face, that is. Will you be all right? I won't be long." Josephine nodded and Harriet walked back down the steep slope of School Hill to the newsagent's. It was cool inside the shop, in every sense of the word, and she was relieved to find only a couple of other customers there before her. Obviously, the man behind the counter didn't feel that he could be overtly rude, but neither did he want to offend his existing clientele, and his brusque grunt of acknowledgment was a halfway house between civility and insolence. He turned to serve her immediately, bypassing the woman already at the counter as if he wanted her out of his shop as quickly as possible, and she opened her mouth to ask for some cigarettes, but a pile of local newspapers stopped her in her tracks. A school photograph of Dorothy Norwood stared back at her from the front page, inset with a picture of Charleston, and although there was no image of her or George as far as she could see, the headline was damning enough without it: *"Tragic Schoolgirl's Final Hours at College of Shame: see inside for the full story."* The pictures took up two-thirds of the page, eclipsing even the heroic reports of Sussex regiments that had become the paper's standard fare, and she stared down at them, cold with shock and feeling foolish because she should have expected this and been ready for it. A jolt of anger surged through her when she thought of the story taking pride of place on every newsstand and bookstall in the county, and the only response left to her was contempt. "Fame at last," she said sarcastically, and there was a sharp intake of breath from the woman behind her, which only goaded Harriet further. "Such a shame it wasn't the nationals, but I suppose it's only a matter of time. Twenty Capstans, please, and I'll take this to read over supper."

"We haven't got any Capstans, I'm afraid."

Harriet glanced over his shoulder at the familiar blue and gold packet. "What do you mean? I can see them—they're on the shelf right behind you."

"I think you're mistaken about that."

"Then I'll have Benson & Hedges."

"We're out of those too."

There was a quiet giggle behind her, but it might as well have been as loud as a scream. Harriet threw the money for the newspaper down onto the counter and faced the other customers. "We're thinking of offering guided tours of the greenhouse too, if you're interested," she said, taking a fleeting satisfaction from the horror on their faces, then wishing she'd had the strength to stay quiet. She left the shop, knowing that it had been a mistake to rise to the bait; anything she said would be twisted and distorted, and repeated in the next day's paper as truth, and the last thing she needed was to aggravate the situation. If what she had just said got back to Moira House or, worse still, to Dorothy's parents, they would stand no chance of keeping the college going.

"What's wrong?" Josephine asked as soon as she saw her.

Harriet threw the paper down in disgust. "No wonder we're so universally popular here today—and there was I, thinking it was just our natural charm."

"What does it say?"

"The coward in me hasn't got any further than the headline. Will you read it and tell me the worst?" She lit the last cigarette in the packet and waited for Josephine to finish. "Well?"

"It says that Dorothy had made a complaint about the college she was attending, and although it's not known what the nature of the complaint was, the coincidence of her dying so soon afterward is suspicious. They haven't mentioned your names, but with the photograph of the farmhouse and the college sign outside, I don't suppose that matters." She folded the paper up again and nodded toward their vegetable crates, which were lined with the edition from the week before. "Try not to worry too much, Miss Barker.

That's where this will end up before long, and they'll have moved on to something else. Once the inquest has been held and everyone knows the verdict, no one will be able to print or say anything that isn't true."

"But the damage will have been done by then." There was a silence as they both looked down at Dorothy's photograph. "You've never asked us if any of these rumors are justified," Harriet said quietly. "You must have talked about it, you and Jeannie."

"We've talked about what happened, but that's all. As for asking you about the rumors, we really don't need to. We're there on the spot, and we can decide for ourselves what's fair. If we didn't trust you, we'd have gone back to Moira House when we were told to."

"Thank you, Josephine." She was about to suggest that they call it a day when two women with empty shopping baskets headed in their direction. "Perhaps our luck's about to change," she said, getting up to serve them. "They're actually smiling at us." Either the women were both strangers to the town and hadn't heard the gossip, or they were brave enough to take no notice, but Harriet was so grateful that she didn't care which. She helped them to select the best fruit and vegetables, weighing things out a little more generously than usual, while Josephine and Mags packed the baskets to the brim and kept a tally of the prices. When nothing else would fit, the younger of the two smiled and turned away, signaling to her friend to follow. "Excuse me!" Harriet called after them. "You've forgotten to pay." The women kept walking, throwing back their heads with laughter, and Harriet shouted again, angry this time. "Come back! You can't just take what you want and walk away. That's theft."

One of the women turned round. "And what are you going to do about it? Kill us? You're the one who deserves to be lynched. It's sick, what you two get up to when you think no one's looking." She threw a quick, ugly glance at her partner in crime, and the two of them disappeared out of sight, down Market Lane, swinging their baskets and still laughing. Harriet sat down and put her head in her hands, the taunt still ringing in her ears. She understood now that Dorothy's death had given their neighbors the excuse they had been waiting for to hate them. Any bigotry and prejudice that people might have felt before now had remained in the shadows, always there but kept in check; now they had found a crime they could put a name to, something that warranted their hatred, and for the first time Harriet feared for her own safety. "Let's go," she said, feeling utterly defeated.

"Absolutely not."

To Harriet's surprise, Josephine began to fill a basket of her own, and she couldn't remember a time when she had seen anyone look quite so determined. "What on earth are you doing?" she asked.

"Taking the mountain to Mohammed." Josephine tore off her tie and removed the band from around her hat. When she was sure that she had got rid of all the colors that linked her to the college, she picked up the fruit and headed for the houses at the bottom of the street. "I won't be long," she called back over her shoulder. She was as good as her word, returning twenty minutes later with an empty basket and a handful of coins. "I knocked on each door and told them I was a student from the college in Glynde," she said, grinning at Harriet. "They were delighted not to have to come out in this heat." She handed over the money. "It's not much, I'm afraid, but at least we won't go home empty-handed, and there's still time for Mags and me to do a few more rounds."

Harriet laughed for the first time in days. "I don't know what to be more proud of—your loyalty or your sense of enterprise." She looked at Josephine and spoke more seriously. "And you're wrong about it not being much, you know. These few shillings mean more to me than all the money we took last year, and George will feel the same."

The girls filled two more baskets with the most perishable fruit and went off together, and Harriet sat in the sun and played word games in her head to pass the time. A little girl began to run over to the stall, attracted by the fresh, bright colors, and she got up to give the child a plum, but her mother pulled her back so violently by her hair that she screamed and began to cry. It was an instinctive reaction on her mother's part, borne of genuine abhorrence, and it hurt Harriet more than any of the conscious attempts to humiliate her. She realized, to her horror, that she was afraid to touch a child now, in case her affection was misconstrued. She was afraid of being alone with one of the students, when she had never thought twice about it before; afraid of laughing with the girls and appearing too intimate; of saying George's name in public in case her tone gave her away. In everything that mattered, she felt her true self slowly but surely disappearing, and there was nothing she could do to stop it.

By the time Mags and Josephine returned, Harriet had loaded most of what was left unsold back into the van, determined now to leave as soon as possible. She went round to the driver's side to get in, and a car coming the other way swerved toward her, sounding its horn as a threat rather than a warning; it had been done deliberately, she knew that—done to scare the "brazen bitch" and make her run—and suddenly they were surrounded by jeers and laughter, by a slow handclap which began as a small ripple of protest and gathered momentum until she felt the hatred as a physical force. She threw herself behind the wheel, longing to mow them all down and caring so little for her own safety that only the presence of two innocent people in the van kept her sane enough to drive away from the trouble and not toward it.

No one said anything on the way back to Charleston. Josephine, in particular, was pale and withdrawn, and Harriet was all too aware of how she must be feeling as the possible consequences of her relationship with Jeannie began to dawn on her. Most mornings, when she came downstairs to make breakfast, Harriet heard Josephine stealing quietly from Jeannie's room, going back to her own bed before the house came to life; she had seen how her face became animated—beautiful, even—the minute that Jeannie entered the room, how she had grown in confidence until it was Jeannie now who seemed happy to follow. It was wrong that their love should be tainted by the scandal going on around them, but inevitable that it should leave Josephine feeling confused and afraid— and she was right to be worried. Nothing that intense could stay forever hidden, and even Peter had noticed the affair. It was only a matter of time before they gave themselves away in less forgiving company. If they had been alone on the journey home, she might have tried to say something reassuring, but Mags was too bright to miss even the most veiled of hints, and any general words of comfort that might have helped died in her throat long before she could give voice to them.

"We'll unload," Josephine said when they got back, and Harriet was glad to let her. She made her way through to the gardens to look for George and tell her what had happened, but her attention was caught by shrill cries coming from the orchard—not the usual conversation of the girls at work, but something strident and more disturbing, the sounds of children in a playground. She changed direction to take a look, and found a group of small boys playing among the trees, some of whom she recognized as the farmworkers' sons. They were waving sticks at one another and yelling, and one of them was holding a tin of what looked like paint or creosote and flicking it at the trees; on the far side of the orchard, the word "witch" had been crudely daubed onto one of the trunks, and God only knew what insult they were trying to spell next. "Stop that at once!" she shouted, her anger flaring again. "Go away now, or your parents will hear about this." It was an idle threat—their parents had probably sent them in the first place—but they ran off when they saw her, tossing the tin of creosote onto the ground, where it spilled out into thick, poisonous puddles on the grass.

Harriet went over to pick it up, and that was when she saw him, hanging from the branches of an apple tree, his fur covered in sticky black liquid until he was barely recognizable as the cat she loved. A noise came from her throat that she seemed to have no ownership of, primal and raw, a mixture of rage and pain and disbelief that was at the same time beyond any emotion she had ever known. She ran to him, hoping for his sake that he was already dead, and tore the leather whip down from the tree, noticing how tightly it had been pulled around his neck. The creosote was everywhere—in his ears and mouth, matted in his fur—and the strong, smoky smell of the tar filled her nose as she clutched him to her and tried to wipe it from his eyes. She held him tight—something that he had never allowed her to do when he was alive—and stayed with him under the trees until George came to look for her.

CHAPTER 4

Harriet had assumed that a verdict of death by misadventure, when and if it came, would be a relief, but she was wrong. As the coroner announced his decision and a murmur of conversation broke out around the courtroom, all she felt was a depressing certainty that nothing really had changed. They were still outcasts and likely to remain so. She felt George tremble at her side as the tension of the last few days broke, and glanced anxiously at her lover, aware of how carefully they were being scrutinized from all directions. "Come on," she said gently, risking a hand on George's arm. "Let's go."

All the girls had turned out to support them, even those not called to give evidence, and Josephine and Jeannie began to shepherd them toward the railway station, where they would catch the train for Glynde and walk back to Charleston from there. Harriet had declined the offer of a lift from Dr. O'Brien, knowing that they would want to be on their own when the inquest was over, and she led the way back to the small side street by the castle, where they had left the van. It had escaped relatively unscathed, with just a scratch down one side that could almost have been accidental, and she slammed the door firmly on any attempt at conversation by the stragglers who had followed them from court. "Thank God that's over," she said, rubbing her temples against the headache that had been threatening all morning. "Perhaps now they'll leave us in peace."

It was a vain hope, but she had taken to saying things that she no longer believed to be true, and she clung to it anyway. Tuesday was half-day closing in Lewes, and the streets were pleasantly quiet. She headed out on the Firle road, then changed her mind about going straight home and took the lane that led up to the Beacon instead; they needed space to talk, away from the farmhouse and any reminders of what had happened, and George raised no objections. "I thought we could both do with some time on our own," she said. "We don't seem to have had a second for weeks without somebody's eyes on us."

There was no answer, and she looked at George, horrified to see the tears silently streaming down her face. She pulled the van over onto the grass and took George in her arms, desperate to carry some of her pain, but she seemed inconsolable, and Harriet could only wait while her grief played itself out. "I'm sorry, Harry," she said at last, when she was calm enough to speak. "I'm so sorry for everything you've gone through because of me. I've asked too much of you—I always do—but I swear it was never meant to go this far."

"You haven't asked for anything that I wouldn't willingly have given a thousand times over."

"But you've made so many sacrifices, risked everything to protect what we have, done things you should never have had to do, and you've never once thrown it back in my face."

"And I never will. I don't blame you, George. You understand me, don't you? I don't blame you for *any* of this."

"Not now, perhaps, but you might wake up one day and wonder if it was all worth it."

"As long as you're there beside me, I'll know that it was worth it." She held George's hand to her lips, troubled by how lost and defeated she seemed. Since Dorothy's death, she had watched George fade, day by day, minute by minute, until it was like living with the ghost of their love. The sudden outburst of emotion frightened her even more than the quiet despair which had preceded it, and Harriet began to fear what George might be driven to do.

"We'll share the burden of this, just like we share everything else," she said. "Don't you dare make me carry that on my own." To Harriet's relief, her words seemed to make an impression. "Let's walk for a bit," she suggested. "We haven't done that for ages. It'll do us both good."

It felt wrong, somehow, to be out in the open and breathing in the sweet, fresh smell of gorse on this of all days. Her mind kept going back to the courtroom and the stricken look on Mrs. Norwood's face as first Josephine and then George testified to her daughter's final moments. Betty's evidence had been given between sobs, and her ordeal in the witness box was as distressing to Harriet as the words themselves; she had looked continually to her parents for support, but the Norwoods only seemed to have enough grief for one daughter, and it was Charity who comforted her when she went back to her seat, and who raised the loudest objections when the verdict was eventually announced. As the crowd dispersed around them, Dorothy's parents remained in their seats, holding hands and staring straight ahead, at a loss to know where their life had gone, and although it shamed Harriet to compare her pain with theirs, she knew exactly how they felt.

"We need to talk about the future," George said. "Cassidy told me last night that he won't be recommending any investment from the government, but I suppose that scarcely matters now."

"Surely when he knows the verdict—"

"The verdict won't make any difference, Harry. We're tainted by this, although he's far too much of a politician to be honest about his real reasons. Apparently we simply haven't got the capacity to expand in the way that the Ministry would want us to. There's no argument to be had."

Harriet wondered how George could sound so sanguine about the very thing that had, until recently, been all she ever dreamt of. For a fleeting moment, the smallest flame of resentment flickered at the back of her mind, but she fought against it. "So what do you want to do?" she asked. "Give up and run away? Start again somewhere else, and live happily ever after until someone works out that I'm not your sister and more than your friend? Until they hear where we've come from and why we left?"

Her voice was heavy with sarcasm, and George looked sadly at her. "You *do* blame me. That didn't take so long after all."

"Christ, George, don't you dare tell me how I feel. You can't possibly imagine it. And just so we're clear—I don't blame you for what you *have* done, only for what you haven't."

"What do you mean?"

"Why won't you fight? You've always been so strong. You've always stood up for what you believed in, no matter how hard it was. You've always fought for your dreams. Why not now?"

"Because I haven't got the heart for it any more—don't you understand that? It's easy to fight when you believe in something, but my dreams are what brought us to this mess. We don't deserve to be happy, Harry—not now. A girl is dead because she dared to stand in our way, and there's nothing *I* can do to put that right. You know what I mean, don't you? I don't have to spell it out."

Something in Harriet longed to make her do just that, if only to stop the words festering between them, but she didn't have the energy to argue. "Yes, I know." She turned away and headed for the road. "I'm going back to the house. You can do as you like. You usually do."

★   ★   ★

After the tension in the courtroom and the flurry of interest that followed the girls' progress down Lewes high street, the comparative peace of Glynde Station was a welcome relief. "Thank God that went the right way," Jeannie said as they followed the trail of students across the fields. "I don't think I could have stood another day of worrying about what might happen to us if the college had to close."

She squeezed Josephine's hand, but Josephine pulled away. "Don't do that here. One of the girls might see."

Jeannie stared at her in surprise. "So what if they do? They'll think nothing of it. They're as happy as we are—just look at them." It was true. There was a jubilant atmosphere among the students as they wound their way along the edge of a wood, taking advantage of the shade, and Josephine watched as Joyce and Mags linked arms, leading the other girls in a medley of morale-boosting war songs that they had hijacked for a different sort of victory. Suddenly Jeannie stopped walking, forcing Josephine to turn back to her. "What's the matter, Josephine? You've been acting strangely for the last few days. I thought it was the pressure of the inquest, but all that's over now. You should be relieved."

"Why? I don't see what's changed."

"Everything's changed. Harriet and Miss H have been cleared of any responsibility for Dorothy's death, and there's no stain on the college's reputation. We can get back to normal, the way things were before this all started. Surely you want that as much as I do? We've got the whole summer ahead of us."

"There's nothing remotely normal about what you and I have been doing." The words came out before she had a chance to consider their impact. Jeannie looked at her with such hurt in her eyes that Josephine had to turn away. "You don't really believe that all this scandal is just going to blow over, do you?" she said.

"Of course it will, given time." Jeannie spoke evenly, a degree of challenge now in her voice. "And even if it doesn't, even if George and Harriet are still guilty in some people's eyes and always will be, what has that got to do with you and me?"

"You wouldn't need to ask that if you'd been at the market with us. Dorothy's death was only the half of it." Josephine closed her eyes, remembering the hatred in the streets, the soul-destroying moment in the van coming home when she had realized that she wasn't strong enough to follow her heart, and never would be; since then, every minute she had spent with Jeannie had felt like a lie, the sort of smile you offer a dying man. "If we carry on as we are, that's the life we choose," she said. "Everyone would hate us if they knew how we felt."

"Not necessarily. There are other people—"

"Like us?" Josephine laughed, her frustrations with the world and with herself making her more scornful than she intended. The confusion and vulnerability of the last few days had laid bare a streak of callousness that she had never noticed in herself before, and while she hated it, she was powerless to stop it. "So where are these people, Jeannie? Living happily ever after somewhere with no one to bother them? You're not being realistic."

"Don't think for a minute that I'm going to apologize for that. And anyway, George and Harriet—"

"George and Harriet have been completely destroyed by this— haven't you noticed that? They're bickering about nothing all the time and silently blaming each other for the way that their world has just been pulled from under them." She forced herself to speak more gently, willing Jeannie to understand how she felt. "The man in the pub, your father—they're not the exception, Jeannie. That's what most people would think of us. It's what my family would think."

"And they're hundreds of miles away. They don't ever have to know." Jeannie's words were meant as an argument in favor of their future, but they only served to strengthen Josephine's resolve. The trauma of witnessing Dorothy's death and the violent reactions that followed had left her feeling isolated and alone, and she longed for the safety of home. The urge to return to something more familiar was suddenly as strong in her as the pull of the south had been when she first arrived, and her newfound freedom—synonymous with Jeannie's love—now seemed alien and dangerous. "So what are you going to do?" Jeannie asked defiantly, apparently reading her thoughts. "Pick up with the soldier from the next village just to make life easier?"

Ashamed of her own transparency, Josephine quickened her pace. "This has to stop," she said, hoping to get within earshot of the girls so that Jeannie couldn't argue. "I can't do it any more. It's too much."

"Of course it's too much. That's why it's so precious. And you'll change your mind," Jeannie called after her. "We love each other. You can't just turn your back on that."

Josephine kept walking, wondering if there would ever come a time when she stopped wanting to believe her.

★   ★   ★

George and Harriet drove back to Charleston in silence. The first sign of something amiss was the college sign, which had been daubed with red paint until it was no longer legible. "They knew there'd be nobody here during the inquest," George said when she saw it. "Of course they knew. How could I have been so bloody stupid?"

She opened the door before Harriet had even brought the van to a standstill, and ran past the house to the gardens. Harriet went after her, fearful for what she would find after Byron's death, but not even that could have prepared her for the devastation that greeted her. Everything that was beautiful or productive had been completely destroyed. It was as if the garden screamed. The flowers and shrubs around the top terrace had been savagely pulled from the earth and scattered across the lawn, and the roses that meant so much to both of them were torn down from their arch and severed at the base. The vegetable plots were barely recognizable, their neat lines and promise of abundance obliterated in a matter of minutes. Runner bean poles had been snapped and their plants trampled into the earth; and any produce that was nearly ready had been roughly dug up and left on the surface, where someone had doused it in bleach, rendering everything inedible. Harriet heard the gate open at the bottom of the garden and went to join George by the potting shed, following a trail of broken terracotta where flowerpots had been thrown to the ground. If possible, the damage here was even more extreme. Most of the glass in the greenhouse and cold frames had been smashed, and the water butts were upended so that all the precious water flooded out onto barren ground. The vandals had ransacked the shed and used some of its contents to build a bonfire around the bench that George had always loved to sit on; it was burning steadily still, and someone had placed the scarecrow on top in an eloquent gesture of mockery and contempt. Through the flames, their figures distorted by the shimmering heat, Harriet could see a group of farmworkers and villagers standing silently at the edge of the field; to her horror, most of them were women.

"I don't understand," she said helplessly. "Why would they go this far? How do they think they can get away with it?"

"Who's going to stop them? They hate us. They've always hated us."

George's voice was tight and strained, and her face was white with rage. Before Harriet could stop her, she headed back toward the house, returning minutes later with a shotgun. "George, no— for God's sake, don't," Harriet shouted, trying to catch her arm. "Can't you see? That's exactly what they want you to do. Don't give them the satisfaction."

George took no notice and leveled the gun at the gathering. There was a moment of stillness that seemed to last an age, a perilous stalemate that no one seemed inclined to break. Then one of the women took a provocative step forward. Harriet closed her eyes, listening to the taunts of abuse and waiting for the explosion, but it never came. When she dared to open them again, George had lowered the gun and sunk to her knees, and her tormenters—sensing victory—began to drift away.

CHAPTER 5

Harriet sat on the end of Peter's bed and watched as he put the last few things into a holdall. "I've lost count of the times I've seen you pack," she said, absentmindedly straightening the bed-clothes, "and it never gets any easier. I wish you didn't have to go."

"For two pins I'd tell the British army what to do with its call-up notice."

"And end up with a court martial? Or worse? That would really help."

"But I hate leaving you here like this, Harry. It's not safe."

"We won't be here much longer. Dr. O'Brien has found us a house in Devon with a couple of months left on the lease, and we can go whenever we like. He's been so kind and it will give us a chance to think about what we want to do next." She smiled, a little bitterly, and added, "Not that we're exactly inundated with options."

"Whatever you do and wherever you go, you'll still be with her."

She touched his cheek and made him look at her, tracing the lines around his eyes that were the only overt signs—so far—of the toll that the war had taken. "Peter, this is destroying George. I've never seen her so beaten before, and she needs me. I couldn't leave her now, even if I wanted to. And I *don't* want to—ever. I love her. I've loved her from the moment I set eyes on her, and that will never change, no matter how much you might want it to."

"Even though she's killed someone?"

She glanced toward the open bedroom door, horrified by his lack of discretion. "I didn't say that. You know I didn't."

"But that's what you were thinking, isn't it, when I came home that night and found you beside yourself. You were literally sickened by what she might have done. A sixteen-year-old girl, for God's sake. Have you forgotten that so easily, Harry? Doesn't it come back to you whenever she touches you? I can't believe you're still standing by her."

She set her face to a lie, knowing how rarely she fooled him. "I was in shock that night. Everything was out of kilter, but it was an accident, and you mustn't say it was anything else—promise me, Peter, or we'll both suffer for it, not just George." He nodded, and she knew she could trust him. "I'll be all right—honestly, I will. We just need to get away from here and get on with our lives. And anyway, it's *my* job to worry about *you*—remember? I'm not ready to change places with you yet. There'll be plenty of opportunities for you to boss me around when I'm in my dotage. Don't make me old before my time."

"You're *not* old—that's what I mean. You could do much better for yourself."

Harriet laughed. "Now you're sounding like my father."

"Yes, I suppose I am." He smiled grudgingly, no more capable of staying angry with her now than he had been when he was a boy, resenting her half-hearted attempts to discipline him. They had always been more like brother and sister than cousins, thrown together by a family that seemed devoid of all the usual ties, and she had happily taken responsibility for him when no one else would. Until now, it was the only thing that had ever come between her and George—a longing for children on her part to which George could never be reconciled. For a while it had threatened to break them, but she had accepted her lot eventually, deflecting those instincts first to Peter and then to the stream of girls who passed through the college, glad of her care and guidance. And that had been enough in the end, or so she had told herself, knowing in her heart that—whatever the crossroads—she would always choose George.

"Do you remember these?" Peter asked, taking a pile of dog-eared pocket books in matching covers down from the shelf.

"You've still got them!"

"Of course I have. I take them everywhere. They were the first thing that anyone ever bought me, and the most important." He flicked fondly through the pages of the Gowans and Gray art books, and she took one from his hand, looking for the inscription that she had written in the Christmas of 1903. "They'll be printing one of these about you some day," she said, "as long as you don't get yourself killed first."

"I'll be more famous if I do."

"Don't joke about it." She took his hand, and all the fear for him that the events of the last few days had briefly displaced suddenly resurfaced, stronger than ever. "Promise me you'll be careful."

"I promise." He put the books in the side pocket of the holdall and stood up. "Come with me. I've got something to show you." She followed him downstairs and out to his studio. "You asked me what I've been spending so much time on, and this is it." He removed a sheet from his easel, revealing a small canvas underneath, and she saw her own reflection staring back at her—except it was her younger self, carefree and happy. "I wanted you to have a reason to think of me while I'm gone." He hadn't meant the words to sound so final, but they struck her as ominous, and she found it hard to separate the painting and his gesture from the knowledge that it might be a parting gift. She forced herself to look critically at the portrait, inevitably comparing it with the face she saw each morning in the mirror, and wondered where those years had gone.

"Do you like it?" he asked impatiently.

"I love it," she lied, "but I wish you hadn't finished it."

"Why?"

"Because then you'd have a reason to come back."

There was a knock at the door, and Harriet heard Josephine's voice calling a hello. "Come in," she said, relieved that Peter hadn't had the chance to make a vow he couldn't keep.

"Oh sorry—I didn't realize you were here. I can come back later if I'm interrupting."

"Of course you're not interrupting. Come and have a look at what Peter's just given me, and tell us what you think."

"Be kind, though," Peter said, winking at her as she walked across to the canvas. "I know how harsh you can be."

"I don't need to be kind. It's stunning."

"Not bad for a work in progress," he agreed, looking at Harriet.

"It looks finished to me."

"Not quite. The skin needs a richer tone, but I ran out of time. Is that the letter you want me to take to Summerdown?" he asked, nodding toward the envelope in Josephine's hand.

"Yes, please, if it's not too much trouble."

He read the name on the front. "Private Jack Mackenzie. Is he a relative?"

"No." Josephine hesitated, and Harriet looked at her curiously. "No, he's a friend from back home in Inverness."

"Consider it delivered."

"Thank you."

She turned to go, but Harriet called her back. "Can we talk about something before you leave for Moira House?"

"Yes, of course."

Harriet squeezed Peter's arm. "Don't you dare go without saying goodbye this time." He nodded and she walked out into the garden, still shocked by the thoroughness of the devastation. "There's something I've been wanting to ask you," she said. "You strike me as a good judge of character—what did you think of Dorothy Norwood? And I want you to answer honestly, as if she hadn't died. None of that sentimental rubbish that people use in hindsight when they don't want to be disrespectful."

The question obviously took Josephine by surprise, and she took some time to consider her answer. "I didn't have long to get to know Dorothy, I suppose, but I'm very glad she was my pupil and not my sister or my friend."

"What do you mean by that?"

"That she was bright and keen and quick to learn—the ideal student, capable of excelling at whatever she chose to turn her hand to. But on a personal level, there didn't really seem to be anyone else moving in her orbit—at least no one she'd noticed."

It was an insightful comment, which chimed very much with Harriet's own impressions. "Were you surprised to hear that she'd complained about us?"

"Yes, very. Partly because she seemed happy here, but mostly because she was far too selfish to care about something that didn't directly concern her."

Harriet smiled. "Yes, that's what I thought too." She sat down on the wall around the terrace, facing back to the house so that she didn't have to look at the slowly dying roses. "Does Jeannie know your friend from back home?"

Josephine reddened. "No, they've never met. She was off looking for—"

She stopped abruptly, realizing her mistake, and Harriet finished the sentence for her. "Off looking for Lomax and Norwood. Yes, I know—Peter told me, so you can stop pretending. Anyway, a spot of truanting hardly matters now. I'm not in charge any more, so you and I can be friends. And speaking as your friend, I'd like to give you some advice, if I may. It's up to you whether you take it or not."

"Go on."

"George and I have been grateful for everything you've done while you've been here—not just your teaching and your rapport with the girls, but your personal support for us through some difficult times. You've witnessed a lot of terrible things—things that no one should have to put up with—and it's one of my biggest regrets that we've shown you how much hatred and prejudice exists in the world."

"It wasn't your fault," Josephine insisted, "and you've shown us plenty of more admirable things as well. That's what I'll remember. I'm glad to have been here."

"Good, but that's not why I'm speaking to you like this. I wanted you to know that it's worth it. All the taunts and the abuse, even the violence—I'd put up with it all over again for the happiness and the love. Do you understand what I'm saying to you?"

"Yes, I think so."

"There were times when I was tempted to take the easy way out, but I'm so glad I didn't." She leant over and gave Josephine a hug, noticing that there were tears in her eyes. "You'd better go and finish packing. Jeannie will be wondering where you are."

"What will you and Miss H do now?" Josephine asked. "Will you stay here?"

"No, but other than that, I'm not sure of anything."

"Whatever you decide, I hope you'll be happy."

"Thank you. And Josephine . . ."

"Yes?"

"If you can't be brave, at least be kind. Don't blame the person who loves you for what you can't face."

1938

CHAPTER 1

The handful of houses at Birling Gap was scattered untidily across the landscape, as if someone had thrown a pile of stones into the air to decide where they should be built. There was a small hotel by a row of coastguards' cottages, serving the summer visitors who came to walk the dramatic stretch of coastline, but otherwise, it was a remote and lonely spot, a good three or four miles from the Eastbourne to Seaford road, and that didn't surprise Josephine. After the stories she had heard about those restless years following their departure from Charleston, she would have been surprised to find Harriet and George living at the heart of a community. Marta turned into a makeshift hotel car park that overlooked the shingle beach below, and they got out to take in the view. "This is stunning," Marta said. "Quite a change from a rural farmhouse, though. I can't see many gardens flourishing this close to the sea."

Josephine agreed. "Although we only know for certain that Vera lives here. When she answered my letter, she said that Harriet was 'nearby,' but wanted to meet here." She looked westward, back toward the rhythmic splendor of the Seven Sisters cliffs—sheer white precipices that seemed to have been cut sharply from above rather than shaped naturally by the sea—and wondered what had given the women the courage to return to a part of the world that had caused them so much heartache. "Perhaps a contrast is exactly the point. They were both devastated by what happened to the college gardens. I can understand why they wouldn't even try to recreate that. It was probably just too painful."

"Do you want me to come with you, or would you rather go and see them on your own?"

"I think I'll get more out of Harriet if I go on my own. Vera didn't mention George, so with a bit of luck it will be just the two of us. We always got on well, so I hope she'll feel she can talk to me."

"I hope so too. The sooner you come to some sort of peace about this, the better."

It was unlike Marta to be quite so terse about anything, and Josephine glanced at her, concerned by how far she had pushed her lover's patience. "You do understand why it took me so long to tell you about Jeannie?"

"Yes, I understand. I wish it hadn't, but I understand. As for lying about what happened on the night, though—"

"We've been through all this. What choice did I have?"

"Telling the truth or saying nothing are two that immediately spring to mind. It's not as if Charity Lomax—or any other journalist, for that matter—is doing this officially. You're not obliged to answer."

"I know, but I was frightened. She was accusing Jeannie of—"

The name was an irritant, and Marta held up her hand, effectively removing herself from the conversation. "I just want you to be safe, Josephine. If you insist on doing this alone, at least promise to be careful."

"Of course I'll be careful." She wondered what Marta's response would have been if the false alibi had concerned anybody else, but knew that she was in no position to argue. "What will you do while I'm gone?"

"Sit and worry until you come back." Marta reached into the car and took out a book and some glasses. "I've got some reading to catch up on."

Josephine looked at the copy of *Rebecca*. "Haven't you had enough of Daphne du Maurier?"

"Alma asked me to read it. Anyway, it might give me a few tips on how to live up to the woman who comes before me."

"Marta, don't. You have nothing to live up to."

"Assuming Jeannie *is* that woman, of course. There are plenty of years still unaccounted for."

Josephine was about to deny the suggestion, but it would have only made things worse to admit that her grief for Jeannie and the fear of being found out had scarred her so deeply that it was a long time before she allowed herself to feel anything for another woman. "What does it matter?" she said. "It's now that counts."

"Just do one thing for me, Josephine. When the next old flame crawls out of the woodwork needing your urgent attention, at least have the decency to tell me yourself, rather than letting me find out from someone else—and preferably before you introduce me to her at the theater."

Marta started to walk away, but Josephine caught her arm. "What do you mean? Who told you about Jeannie?"

"It's not important."

"Of course it is. Was it Charity? Did she speak to you the other night, because if she did—"

"If you must know, it was Archie."

"Archie?" Josephine stared at her in bewilderment. "When did you speak to Archie? And what on earth did he tell you?"

"I saw him when I was in Cornwall," Marta admitted.

"What? He just happened to be strolling across Bodmin Moor?"

"No, of course not. I asked him to meet me there. I was worried you might be putting yourself in danger by raking up the past, and I knew he'd want to help if he could."

"How dare you go behind my back where Archie's concerned?" Josephine's anger flared quickly, but she had the presence of mind to realize that very little of it was Marta's fault. The idea that Archie had somehow known about Jeannie and that he might have told Jack horrified her. As painful as it had been at the time, she had made her decision and stuck to it, and the last thing she wanted was to hear that Jack might have died doubting her loyalty to him.

"I wanted to help," Marta reiterated. "Apart from anything else, you and Archie needed to make your peace after Bridget's death. He misses you as much as you miss him."

"It was your fault we argued in the first place. If you'd told me about Phyllis as soon as you found out, he wouldn't have felt so betrayed."

"I really don't think you're in a position to complain about withholding information."

"So what did he tell you?"

"That Jeannie obviously cared for you. He thought I knew, and of course I should have. It was obvious from the way she looked at you the other night. She still cares for you."

Marta turned away and walked toward the hotel, and Josephine understood for the first time how frightened she was—not angry or jealous, but frightened. "Why are you still reading books for Alma Reville?" she called after her, ashamed now of being so caught up in the past that she had failed to give Marta the reassurance she needed. Marta stopped but refused to look at her, and it was left to Josephine to guess at the answer. "You're going with them, aren't you? You're going to America."

"I haven't made my mind up yet."

"But you'd made your mind up before all this started."

"Yes, I had."

"Please don't go." She took Marta's hands, suddenly as frightened as she was. "I've given you every good reason to doubt me these last few weeks, and I'm sorry, but I've never loved anyone the way I love you, and I never will."

Marta seemed convinced of her honesty, but her hesitation proved to Josephine that it had come too late. She opened her mouth to say more, but Marta stopped her. "There's something I've been too afraid to ask you," she said.

"Then ask me now."

"All right. Are you going to see her again?"

Josephine shook her head. "No, I'm not, but seeing Jeannie or not seeing her makes no difference to you and me. There's no choice to be made, Marta, and there never will be—not for me, anyway. I made my mind up a long time ago."

Marta nodded, acknowledging the question in the answer. "Yes, so did I."

Only when the tension between them relaxed did Josephine allow herself to consider what she had come so close to losing. "I'm sorry," she said.

"So am I. Jealousy is my least favorite trait, but I've surprised myself by excelling at it recently." She smiled and brushed the tear from Josephine's cheek. "Go and do what you need to do. I'll wait for you in the hotel, but if there's the slightest sign of trouble, come and get me. I mean it, Josephine—don't take any risks."

Josephine reiterated her promise and walked back up the lane they had driven down, looking for Thistle Cottage. She found it on the left-hand side at the end of a terrace of three, built of soft red brick and pleasing to the eye, with an air of quietness and order. The white picket gate stood open, inviting her into a small front garden that—though carefully tended—lacked the natural exuberance of its neighbors, and she walked up to the front door, feeling slightly apprehensive. She had never really known Vera Simms and would have much preferred to call directly on Harriet, but she could understand the instinct for caution or safety in numbers, and resolved to make the best of whatever time they allowed her. Her sense of anticlimax grew stronger as the first knock went unanswered, and she tried again, then followed the herringbone path round to the garden at the back. A child's laughter greeted her as she rounded the corner of the house, and she stared in astonishment at the man with a little boy on his shoulders. He looked older, obviously, and his once jet-black hair was now streaked with gray, but there was no mistaking Peter Whittaker. He waved when he saw her and swung the boy down to the ground, bringing forth another squeal of delight. "Go and find your brother, Tom," he said, ruffling the child's hair. "Granny's friend is here, and I need to speak to her." Tom looked as if he was about to protest, but Whittaker grinned and pointed to the house, and the boy ran obediently inside. "You look surprised to see me," Whittaker said. "I told Vera that she should have mentioned our marriage when she wrote to you, but obviously she hasn't."

"It's not just that," Josephine admitted, although her mind was having trouble contemplating such an unlikely union. "There's no gentle way to say this, but I thought you were dead. Charity Lomax said you'd been killed toward the end of the war."

"I think we both know she's not the most reliable source of information, but in this particular case I have to take some of the blame. God knows why, but Charity seemed to think that there was some sort of understanding between us. In the end, it was easier to let her believe that I was no longer here. As you can see, though, I'm very much alive."

Perhaps it was childish of her, but Josephine took great satisfaction in knowing that someone who was as skilled in telling lies as Charity could also be fooled by one. "I'm glad to hear it," she said. "Alive and happy—that's very obvious."

"Yes. I never thought family life would suit me, but it does."

"Is Vera at home?"

"No, she's working. She and our eldest daughter have taken over the horticultural business from Harry, and they're fanatical about it. Some things never change. I expected them back by now, but they must have been held up."

"How many children have you got?"

"Four. Two of each. Tom's the youngest, and Rose will be nineteen in December." So the marriage had been a long one, Josephine thought; she would never have believed that someone who had despised George so much could live in harmony with someone who obviously adored her, but perhaps emotions had softened over the years, and in any case, she had never known Peter to allow his hatred for George to come between him and Harriet. She remembered what Joyce had told her about Harriet and the children, and was pleased to think that the bond was even stronger than she had realized.

He seemed to guess a little of what she was thinking, because he said, "Sometimes you miss what's right in front of you, don't you? It took me a long time even to notice Vera, and then suddenly I couldn't imagine life without her." Could that explain what she had heard that day by the shepherds' huts, Josephine wondered? If Vera and Peter were already involved, Harriet could easily have been discouraging Vera from making the relationship public in case George disapproved. And that might also explain why Peter had seemed to be stirring things up. "All this—our family and our marriage, being close to Harry and finding some peace—I never thought I'd have that. Actually, there were times when I thought it had gone from the world forever, but you know that. You saw my paintings, although you probably don't remember them."

There was no false modesty in the comment, just a simple recognition of how much time had passed. "Of course I remember," Josephine said. "In fact, I was admiring one of them again recently." She told him about her visit to Charleston and how much it had changed. "You've got some ardent admirers in Bloomsbury. Duncan Grant told me how sorry he was never to have met you or exhibited with you. Now I think about it, a lot of people assume that you're dead."

The smile transformed his face, just as it used to, and she remembered how dismissive Jeannie had been of his charm, and how readily Joyce had succumbed to it; he had always been someone who attracted extremes of opinion. "As far as galleries are concerned, I might as well be dead," he said. "I don't paint any more. I'm happy, so why would I need to?"

Josephine couldn't decide if that was a positive or negative reflection on art, but there was certainly no denying that the inspiration for Peter Whittaker's painting had been violence and pain. "I have a confession to make," she admitted. "I stole two of your sketchbooks from the portfolio while I was there."

Peter laughed. "I'm flattered to have driven you to something so underhand."

"I wasn't sure that you'd want anyone to see them, bearing in mind what's been happening in the newspapers recently."

"Why?"

"The drawings of Dorothy Norwood . . ."

"Oh, that. Yes, of course—I drew her in the greenhouse, didn't I? I'd completely forgotten. It's kind of you to consider it, but if you look at that sketch in the context of everything else I was doing at the time, it's not so very shocking. I was more than used to drawing dead bodies, even if they were never recognized in any of the official war art."

"But what about the others?"

"What others? I only remember that one." He shrugged, and Josephine genuinely believed that he had no idea what she was talking about. "You're welcome to do what you like with my sketchbooks. Keep them or destroy them. I've got no more use for any of that stuff." There was a wail from the house, followed by some shouting, and he looked apologetic. "A ceasefire only lasts for so long at that age, I'm afraid. Will you excuse me? Harry's out walking on the cliff. She said to point you in the direction of the lighthouse if you arrived before she got back, or you're welcome to wait here if you prefer."

"I'll go and look for her. I could do with a walk myself after the journey. Is George with her?"

He paused, ill at ease for the first time since she'd arrived. "I'll let Harry explain. It was nice to see you again, though."

"And you." She watched him disappear into the house, trying to guess why he had avoided the subject of George when he had been so open about everything else; the obvious answer was to prevent himself from saying more than Harriet wanted her to know. Intrigued, she left the houses behind and started the steady climb toward Belle Tout, the disused lighthouse that graced the cliff at Beachy Head. She had only been to this part of Sussex two or three times before, but each time she had found the wildness of the place exhilarating, and today was no different. There was a stiff breeze on the headland, with the air pure from the sea, and she walked as close to the cliff edge as she dared to enjoy the graceful sweep of coastline and the flocks of birds that seemed to hover and dance on the wind.

Up ahead of her, Josephine saw Harriet standing a few yards from the old lighthouse, and her solitary, silhouetted figure seemed to emphasize the headland's sense of loneliness and desolation. As she walked across the soft, salt-sprayed turf, Harriet turned and raised her hand in greeting. She was wearing an old raincoat as protection against the wind, and as she removed its hood, Josephine was shocked to see how much she had aged; somehow, whenever she had thought of Harriet during the past couple of weeks, she had seen in her mind's eye the attractive, youthful woman with the laughing eyes who had welcomed her to Charleston. Her greeting was as warm as ever, in spite of the circumstances, but now Harriet looked every moment of her sixty years, weary and defeated by the world, and somehow Josephine knew that—for whatever reason—the woman who was standing in front of her no longer had the companionship of the person she loved.

"That photograph in the paper doesn't do you justice," she said, releasing Josephine from a hug and holding her at arms' length to take a good look at her face.

"I'm not sure justice is the *Daily Mirror*'s main objective." Josephine returned the appraisal, concerned by a vulnerability that she hadn't expected to see, and all her old loyalties returned in an instant, no matter how determined she had been to remain open to the possibility that Harriet and George were involved in Dorothy's death. "Has it caused trouble for you? Other than bringing it all back, of course."

"I've never needed Betty Norwood's help to relive that night."

"And what about George?"

Something in her tone gave away her suspicions. "Peter didn't tell you?"

"No. He said you would."

"He still doesn't trust himself to hide his relief, I suppose, although he's been very good about it. George took her own life— three years ago now, just before we moved back here. It wasn't the first time she'd tried it, but one of us always managed to stop her. She was determined to do it, though, and I always knew she'd manage it somehow. Her life was too much to bear."

The emotions that Harriet managed to keep out of her voice were written all over her face, and Josephine could only imagine how much self-possession it took to talk about the suicide. "What couldn't George bear?" she asked, although she thought she already knew the answer.

Harriet was silent, staring down at the turf, which was dotted with pieces of chalk from the cliff. "Shall we walk for a bit?" she suggested eventually. "There's a lot I'd like to tell you, and it helps me to think more clearly. I need to be honest with someone after all the lies, and your letter came at just the right moment." They turned inland, past the redundant lighthouse, then picked up the route along the cliff. "I don't know how much you know about what happened after we left Charleston."

"I know that Dorothy's parents took you to court for negligence, and you won. And I know you were in Devon for a while."

"Devon, Dorset, Somerset, Wiltshire—we couldn't settle anywhere because sooner or later someone always found out that a young girl in our care had died. Or they guessed that we were lovers. We even tried changing our names a couple of times, but once the Norwoods had lost in court, they were determined to make our lives miserable in other ways, and they always found us in the end. I don't blame them. If anyone hurt Vera or her children, I'd be exactly the same."

Perhaps she was reading too much into it, but there seemed to be an unconscious acknowledgment in the phrase that Dorothy's death was no accident. "Has Vera been with you since Charleston?" she asked, interested to hear that Harriet thought of their former assistant as a daughter.

"Yes. She stuck by us when we left, and I don't know what we would have done without her."

"She's obviously made Peter very happy. I have to admit, that was a surprise."

"To all of us, I think, although she told me that she'd always been fond of him. When the war ended, he came to live with us, and they fell in love. He was angry and bitter and damaged, but somehow Vera knew how to cope with that in a way that even I didn't. I was worried at first that he'd hurt her—he'd always been restless and volatile, even before the army—but she was so patient with him, and by the time Rose came along, he was a different man." She smiled to herself, and just for a moment there was a glimpse of a different time. "It reminded me of how George and I were when we first met, if I'm honest, although that's the last thing he'd want to hear."

"How did George feel about their marriage?"

"It reconciled her with Peter to a certain extent, I think. There was what you might call a truce of convenience once it became obvious that our lives were always going to be linked. She would have preferred it to be just the two of us, like it had always been—George had too many problems with her own family to want to be part of anybody else's—but she knew how much it meant to me. And she always felt that what our life had become was her fault."

"Is that why she killed herself?" Josephine asked quietly. "Because she felt guilty about something?"

"She felt that she was a burden," Harriet said, avoiding a direct answer. "She had a stroke, you see, and she found it impossible to come to terms with her incapacity—you knew her well enough to appreciate that. She never regained the strength on her left side, and speech was difficult. She had no stamina, and it made her clumsy. A George who couldn't rant and rave or stride about like she used to, a George who couldn't garden properly or manage her share of the business—that was no life. She endured it for my sake, but that's all."

"When was this?"

"Fifteen years ago. I blame the stress of what happened and the constant moving from place to place. She'd always been so fit until then."

"And you cared for her all that time?"

"Of course I cared for her. I loved her. What else would I have done?" Josephine had only meant to sympathize with how hard it must have been, and Harriet acknowledged her abruptness. "I'm sorry, and you're right—it was a struggle. I could have coped with the physical strain of it, and Vera was a tremendous help, but it was George's depression that I found so difficult. She was utterly broken, and I don't blame her for it, but I couldn't find the person I'd fallen in love with, as selfish as that sounds."

"It doesn't sound selfish at all. Devastating, yes, but not selfish."

"Somehow I thought you'd understand." She glanced gratefully at Josephine, and then said, "I did my best to be brave about it for Vera, but it got harder when I could see how badly George wanted to die. She found the most amazing strength from somewhere once she'd made up her mind. I stopped her every time because I didn't want to lose her, but whenever it happened, I could feel her daring me to prove how much I really loved her by letting her go." Josephine wanted to ask if she had helped George to end her life, but it felt too intrusive, and that wasn't the truth she was here to discover. "In the end, she waited for the one weekend of the year that I had to go away. Vera found her, and I wish to God it had been me. She shouldn't have had to suffer that."

"Why do you consider Vera's feelings so much more than your own?" Josephine asked. "I know Vera always admired George, and

I know how loyal she's been to you both, but you loved George for years—and she, you. You went through so much together. Surely there can be no doubt about who really suffered?"

Harriet took a long time to respond, and Josephine wondered if she was having second thoughts about the conversation. "Vera is George's daughter," Harriet said eventually. "George never knew that, but Vera did. That's why—when you first met us—Vera was so desperate to have a relationship with her. It wasn't at all what everyone thought, but it was love all the same. Unrequited love, with all the pain and rejection that involves."

Josephine looked out across the multi-colored fields stretching inland, trying to make sense of what she had just heard. "I don't understand," she admitted.

"Why would you? You don't know anything about us—not before that summer, anyway."

"So tell me. How did George come to have a child? Was it before you met?"

"No, afterward. I suppose you could say one was a direct consequence of the other." She saw Josephine's bemused expression and tried to explain. "George came from a good family in Oxfordshire. Good in the sense of traditional and respectable rather than any true sense of the word—well-off, with houses all over the place, distinguished naval careers going back generations. You know the sort of thing I mean."

Josephine nodded. "Money and breeding. I suppose I always assumed that."

"Quite. We were worlds apart when it came to class, although that never mattered to either of us. When I was eighteen, I got a job as housekeeper in their London home."

"That's how you met?"

"Yes, although not straightaway. George hated the city and very rarely left their main residence. That's where she loved to be and where she learnt everything she knew about horticulture. They had an old gardener there, apparently, who took her under his wing from when she was a little girl, and she never looked back. I didn't see the gardens she created there, but I gather they were beautiful.

"Yes, I imagine they were."

"Her father was on his second marriage by the time I joined them, and his new wife was much younger, so they spent more time in London—and that was another good reason for George to avoid it. She and her father hated each other, and she could never reconcile herself to the fact that he had started another family so soon after her mother died. They had a young son, and I used to look after him as well—by choice rather than expectation. He was a nice child, a bit like Peter when he was a boy. Then George came to stay for the first time, and everything changed. I'd never met anyone like her. I still haven't." Josephine heard the warmth in her voice and envied her the simplicity of loving one person her whole life, no matter how testing the circumstances; the closer she and Marta became, the more she resented how long it had taken them to find each other. "From then on, George spent a lot of her time in London. We hated being apart."

"Did her family know what was going on?"

"Good God, no. Not at first, anyway, although I suppose it was inevitable that they'd find out. Her little brother must have seen us together because he said something to her father—something perfectly innocent as far as he was concerned, but enough to have us watched. We were caught together, and all hell broke loose. I could never work out which they objected to more—my being a woman or a servant, but the combination of the two was as bad as it could get. They sacked me on the spot, of course, and turned me out of the house without a penny, and George came with me. I think that's what really provoked her father in the end—the fact that she wouldn't give me up. If she'd stayed and toed the family line, he could have blamed it all on me—the wicked commoner, leading his daughter astray. But she made that impossible, and the shame was unbearable once word got out. He was never going to allow a daughter of his to show him up like that."

"What did he do?"

"Small things at first. I tried to get another position, but wherever I went, someone seemed to have a discreet word in the right ear, and I was shown the door. We had no money, so in the end George went back and asked for what was hers from her mother's trust fund. I didn't want her to go anywhere near her father, but she said she had a right to the money, and I couldn't argue. He agreed on the condition that she stay under his roof until her twenty-first birthday. It was only a few weeks away, so she thought she could put up with it. At least then we'd have enough to make a start on our own. She already had plans to set up the college, and I knew I could help her make it work. It seemed like the perfect future."

They had walked a long way, and whether from the distance or the effort of reliving painful memories, Harriet seemed suddenly weary. Josephine took her arm and changed their course toward a bench overlooking the lighthouse at Beachy Head, which stood small and forlorn by day. "I'm guessing that something terrible happened during those few weeks," she said, hoping to make the story a little easier for Harriet to tell. "Something that led to George having a child she didn't want."

Harriet nodded. "Yes. It was one of her father's friends, although she could barely bring herself to say his name. She made me vow never to tell a soul while she was alive. *That* was her shame, not the love that she and I shared. She couldn't bear the thought of anyone finding out. I swear she only told me because she had to—she came back to me on the night it happened, and she was in the most terrible state. She kept apologizing, Josephine. I can't bear that, even now—the fact that she blamed herself for being raped. And I wasn't as supportive as I should have been."

"In what way?"

"When she realized she was pregnant, I begged her to keep the baby. I'd always wanted children, but I knew that I'd probably never have any of my own, and this seemed like a miracle—a child by the woman I loved. I should have realized how she'd feel about it and what a painful reminder that baby would be, but I didn't. She refused, of course. When the time came, she didn't even want to know if she'd had a boy or a girl. I honestly think she would have killed the baby at birth if there hadn't been an alternative."

"She had Vera adopted?"

"Yes. I made all the arrangements, and we never spoke of it again. I tried to put it out of my mind too—until that child walked back through our door seventeen years later."

"How did you know it was her?"

"I didn't at first. I assumed what everyone else assumed—that Vera had a faintly embarrassing fixation on George, which would pass in time. When it didn't, it began to bother me more, and I had it out with her. That's when she told me who she was."

"And you believed her?"

"Yes. Her adoptive parents had told her early on that she wasn't theirs by birth, and she'd found her birth certificate to prove it. She said to me once that she spent most of her childhood waiting for the moment when she could go out and find her real mother. She saw something about the college in the newspaper, and there aren't many people called Hartford-Wroe. It didn't take her long to work out that George was the person she was looking for."

"But she didn't announce herself to George?"

"No, thank God. She answered the advertisement and came to work for us, but she had the sense not to plough straight in. Deep down, she must have known that she was unwanted and that it might be wise to tread carefully. Looking back on it now, it breaks my heart to remember how hard she tried to impress George and how pleased she was to be noticed. Even the smallest bit of praise was like air to her."

And the smallest criticism so damning, Josephine thought, remembering Vera's face on the day that George had humiliated her in front of everyone. "But Vera wanted to be honest, didn't she? You fought with her about it."

"Yes, that's right. How did you know?"

"I heard you discussing it, although I didn't know what you were talking about at the time. In fact, I couldn't have been more wrong."

"In the end, I had to tell Vera the truth about her birth and the adoption. It was the only way I could persuade her that if she wanted any part in George's life, she could never reveal who she was."

"That must have been a difficult decision to make."

"Not really. I was desperate. I could see how much Vera had come to value her relationship with George, even though it was far from the one she really wanted, but my motives were selfish too. George would never have forgiven me for betraying her trust by letting Vera stay in our lives once I knew the truth, and I knew I'd end up losing them both. Vera coming back like that was a second chance for me, and I loved her as if she were my own. I was a substitute at first for the mother she couldn't have, but I was happy to settle for that, and it grew into something more, especially after she and Peter got married. I can't tell you what a comfort that is to me now, Josephine. Vera's like George in so many ways—determined and hardworking and brave, even if she goes about it in a quieter way than her mother did."

"Does Peter know?" Josephine asked, struck by the irony of the marriage when he had always hated George so much.

"Yes. To my shame, I didn't want Vera to tell him, in case he used it against George, but she was right to insist on it, and I should have had more faith in him. I think he understood George better after that, even if he could never bring himself to like her." Harriet looked earnestly at Josephine. "You're the only other person who knows, though. Can I rely on you not to tell anyone? It wasn't what you came here to find out, and it's got nothing to do with Dorothy's death. Well, nothing except . . ."

She tailed off, preoccupied by whatever had occurred to her, and Josephine took the risk of pushing her. "Except what?"

"Except that the night of Dorothy's death reminded me of the night that her father's friend decided to teach George what women really wanted. Her rage was the same each time, and each time it stemmed from fear."

Fear for the college's future, Josephine wondered, or fear for her own? For as long as she had known her, Harriet had always despised prevarication and dissembling of any kind, and she decided not to insult her now by beating about the bush. "Did George kill Dorothy?" she asked gently. "Is that why she was so frightened?"

Her directness was rewarded. "Yes, she killed her." Harriet took a folded sheet of notepaper out of her pocket and handed it to Josephine. "This is all she left behind, after everything we went through. It's funny, but that's what hurts me most, far more than what she actually did. I can't reconcile it with the woman I loved. It's the only time she's ever disappointed me."

Josephine read through the suicide note, a simple confession to Dorothy's murder and a request for Harriet's forgiveness. Its brevity and matter-of-factness surprised Josephine too. She would have expected George's final letter to Harriet to have said more about their love and all it had meant to her, to offer some sort of comfort, no matter how false, but perhaps she had been so wracked with guilt by then that she could think only of one thing. "Did you suspect anything at the time?"

"Yes, but we never talked about it. I wanted George to tell me, if only to share the burden with her, but she cut me off every time I tried to raise the subject. I know she was trying not to implicate me in what she'd done, but I was already implicated." Josephine was about to ask how, but Harriet answered the question without prompting. "We both said things we didn't mean before it happened. I was furious with Dorothy for complaining about something that was none of her business and threatening everything we'd worked so hard for, and I made no secret of what I'd like to do to her, given the chance. I encouraged George to kill her, even though I didn't mean to. It's as much my fault as hers, and I suppose that's why I wasn't brave enough to force the subject. If

George never actually said the words, I could almost convince myself I didn't know."

In her heart, Josephine had found it hard to believe that the conversation Jeannie had overheard was as damning as it seemed; from what she remembered of that night, George had seemed as shocked and upset as she was, but there was no misconstruing the note in her hand, and she realized now how naive and foolish she must have been. "So you never believed it was an accident?" she asked, torn between sadness for Harriet's loss and anger at her own gullibility.

"Not with the way George was behaving. She was so on edge, so frightened. Then it all started to add up. The missing window pole—she found that very easily. And the temperature in the greenhouse—you must have noticed how hot it was?"

"Yes. Hot enough to make Dorothy take her oilskin off."

"Leaving her unprotected—exactly. I saw George turn the heating down while we were deciding what to do, and there was something in the way she did it—surreptitiously, guiltily. That chilled me at the time, you know. I could believe she'd lash out in a moment of panic or anger, but to have planned it all like that . . ." She took the letter from Josephine's hand. "And you can't argue with this."

"No, I suppose not." Still Josephine hesitated, unconvinced in spite of the evidence that someone as intelligent and practical as George would risk everything when the damage was done. "It just seems so senseless," she objected. "The tales had already been told. Gertrude Ingham already knew. Why would George kill Dorothy when there was nothing left to salvage?"

"Anger, revenge, desperation—who knows?" Harriet seemed irritated by her arguments. "I appreciate what you're doing, Josephine, and it's kind of you, but I've had years to try to come to terms with what I know in my heart George did—for our future, for our love. The shame of our summons to Moira House—it was all starting again, just like it did when we first fell in love and her family set out to make our lives hell. You were in Lewes that day at the market, and you saw what those women did to the gardens. They hated us." She gave a hollow laugh, as far from joy as was possible. "No doubt it would comfort them to know that we lost everything in the end."

Josephine watched her staring down toward the sea, and wondered how often she had contemplated leaving the world as George had done. The strength that it must have taken to live when so much had been lost was remarkable. "Not quite everything," she said. "You've got another family now. I know it's not the same, but it must count for something."

"It counts for everything, but even that plays on my conscience. I know my relationship with Vera is a betrayal of everything I had with George, and sometimes it feels as if I've stolen all the joy that should have been hers."

"Does Vera know what her mother did?"

"Yes. She found the note, although I'll make sure she denies it if this all comes out. *When* it comes out. Now the newspapers are involved, it's only a matter of time before someone puts two and two together, and then there'll be no peace." Harriet shivered and stood up, and they began to retrace their footsteps across the headland. "I sat with George for hours in the chapel of rest, and all I could think of was how perfect her hands were—no soil under the fingernails, no blisters from a spade or cuts from a bramble. They didn't really look like her hands at all, and I'd never noticed that before. It was a funny sort of comfort, but it told me she'd done the right thing, in spite of everything else. And I'm pleased that she doesn't have to go through this. Her memory will be disgraced, and no one will ever believe I didn't know, but at least she doesn't have to live with the fear."

"It might not come to that," Josephine said without conviction.

"It *must* come to that." Harriet stopped walking and surprised Josephine by handing back George's suicide note. "You should have this. You came here to get to the bottom of what happened, and now you know. It's not fair that other people should be living under suspicion, and I trust you to do the right thing with it."

"But it's the last letter you have from George."

"And it brings me only sadness. I've kept it to myself for as long as I could, but I knew from the moment Vera showed me the newspaper that we were living on borrowed time. The lies have gone on for long enough, Josephine. I want this to be over. You said in your letter that you'd already been to see Betty, so perhaps you'll do me the favor of explaining everything to her. I should do it myself, but I'm afraid I can't face her. Tell her what happened to her sister. Give her some sort of peace. George is out of her reach now."

"But you're not." Josephine forced Harriet to look at her. "Surely you know what will happen if this letter goes anywhere near Betty or Charity? It's not only George who will pay. They'll find a way to incriminate you too."

"So what are you suggesting?"

Josephine could hear in her voice that Harriet was daring to hope, and she took time to consider what she was about to say in case she might live to regret it. To her left, rival flocks of jackdaws and herring gulls struggled for mastery of the cliffs, and the shifting blur of black and white seemed to underline her moral dilemma. "If they suspect you of being involved, they could hang you. At the very least, they'll send you to prison."

"I've had my life . . ."

"But I can't take any part in ending it." She held the letter out, insisting that Harriet accept it. "Nothing will bring Dorothy back, but George has paid with her life, and you've suffered enough. If your conscience tells you to bring it all out into the open, then that's what you must do, but as far as I'm concerned, we haven't had this conversation."

"What about Betty?"

"Perhaps I'm only trying to justify what I would have done anyway, but part of this is for her."

"I don't understand."

"It was Betty who made the call to Moira House all those years ago," Josephine explained. "She started this, and she's already wracked with guilt about it. Finding out beyond the shadow of a doubt that she was the cause of her sister's death won't give her the peace you want to offer—just the opposite. It's kinder to leave things as they are, and without a confession, no one can prove anything to the contrary. Charity will give up eventually and find some other lives to play with."

Harriet read through the letter one last time and seemed to come to a decision. Before Josephine could stop her, she tore the page into tiny pieces and scattered them to the wind. "That was the proof of your innocence," Josephine objected. "What will you do now if someone *does* accuse you of being more involved than you were?"

"Take my chances with George, like I always have. Everything was an adventure when we were together—that's what I meant when I told you it was worth it." She looked at Josephine, and already some of the burden seemed to have lifted. "Did you and Jeannie last beyond that summer?" she asked. "I've often wondered."

"No, we didn't."

"I thought not. George and I played our part in destroying that too. Not many people would have followed their hearts after living through that."

"*You* didn't destroy it. I was perfectly capable of doing that myself. You gave me some good advice, and I only wish that I'd worked harder at taking it."

"But are you happy with someone now?"

"Yes, very."

"I'm glad." They began the descent to the tiny hamlet at Birling Gap, and Josephine said, "You already suspected that Dorothy wasn't your accuser, didn't you? That's why you asked me what I thought of her."

"It certainly wasn't in character, and I began to wonder about that," Harriet admitted. "I just thank God that George never guessed. It would have destroyed her to know that the wrong girl had died."

The coldness of the phrase unsettled Josephine. For a moment she couldn't help but consider Harriet's strength and how it had been she, not George, who had seemed so determined to keep the college going in spite of everything, almost as if she was making sure that Dorothy hadn't died in vain; she was still thinking about it when they reached the foot of the hill. "Charity and Betty seem to have had a knack for meddling in things that were none of their business," she said. "Do you think they knew about Vera and George?"

There was a brief hesitation, so brief that she might have imagined it, then Harriet turned and looked her squarely in the eye. "I really don't see how they could have found that out, do you?"

An unguarded conversation like the one she had overheard would have been enough, but there was little point in further speculation, or in worrying Harriet needlessly about things that might or might not emerge in the press. They finished the rest of the walk in silence. "Are you heading back to London tonight?" Harriet asked as they reached the hotel.

"Yes."

"Then I'd better let you go." She hugged Josephine like an old friend, just as she had done the last time they parted. "I can never thank you enough, but please know how grateful I am. Will you stay in touch?"

"Yes, of course. I'd like that."

"So would I."

They said goodbye and Josephine watched her go, wondering how she was going to explain the choices she had made to Marta. Just for a moment, she considered lying about what Harriet had told her, but if she had learned one thing over the last few weeks, it was to be honest from the start. She walked over to the hotel and found Marta in the corner of the lounge.

"Are you all right?" Marta asked, noticing her anxious face.

"Yes, I think so, although I have no idea if I've done the right thing."

"Do you know who killed Dorothy?"

Josephine nodded and sat down. "It was George. She committed suicide three years ago, and she left a confession behind. Harriet showed it to me."

"And you've promised not to tell anybody because she's suffered enough."

"How do you know that?"

Marta smiled. "Just a lucky guess. Come here." She held Josephine tightly and kissed her hair. "You did the right thing, but now it's over. Let's go home."

1948

"Women who live lonely lives do insane things."
—Josephine Tey, *The Franchise Affair*

CHAPTER 1

"The new issue's just arrived, Miss Lomax."

"Thank you, Barbara."

Charity turned away from the window and stubbed out her cigarette in an already overflowing ashtray, then picked up the magazine that her secretary had placed on her desk. There was a time when it would have filled her with a sense of pride—the gradual fashioning of order from chaos as features took shape and photographs were selected, all under her guidance—but those days were long gone. Now, each working week bored her a little more than the last.

This month's cover had the usual skillful blend of elegance and mystery—a picture of perfection that would have women scrambling for the newsstand shelves, yet sufficiently grounded in reality to convince them that the life was theirs if they wanted it. The model wore a gray belted dress, chic and of the moment, with a nipped-in waist and bold shoulders, but it was the accessories and scene setting that gave the image its narrative: the white, elbow-length gloves and string of pearls that promised purity and status; the scarlet buttonhole that emphasized bright red lips and hinted at danger; a bird cage standing next to an open window, conflicting symbols of the freedom and constraints that most of the magazine's readers spent their lives trying to navigate. To her surprise, Charity found the overall effect faintly unsettling, partly because women on her covers now were invariably much younger than she was. At one time, she might have been mistaken for a model herself, but these days—a few months shy of her fiftieth birthday—she stood among the ranks of those looking back at their lives with a bewildering muddle of panic and emptiness.

There was more to it than that, though. The model was poised and confident, as models always were, but she radiated a determination that reminded Charity of Betty when she had last seen her— just before she moved to Hollywood at the height of the war, with bombs falling on London and no end to the conflict in sight. She had never called or written, in spite of how close they once were, and Charity missed the only true friendship that she had ever known—a casualty not of distance or Betty's success, but of the disappointment and recriminations that had followed their attempts to resurrect the past. The rift had been sudden and unequivocal, and the last time Betty had returned to England to promote a film, Charity was the only influential journalist not to be granted an audience. She looked again at the cover girl with the expression that was so like her friend's, and acknowledged what troubled her: the magazine reminded her of her biggest professional failure. There had been plenty of personal failures—divorce and the grief of her father's death, a hasty remarriage, then divorce again—but only on a handful of occasions had she failed to get the story she wanted, and this one rankled more than most. In her heart, she knew that one or both of those women were guilty of murder, but she had never been able to prove it.

She tossed the magazine to one side and went out for lunch, telling Barbara, on a whim, to cancel her afternoon appointments. Even now, five years on, the square outside her office felt exposed and incomplete from the removal of its iron railings for the war effort. It was such an insignificant part of the city's disfigurement compared to the fallen masonry and open skies, but it was the one that Charity saw most often, and these small, everyday reminders of how the world had changed were somehow more affecting.

The spring day was irresistible, with fresh, powder-blue skies and a generous sun, and instead of choosing one of her usual restaurants, she struck out down Piccadilly, heading for the park. Once inside its gates, she slowed her pace, trying to remember the last time she had wandered aimlessly like this, with nowhere to be and no one demanding her time. Perhaps it was the frustrations that the day had triggered, perhaps simply a feeling that she had achieved all she could in her current position, but Charity suddenly longed to do something different with her life—now, before it was too late. Lost in her thoughts, she was aware of someone coming up behind her, and she moved to the side of the path to allow the person to pass, but the footsteps slowed before they reached her, and she heard a woman calling her name. Surprised, she turned to see who it was, then recoiled instinctively as something was thrown in her face. For a few precious seconds she thought it was water, but then she smelt the pungent odor of bleach, and her skin began to burn with unimaginable pain. She opened her mouth to scream, but another shower of liquid hit her and it was impossible even to beg for mercy as she felt her throat begin to swell and constrict. The poison blinded her, and in her panic she put her hands to her face, desperate to wipe it away, but the gesture only served to spread the pain, as if the chemical were a living thing, crawling all over her body and eating away at her skin with its insidious, deadly advance. Charity felt her chest tighten. She could only breathe in short, desperate gasps, but she was aware of another face close to hers and a woman's voice, threatening and vaguely familiar. "That was for George. Now you know what poison feels like."

In a second, her attacker was gone. She heard screams breaking out around her as people began to realize what had happened. Footsteps approached from all directions, running to her aid, but it was already far too late. Charity was unconscious long before they reached her.

CHAPTER 2

Josephine hardly ever accepted invitations to literary parties, disliking small talk and poor sherry in equal measure, but it was virtually impossible to find an excuse when the book being launched was her own. Her publisher wanted to make a fuss of *The Franchise Affair*, building on the success of her previous effort, and it would have been ungracious to refuse, so she gritted her teeth and took solace in the quality of the wine. She looked round the elegant rooms in Bedford Square, where the offices of Peter Davies were based, and noticed how few of the people present she actually knew; most of them were critics or booksellers, but there was a smattering of other writers and one or two theater friends from her personal guest list, and already several of them were happily clutching a copy of the book. The cover was a clever design incorporating key features from the story—the driveway at the house called the Franchise; a watch which provided an important clue—and seeing the book finished and out in the world gave her the same feeling of pride and excitement that she had experienced when the name "Gordon Daviot' first went up in lights above the New Theatre. She missed the spirit of common endeavor that was peculiar to the stage, but the more crime fiction she wrote, the more she enjoyed its combination of discipline and subversion—even if she did feel an increasing sense of disloyalty to her stage pseudonym, like turning her back on a faithful lover.

She saw Harriet across the room and waved. The two of them had written to each other now and again over the years and met on one or two occasions, but still Josephine was touched that she had bothered to make the trip to London. She pushed her way through the crowd, waylaid periodically by congratulations from one stranger or another, and Harriet gave her a hug. "A story about two women who are victims of an amazing accusation?" she said, reading from the book jacket. "Are you sure you got the idea from a notorious eighteenth-century cause célèbre?"

She raised an eyebrow, and Josephine was struck by how much better she looked each time they met—younger, if that were possible, and certainly more content, as if the years that had been dogged by grief and suspicion were finally beginning to fade. "Yes, I'm sure—although I won't deny that some of the things I've put my characters through didn't happen a little more recently and a lot closer to home."

"And are your women innocent or guilty, I wonder? Don't tell me. I'm looking forward to reading it." She accepted a drink from a passing waiter and glanced round the room. "This is quite a crowd. I'm so pleased for you, Josephine, but don't let me monopolize you when you must have guests to speak to. I just wanted to come and wish you well."

"I'm glad you did, and don't rush off. I have no idea who most of these people are, and I was just wondering what on earth we might find to say to each other." They talked for a few minutes about family and work, and Josephine was pleased to hear that Peter had just become a grandfather for the second time. "And are *you* more settled now?" she asked. Several of Harriet's letters had talked of how homesick she was for the countryside she loved. When war broke out and the threat of invasion loomed, the coastline at Birling Gap had been taken over by the Canadian Artillery, and Peter and Vera were forced to move inland. Harriet went with them, eventually taking a cottage in Lewes, which she had struggled to feel at home in. "I thought you might move back to one of the villages after the war."

"To be honest, I couldn't face the upheaval, and now I'm older, it suits me to live in the town. It took me a while to get used to a smaller house and so little garden, but the war spoilt things forever. You must have experienced that."

"Yes, although we were luckier than most at home."

"I can never look at that headland now without remembering the barbed wire. I'll always associate it with our conversation, though. That was a new start for me, Josephine, and I'm still eternally grateful. I don't want to go back." She squeezed Josephine's hand in thanks. "It looks like you're needed. You can sign this for me later."

Josephine turned to see her publisher beckoning to her from across the room. "Time for the speeches," she said without enthusiasm. "Don't go away, though. Mine, at least, will be very short."

Peter Davies was chairman of the firm that had now handled two of her novels, and Josephine had come to like and respect a man whose life story was as fascinating as most of the books he published. Cousin to the du Mauriers, he was also one of the boys befriended and adopted by J. M. Barrie, and had spent most of his life trying to shake off the notoriety of being the original Peter Pan. Although she couldn't claim to know Davies well, she appreciated his humor and was intrigued by the darker streak that surfaced occasionally in his conversation, and his loyalty to her books had been unwavering. "Ladies and gentlemen," he said, calling the room to attention, "thank you for joining us today to celebrate the publication of a very special book. *The Franchise Affair* is the fourth detective novel that Josephine has written and the second that we have had the privilege of publishing. Readers of its predecessor, *Miss Pym Disposes*, will know not to expect an orthodox detective tale from this most unorthodox of writers, and I can assure you that *The Franchise Affair* is as disturbing and exciting a novel as any you are likely to read this year." There was a murmur of expectation from the audience, and Davies paused to savor it. "The book makes a fascinating modern story out of an eighteenth-century case, popularly known as the Canning mystery, which remains unsolved to this day. With all the skill that we have come to expect from her, Josephine has us doubting in turn the victim and the victimized. One minute her central characters seem capable of almost anything; the next we are firmly on their side as they battle the poisonous atmosphere of small-town gossip—something on which I suspect the book's author has very strong opinions." A ripple of laughter ran round the room, and Josephine smiled in acknowledgment. "What is certain, though, is that *The Franchise Affair* could only be the work of one person, and it gives me great pleasure to call on her now to tell you a little more about this remarkable book."

Josephine thanked him and did as he'd asked, outlining the details of the book's inspiration and expanding on why she had become so interested in the story of a young servant girl whose month-long disappearance became the basis of one of the most notorious criminal cases of the eighteenth century. She was about to bring the speech to a close when she caught Harriet's eye, and something in her wanted to acknowledge what had really been most in her mind during the writing of the book. "I once made the mistake of describing my crime novels to a friend as "yearly knitting,'" she added, "and I've since learned never to say something to an actor if you don't want it repeated word for word every night and twice on a Saturday." She waited as the audience laughed again. "By knitting, I simply meant that discipline and structure are important, but what's more important still is to write about what interests you and what troubles you. This book is about what happens when you're judged for who you are as much as by what you do. It's about prejudice and hatred, and it's about what happens when people take the law into their own hands. I witnessed that myself once when I was very young, and it's always stayed with me; more recently, we've all seen it at work on a terrifying scale. Nothing is ever quite as straightforward as it seems, and sometimes justice and the law are very different things, but we all know what *injustice* is when we see it, and ultimately *The Franchise Affair* is about having the courage to stand up to it."

During the applause, she noticed that Archie had arrived, slipping effortlessly into the party atmosphere despite having come straight from Scotland Yard. "Sometimes justice and the law are very different things?" he repeated wryly. "I can't think what gave you that idea."

"I rather hoped you'd missed that part. Please don't take it personally."

"After the day I've had, I'm far more likely to be agreeing with you. A lot of people will be talking about justice and the law when they understand the full implications of what's going through Parliament at the moment." The Commons had recently passed an amendment to the criminal justice bill to suspend capital punishment for five years, and Josephine knew how torn Archie was on the subject. "Sorry I'm so late," he said. "Has it gone well?"

"As well as these things ever go, but I'm looking forward to dinner. You're still giving me an excuse to leave early, I hope?"

"Of course. The table's booked for seven thirty." He took her to one side, away from the crush. "I don't mean to spoil the evening, but I think you'll want to hear this. The woman who once caused you all that trouble—what was her name?"

"Which one? There have been so many."

He smiled. "The journalist who was hounding the women in Sussex."

"Ah. Charity Lomax."

"Yes, I thought so. Keep this to yourself for now, but she was attacked this afternoon. Someone threw bleach in her face in Green Park. The chaps on the case think she must have been followed from her offices when she went out for lunch."

Josephine stared at him in horror. "How serious is it?"

"Very. She's still alive, but only just—and if she does pull through, I'm really not sure what sort of life it will be. They've got her on an iron lung at the moment—the bleach got to her throat and chest, and her facial injuries are too horrific to contemplate. Whoever did it really meant business."

"So they haven't caught anyone?"

"Not yet."

"And they don't know why it happened?"

Archie shook his head. "Her secretary said that Miss Lomax had made herself very unpopular over the years, but I don't know a successful journalist who hasn't, and they're not all subjected to this." He looked round for a waiter. "I'm going to get a drink. Would you like one?"

She handed him her empty glass. "Yes, please. I think I need it."

His place next to her was soon taken by a succession of well-wishers. Josephine did her best to concentrate on their questions, but *The Franchise Affair* had trouble competing for her attention with the real-life mystery she had just been told about, and she was pleased when Harriet sought her out again. "I thought I'd better get this signed before I leave," she said, passing Josephine her book. "Whatever's wrong? You look as if you've had a terrible shock."

"I have." She hesitated, remembering Archie's request for discretion, but the incident was bound to be in the evening paper, and she was interested in Harriet's reaction. No matter how hard she tried to put it to one side, the coincidence of her friend being in London on the day that Charity was assaulted bothered Josephine, and she desperately wanted to put her own mind at rest. "It's Charity Lomax."

"Good God, she's not here is she? I thought all that was over and done with."

To Josephine's relief, there was nothing forced or artificial about the response. "No, she's not here," she said, more relaxed now. "I've just heard that someone threw bleach in her face at lunchtime, while she was out walking. She's in hospital, fighting for her life."

Harriet went so pale that Josephine thought she was about to faint. She put a steadying hand on her arm, but Harriet shook it off. "I'm sorry, but I'm late for my train." She turned and left the room, without another word, and Josephine watched her go, debating whether she should follow.

"Is everything all right?" Archie asked, handing her a glass of champagne.

"Yes, I think so, but I'm still trying to take in what happened to Charity. I can't help wondering if it had anything to do with her articles about Charleston and Dorothy's death."

"But that was years ago. I imagine this is connected to something much more recent. You never did get to the bottom of what really happened there, though, did you?"

"No, I didn't." Josephine hated lying to Archie, but she was loathe to compromise him where his job was concerned, or to risk sharing a confidence that he would feel obliged to betray. Now, remembering the fear in Harriet's face, she found herself wondering if her denial was actually a lie after all.

CHAPTER 3

The journey to Victoria seemed interminable, and when the doors of the underground train finally opened, Harriet felt as though she had been set free from a prison of her own making. She pushed her way through the rush-hour crowds to platform nineteen, where she had arranged to meet Vera by the entrance to the station's tiny news cinema, all the time desperately hoping that she was wrong—but even from a distance she could tell that her worst fears were justified. The girl—strange how she always thought of Vera as a girl, even though she was fifty now, with grandchildren of her own—was pacing up and down by the staircase that linked the concourse to the small first-floor auditorium; she was ashen-faced and apparently oblivious to anything but her own tortured thoughts, and, when she eventually lifted her head in response to her name, Harriet could see that she had been crying. "Vera, what have you done?" she said, taking her by the shoulders and resisting the urge to shake her like a child. "What in heaven's name have you done?"

At first, Vera seemed bewildered by the fact that Harriet knew anything at all, but her confusion was soon replaced by relief at not having to make a confession, which she had obviously been dreading. "I'm sorry," she said. "I'm so sorry. I don't know what came over me." She clung to Harriet as if her life depended on it, and any last-minute hopes of a misunderstanding vanished as Harriet saw the red weals on her arm where her skin had been splashed by bleach. Anger and panic and love overwhelmed her, and she pulled the sleeve of Vera's cardigan down over her wrist to hide the injury, torn between keeping her safe and wanting to punish her. "How could you be so stupid?" she demanded as she held her close. "It was over, Vera. George made that possible for both of us—don't you understand? If you've ruined that by hurting Charity, her sacrifice will mean nothing."

"But the bitch deserved it. You don't know what she did. What her father did . . ."

"What?" Harriet released her, suddenly aware that people were beginning to throw curious glances their way. "I have no idea what you're talking about, but I don't want you to say another word about this until we're home. Do you understand me?" Vera nodded. "Not another word."

They boarded the six-thirty train to Lewes in silence. It was a beautiful evening, but the familiar return to the Downs from the city gave Harriet none of its customary pleasure, and the fading of the suburbs into open countryside simply brought closer the moment when she would have to face this latest, unexpected crisis. She studied Vera's face, with all its competing emotions, as they traveled, and noticed that each mile of the journey seemed to quell the fear a little more and foster defiance in its place, paving the way for an anger that flared whenever the family was threatened. They waited for a taxi at Lewes Station, and Harriet prayed that the driver would be a stranger to them; the last thing she trusted herself with at the moment was small talk. "Is Peter at home?" she asked, her voice unnaturally tight. Suddenly she didn't want Vera under her roof; whatever conversation they were about to have, and no matter how devastated it left them, Harriet needed to be able to get away to think.

"No, he's out with Tom. He won't be back until later."

"Good. We'll talk there."

She paid the driver at the door and followed Vera into the house. It was unnaturally quiet, as if it too were waiting for an explanation, but the stillness seemed to trigger the storm that had been building during the journey, and Vera rounded on Harriet almost as soon as the front door was closed. "I won't apologize for hurting that bitch," she said, no longer on the defensive. "My mother wouldn't be dead if it weren't for her. She hated both of you—you know she did. She set out to destroy everything you'd worked for simply because she despised what you stood for, and you dared to stand up to her. *She* should have been the one who died all those years ago, not Dorothy. All I was doing was putting things right."

Harriet stared at her, frightened by her fury and wondering if she had actually gone insane. "How can this be putting things right?" she asked. "The violence has to stop, Vera. You can't fight hatred with more of the same. Think about what you've done—if they find out it was you and everything comes out, George's memory will be worth nothing. She'll have *died* for nothing, not to mention the danger you've put yourself in."

"I don't care about that."

"Well, you should care. You're a mother yourself now, for God's sake, and *your* children were brought into the world with *love*. You've had the chances that George never had, and yet you risk it all—Peter, your family, me. How could you be so selfish?"

"What about the chances *I* never had? The chance to get to know my mother. The chance that she might actually tell me she loved me."

All the guilt that Harriet had tried to suppress over the years surfaced with a force that took her completely by surprise. This was her fault, she saw that now. The halfway house that she had offered Vera by bringing her into their home as an outsider had proved more destructive in the end than turning her out into the cold; at least that would have been honest. "I'm so sorry," she said. "I know how much it hurt you, but that's no excuse for what you did today. None of that was Charity's fault."

"But it *was* her father's."

"What?"

"Charity's father, William Lomax. He's the one who raped George. He was a friend of the family. It was his fault that my mother hated me."

Harriet looked at her, trying to understand her reasoning. "No, Vera. Listen to me . . ."

"It must be him. I've worked it all out. Charity was always going on about how her father didn't want her at the college and how he was going to come and take her away. He wrote to you about that, didn't he?"

"Yes, but—"

"That's obviously why he hated you both and why he wanted to get her out of there—he was worried she might find out what he'd done. It all makes sense, but I didn't understand at the time— not until he died, and there were articles about him in the papers. I've got them here somewhere. Wait a minute, and I'll show them to you." She went through to the kitchen and took a box file out of one of the cupboards, and Harriet watched her as she searched through a pile of news clippings and other papers. "The Lomax family lived in Oxfordshire, which made me wonder, but then I found out from his obituary that he was in the navy, so I looked him up, and he served with George's father."

"Vera, please—stop it." Harriet went across to her and gently took her hands. "George told me who raped her. It was a man called Roger Bentinck. She only ever brought herself to say his name once, but I'll never forget it. How could I? He hurt the woman I loved."

"No, that can't be right." Vera looked up from the papers, and Harriet saw her own desperation staring back at her. "I tracked it all down to make sure. He *must* be the one." The horror of her mistake made her more vehement than ever, and she turned on Harriet. "Don't lie to me."

"I'm not lying."

"Stop saying that, and stop pitying me. That's all you do—all you've ever done." Harriet opened her mouth to object, but she knew there was a grain of truth in Vera's claim. "Have you ever stopped for a moment to wonder what it's like to be me? How it must feel to know that your mother hated you so much that she killed herself rather than face the truth?"

"That's not why she did it."

"All that time at the college you let people make fun of me, let them think I had some sort of crush on George, when you knew perfectly well that I had a right to her love. By the time you'd finished, I hated myself as much as she did."

"George didn't hate you, Vera. She didn't know who you were, so why would you think—"

"But she *did* know."

She screamed the words, and Harriet's heart went cold. "What do you mean?"

"George knew exactly who I was. I told her the day she died. I was reading to her in the garden, and she asked why I'd always been so kind to her. I told her I loved her, and she misunderstood at first, so I had to tell her everything. I'll never forget her reaction."

Vera's face clouded over, and Harriet tried to remember a time when she had ever seen someone look so sad. "What was it?"

"Disbelief. Disgust. I tried to make it right, but she sent me away. I went back a few hours later to try again to make my peace with her, but by then it was too late." Vera began searching through the newspapers again, as if only that could distract her from her memories. Eventually she found the obituary she was looking for, and Harriet took it from her, wondering how she could have missed this obsessive streak in someone she loved. Why hadn't she spotted it and stamped it out before it could cause such heartache? "This proves nothing," she said, trying to keep her voice even. "Your father's name was Roger Bentinck, and he had nothing to do with Charity Lomax or her family. Charity hated George and me because she was prejudiced and spoilt and ambitious. She hated us because that's what some people do—they hate, and they try to destroy. But she didn't succeed—not until now, anyway. She didn't deserve what you've done to her." Vera's lack of remorse angered Harriet, and she took her by the shoulders and forced her to pay attention. "What if Charity dies—have you thought about that? They'll come for us again, and this time they'll work it out—all of it. Josephine already thinks it was me—I could see it in her face. She's protected me once, but she won't do it again, and this time she'll give George away too. It's you who's destroyed everything, not Charity." She sat down, defeated by the impossibility of her situation, and suddenly only one thing mattered. "Did you tell George that I knew who you were?"

Vera hesitated, then nodded. "She asked me. I had to tell her."

So that was what George couldn't live with: not her depression or her guilt over Dorothy's murder, and not the reminder of the worst night of her life, but the knowledge that her lover had betrayed her. Harriet had never been able to bear the idea of George dying alone, but only now did she realize how truly isolated she must have felt, stripped of the one thing she believed in and trusted: their loyalty to each other above everything else. "Get out," she shouted, no longer trusting herself to be in the same room as Vera. "Get out of my sight. I can't even bear to look at you."

Vera ran upstairs and Harriet heard her sobbing in the room above. She pulled the box file toward her and started to sift through it, finding things that went back much earlier than the clippings on Charity's father. There were press announcements on anything to do with George—the founding of the college, her victories in various gardening shows, even the slightest mention of her name—and she realized that Vera's quest to know her mother had begun long before she came to Charleston. There were drawings of George on pages torn from Peter's sketchbooks, done in the early days when Vera had asked him to teach her, and a bundle of photographs that Harriet had taken during the college years and thought were lost. She flicked through them now, noticing for the first time how often Vera appeared next to George, how desperately she had tried to be like her in the way she dressed, in the stances she took, and the way she held a spade, as if the earth were an enemy to be conquered.

The collection was a tinderbox of suppressed love and desperation, and it had only been a matter of time before it forced its way out into the open. Harriet's anger disappeared in an instant, leaving guilt and regret in its place, and she was about to go upstairs to make her peace when she saw something in George's handwriting. She opened the folded page, wondering why George had written to Vera, then saw that the letter was actually addressed to her. A single glance was enough to tell her that she had never seen it before, and she read on in disbelief, bewildered to think that Vera could have kept something so important hidden from her.

My darling Harry,

It breaks my heart to leave you, but I've always known that this moment might come, and so—in your heart—have you. Forgive me for doing this alone when we've faced so much together, but I can't go on now, knowing what I know, knowing that your love for me has driven you to such extremes over the years. You shouldn't have to live in fear and deceit, and it comforts me to know that some good will have come of my death if I can finally free you of those shadows. At least by leaving the world now, while I'm still able to decide for myself, I can protect you like I've always wanted to, and my peace comes from knowing at last that you'll be safe after I'm gone.

We've circled round the truth of that terrible night, and I'm sorry for lacking the courage to let you say the words that might have eased your conscience, but I couldn't bear to hear them. You killed a girl for me, and for our love, and I've always blamed myself for that; they were my dreams that you were trying to salvage, as you once reminded me. You've carried that burden so bravely all these years, but now it's my turn. We've spent the last part of our lives looking continually over our shoulders, waiting for our past to catch up with us, living in fear of the day we would be asked to prove our innocence. I know you would never let me lie for you while you had breath in your body to deny it, so I'm leaving you no choice, and I gladly give my life to save yours. Destroy this letter and give the confession you find with it to the police. Don't worry about my memory or my name. The only person who matters knows the truth.

For too long I've been helpless and dependent on your strength, and you know that was more than I could bear when we have always been equals, always lived as one. Our love has meant the world to me from the moment you came into my life. You have brought me joy, passion and understanding, comfort at the darkest times, and courage when I needed it most. And we will be together again, Harry, even though you doubt that now. A love like ours can survive anything.

George

Harriet read the letter again, taking in the full implications of George's last words: that she had been innocent of Dorothy's murder; that they had each wrongly believed the other to be guilty; that someone else must be to blame—and that even at the end, after her betrayal over Vera, George had still loved Harriet enough to die for her. She put her head in her hands and wept for her lover, knowing that—in spite of George's faith, a faith which she didn't share—there would never be a chance to correct all the misunderstandings between them, to prove herself worthy of what George had done. Eventually, when there were no tears left, she lifted her head and saw Vera standing quietly at the kitchen door. "You found this with George's body?" she asked, just to be sure. "There were two notes?"

"Yes."

"Why did you keep it from me?"

"I didn't want you to know that George thought you were capable of murder."

"There are far worse things. I thought George had killed Dorothy. I thought she was a coward. I thought our love wasn't even worth a mention on the day she left this world. This would have made all the difference."

She held the letter up, amazed by how calm she suddenly felt, and Vera seemed to notice the change in her. "I'm sorry," she insisted. "I didn't know what to do, and I was so upset when I found her. The only thing that seemed right was to make sure that her final wish was carried' out. She wanted that destroyed and the other one left in its place."

"I know what she wanted. And yet you didn't destroy it. You kept it. Why, Vera? Why would you keep something that wrongly incriminated me for murder? To protect your mother's name if you needed to? Or was it a safeguard in case someone discovered the truth?"

"What do you mean?"

"You killed Dorothy, didn't you?" Until she said it, she hadn't actually believed it to be true, but once the words were out in the open, she wondered how she could have failed to see it before. "George obviously didn't, and I know it wasn't me, so who else could it have been?" Vera had been so calm and collected that night, she remembered now. She had lied to the police without turning a hair, played up the ill feeling between the Norwood sisters, and— most significantly of all—she had been at the hub of all the comings and goings, with the knowledge and the opportunity to set up the death in the greenhouse and cover her tracks. Even so, to the last second Harriet hoped that she was wrong; she longed for Vera to deny it or simply to lie—anything to save her from the truth and all the dilemmas which that would bring—but she didn't.

"I did it for you and George," she said, so matter-of-factly that she might have been talking about fetching a pint of milk. "I heard you talking in the kitchen when you still believed that Dorothy was causing all the trouble. You said you wanted to stop her from destroying everything, and I knew that if the college failed, I'd have to leave you. I did it to save our family, and I thought one day I'd be able to explain that to George. I thought it might make her love me."

Her voice broke with the final admission, and she threw her

arms around Harriet, but Harriet couldn't bring herself to return the embrace or offer comfort of any sort. She stood stock-still with her hands by her sides, waiting for the moment to pass, and eventually Vera gave up hope and moved away. "I have to go," Harriet said.

"But you can't leave me like this. We have to talk. You're the only one who understands."

"I can't be near you at the moment. Peter will be home soon."

"What are you going to do?"

The fear in her voice was obvious, but Harriet ignored the question. "No one has a *right* to be loved, Vera—not by birth or by any other act of chance. Love has to be earned, just like trust, and I think we've both fallen short on that score, don't you?"

CHAPTER 4

Josephine went to Suffolk for a few days after the obligations to her book were fulfilled, and she was grateful for the peace that greeted her there while she waited for Marta to return from an assignment in Wales. It was hard to believe that she had owned Larkspur Cottage for more than a decade now, and it grew more important each year—a place where she could be herself, neither Josephine Tey nor Gordon Daviot, with all the expectations that each name conjured, someone who answered to no one and who loved as she pleased. The restrictions on travel during the war had made it difficult for her to come south as often as she would have liked, but she had made up for it since, and Marta had begun to spend more time here too, even when Josephine couldn't join her. Her presence showed in the garden, in the beautifully planted borders and profusion of flowers that surprised and delighted Josephine with each new season. It wasn't quite the life together that she had once envied in Harriet and George, but it was more than she had ever dared to hope for, and she cherished it.

The typical April day was neither warm nor cold, and the afternoon light seemed especially designed to sharpen the youthful greens of a new spring. The wind had a softness that rippled the water on the pond, creating choppy seas for the moorhens that gathered there, but leaving everything else untroubled, and Josephine went for a walk through the fields, then returned to the garden until the ringing of the telephone called her inside. It was Archie, and she could tell by the tone of his voice that he had rung with bad news. "You asked me to keep you up to date on Charity Lomax," he said. "I'm afraid she died this morning. She never regained consciousness, which is probably the only blessing."

"I'm so sorry to hear that," Josephine said, realizing that the dilemma she had been wrestling with about Harriet would now have to be resolved, one way or the other. "We were never the best of friends, but no one should die like that. Do they have any idea who did it?"

"Not yet, I'm afraid. They're chasing up the most recent stories that she was working on to see if anything controversial emerges, but there's been nothing promising so far."

Josephine was silent for a moment, remembering how angry she had felt after her own encounter with the journalist. It would only take a different personality or marginally higher stakes to goad someone into reacting more violently, and Charity's stories these days carried a much higher profile. Perhaps she was wrong to link her death to a distant past; perhaps Harriet's presence in London on the day in question had genuinely been an unfortunate coincidence. Then she remembered her friend's hurried departure and obvious fear, and knew she would never be satisfied until she had spoken to her about it. "Can I pick your brains about something?" she asked casually, hoping that her tone was sufficiently light for Archie not to link the conversations.

"Of course."

"You were talking about the suspension of the death penalty the other day, and it got me thinking—what will happen to anyone who's convicted of murder during that time?"

"He'll be granted a reprieve by the Home Secretary. We've just had our first one, as it happens. Nice chap. Killed his wife. Why do you ask?"

She smiled at his sarcasm. "No particular reason. I was just thinking about some ideas for a new book, and that struck me as an interesting thing to explore. If you were going to commit murder, this might be a very good time to do it."

She heard him laugh. "It's rather a cynical approach, and I hope it doesn't catch on, but yes, I can see that might work in a novel."

"And if the government changes its mind and reinstates hanging, what will happen to the people who've already been reprieved? Will they have their sentences changed?"

"Are you sure this is hypothetical?" he asked, sounding suddenly suspicious.

"Yes, of course." She turned the tables on him, trying to make light of the question. "You surely don't think I'm about to go out and kill someone, do you?"

"That's not what I meant, and you know it. But speaking purely hypothetically—no, the original sentence will stand, and he or she will cheat the gallows. You'd better get your story in quick, though. My money is on the Lords voting this down at the earliest opportunity."

Josephine spent a restless night thinking about what Archie had told her and decided to travel to Lewes in the morning, before she could change her mind. She made good time, and it was just before two when she got out at the station. The part of town which greeted her was uncharacteristically devoid of charm, but the view improved as she crossed the railway bridge and saw the keep of the castle to her left, surrounded by a cluster of red roofs, sloping lawns, and trees, all facing to the southern sun. The high street was busy, but not too prosperous to lose its character; old, bow-fronted windows ranged out onto the pavement amid a mixture of houses and shops, and occasionally she caught a glimpse of peaceful walled gardens through an open front door. She liked the town immensely and wondered why fate invariably marred her visits there with trouble.

She headed for Castle Gate, aware that she was procrastinating by taking the long way round. Banks of pale primroses covered the steep mound of the keep, and she paused by a sheltered old bowling green, looking down toward the town's ancient heart. One of those tiny cottages was Harriet's, and she knew she could put off the visit no longer.

At the head of the narrow street, she stopped abruptly when she saw Harriet's front door open up ahead of her. A young woman holding a baby came out, followed by Peter and Vera—a middle-aged woman now, but still trim and healthy from her outdoor life. Harriet joined them in the street to wave them off, and the small group talked for a long time in the sunshine. It was a touching scene that reminded Josephine of everything she would be taking from the family if her suspicions proved correct, and it was almost enough to make her change her mind—but she had let her heart rule her head once before, and she couldn't do it again. As soon as Peter and his family were out of sight, she made her way to the front door and knocked.

CHAPTER 5

Harriet looked out of the window before answering the door, hoping that Vera or Peter hadn't come back for something. She had said her goodbyes, somehow managing to fool them into thinking that this was just another day, but she didn't trust herself to continue the charade a moment longer. To her relief, Josephine was standing outside in the lane, obliging Harriet by turning up on her doorstep earlier than she had even dared to hope. One more conversation and she would be free to go.

"I've been expecting you since the party," she said, obviously unsettling Josephine with her directness. "Come in."

Josephine did as she asked and handed over a parcel wrapped in brown paper. "I've brought your book," she said. "You left in too much of a hurry to take it." She looked curiously at Harriet. "How did you know I'd come?"

"Because there's a question you want to ask me, and I've been waiting to give you your answer. Somehow, I didn't think you'd let me down. You never have."

She showed Josephine through to the sitting room and watched as she stood in front of the painting above the fireplace, the portrait that Peter had painted of her at Charleston before going back to war. "I'd forgotten quite how good this is," Josephine said admiringly. "It's nice to see it again."

"Is it? I don't like it, if I'm honest. It reminds me of a very sad time, but it was his gift to me, and it seems ungrateful to hide it away." She looked at the cups and half-eaten fruitcake which she hadn't had time to clear away. "I can make a fresh pot if you'd like some tea," she offered, but Josephine shook her head and sat down, apparently keen to get to the point. To Harriet's surprise, bearing in mind the circumstances under which they were meeting, her visitor seemed more anxious than she was, and she was sad to have made someone she cared about the instrument of her own torment. "Ask your question, Josephine," she said gently. "Neither of us is up to prolonging this any more than we have to."

"Was it you who attacked Charity?"

"Yes, it was."

"She died yesterday morning." Harriet closed her eyes. It was the news she had been dreading, and she felt the panic and guilt well up in her; somehow she kept them under control, but not before Josephine had noticed her distress. "Why did you do it?" she asked. "You told me that our last conversation was a new start for you, so what's different? Killing Charity can't bring George back or change what she did, so why would you risk your life and your family to do something so senseless?"

"My life and my family don't mean as much as I thought they did. I lost everything when I lost George—I can see that now, and Charity played her part in that." The words were the truth and Harriet found the role she had given herself much easier to play than she had ever imagined—almost too easy, in fact; she could see that Josephine was still skeptical about her explanation. "It's not just that," she added. "I lied to you when you came to find me last time."

"What about?"

"I killed Dorothy too."

Josephine stared at her in disbelief. "But you can't have. What about the note you showed me?"

"George wrote that to protect me," Harriet said truthfully. "She guessed that I did it to save what we had, and she wanted to take her share of the blame, so she sacrificed her life to save me. She loved me, Josephine. Even I never really understood how much until then. I only wish I had." She took George's note out of her pocket and handed it over, struck by the sorrow in Josephine's eyes as she read it. For reasons she couldn't explain, she felt as bad about deceiving her as she did about any of the events that had made it necessary; it was wrong to exploit a woman who had done so much to help her, who had been fair and kind and loyal from the moment they met, but she needed to make sure that Vera and her family were safe. "You once refused to take any part in ending my life, but surely now you must see—"

"And I still can't. I could no more send you to the gallows than I can justify what you've done."

"But you must," Harriet insisted, horrified to think that everything she had planned so carefully might be for nothing. "Why are you here if not for justice? Now you know everything, you *must* go to the police. You've got the proof there in your hand, and you have to tell the truth."

"I will, but they won't hang you. You'll get a reprieve and a prison sentence, and I *can* do that. I must do it." To her shame, Harriet was tempted to clutch at the straw that was being offered her, but then she remembered everything that had driven George to her death. "It will look better if you give yourself up," Josephine continued. "I'll let you have until tonight to make your peace and talk to Peter and Vera. Then I'll go to the police." She slid the letter back across the table. "This is yours to give them, not mine."

"You trust me? What if I simply destroy it and run away?"

"You won't, though, will you?"

Harriet smiled sadly and reached down to stroke Percy as he rubbed round her legs. "No, I won't. I'll be here when they come for me."

The cat jumped onto her lap and nuzzled her hand, and his reliance on her was suddenly too much. The tears took her by surprise, offering her no choice but to give in to them, and she let Josephine hold her until the crying stopped. "Do you want me to stay?" Josephine asked quietly.

For a moment, Harriet wondered if her friend knew perfectly well what she intended to do, but she shook her head. "No, you've done enough. Thank you, but I need to be alone now."

Josephine nodded, accepting her answer, and Harriet stood up, feeling calmer and more certain than ever that she was doing the right thing. There were preparations to make, and she was grateful for a visitor who showed no inclination to linger. She waited on the step until Josephine was out of sight, then closed the front door behind her.

Acknowledgments

Ideas for a book come when you least expect them, and I'm grateful to the Charleston guide who—on a tour of that beautiful house—mentioned that it was once run by two women as a boarding house; as Josephine notices during her visit, the ceramic number plates are still visible above the bedroom doors. Further valuable information on Charleston came from Quentin Bell's book on the house; Frances Spalding's biographies of Duncan Grant and Vanessa Bell; Angelica Garnett's *Deceived With Kindness*; and Stewart MacKay's book on Grace Higgens, *The Angel of Charleston*.

The horticultural history of Charleston is entirely my invention, but is closely based on the work of several pioneering women and their gardening colleges, most notably Viscountess Frances Wolseley at Ragged Lands, Glynde, and Beatrix Havergal and Avice Sanders at Waterperry in Oxfordshire. The peace of the walled garden and spirit of a country estate during the First World War were inspired by the beautiful Lost Gardens of Heligan in Cornwall. Gertrude Ingham—a remarkable woman—was Principal of Moira House School for more than 30 years, retiring in 1939; the school—now Roedean Moira House—is still flourishing. Kate Adie's fascinating book, *Fighting on the Home Front*, is a brilliant account of women's achievements during the Great War, on the land and in many other arenas.

My thanks go to Shirley Collins for such a warm welcome to

Lewes and the Downs, and to everyone at the Ram Inn, Firle, for their hospitality.

As always, I'm indebted to the people who work so hard to make these books a success: Veronique Baxter at David Higham and Grainne Fox at Fletcher & Company; Walter Donohue, Sophie Portas and all at Faber & Faber; Matthew Martz, Jenny Chen and Sarah Poppe at Crooked Lane Books; and everyone at W.F. Howes. My thanks go, as always, to my family for their love and support, and especially to Mandy, my favourite gardener, who creates something beautiful wherever she goes.

Finally, it's been lovely in this novel to pay tribute to the book that first introduced me to Josephine Tey and, by a circuitous route, inspired this series. *The Franchise Affair* is a brilliant, complex and original crime novel, a chameleon of a book which shifts and changes with each new reading. If you've never read it, go and find a copy; you're in for such a treat.

·